"A Chamber of Summoning? For summoning what?"

Again the mage looked quickly around. "I don't want the holier-than-thou types to know of my concerns," he explained, "but this spell that will release their god is not unlike the spell of Summoning." Sordaak paused, unsure as to how much the ranger would understand.

"That still does not explain the—"

"It will if you give me a minute!" Sordaak glared at the ranger, who said nothing more. "A summoning works best if the creature being summoned is held at bay until the submissive relationship between the summoner and the summoned is properly established." Breunne nodded. "Generally a pentagram is used in one form or another, drawn or painted on the floor by preference."

The fighter scratched his head, perplexed at the explanation. He was about to say so when the mage continued. "In this case, the shape of the chamber will be the pentagram." His finger traced the markings on the diagram for the walls of the chamber.

Breunne's eyes opened wide. Remembering something, he leaned forward and lifted the sheet of parchment currently on top of several others. He sorted through the stack until he found the one he wanted. "The outer walls of the keep are to be in the same shape?"

Sordaak nodded. "Call them the 'backup plan'. You don't want the creature—or being—that was summoned to escape without that relationship properly established."

"You do if the being summoned is a god and he's pissed!"

THE PLATINUM DRAGON

VANCE PUMPHREY

Kellie,

Thank You SO Much For Your Support For This My First Series. Now It's On To Book 5!!! Thanks For Reading!

Vance R Pumphrey

LEAPING WIZARD PRESS

The Platinum Dragon

Book Four in the Valdaar's Fist Series

Published by Leaping Wizard Press

ISBN-10: 0692604782
ISBN-13: 978-0692604786

This book is also available in digital formats.

Discover other titles by the author at
VancePumphrey.com

I would like to dedicate *The Platinum Dragon*—
the last book in this first series—
again to friends and family, for they make life worth living.
Friends and family also provide the spice to keep that life from being bland.
There are those of you that will recognize yourself—
or perhaps others—within the pages of my books.
If you do not, rest assured that I will get to you.
I have at least another dozen or so books to pen.

The Platinum Dragon

What has Gone Before

Forged by mortals. … Enchanted by Drow. …
Wielded by a God. …. Lost by man…

Or was it?

If you have not read *Dragma's Keep*, *The Library of Antiquity* and *Ice Homme*, then I would suggest you do so! You will not be disappointed.

The Platinum Dragon is the fourth book in a series called Valdaar's Fist. However, in the event that it has been some time since you read the first three books in the series, here is a synopsis of what has gone before.

Sordaak, the sorcerer in this story, pulls together a group to make a raid on Dragma's Keep in book one of the series. He's after the ancient wizard's fabled staff, *Pendromar, Dragon's Breath* and his spell books. Sordaak meets up with a rogue, Savinhand, under nefarious conditions, and they end up working together. In the process of escaping from the aforementioned nefarious situation, the mage steals a horse—ostensibly with the intention of returning it. The owner of the horse, Thrinndor, a paladin of the Paladinhood of Valdaar, takes exception to such thievery and is intent on exacting appropriate payment from the caster's hide. But, smooth talker that he is, Sordaak not only worms his way out of being exacted but persuades the paladin and his best friend Vorgath—a barbarian dwarf of the Dragaar clan—to join with them.

Together, they begin their assault on the Keep, but they don't get far before they realize the folly of their ways in making the attempt without some healing power. Lo and behold, what do they find deep in the bowels of this keep? You guessed it! A healer—Cyrillis by name. Not just any healer, either, but a servant of Valdaar, the same god that Thrinndor serves. There is a minor discrepancy, though. This Valdaar has been dead for many centuries, slain by his brother Praxaar in the war to end all wars. But that is another story.

Anyway, the companions make their way through the underground labyrinth, battling orcs, sea monsters, a fire demon and another wizard consorting
with assassins. Along the way, they discover that the paladin is a direct descendant of the dead god Valdaar and are surprised to also learn that Sordaak is a
direct descendant of Dragma—a powerful sorcerer who served on Valdaar's
High Council. When the paladin tells the story of his master's demise, it is
revealed that he is after the immensely powerful sword of his master, *Valdaar's
Fist*. With it, he and a person from the line of Dragma (assumed to be Sordaak
at this point) and another from the line of Angra-Khan—the High Priest from
the god's Council—will attempt to raise the god from his prison in death. In the
end, it is surmised that Cyrillis must be the third person—but she was orphaned
at an early age, and knows nothing of her heritage.

After they fight their way to the treasure room, it is discovered that neither
the staff nor the sword is in the booty. However, the powerful greataxe *Flinthgoor,
Foe-Cleaver and Death Dealer*, which once belonged to Kragstaadt, Valdaar's mighty
general of armies, is there.

Upon exiting the Keep, the companions are beset by Sordaak's mentor, who
is also after *Pendromar*. A huge battle ensues, but alas our heroes prevail. But now
Sordaak needs a new mentor, and must go in search of one. The group agrees to
meet again in a few weeks' time after getting with their respective trainers.

That's where book two, *The Library of Antiquity*, picks up. Vorgath is early
to Farreach, the agreed-upon meeting point. He makes friends with a ranger,
Breunne, and then manages to upset the locals, getting into a barroom brawl.
Big surprise there!

Meanwhile, Thrinndor and Cyrillis attempt to squeeze some information as
to her past out of the local Temple of Set, but the Minions don't care for being
squeezed, so the paladin and healer must fight their way clear. In the process
they slay the twin clerics who run the place and burn the temple to the ground.
This, of course, upsets the Minions of Set back at headquarters, and vengeance
is promised in the usual manner (not generally pleasant for those involved).

While all of this is taking place, our rogue learns he has been selected to be one
of the contestants in the Rite of Ascension—the process whereby a new leader is
chosen for Guild Shardmoor. Savinhand wins this death match. However, in order
to complete his rise to power he must gather a team and gain access to the Library
of Antiquity—a process that makes him the new administrator for said library.

So the remaining companions meet him in Shardmoor and are sent on their
way. They are led to the secret entrance, only to find out that this is but the
beginning of a vast quest during which they are teleported to…where? They
have no clue. The only way out of the labyrinth is to finish the quest, or die.

The companions prevail, of course. And, of course, it is not easy. A hydra,
a drow-filled maze, traps out the (never mind where) and a horde of nasty

creatures called rakshasa stand in their way. Oh, and a dragon—you mustn't forget the dragon.

The Library contains information that exceeds even what they had hoped. Cyrillis is indeed of the proper lineage. Thrinndor discovers clues as to the location *Valdaar's Fist*. Breunne finds in the dragon's lair *Xenotath*, Bow of the First Ranger. And Sordaak goes gaga over the information overload—refusing to sleep while he studies. He has to be dragged from the library, kicking and screaming. Vorgath volunteers to do it another way, of course, but Thrinndor won't allow it.

The companions compare notes, and Thrinndor reveals that his prized sword was seen less than four hundred years earlier in Ice Homme—headquarters of the Minions of Set. So they decide that is where they must go, at least right after they make a detour to rough up some Storm Giants for their outerwear.

In book three, *Ice Homme*, the companions continue their quest by departing the entrance to the Library and heading for the Isle of Grief. Along the way they clear out a bunch of undead from a ghost town known as Ardaagh and send a Lich Lord back to the netherworld. They also do battle with another dragon, but this king of the lizards already had one foot in the afterlife and did not task our heroes much.

Finally they make their way to the Isle of Grief only to discover that the construction team Sordaak had hired to build his keep had gone missing. A search ensues that leads them to a Troglodyte Lord, but instead of a much anticipated battle, Sordaak persuades the lowly creatures to take over the security on his island so his men can work unimpeded on his keep. Smiles all around, except for the barbarian—he would have greatly preferred the much-anticipated battle.

Sordaak reveals his plans for the keep and that the native rock to be used for its walls is rich in precious metals. He and Vorgath teleport to his clan in the Silver Hills and persuade the dwarves to help build the keep in exchange for the right to work the mines for the ores they prize so dearly.

That settled, the companions set sail for the Cliffs of Mioria to do battle with the storm giants and obtain their cloaks—powerful talismans granting the wearer many powers. But the giants are aware of their purpose and conjure a massive winter storm that blows Sordaak and company far off course—but not killing them, as intended. Another struggle ensues from which our heroes again emerge victorious, stopping just short of wiping out the giant clan. Instead, Sordaak signs up the four remaining storm giants to aid he and his companions in the coming battle with the Minions of Set.

That battle was indeed epic, pitting our heroes along with the four giants against a force of well over a hundred Minions—conveniently split into two factions. Again, they win the day and begin a quick march on to Ice Homme—Headquarters and University for the Minions of Set in the land.

Once there, Sordaak does battle with the powerful priestess Kiarrah and barely escapes with his life. He also discovers that he has two sisters he knew nothing about—one of them being the now deceased Kiarrah. The other a beautiful sorceress named Shaarna.

That catches you up. So, without further ado, here is the fourth book of the Valdaar's Fist Saga, *The Platinum Dragon*.

Chapter One

Reunited

Sordaak had taken his leave from his companions once they were safely back at the cabin. It had been especially hard to leave Cyrillis, as his burgeoning relationship with the healer brought tears to the eyes of both. Yet both knew they had tasks to perform with their masters that required weeks of training. For the mage it was even more so, as he had to learn how to use his new staff, *Pendromar, Dragon's Breath*, before their quest could continue.

Despite the protests of Cyrillis and Thrinndor, the sorcerer had adamantly insisted that they not resume their quest until spring—then still some three months hence. Not only did Sordaak despise traveling in winter, he knew he needed to be in two places at once: at the Isle of Grief overseeing the construction of his keep and at his master Rheagamon's tower. Yes, there was much to do, and three months would probably not suffice.

The mage took Vorgath with him on the first leg of his journey to the island. The barbarian intended to ensure that the Dragaar dwarves got settled in at their new home before sailing on to Pothgaard to work with his trainer.

Cyrillis and Thrinndor would travel together to Khavhall, Paladinhome. There, they would winter with their people, each taking the much needed time off to spend with respective masters. Savinhand agreed to travel with them as far as Grandmere, where he would leave them to take up the reins of his Guild for the first time.

Breunne took his leave to travel east, where he would meet up with his mentor. He preferred to travel alone, although leaving these who had become his friends behind was unusually difficult for him.

The giants left to return to the cliffs at Mioria, promising to join the troupe on the Isle of Grief in a few days.

Before the party members went their separate ways they agreed to meet the first week of spring, this time on the Isle of Grief.

*

Sordaak alternated his attention between the engineer's drawings spread before him and out the window to stare down at the construction going on below. It was for that reason he had made the trip by teleportation at least once a week—much to the consternation of his master. This was not to be helped, insisted the student. While everything seemed to be in order, he knew he could not leave that to chance.

Construction of the temple progressed nicely. The Storm Giants had come in handy on more than one occasion by diverting major winter storms around the island. As such, the good townsfolk of Farreach had had the worse winter on record as inexplicably those same storms, usually tempered by losing some of their intensity on the island just over the horizon, hammered the coast one after another.

The Dragaar dwarves had thrown themselves into the work of building the temple, working around the clock in multiple shifts as if it had been their destiny to do so—a concept Sordaak allowed them to believe.

The dwarves were given one day off for every four they worked, allowing them time to work the mines far below for the precious metals and gems that were in abundance there. Rumors occasionally floated to the surface of an especially large gem, or maybe of a rich vein of platinum. Vorgath claimed he had never seen his father or his people happier.

As such, the walls of the temple were nearing completion and another crew had begun working on the roof. As fewer craftsmen could work the temple now, work had begun in earnest on the keep's outer wall. Sordaak had insisted this wall must be next, as he was secretly worried that once their work on the island was discovered, they would be paid a visit by those who had striven so hard for the past two millennia to stop what was now happening here—the rebuilding of The Keep.

He couldn't allow them to stop him.

And they would certainly try. Of that he was certain.

The magicuser reached up to scratch his head, but suddenly sensed someone else in the tower. Sordaak tensed as he turned slowly to see Breunne peering over his shoulder. The ranger smiled a greeting.

"It would be much easier on my heart if you would announce your presence," the mage said. "That damn rogue likes to sneak up on me just to piss me off."

"I assure you I meant no harm," the leather-clad man with speckled green eyes said, raising his hands to waist height. "I was merely loath to disturb your concentration."

Sordaak raised an eyebrow and smiled. "Well, thank you for that anyway." He turned back to the drawing. "The dimensions for this temple are *so* precise! If any one of these is off by so much as an inch, everything we're doing could end up being a waste of time!"

Breunne whistled. "That's a *lot* of dimensions! Just what is it you are trying to build, other than a strange-shaped keep?"

The sorcerer took in a sharp intake of breath and checked around the tower for other pairs of ears. "Essentially is it a massive Chamber of Summoning."

"A Chamber of *Summoning*? For summoning *what*?"

Again the mage looked quickly around. "I don't want the holier-than-thou types to know of my concerns," he explained, "but this spell that will release their god is not unlike the spell of Summoning." Sordaak paused, unsure as to how much the ranger would understand.

"That still does not explain the—"

"It will if you give me a minute!" Sordaak glared at the ranger, who said nothing more. "A summoning works best if the creature being summoned is held at bay until the submissive relationship between the summoner and the summoned is properly established." Breunne nodded. "Generally a pentagram is used in one form or another, drawn or painted on the floor by preference."

The fighter scratched his head, perplexed at the explanation. He was about to say so when the mage continued. "In this case, the shape of the chamber will be the pentagram." His finger traced the markings on the diagram for the walls of the chamber.

Breunne's eyes opened wide. Remembering something, he leaned forward and lifted the sheet of parchment currently on top of several others. He sorted through the stack until he found the one he wanted. "The outer walls of the keep are to be in the same shape?"

Sordaak nodded. "Call them the 'backup plan'. You don't want the creature—or being—that was summoned to escape without that relationship properly established."

"You do if the being summoned is a god and he's *pissed*!"

The mage scowled as he looked out the window at the construction below. "I hadn't thought of that." He shrugged. "We're just going to have to assume that he won't be pissed, I suppose."

It was the ranger's turn to scowl.

"Who are we hoping to not piss off?"

Breunne and Sordaak turned to see Thrinndor step into the chamber from the landing at the top of the stairs.

"You, of course," lied the sorcerer, his eyes beseeching the ranger to follow his lead.

Breunne caught the look and nodded slightly to indicate he understood and would comply. He was sure the mage would continue the explanation at a later time. Particularly if he was prodded to do so.

"Why would there be concern about—"

The paladin was roughly shoved aside and a woman clad in white robes charged past and threw her arms around Sordaak's neck, hugging him tightly. "I have missed you so," came the muffled voice of Cyrillis. The cleric pushed herself back so she could look into the mage's eyes. His look of surprise and concern combined to cast doubt into the heart of the young woman.

Her smile changed to chagrin, and she quickly took a step back. "I am sorry," Cyrillis said, her voice demure. "I—I do not know what—"

Sordaak, realizing her plight, took the necessary step between them, threw his arms around her and kissed her passionately on the lips. The healer's eyes opened wide in surprise, but they quickly closed as she again threw her arms around the mage's neck and returned his kiss.

Thrinndor cleared his throat noisily and Sordaak slowly disentangled himself from Cyrillis' embrace. The mage's eyes found hers. "I missed you as well."

The ranger smiled and winked at the paladin. "Perhaps we should take our leave and give them some privacy?"

Thrinndor lifted a not amused eyebrow and said quietly, "Perhaps." He didn't move.

Suddenly both the cleric and the mage realized they were not alone and pushed away from one another, each brushing at imaginary wrinkles in their robes. "No, no," stammered Sordaak. "We're good." He frowned at his words, knowing not even he believed them. Quickly he turned and pointed out the window. "Look at all that has been accomplished."

Cyrillis obediently moved to the ledge, but the paladin lagged behind. While he had expected the healer and mage to renew their relationship somewhat, he had not expected it to be renewed so enthusiastically. His right eyebrow still perched over his left, he shook his head and moved forward to stand beside the cleric at the window.

There was ample room for them all, yet Sordaak chose to stand behind Cyrillis, his arm raised over her shoulder, pointing out significant points of interest as he spoke.

When he was done, the paladin nodded. "Indeed, the Dragaar Dwarves have availed themselves well. Progress is better than I had expected." He turned so that his eyes caught those of the magicuser. "Yet, will the temple be ready when we are?"

Sordaak took in a breath and held it. "I believe so," he said, exhaling noisily. "There are several factors that will affect the final answer to that question, however."

The sorcerer moved back and circled the table so that he was again able to sort through the drawings there. "First, there is yet much to do. While the dwarves have made phenomenal progress, the roof remains to be finished and there are several details that must be worked out for the altar and dais structures."

"Which brings up another question: Just how did you come by these details?" Thrinndor's tone suggested he had more than a passing interest in the answer to that question.

"The Library of Antiquity, of course," answered the mage. "This temple— and the entire island and keep, actually—was the focus of much of my study in the days the Library was made available to me—us." Sordaak paused as he looked down at the drawing of the temple. Clearly something was bothering him as he fidgeted with the papers on the desk.

Thrinndor waited patiently, certain the sorcerer would speak when he was ready. He had become accustomed to the man's theatrics. Somehow this seemed different, however.

Finally the mage looked up, his eyes a mixture of excitement and concern. "One of the things I discovered is that Valdaar's Keep was not the first structure to be built here."

"What?" Cyrillis was first to react.

"You are certain?"

"I wouldn't have mentioned it were I not!" Sordaak's tone softened. "What I'm *not* certain of is how *many* times a temple has been built here."

Even Breunne got involved in the ensuing commotion as suddenly everyone was speaking at once.

The magicuser held up both hands, having known their reaction would have been as it was. When an uneasy but excited silence was restored, he continued. "I found records dating back more than *five thousand years* that indicate a temple in this place then was old *at that time!*" He paused, expecting another outburst, but he was disappointed. The sorcerer sighed. "Since that time in a different age, the temple has been torn down and rebuilt at least three times—with Lord Valdaar's being the most recent rebuild some two thousand years ago, give or take."

There was no longer any contention for speaking time as a hush settled on the chamber. The workings and an occasional shout from the dwarves far below wafted through the window on the spring breeze.

"But why here?" Breunne asked.

"I'm glad you asked," the sorcerer said, smiling at the ranger. "When we were here a few months ago I showed these two a place below where some sort of power can be felt if one tunes one's senses properly."

Breunne glanced at the paladin, who nodded.

"As best as I can discern, the walls of both the keep and the temple serve to focus this power in some way." The mage scratched his head. "Even the structures within the temple—the dais, the altar and the urn on the altar—must be of the same exact shape. See how the points of each align precisely, with exactly the same distances between the points."

Thrinndor sifted through the documents on the desk and removed one. "I see from this that my lord's keep was built as a perfect square. Yet your design has five sides. Why pentagonal?"

"Another good question," said the mage. *Damn! I should have put that drawing away!* "As I said, the structure serves to focus the energy. A square is not ideal to do so. A circle would be best, but building a perfectly circular keep with concentric circles inside from cut stone would be difficult at best."

"And hard to defend if attacked," mused Breunne.

Sordaak shot the ranger a glance of thanks. "Correct. My research took me through the past four structures built here, and each was different. A circle was even tried, but the builder acknowledged the flaws in design and that keep survived only a few centuries before falling before a horde of enemies."

"That seems to be a common theme." All eyes turned to the cleric, who was the one that had spoken. "I mean, from what we know about what happened here when Valdaar fell and the keep you just described, any structure built here seems to attract those that want to destroy it." She looked up and met the eyes of the sorcerer. "Why?"

"Jealousy," answered the mage. "If I am correct, this source of power from the ground can be used by those that understand it."

"To what purpose?" Thrinndor asked. "And why did not Praxaar build here following the death of his brother? Surely he could have made use of this power?"

Sordaak shook his head. "I'm sure he could have had he wanted to. But he left this realm following that war, remember? I believe he didn't want the power to be available to man for fear of its possible misuse."

The paladin nodded. That he understood. It also aligned with what he knew to be true from what had been passed down to him following those final days.

Sordaak did some mental brow-wiping as he rolled the plans from Valdaar's Rest and stuffed them into a tube under the desk. Those would no longer be needed.

"How much longer do you figure before the temple and the surrounding walls will be sufficient for our purpose." Thrinndor had grown weary of beating around the bush. He was ready to claim his sword.

That question Sordaak had been ready for. "Another month—two at most."

The paladin hooked a dubious eye out of the window at the construction below.

"I know what you're thinking," Sordaak said before the paladin could speak. "But understand I don't need the *entire keep* built—just the temple and the outer walls. The rest can be built at a more leisurely pace."

Thrinndor hesitated, but then he too nodded. "Very well. What then of our preparation for the dragon?"

"I thought you'd never ask." The sorcerer smiled as he extended his right hand and suddenly *Pendromar, Dragon's Breath* was in it. "While overseeing construction of the Keep was of great importance to me, it was not my only concern. Learning how to use *Pendromar* took substantial time, as did studying new spells and taking many long hours in counsel with Rheagamon. Together he and I began to form a plan. It still has some rough edges, but with proper preparation, some outstanding timing and just a little luck, I now believe we can prevail."

"Against Bahamut?" asked the ranger. "This I want to hear."

"Patience, my dear Breunne." Sordaak smiled at the man. "Patience. Even these walls have ears. I will not reveal my plans until we begin this our final quest."

Thrinndor raised an eyebrow at that. "Final? What makes you believe this will be our final quest?"

The mage turned slowly until he faced the paladin. He squared his shoulders and said, "It will be mine. I will have my keep, the beginnings of a library and the spell books from both a high sorcerer and the most powerful dragon in all the land to study." His eyes twinkled as he continued. "What else could a sorcerer ask for?"

The paladin did not return the smile as his eyes shifted to the cleric. "Yes, what else indeed?"

An uncomfortable silence ensued, and suddenly Sordaak's cheeks were tinged with red.

Breunne again came to his rescue. "Has anyone heard from Vorgath or Savinhand?"

"Yes and no," the mage answered quickly. "Vorgath stayed here with me for almost a month before departing for Pothgaard. He promised to return by—" he looked over at a crude calendar that was pinned to a wall "—last week." He shifted his staff to his left hand as he walked up to the calendar. "Wait, that can't be right." He began counting the weeks.

After doing so twice, he turned to face the paladin. "That's not good. He should have been here at least a week ago. He said he'd be early, if anything."

The paladin's face took on a grim expression. "Savinhand?"

"Him, I haven't heard from. Wait," the mage glanced around quickly, his eyes settling on an area near the doorway. "You can quit hiding, Savin!"

"Drats!" the rogue said as he stepped into the light. "Either you're getting better or I'm slipping!"

"Or both." Sordaak grinned as he stepped forward and clasped forearms with his old friend. "Good to see you still in one piece."

"Thanks, it's good to be seen."

"How long have you been there?"

"I just came up," answered the thief. His face turned serious. "I do have news concerning our barbarian friend, though." He had everyone's attention. "And it's not good, I'm afraid. My ears in Pothgaard report that he went into battle with a young clan against a powerful overlord. Something about taxation and land rights."

"That sounds like Vorgath, all right." Thrinndor grinned. "Should not be anything to worry about."

Savin shook his head. "The clan was decimated. Less than a dozen of the more than fifty that marched, returned." His expression was grim. "Vorgath was not one of them. One of the returning said they saw him taken captive."

Thrinndor frowned. "You could have led with that." He turned to the caster. "How soon can a ship be ready?"

Sordaak licked his lips. "Within an hour."

"Very well, we sail in an hour." The paladin turned, walked through the door and went down the steps.

Chapter Two

Pothgaard

The trip across the open water had been uneventful. The winds were favorable and the party made good time. Still, it was two days before the hills on the western shore of Pothgaard loomed on the horizon.

They tied their ship at a dock in the waterfront city of Klarrooft. From there, the companions hired horses and rode for another day non-stop until they arrived at a small village known as Riversedge.

Savinhand made private contact with his informant, leaving the others at the only tavern in town to get something to eat and rest. The man led Savin to the outskirts of the village, where he knocked lightly on the door of a dilapidated building.

Savinhand heard the shuffling of footsteps inside. Soon a latch was lifted and the door creaked open a few inches. "Go away," a harsh voice said. Savin was fairly certain it was a woman's voice.

The rogue stuck his boot toe into the opening before the door could be slammed in their face. He winced slightly as the person on the other side tried to close it anyway.

"Please," Savin said, "we must speak with Egredt." That was the name he had been given.

The face appeared in the crack again. This time Savin was sure it was the face of an elderly female. "I said go away!" she said.

"Please," Savin repeated.

The woman hesitated. "Get your foot out of my door before I sic my dogs on you!"

Dogs? That had not been part of the plan. "Please don't. I need to speak with Egredt—it's of vital importance." He put his left hand on the door and was prepared to push.

"You can't," spat the old woman. "He's dying."

That news he hadn't been prepared for. "All the more reason to let me speak to him," lied the rogue. "Perhaps I can help him."

"You a healer?" the voice demanded.

"No, but I have helped save many battle worn soldiers in my day."

"Go away," the woman repeated. Savin felt the pressure on his foot as the woman tried again to close the door.

"Wait!" he cried. "We have a healer." Savin turned to his informant. "Run back to the tavern. Bring the woman I came in with. *Hurry!*"

The man obediently scampered off, and Savin could hear the receding footsteps as he turned again to face the woman on the other side of the door. "Please, I must speak with him. A healer will be here in moments."

Suddenly the woman kicked his toe out of the crack and slammed the door shut. Savin heard the latch slide home. "Bring a healer and I will let you in. Not before," the woman said through the door.

Savinhand looked down at his booted foot and wiggled his toes to verify everything still worked. He took the time while waiting for Cyrillis to study the building. It was probably an old cabin, he decided. The wood was unpainted and weathered beyond its years. He walked around to the side and discovered the cabin was larger than he first thought. The walls extended to where they joined with the side of a hill. The rogue suspected they might even go back some distance further than that.

The rogue was brought back to the front of the cabin by the sound of running footsteps. Damn! The whole crowd had come.

Savin quickly stepped into the path and put his hands up. "Only Cyrillis, please!"

"But," began the sorcerer.

"No 'buts'," the rogue said sternly. "We have a woman inside with a person who is injured. That person is the one I am here to see. The woman already doesn't trust us, and only by promising a healer did I get her to agree to let us in." His eyes went to the paladin. "So, the rest of you *please* go back and wait for us at the tavern."

Sordaak made to argue further, but Thrinndor nodded his understanding and clamped a massive hand on the sorcerer's shoulder and turned him aside. "We will do as requested. Shout if help is needed."

"Thank you, I will," promised the relieved rogue. He grabbed the cleric's hand, turned her and said, "Let's go. There's a man dying inside."

Cyrillis nodded and allowed herself to be led to the door as the others did as requested and departed. Savinhand rapped lightly on the old wood.

The shuffling was again heard, the latch was lifted and the door cracked open. A suspicious eye appeared in the crack and settled on Cyrillis. "You a healer?"

"Yes," the cleric replied. "I understand there is someone here who requires my services?"

The door was pushed almost shut again and Savin feared the woman had changed her mind, but the rasping sound of a chain being lifted informed him otherwise. *Secondary locking mechanism. Nice.*

The door swung inward and Savin could see the woman was not as old as he had thought. She wasn't young, either, but the years had not been kind. However, the extra-large kitchen knife she held in her right hand looked sharp and the way she held the blade indicated she knew how to use it.

"This way," she said gruffly. "Hurry." She led the way through a curtained doorway across from the entrance. She brushed aside the curtain and went down a dimly lit hall. There were other curtains covering passages along the way, but the woman scurried past them.

She paused at the end and turned to face the two following her. "Forget you ever saw this." Without waiting for an answer, she rapped on the plank wood at the end of the hall with the handle of the knife in code. After a moment the wall swung inward on noiseless hinges.

A bulls-eye lantern was uncovered, shone on the woman's face and an unkempt man of indeterminate years nodded. "Who're they?" he demanded.

"He's here to talk to Egredt, but she is a healer. Now *move*!" Without waiting for the man to comply, she pushed past him. Savin shrugged at the man as he too walked past, Cyrillis behind him.

Savin had been correct; this place was much larger than it appeared from the outside. The area behind the secret door was also much newer and cleaner.

After several twists, turns and opened doors, the woman stopped in front of one that was closed. She turned and eyed the two suspiciously. Again she tapped on the door with the butt of the knife, this time in a different staccato pattern.

Savin heard a series of bolts being slid back as the hairs on the back of his neck rose. *Something was not right!* He was about to turn when a blinding pain exploded on the side of his head and everything went dark.

Cyrillis turned at the sound and was about to scream when a bag dropped over her head, a hand covered her mouth and *Kurril* was ripped from her hands. She heard a curse as the person that grabbed the staff was instantly burned by its touch. Roughly, she was shoved through the door that had opened in front of them.

"Make no sound, do as we say and you may yet live to see another day," a harsh voice grated in her ear. "Do you understand?" The voice turned away. "Use a rag and bring that staff. *Now!*"

Scared, Cyrillis nodded and took hesitating steps when pushed. "Is this mask necessary?" she asked, her voice more mad than afraid.

"Shut up and do as told or both of you will die before night falls."

Cyrillis nodded tentatively and walked when her arm was grabbed and pulled. Abruptly they stopped and she was turned several times in succession, and then back the other way. Soon Cyrillis had no idea which direction she was facing or from which direction they had come.

"Bring him," the male voice said as she was pulled back into motion. Cyrillis could hear the sound of the rogue being dragged along the floor behind her.

They went down a circular set of stairs, through several doorways and across a lot of hard planked floor. The cleric tried to count steps, but every so often she was stopped and spun some more and realized the futility of doing so. She simply allowed herself to be led, trusting these people were just being overly cautious.

Abruptly, they stopped and she could hear the butt of the knife again knocking on wood.

Bolts were slid back, the door was opened slightly and Cyrillis could hear whispers but couldn't make out what was being said. She was shoved and almost tripped but someone caught her. The bag was jerked off of her head and she blinked rapidly as the light in the chamber momentarily blinded her.

"Be careful, you idiot!" snapped the woman who had met them at the front door. "If she's a healer, we need her!"

"If she's *not* a healer, then she's *dead!*" replied a new voice. The voice was attached to a man who now stood in front of the cleric, appraising her with suspicious eyes.

"If she's not a healer," the woman replied, "then *he's* dead." She walked over to a man lying on a bed who Cyrillis noticed for the first time. The man's face was ashen and covered in several days' worth of stubble. A blanket covered the rest of him, yet the healer could see he shivered with the cold of impending death.

The woman turned and locked eyes with the cleric. "Can you heal him?"

Cyrillis walked over and knelt by the side of the bed. "I do not know," she said. "He is very sick." Her face was grim. Without turning, she held out her right arm behind her. "Give me my staff."

"If you are a *true healer*, you don't *need* the staff," replied the man who was apparently in charge.

Cyrillis turned her head slowly until her eyes locked with those of the speaker. "What you say is true." Her eyes bored into the man's until he shifted uncomfortably. "Yet, its power increases my ability to heal. Surely you want me to be at my best."

The man glared back at her, weighing her words. Abruptly he turned to the man holding *Kurril* at arm's length, wrapped in a rag. "Give it to her," he spat as he turned back to the cleric. "If she tries to rise before Egredt is healed, kill her." He folded his arms on his chest and waited.

The second man nodded and sneered at Cyrillis, then handed her the staff. "*Please* try to rise!" The healer could see the man's hands were badly burned from his earlier encounter with the staff and that he was in a lot of pain.

Cyrillis accepted the staff and looked back at the supposed leader. "Are you so eager to kill that even a stranger trying to help is subject to your ire?"

Not waiting for a reply she waved a hand and the man whose hands were burnt yelped in surprise. "Hey," he exclaimed, "she healed me!" He stared at his now whole hands in wonder.

As the healer turned to assess the man on the bed, the leader said, "You could be a stranger trying to help, or you could be a spy from Arrahaft!"

"Who is Arrahaft?" Cyrillis asked absently, not really caring about the answer; her mind was already on her patient.

"He's the cowardly overlord responsible for taxes, this war and the injuries to that man lying on the bed in front of you."

"Ummhmm," Cyrillis said as she pulled back the blanket to see what she was dealing with. "Generally it takes two sides to have a war." She sucked in a breath as she saw what the blanket had been hiding and didn't hear the reply. The man in the bed was naked save for a loincloth that covered his lower body and a blood-soaked bandage that loosely covered his entire midsection.

She gently removed the bandage and the healer could immediately see why the man was in such bad shape. The wound was very deep, penetrating the fleshy part of his lower left side. She was certain there would be internal damage as well. The wound was also badly infected.

"This man may be too far gone," she said aloud as she called forth her healing power. Gently, she wafted her hand over the prone man's side, first purging the infection. Again and again she called forth her power, drawing from her staff when indicated, pouring her healing into the man's body. Death had been near for him, perhaps only minutes away.

Cyrillis could see the immediate effects of her ministrations. The wound turned less green, the vital organs inside resumed working, and lastly the skin knitted together. His breathing, which had been shallow and labored, eased. Yet still his eyes remained closed.

The cleric pushed aside a strand of wayward hair and sat back on her heels. She looked around at the would-be leader. "Have you no healer?"

The man shook his head, his eyes wide in wonder at what she had just done. "No. Arrahaft makes sure any that attempt to train in those arts are either brought in to support his army." His lips formed a thin line. "Or killed."

"How barbaric!"

"Yes ma'am," the woman said as she flashed white, even teeth. "It is our chosen path, after all." Seeing her confusion, she added, "Barbarians. We're all barbarians!"

Cyrillis nodded slowly, understanding at last. Then she shook her head as she turned back to her patient. She was somewhat concerned at his continued unconsciousness, but she could tell he was simply weak from blood loss and his near-death experience. "He will live, but he needs lots of rest."

"He's done nothing *but* rest for the past five days!" protested the man whose hands had been burned.

Cyrillis' voice was stern when she continued. "That was not rest. His body shut down unnecessary functions in its effort to heal itself." She turned and looked at the woman, who smiled gratefully. "He must rest."

"I promise you he will!" The woman choked up briefly but fought back tears. "Thank you," she whispered. Seeing the cleric's silent question, she added, "He's my mate. I thought for sure I was going to have to find another."

"And our cause another leader." It was the man standing guard who spoke. "We owe you."

"You owe me nothing except my freedom," answered the cleric. Her tone softened her words, however. Her eyes shifted to where Savinhand lay on the floor. "May I tend to my companion?"

The man seemed to ponder the question. "He will yet live." He turned to the other man in the room. "Bind him."

"*What?*"

The would-be leader turned back to the cleric after verifying his command was obeyed. "We have a desperate need for one with your skills."

"Not this way," protested the woman.

"Silence!" The man was thinking fast. "What other way is there? Would one such as her willingly join our cause?"

The woman appeared to ponder the concept. "A priest can't be *forced* to provide the services they do."

"Sure they can," sneered the man. "They just need the right motivation." He took a step toward the cleric.

Cyrillis dropped into a crouch, *Kurril* held before her. "Touch me and I will bring the wrath of Valdaar down upon you and *all* those that side with you!"

"Valdaar?" he laughed. "You serve a god that is no more?" He paused, however, as his eyes didn't leave the staff in her hands. "Guards!" he shouted.

A noise was heard outside the room, and then the door burst open and two more men stepped in. Armed men.

Cyrillis knew she was in trouble, and her mind began to race as the rogue stirred, testing his bounds. "Yes, Valdaar," she said, looking right and left for a possible way out. "However, he is not your immediate concern." She let that sink in as she turned to the woman. "Remember my comrades outside the cabin?" The woman nodded. "Those three are companions of mine. Breunne, a mighty ranger wielding *Xenotath*, bow of the First Ranger, Thrinndor, a High Paladin and Sordaak—perhaps you have heard of him?—a powerful sorcerer who will stop at nothing to ensure my safety."

The man hesitated. "They can't find you here." He didn't sound convinced.

Cyrillis sensed his doubt and pressed forward. "No? Did they not see where we came in? These men have entered and solved Dragma's Keep, assailed and

defeated the Storm Giants at Mioria and walked into Ice Homme and slew several
legion of their host—including their new High Lord." She paused. "Not to mention two—not one, but two—*dragons!*" She leveled her gaze at the would-be leader.
"Do you really think you and your men would pose a serious obstacle to these?"

"Fred, are you daft, man?" Egredt spoke from his place in bed, his voice
coarse from lack of fluids.

The man known as Fred licked his lips. "I've heard of this Sordaak." His
eyes found those of the healer. "He's with you?"

"I forgot to mention," Cyrillis replied as she pointed to Savin. "That is
Savinhand, leader of Guild Shardmoor, you have bound on the floor." She
smiled at Fred. "That is an egregious error on your part, I am afraid."

"Savinhand?" Egredt spoke again, his voice stronger. "Release him!" When
his men hesitated he shouted, "*NOW!*"

In a flurry of movement, one of the guards produced a dagger and cut the
leather thongs that bound the rogue's hands and feet.

Egredt sat up in bed and put his head in his hands. "Fred," he said quietly,
"we're going to have to have a little talk."

"Water!" Cyrillis said quickly. "Give him something to drink."

The woman grabbed a waterskin from a hook on the wall, removed the cork
and held it out to her mate. Egredt took it and nodded gratefully as he tilted his
head back and took a pull at the skin. Instantly, he put the flask aside and spewed
most of the water in his mouth all over the floor.

"Slowly," chastised the cleric.

Egredt smiled and put the skin back to his lips and took small sips.

"I only did what I thought was right for the cause," Fred protested when
he was able to get in a word. He looked at Cyrillis, and his eyes begged her to
understand. "We need a cleric so badly! This past fight would have gone differently had we had aid such as yours!"

Egredt put down the skin. "In that Fred speaks sooth. We would have prevailed and won the day had we but had a cleric for support." His eyes softened.
"Perhaps you can train some of our people?" His voice held hope.

Cyrillis hesitated. "I would like that," she said, "once I complete my current quest."

Sensing it was time to change the topic, Savinhand spoke while still rubbing
his wrists. "Fred?" he smiled as he looked at the man who had ordered him
bound. "What kind of name is that? Did your parents not want children?"

Fred returned the smile with an uneasy one of his own. "That remains to be
seen. If I ever catch up with my father, I'll be sure to ask him!"

"And that brings us to why I'm here." All eyes shifted to the rogue. "Vorgath,"
he said simply. When he got no response he added, "It was spoken to me that he
went into battle with your people and was taken captive."

Egredt tried to swallow a couple of times, and then put the skin back to his mouth and drank some more of the water. When he set the skin aside, he spoke. "You know Vorgath?"

Savin nodded. "Yes. He is one of us." He squared his shoulders. It was clear he enjoyed saying that. "What can you tell us of him?"

Egredt shook his head. "Not much more than you already know. He came here looking for a cause to back and we took him in. We went to Beordgoff to confront the overlords about their taxes, things escalated, and we ended up going at it." He bowed his head. "We lost many good men that day." When he looked back up, a tear was in his eye. "I went down with a poleaxe in my side. The last thing I remember was your Vorgath charging into a group of at least ten men, his greataxe swinging wildly all about him." He again paused. "He was hit on the head and knocked unconscious. The last I saw of him he was being drug by the heels into their keep."

Chapter Three

Beordgoff Castle

"Then you know not whether he yet lives?" Cyrillis' tone was demure.

"No," admitted Egredt. "However, our spies tell us that he's alive. He's a mercenary, after all. Arrahaft is trying to convince him to fight for them."

The healer nodded. "That is good news." She looked over at Savinhand. "We must alert the others and be on our way." The rogue leader nodded.

"Be on your way where?" Fred demanded.

Cyrillis turned a disdainful eye on the man who had tried to hijack her very life. "Why, to this Beordgoff Keep, of course."

The man's jaw fell open. "*What?* You can't possibly be serious! Arrahaft has more than one hundred men under his command!"

The cleric allowed her disdainful eye to switch to withering. "I see you are not aware of the concept of no man left behind, are you?"

Fred set his jaw stubbornly. "I am so! I had *you* brought here to save our leader, did I not?" Before Cyrillis could answer, he continued, "But a frontal attack on Beordgoff is *suicide*!"

The healer folded her arms on her chest. "Yet you tried it."

"We had more than one hundred men ourselves, and we had surprise and a well-laid trap on our side!"

"And yet we failed." Egredt stepped into the conversation, trying to alleviate a growing situation.

Cyrillis turned to the leader, still sitting on the bed. "Have you tried reasoning with them?"

"*Reasoning?*" Fred was apoplectic. "There is no *reasoning* with *them*! You pay your taxes and keep your mouth shut! Anything else results in imprisonment."

"Or death," Egredt finished for him. "Fred's right. There is no reasoning with Arrahaft."

Cyrillis' stance did not change. "For you, maybe. But *we*—my companions and I—do not pay taxes. Mayhap he will listen to us."

"You're daft, girl!" Fred sneered. "They will listen to *no one!*"

The healer backed off on the withering stare, but not by much. "That is the problem with you *barbarians*. There is only one way for you: Go in with your weapons swinging. The only way for your side to prevail is for you to kill more of them than they kill of yours."

"So?"

Cyrillis rolled her eyes. "I realize that intelligence is not an attribute you cherish, but for those who hold winning the day so dear, I would have thought you would have figured this out long ago. Diplomacy is a tool like any greataxe or longsword. It is just another way to get your point across." She shifted her gaze from Fred to Egredt and back. "Then if diplomacy fails, knock their heads off. With diplomacy, you have two ways to accomplish your goal."

The four men and one woman in the room looked at the healer as if she had two heads, one green and one red.

"We'll stick with what has worked for us, thank you very much." Egredt shook his head in wonder. "However, you are free to try talking to them. Who knows? If they don't kill you outright, you might have a chance to make that work for you." He shrugged.

"We are free to go, then?" Cyrillis asked, trying not to sound relieved.

"Yes, of course," Egredt replied.

"How do we get to this Beordgoff keep?" Savin asked as he did a brief inventory of his weapons, remembering he had been unconscious during his trip into this room. He rubbed the side of his head where a good-sized knot now stood.

"And can you take us there?" the cleric asked.

"If you're going to try this 'diplomacy' thing," Egredt said with disdain edging his voice now, "you probably don't want any of us along." He smiled. "They won't take too kindly to any approach with us in the party."

"Beordgoff is actually an old castle," Fred answered the question. "You can't miss it. Take the road north out of town and ride for about a day. It's the only thing that road is for."

"If you don't mind my asking," Egredt said, "when diplomacy fails, what are your intentions?"

Cyrillis leveled a stare at the barbarian leader. "Why, we will have to get our companion back by force, then." Without waiting for a reply, she turned and headed for the door.

Savinhand smiled at Egredt, shrugged and followed the cleric.

"Good luck with that, too," muttered the barbarian leader.

Cyrillis looked at the rogue and asked haughtily, "How did this group ever convince Vorgath to side with them?"

Savin shrugged. "My guess is they mentioned there would be fighting." Now he smiled.

Cyrillis glared at the thief and then laughed. "Yes, I suppose that would do it."

The cleric and rogue were shown to the door with far less elaborate precautions concerning secrecy. They exited to find Breunne, Sordaak and Thrinndor outside talking quietly among themselves.

Thrinndor looked over at the duo as they exited. "We thought you gone longer than expected. We were about to ascertain your location."

"We're here," Savinhand replied, an easy smile on his lips.

The paladin glared at the thief.

Cyrillis put a hand on the rogue's arm. "Our friends had a very sick leader. There was more to his healing than at first thought." She winked at Savinhand.

Savin caught the gesture and nodded almost imperceptibly. "That and I had to wait for her to accomplish her task before I could get the required information out of him."

"Do you know where Vorgath is, then?" Sordaak asked.

"Yes," replied the rogue. He turned and pointed down the road that ran by the cabin. "That way."

"How far?" Thrinndor asked.

"About a day's ride," answered Egredt from the open door. He had relaxed somewhat once he knew the cleric was not going to discuss their attempted abduction.

The ranger looked up at the sun; it was approaching noon. "If we leave now, it will be well after dark before we get there."

"Then we'd better get moving," the mage answered as he turned and led the way back into town to where their horses waited.

The ranger and paladin exchanged glances. Thrinndor shrugged and quickly followed the sorcerer. The remainder of the companions followed suit.

"If they're half as good as she said they were," Egredt said to his mate who stood beside him, "I would like to see how they do."

"As would I," replied the woman, her eyes thoughtful.

Within a half hour the companions were riding north, driving their mounts hard. They ate as they traveled in silence, Breunne having procured packs for each of them containing the usual dried meats, cheeses and breads.

Nightfall found them approaching the castle—they could see the light of several fires in the distance—on horses that were well-lathered and almost done. As they approached they came to a small river that blocked their path. On the opposite bank were the walls to the castle. The drawbridge was up, blocking access to the main gate.

Thrinndor didn't hesitate. "Hello in the keep!" he shouted.

There were guards stationed along the top of the wall. Two turned to face them and one shouted back. "Go away."

"That seems to be the standard response in this province," Cyrillis announced dryly.

The paladin ignored her. "We would like to speak to the master of the house." He no longer shouted, knowing he had the attention of those on the wall.

"He says 'go away'." This brought laughter from several guards.

"Bring Arrahaft out to speak to me or I will come and get him." Thrinndor's voice was not excited—in fact, he could have been talking about the weather.

That caused the men they could see to stand straighter, and now they were peering into the darkness trying to see who—and how many—stood on the far side of the water. Thrinndor could hear a lot of harsh words being spoken.

"Who should we say is calling?" the same voice replied. That drew several more snickers. "Shut up!"

"Thrinndor, Sordaak and Cyrillis." The paladin knew that Savinhand and Breunne were hidden from the guard's view.

"And what do you want?"

"To speak to Arrahaft."

More subdued voices. "I will send word to his lordship," more snickers, "and see if he is expecting company."

"He is," assured the paladin.

Several minutes passed; Thrinndor and his companions didn't move.

"Arrahaft says to go away."

"I thought that might be your answer," the paladin said. Without turning he said in the same voice, "Sordaak, if you please."

The magicuser didn't speak. Instead he slowly raised *Pendromar* in his right hand and then slammed the heel of the staff to the ground.

A loud concussion was heard at the point of impact and the earth shook. In a clatter of sound and movement, the drawbridge rapidly descended and crashed to the ground at the companions' feet.

Alarmed shouts rang out as Sordaak again raised the staff and again brought the heel to the road with a thud. This time the wooden gates to the castle exploded inward, ripping from their massive hinges as they did.

Thrinndor leaned toward the mage and said without expression, "Something you have been working on?"

"Yep."

The paladin straightened. "Nice."

As the companions began to cross the bridge, guards recovered and arrows began to rain down on them from the parapets. The mage was ready for that as well, holding his empty left hand above his head. All arrows and spears were deflected aside by some unseen force as they walked steadily along.

Deliberately the three crossed the bridge and approached the splintered gates. At a shout from inside the portcullis began to clank down.

Sordaak raised his staff again and the spiked wrought iron gate reversed course and began to rise.

More shouts and quickly a formation of greatsword and greataxe wielding men blocked their path.

Thrinndor stopped fifteen feet from the first of the men. "We can do this one of two ways," he shouted. "You can bring Arrahaft out of hiding to speak to us, or we can decimate this sorry excuse for an army and afterward chase down the coward."

Silence settled on the group opposite them as more torches were brought to bear, lighting the courtyard behind the formation that blocked the companion's path. The torches external to where the gates had stood were also lit, giving the occupants of the keep a better idea of what they faced.

Suddenly, an enormous man pushed his way through the gathering until he stood between them and the three outside the gate. He was at least as tall as the paladin, but more muscular. The man had a thick, unkempt beard that covered more of his face than was normal for most men, giving him the appearance of a bear.

"I'm Arrahaft," he said in a booming voice. "Who are you to threaten me so and to destroy the gates to my castle?"

"I am Thrinndor," the paladin said. Without taking his eyes from the man, he nodded to his left. "This is Sordaak, and she is Cyrillis."

"What do you want?"

"You took a prisoner several days ago. Vorgath. He is a friend of mine."

Arrahaft's eyes opened wide. "He's dead."

Thrinndor hesitated. "I do not believe you. If he is, you will soon join him in the afterlife." The paladin drew his flaming sword. "I sincerely hope you are prepared to meet in death whatever god you chose to ignore in life."

Clearly this brute of a man was not accustomed to being spoken to as such. He hesitated. "You are only three," he said finally.

"Are we?"

This caused the man to squint to see behind the three that stood on the edge of his bridge. Try as he might, he could see no one behind them.

Suddenly, in the blink of an eye, Breunne was standing next to the paladin with an arrow notched and his bowstring drawn. The arrow was pointed straight at Arrahaft's head.

Thrinndor didn't look over at the ranger. "You will be the first to die, your *lordship*! You need to ask yourself, is today a good day to die?"

"It's as good as any," said the big man. He too did not blink. Arrahaft ignored the ranger, instead staring into the eyes of the paladin, trying to ascertain whether he was being bluffed.

Without taking his eyes from the paladin, he turned his head slightly to the left. "Bring the dwarf."

"And his weapons and other personal items," Thrinndor added for him.

Arrahaft stared at the paladin for several heartbeats, and Sordaak was certain his friend had pushed too far. The big barbarian merely nodded, and running footsteps could be heard leaving the courtyard.

While they waited Arrahaft fidgeted. Finally, unable to contain himself he strode purposefully forward until he was face-to-face with the paladin. Breunne's arrow followed the big man.

They stood that way for a few moments, Thrinndor wondering just what this was about. "You realize," Arrahaft said quietly so that only the three in front of him could hear, "that I need to do something to save face with my men?"

The paladin eye's opened wide in mild surprise. He nodded. "Just what do you have in mind?" He kept his voice quiet as well.

"I don't have a clue!" admitted the barbarian. "I was hoping you did." Arrahaft smiled, showing amazingly straight and white teeth. One didn't expect such from a barbarian.

Thrinndor was about to shake his head when a thought struck him. "We were followed here. I have an idea." He winked. "Follow my lead."

Arrahaft nodded slightly.

The paladin shoved the barbarian so hard he had to take a couple of steps back to keep from falling. "Get back to your men or I will order my army to attack!" Thrinndor shouted.

"Your *army*?" Arrahaft bellowed. "Since when does one trickster, a woman and a ranger count as an *army*?"

"You neglected to mention these," the paladin shouted, raising his huge arms above his head.

Arrahaft raised his own arms, and they were significantly larger than the paladin's. "Whatever!" the barbarian shouted. "Those two *little* armies had better have some backup, or I'm changing my mind!"

Without turning, Thrinndor shouted even louder. "Egredt! Show yourself and some of the men." Silently the paladin said a prayer to Valdaar that this would work. He knew Egredt and several of his men had followed them, but he hadn't actually spoken to them.

"Egredt?" Arrahaft said, somewhat confused. "Now I know you're bluffing! I killed that skinny little shit myself a few days back." He grinned hugely, and Sordaak was fairly certain the barbarian was no longer simply playing along.

"Is that so?" Arrahaft's eyes narrowed as a voice, accompanied by the sound of several men stepping out of the trees behind the paladin. "My mother would be disappointed to hear that."

The circle of light from the torches barely reached that far, and Arrahaft squinted to penetrate the gloom beyond. He could see several armed figures astride horses but could discern no details.

"Show yourself, whelp!" Arrahaft shouted. "I ran a young man bearing that name through with my blade less than a week ago. There is not a chance he survived!"

Thrinndor heard the steps of a single horse advancing behind him. He didn't turn as it stopped behind and to his right.

"Impossible!" Arrahaft bellowed. "I saw the life light leave your eyes myself!" He glared at the paladin. "What manner of trickery is this?"

Thrinndor started to reply, but Egredt spoke first. "This young lady standing before you is a cleric of the first order. Indeed I was nigh death, but she brought me back and made me whole." A smile crept into his voice. "Whole enough to kick your fat ass!"

"Fat?" Arrahaft was apoplectic. "You crawl your narrow ass down off of that flea-bitten excuse for a horse and I'll show you *fat!*"

Thrinndor raised his hand for silence before the barbarian behind him could speak. "Enough!" the paladin said. "Bring Vorgath out here or we will have to go get him." He lowered his voice. "And you will not like how that is done."

There was a rumbling from the ranks behind Arrahaft and it was clear they would rather fight than surrender anyone—or anything. But the big barbarian had become their leader not only by his brawn. He had learned over the years to trust his instincts, and right now his were screaming at him he would be on the shorter end of the stick should things go south.

The strained silence was broken by the sound of metal chains clanking together and being drug across the stone of the courtyard.

Arrahaft turned at the sound and smiled disapprovingly as a shackled Vorgath came into his line of sight. Abruptly the guard behind the dwarf shoved him with the butt of his pole-axe, causing diminutive barbarian to stumble and fall to his knees.

"Ah," said the barbarian leader as he shook his head, "had you but gotten to that position days ago, we would not be having this conversation."

Vorgath glared up at the clan leader while he struggled to regain his feet. "You could never put me in that position."

The guard that brought the dwarf out raised his weapon and stepped up to smack Vorgath on the back of his head, but the dwarf had other ideas. Unbelievably quick, he raised both hands and spun around. In one motion the chain whipped around the guard's neck and the dwarf crossed his arms, jerking the chain tight. Before anyone could react, Vorgath dropped to his back, ripping the guard from his feet.

Vorgath twisted the chain again and the man's neck snapped like kindling. In one fluid motion, the dwarf was back on his feet, glaring at Arrahaft.

The barbarian leader shook his head and clucked his tongue. "Thorrad was less than intelligent." He turned to cast almost indifferent eyes on the paladin. "Yet, he was one of *my* men. This dwarf has cost me far too many to allow another to be slain without recompense."

Thrinndor set his jaw. "What is it you seek?"

Arrahaft was silent for a moment. An idea came to him and he pointed to the mounted barbarian. "Egredt," he sneered. "He's the instigator of all this unrest. Hand him over to me, and you will all go free."

Before anyone could answer, Thrinndor spun, grabbed the barbarian by his tunic and yanked him from his horse.

"Hey!" shouted several of Egredt's men, a couple of whom started forward to come to the aid of their leader.

In a flash the paladin spun the man in his hands and again drew his flaming sword. This he held at Egredt's throat. "Stay where you are," he commanded. They did as directed, unsure what to do.

"Take him!" spluttered Egredt in a rage.

"Another step and he dies," Thrinndor said calmly. "Sordaak, watch them while I deal with Arrahaft."

Sordaak nodded and turned slowly to face the men along the trees. He planted *Pendromar* in the ground out in front of him to make sure it was seen. "I wouldn't test him," the mage said, shrugging. "He has eyes in the back of his head." He smiled a smile that showed no humor. "But, do what you must."

No one moved.

Thrinndor turned to face Arrahaft and nodded at the dwarf. "Release his bounds, return all that is his, and Egredt is yours."

The barbarian in his arms began to thrash about, but the paladin slid his left hand up to the man's throat and began to squeeze. Egredt's motions grew more frantic, yet he couldn't break free of the paladin's grip.

"Quit struggling or I will snap your neck like my companion did that guard's," Thrinndor said evenly.

Seeing he was not going to escape and that he was beginning to feel faint from lack of air, Egredt complied.

"That is better."

Arrahaft watched the struggle with amusement. He briefly considered attacking while the paladin was distracted, but noticed the ranger again had an arrow pointed at his left eye. "How do I know you will stand true to your word?"

Finally Cyrillis spoke, her tone scathing. "Thrinndor is a paladin. As hard a concept as it must be for you to grasp, he is *incapable* of falsehood."

Arrahaft stared at the cleric, trying to make up his mind. That the paladin was willing to negotiate at all bolstered the barbarian leader's thought that his adversary's position wasn't as strong as he'd been led to believe. Yet, he'd lost too many men, and if that that trend were to continue, he would be at the mercy of the other overlords in the vicinity. In the end that argument won out. "Release him," he said without taking his eyes off the paladin.

One of his men hesitantly stepped forward, took the keys off of the dead guard and unlocked the shackles binding the dwarf. Vorgath waited until the last lock had been released and walked over to where his personal items had been unceremoniously dumped onto the stone. "Where's my greataxe?" he demanded as he put his armor back on.

Arrahaft hesitated. "*Flinthgoor* I claim as payment for damage done."

Vorgath bowed his head, and Thrinndor could see the muscles in his friends back knot up as he began to build a rage. "Vorgath, *stop!*" the paladin commanded. He saw the dwarf tense, but he took no further action. *Whew!*

Thrinndor turned back to Arrahaft. "The deal was for my man *and* his weapons," he said evenly. "Return them to us or we are back to us going in and taking them."

The paladin could see the muscles working in the barbarian leader's neck and upper torso as he too began to build a rage. "*Arrahaft!*" he shouted.

The big man visibly forced down his rage. "You ask too much!" The leader's voice was husky with emotion. His rage was further fueled by the growing unrest behind him, as his men were eager for battle.

Without turning Arrahaft reached behind him with his right hand. His teeth grated when he spoke. "Give me the greataxe."

Sordaak snuck a peek over his shoulder and held his breath as there was movement behind the barbarian leader. A barbarian walked forward, *Flinthgoor* hanging loosely from his right hand. The man stopped behind his leader, he too struggling with his emotions.

"C'mon, boss," Sordaak did a double-take. *That's no man; it's a half-orc!* It had been some years since he'd seen one, but the creature was unmistakably a half-orc. The man/monster continued in broken, guttural common. "We can take them; they are *puny!*"

Arrahaft kept his eyes on the stone mere inches in front of his toes and his right arm extended. His breathing came in hoarse gasps.

With a growl that seemed to begin in his toes the half-orc handed the blade to his leader and took a couple of steps back. Back in place, he pulled a nasty-looking greatsword from a hook on his back and stood waiting, the muscles in his neck and chest twitching in anticipation.

Arrahaft held *Flinthgoor* behind him for a few moments and then slowly rotated his shoulder so that the blade was held out toward the dwarf. Still he refused to look up.

Vorgath, having donned his armor and put the balance of his weapons in their places on his back, belt and other standard locations, walked over and put his hand on the haft of his prized greataxe. The muscles in the dwarf's neck bulged as he tried his strength against that of the barbarian leader who refused to release the blade.

To any who did not know the two, there probably wouldn't have seemed anything untoward. But those to who did know, an epic battle of wills ensued; a battle that would have certainly resulted in a bent or broken haft of a lesser weapon.

But, *Flinthgoor* held.

As did both barbarians.

The test of wills continued as both refused to relinquish their grip and neither allowed himself to raise a second hand to the shaft. Muscles bulged, beads of sweat broke out on foreheads, and eyes reflected the determination of entire races.

Sordaak worried that recent lack of food and/or mistreatment might limit the dwarf, but he needn't have bothered. Vorgath pulled the necessary power from reserves deep within. He was not going to lose this battle for his greataxe.

The mage was certain that when one released, the other would tumble out of control. As collective breaths were held by those that watched, Arrahaft suddenly released his grip. Neither tumbled.

The barbarian leader turned his head and locked eyes with the dwarf. "You win this day, dwarf. But, if you ever return to my province, I *promise* you that will not be allowed to happen again."

Vorgath held the bigger man's gaze. He nodded and turned to walk over to stand next to Thrinndor.

Arrahaft's eyes followed the dwarf, respect not quite hidden in his eyes. He sighed, allowed his shoulders to slump and turned to face the paladin. "Your 'requests' have been met," he grated. "Now meet mine."

Thrinndor's jaw worked as unseen forces fought for control inside him. A single tear exited his left eye as he shoved the young man in his grasp toward the barbarian leader.

Arrahaft caught the man, and slung him back to the half-orc. "Bind him."

"Know this, Arrahaft," Thrinndor said, stopping the barbarian leader before he could turn away, "you should take this opportunity to negotiate a truce between your people."

"*Negotiate?*" spat the big man. "We don't *negotiate!*"

"You did with me," the paladin smiled. "And you lived to fight another day."

Chapter Four

Negotiations

Arrahaft sneered, but Thrinndor could tell he had piqued the man's attention. "You have lost many men—undoubtedly some of them good—and therefore are now vulnerable."

"Horse shit!" snapped Arrahaft, yet he glanced quickly around, trying to see if anyone else was paying attention.

Thrinndor walked quickly to stand next to the bigger man. He pulled him aside and spoke sotto-voce. "Unless you have more men than evidenced here, you are in trouble." He looked over a where the half-orc was busy putting the shackles on a desolate Egredt. "Egredt probably has more men out there in the trees than you have here." This drew a sharp, concerned glance from Arrahaft. The paladin nodded. "I know none of this for certain as I have only been in your land for two days. But," he looked over where Sordaak and Cyrillis stood waiting, "it only stands to reason. You hurt their cause badly when you chased them off last week, but their 'cause' will allow them to draw replacements quicker than you can."

"Like your companion Vorgath?" Arrahaft maintained his air of superiority, yet Thrinndor could tell he had the man's attention.

"Sometimes," the paladin agreed. "Vorgath signed up for the sheer joy of doing battle—he would not be concerned with a 'cause.' Egredt must have been actively recruiting to attract the attention of my friend." His eyes locked with those of the barbarian leader. "It is that more than anything else that leads me to assume Egredt has more men than he is showing."

Arrahaft looked suspiciously at the paladin. "Why do you care?"

"Good question." Indeed the question caused the paladin to hesitate—he hadn't expected it. Thrinndor thought about his answer before speaking. "There are too many good men dying here." He rubbed his chin absently. "I believe I will need such men in the not-too-distant future. Alliances can be forged from friendships gained on this day."

Both men turned to look as the half-orc drug Egredt to his feet and shoved the much smaller man—most men were smaller than the hybrid creature—toward a small building in the back of the castle grounds. Presumably the prison.

"That and I don't like what happened to Egredt."

"How so?" The suspicions had been waning for the barbarian, but now they returned full force at the mention of what he assumed as pity for his adversary.

Thrinndor looked down at his feet. "He came to my aid—albeit unwittingly—but he came anyway." The paladin shook his head ruefully. "Now he will be incarcerated for his efforts." Suddenly he looked up and then around at what remained of the barbarian army. "Know that his men will try to free him, and you are ill-equipped for another direct assault."

Arrahaft too looked his men over, now beginning to disperse, as he pondered the situation. Suddenly he called out after the receding half-orc and his prisoner. "Borgat!" The man/creature stopped and turned. The barbarian leader waved him over. "Bring him to me."

Borgat shrugged, grabbed a confused Egredt by his collar, jerked him to a halt and redirected the disconsolate man with a shove. Egredt didn't even complain; he just stared at the ground as he shuffled in the direction told.

Arrahaft leaned toward the paladin and whispered. "What does he want?"

Thrinndor's eyes shone as he realized there might be hope for a truce after all. "Lower taxes," he whispered in return.

"*What?*" Arrahaft nearly shouted. Quickly he lowered it again. "That's how I pay and feed my men!"

"He knows," Thrinndor replied as the half-orc and his prisoner approached.

"I see." The paladin could see that the barbarian truly did.

Borgat jerked on the chain he was using as a leash, effectively stopping the resistance leader. The half-orc cuffed the man roughly on the side of his head to point the human in the right direction.

Thrinndor narrowed his eyes as he witnessed this. As he and the half-orc traded gazes, the paladin felt in his bones he was going to have to deal with this creature someday.

Borat grinned as if to say, '*Bring it on, human.*' Neither spoke.

"Leave us," Arrahaft commanded.

Disappointed, his malevolent glare still on the paladin, the half-orc turned and stalked away in the direction the others had gone.

Egredt, his head held high, entered into a stare-down with Arrahaft. Rolling his eyes, Thrinndor spoke first. He cleared his throat. "If I may be so bold as to point out that you *gentlemen* desire the same thing."

That got both of the barbarians' attention, each shifting a somewhat disdainful look to the paladin.

Before either could speak what was on his mind Thrinndor continued. "Egredt, you want less demands made of your people by Arrahaft, correct?" The opposition leader nodded. "Arrahaft, you need what is demanded to pay your men and hire others to keep the peace in the region." It was the barbarian leader's turn to nod.

"Very well," Thrinndor took a deep breath. "Here is what I propose: Egredt, you swear allegiance to Arrahaft—"

"Never!"

"Hear me out," Thrinndor said sternly. He glared at the barbarian until he backed down. "If you were to accept this allegiance, providing both men *and* goods to support Castle Beordgoff, you would have to provide less of the goods as Arrahaft here would have to hire fewer men. Your men would still get the battle test they need as Arrahaft will still have to deal with the other regions." Both men withheld their tongue, yet the paladin could see in their eyes he had not won them over.

"Arrahaft, you will have to bring in some people to work the land surrounding your castle, and perhaps supplement those you bring in with some of your men—"

"My men...*farmers?*" he spat the word. "That will never happen!"

"Yet you expect others—also barbarians—to work the land for you?" It was Arrahaft's turn to feel the gaze of the paladin. Thrinndor held it until the other man pulled his eyes away.

"Of course," Arrahaft said demurely.

"Surely you have men that are nearing their time to hang up their weapons?" pressed the paladin. "You could ease them into retirement by having them 'oversee' the working of the soil, perhaps even granting them a section of the surrounding lands in recognition of their honored service."

Suddenly both men folded their arms on their chest. Neither would look the paladin in the eye, instead finding some point on the stone path at which to stare.

Thrinndor sighed. "Look, this is not my fight. You two can continue knocking heads with one another until there are no heads left to knock." He shifted his gaze from one to the other and back. Both continued to avert their eyes. "However, it only stands to reason that if you two were to join forces, you would *both* have a bigger say in what goes on in this province."

Thrinndor waited as the two barbarian leaders warily raised their eyes to investigate the interest of the other. Neither appeared willing to budge.

Egredt turned a suspicious eye on the paladin. "What is our fight to you?" he demanded.

Arrahaft answered for the paladin. "He wants an allegiance in Pothgaard."

"What for?" Egredt was not swayed.

"Arrahaft is correct," replied the paladin. "I am building alliances all across the land." He smiled. "No particular reason at this point, but I fear a war may split the land, and I want to ensure there are those that I can count on in the various regions."

"Allegiance in return for what?" Egredt was clearly interested, but his natural suspicions would not just go away.

"Training," replied the paladin. He knew he had them now. "I understand you had requested that my cleric provide some assistance along those lines." Egredt nodded, though his demeanor remained guarded. "Once we get properly established in our new home, I believe we can provide those services, as well as several others."

"What kind of services?" Arrahaft was now listening, as well.

Thrinndor smiled again. "I can think of at least two that might interest you right away. You saw what Sordaak was able to do with his magic powers?" Both nodded, now eager to hear what was being said. "Well, he has talked of setting up a university, as well. Savinhand—leader of Guild Shardmoor—I believe would be interested in setting up a branch of his operation here in Pothgaard." He paused, slightly. "Not to mention Cyrillis and her clerical abilities."

The two barbarians looked at one another and then back to Thrinndor. "You make a good case," Arrahaft said, scratching his head. "I *do* need more men if I'm to expand my operation."

"I'm not so sure I agree," Egredt said.

Thrinndor and Arrahaft looked at the concerned barbarian and waited. Egredt raised his shackled wrists and grinned a lop-sided grin.

"Oh, that," Arrahaft returned the grin. "Borgat!" he shouted at the top of his lungs, startling the two men.

"Damn!" groused the paladin as he stuck a finger in his ear and pretended to rub it. "Was that necessary?"

"It is if you want your friend out of those shackles."

Before either of the men could answer the half-orc reappeared in the courtyard holding a flagon, presumably ale. "What?" he grunted.

The attitude displayed by the half-man/half-orc was really grating on the paladin's nerves, but he bit off a harsh reply, not wanting to erase any progress that had been made.

"Unlock your new co-commander." The smug smile Arrahaft laid on Borgat was probably only interesting to Thrinndor, but the paladin certainly enjoyed it.

The half-orc's face twisted in confusion. "Co-commander? This skinny little shit?" For emphasis he cuffed Egredt on the back of the head, nearly knocking him to his knees.

"I said unlock him," grated Arrahaft, "not knock him to the ground!" He glared at the creature. "Egredt here is going to join our cause, and I'm making him co-commander. He will be in charge of his men." Borgat continued the confused look, and didn't move. "I said *unlock him*, you dimwit!"

The half-orc scowled at his master, reached for the chains binding Egredt's wrists and painfully jerked them high enough so he could easily reach them with the keys.

Thrinndor's rage was building. It wasn't just the mistreatment of a defense-less prisoner, but the monster's attitude that pissed him off. "Easy," he said through clenched teeth.

Borgat turned eyes burning with hatred on the paladin. For a moment Thrinndor thought he was going to let it go. But, as the orc hybrid bent to unlock the shackles on Egredt's ankles, he pursed his flat lips and loosed a wad of spittle that hit the paladin in the forehead.

Thrinndor reached up and wiped his forehead clean as Borgat grasped the chain between Egret's ankles and used it to jerk the man's feet out from under him. The barbarian tumbled to the ground in a crash of chains, arms and legs.

When the half-orc stood upright, Thrinndor back-handed him across the mouth hard enough to split his lips and knock the beast to the stone.

Arrahaft looked on with his mouth agape. Stunned didn't begin to describe... He had never seen anyone strong enough to knock his man to the ground. Well, not since his epic fight with the creature that resulted in Borat submitting to him as his leader many years ago.

Thrinndor ignored the half-orc as the creature put his hand to his mouth, which was bleeding profusely from two split lips. Borat spat out at tooth as he slowly began to rise. "I apologize," the paladin began, still looking at the barbar-ian leader, "you are short on men and here I am about to make your numbers one shorter."

"You needn't worry your empty head about that," Borat said through his bleeding lips, "I'm going to break you in half for that, little man."

Thrinndor, still looking at Arrahaft, raised an eyebrow.

The barbarian leader shrugged. "Just don't kill him. He is useful to the cause."

"No promises," replied the paladin as he turned to face the beast.

The action had drawn a crowd, with several of Arrahaft's men cheering their man on. Thrinndor's companions gathered behind him.

The paladin glanced at Vorgath. "Do not even think about it," he cautioned.

The dwarf looked crestfallen. "Aw, c'mon! At least let me step in if you get winded!" Vorgath flashed an evil grin at the half-orc. "After all, I feel I owe him a shot or two."

"Very well," answered the paladin, "but only if I get winded."

As Borgat watched, Thrinndor took off his armor. "I wouldn't want you to be able to claim unfair advantage," the paladin said.

The half-orc said nothing, instead watching this man for weaknesses. He was surprised to see a mass of well-toned muscles beneath the armor. *No matter...*

Having removed his boots, Thrinndor stood and tested his balance warily on the balls of his feet.

"Ready?" the half-orc asked, his voice dripping with eagerness. He didn't wait for a reply. Instead he launched himself at the paladin, his massive right arm whistling through the air, intending to end this fight with one blow.

Thrinndor ducked under the arm and landed two short—but powerful—jabs to the creature's ribs.

Borgat stumbled and took in a couple of tentative breaths, fearing a rib had been broken. *Damn that human hit hard!*

The paladin, sensing he had hurt the half-orc, followed the jabs with a right cross that nailed his adversary on the chin as he exhaled for the second time.

Lights exploded in Borgat's head as it snapped back. He stumbled back another step and shook his head to clear it. He'd never been hit so hard!

Thrinndor shook his right hand—*that damn orc had a chin chiseled of granite!* But, he knew for certain he had hurt the creature and stepped after him, this time bringing a roundhouse from the left. His fist connected on the beast's ear, instantly splitting it in several places, showering both he and the creature with fresh blood.

Borgat howled in rage and pain as he took a step to the right, his hand going to the damaged ear. The paladin sought to press his advantage, following the maddened monster and aiming an uppercut to his unprotected chin.

But Borgat had other ideas and twisted his face out of the way so that the paladin's hand merely grazed his cheek. Again the monster howled, this time to induce a battle rage.

Vaguely Thrinndor heard his friend Vorgath cluck his tongue. "Uh oh, pretty boy, now you've gone and done it!" He shook his head with mock regret. "He's pissed now."

The miss threw the paladin off balance, giving the half-orc time to recover. The beast grabbed Thrinndor, easily lifted him clear of the ground and over his head, and then launched the fighter at a nearby wall.

Thrinndor twisted in mid-air so that his left shoulder hit the wall first. Lights blared in his head as pain coursed through his body, centering on the shoulder. As he slid down the wall, hitting the ground hard, he feared his shoulder was broken or at the very least separated.

The lights were subsiding somewhat as he felt rather than saw the approach of his adversary. Favoring his damaged shoulder he pitched himself to his left, narrowly avoiding a booted foot meant for his face. He searched for and found Cyrillis in the crowd, noting that she was raising her staff in his direction. "Do not!" he shouted. "I will handle this."

With a rueful shake of her head the cleric slowly lowered *Kurril* back to the stone. Her eyes flashing, she turned and marched with a stiff back toward the draw bridge. *I will not watch this barbaric display!*

As he regained his feet, Thrinndor saw his opponent was now off-balance. The paladin whipped his right fist around, again connecting with the monster's jaw.

This had the desired effect of stunning Borgat and giving the paladin a few precious seconds to assess his injuries. Tentative motion of his left arm revealed the shoulder wasn't broken and any separation was slight. *Damn it hurts, though!* He briefly considered healing himself, but Borgat was on him too quickly. Thrinndor dodged a ham-like fist intent on knocking the paladin into next week by twisting his body and throwing himself to the ground. There, he whipped his legs around and kicked the half-orc's legs out from under him.

Instantly, both were back on their feet and they circled each other warily, looking for an opening. This respite allowed the paladin to heal his left arm, bringing it back to usable status. However, he could see the time also allowed his opponent to clear the cobwebs from his head.

Abruptly, Borgat roared and charged. He no longer cared about openings or trading blows. He was intent on ending this duel. Now.

Thrinndor had time to step aside and put his leg out to trip the creature while at the same time clenching both hands together, he brought them crashing down on the back of Borgat's neck as he stumbled over the proffered leg.

The half-orc was again knocked off-balance, and he went to the stone hard. But instead of landing face first, the creature used his momentum to roll hard away from the paladin, thereby easily avoiding the following kick aimed at his head.

Thrinndor continued the kick, using the miss to spin completely around and prepare for whatever came at him. That was good, because the half-orc continued his tumble and was on his feet in a flash, turning and springing at the paladin.

The big fighter again stepped aside and stuck out his leg, but Borgat had seen this act before. The half-orc managed to change his direction slightly and caught the paladin square in the chest with the top of his head, driving the air from Thrinndor's lungs in a whoosh as he fell back.

The paladin knew he had to react fast or be driven into the stone by the much bigger monster. He reached out and grasped the barbarian's leather armor and pulled him down with him, kicking his legs into the midsection of the creature as his shoulders hit the stone pavement. Thrinndor shoved hard with his powerful legs and launched the half-orc high into the air.

Borgat spun as he sailed through the air, almost landing on his feet. Almost. The half-orc stumbled back where he knocked several of his men to the ground and he tripped, landing on top of them.

Thrinndor fought back the nausea that went with the loss of breath as he worked his way to his hands and knees. The barbarian was busy disentangling himself from his men, and that gave the paladin a brief moment to pull himself together.

As the barbarian stepped free of his men and back into the circle established by his comrades, Thrinndor went on the offensive. From his hands and knees he launched himself at the creature, bringing his right fist around in a roundhouse that exploded onto Borgat's chin.

The half-orc's head snapped back and he again stumbled toward his men. The paladin followed with a blow from his left fist again to Borgat's ribs. The bigger man struggled to regain his balance, but Thrinndor was determined not to allow that to happen. Another step and he delivered a blow to the creature's ribs with his right fist, driving the air from the orc's lips in a rush and his left whipping around to connect with Borgat's chin.

Lights exploded in the half-orc's head as he gulped for air. He flung his arms out as he attempted to keep himself upright, but then the lights went out and he slumped to the ground and lay still.

Thrinndor stood above the barbarian, his chest heaving. "Get up," he said quietly. When Borgat didn't move, he repeated, "Get up! I am not finished with you, yet." He glared at the fallen creature, his hands twitching.

"Yes, you are," Cyrillis said, suddenly standing at the paladin's side. "He is done," the healer said as she put a hand on Thrinndor's arm.

Thrinndor shrugged her arm off as he continued to stare down at his adversary. "Get up," he demanded, still unable to grasp that the fight was over.

Arrahaft moved in as the cleric moved away, shaking her head. "You didn't kill him, did you?" the barbarian leader asked.

"No, he yet lives," Cyrillis replied when the paladin hesitated. "Barely."

His chest still heaving, Thrinndor looked at the barbarian leader. "The man-beast hits like a mountain falling." The paladin rubbed his jaw, not remembering when he'd been hit there. "With some proper training, he could really become a force to be reckoned with."

"*You* train him," Arrahaft said. "I've done all I can with him." He looked up at the paladin, wonder in his eyes. "He's *far* better than when I bested him more than ten years ago."

The two leaders of men looked at one another, sizing the other up.

Thrinndor stepped back and stuck out his hand, which after a moment Arrahaft took and they grasped forearms. "I am glad we are on the same side now," the paladin said. "Remind me not to change that."

The barbarian's eyes widened slightly. "Funny," he said. "I was about to say the same thing." He looked down at his fallen warrior. "That was very impressive. Borgat has not been bested since I did so to bring him into my fold."

Thrinndor looked down at his hands, certain he had at least one broken bone. "He has a chin chiseled of pure granite."

Arrahaft nodded as the two of them turned to walk deeper into the castle grounds. "As is most of his head." He smiled. "Let's go have a beer."

"I thought you would never ask."

"Me, either." Vorgath was suddenly standing next to the pair.

Chapter Five

Isle of Grief

Morning came far too quickly for the companions. That probably had something to do with how long the evening had gone.

Egredt's men had been invited inside the keep and in short order a feast had been prepared and much ale, wine and mead had been consumed. Sordaak and Breunne found themselves hard-pressed to keep up with barbarians, but that didn't keep them from trying.

Cyrillis attended to Borgat, and soon he joined the revelry, all ill feelings set aside as was the way of the barbarian. For now. She even persuaded the half-man to let her put his tooth back in place under the premise he might need it someday to bite an opponent's arm off in battle.

Thrinndor and the half-orc became drinking buddies, and soon they were swapping battle stories with misty eyes at a table off to one side. The paladin took care to make sure he didn't try to match his new friend drink for drink—some modicum of control must be maintained, he reasoned. That had been ingrained into his very being since he was old enough to walk. That didn't stop him from having one or two flagons, however. Maybe three; he'd lost count after three.

Thrinndor and his party gathered at the main gates that next morning, where work had already begun to repair the damage done the previous evening.

"You're going to have to tell me sometime how you did that," Arrahaft said with a side-long look at Sordaak.

"Oh, no," replied the mage, "a sorcerer *never* reveals his tricks."

That caused some raised eyebrows, but soon those turned again to smiles as the companions said their good-byes. Cyrillis had promised to set up a branch temple in the region after telling the barbarian leaders what she was looking for in students. Arrahaft had promised to test all of the youths to determine compatibility before the summer solstice.

Sordaak had promised similar aid if students could be found that demonstrated the acumen required for wizards/sorcerers. However, any training along those lines would have to be done at his new keep when it was complete.

As was the standard practice for barbarians, none wanted anything to do with ranged weapons, so Breunne was let off of the hook easy. However, Savinhand promised to send a delegation to perform a feasibility study as to locating a branch office of his guild in the region.

In all, many smiles were exchanged and forearms clasped as the companions departed. Their mounts had been tended to and were eager to travel, so they made good time back to Riversedge, arriving just before nightfall.

Arrangements were made for the evening meal and quarters for the night. The previous night's festivities still lingered among most of the men, and none was looking for a repeat performance.

Morning found the companions again mounted and ready for their ride to the coast.

Egredt strode purposefully up to the paladin's horse and bade him to dismount. "I wanted to personally thank you for what you did in Beordgoff before you leave," he said.

Thrinndor stepped down and the two clasped forearms. "Think nothing of it," the paladin replied. "I could not stand by and hold my tongue under the circumstances." He grinned. "I *do* need allies in this region, and I saw a means to that end in fostering an alliance between your two peoples."

Egredt raised an eyebrow. "Thanks just the same. Internment by Arrahaft would have been short-lived. I would have either joined their cause or they would have killed me trying to force me to do so." He shook his head.

"Yes," admitted the paladin, "he is most certainly hard of head."

"Agreed." As Thrinndor pulled himself back up into the saddle, the barbarian scratched his head. Clearly he had more on his mind. "I don't suppose you can tell me just what you need alliances for in this region?"

The paladin shook his head. "I have no agenda. I merely want to extend my sphere of influence as wide as possible should I need to call in a favor or two." He smiled reassuringly as he turned his mount and started him on the road that led back to Klarrooft.

Egredt wasn't convinced as he watched the most interesting group of six to visit their little village in a long time—maybe ever. The barbarian shook his head as he turned and went back inside. *An alliance with Beordgoff Castle. Who'd have thought it?*

Vorgath walked next to his friend, and Thrinndor could tell there was something on the dwarf's mind. "Something bothering you, old one?"

The dwarf took several steps before answering. That the barbarian didn't take the "old one" bait was not lost on the paladin.

"Thanks for coming to get me," Vorgath began.

Thrinndor waited for more, but that seemed to be it. "Well, someone had to come rescue your sorry ass!"

"Rescue?" The dwarf looked up at the paladin, his face turning red. "That's what you call that? Why, I had those pea-brained morons right where I wanted them! Another day or two and I'd have been running the place!"

Thrinndor rolled his eyes. "That explains why you were late, then. Just busy taking over Pothgaard?"

"Late?" The barbarian stroked his beard. "I would've been on time except I got talked into one last battle." Vorgath grinned up at his friend. "And then I ended up in their prison."

"There will always be one last battle," chastised the paladin. The smile left his face. "You must know you are needed."

Vorgath's eyes drifted to the dirt on the path in front of him. "Yes," he said demurely. The barbarian took a deep breath. "It wasn't my intention to let you down."

"I know." Thrinndor twisted his foot free and lightly kicked the dwarf in the head. "I trust you got your required training in?"

"Of course," Vorgath said, grinning. "I gained multiple ranks, learned a new weapon and even trained on using *Flinthgoor* in a defensive posture." He was obviously glad to be on a different subject.

As was Thrinndor. That apology was getting weird. He knew his friend regretted his actions; it was just not the dwarf's way to *apologize* for those actions. Not normally, anyway. He decided to let the defensive-posture thing go, even.

The journey back to the Isle of Grief was uneventful. However, the prevailing winds worked against them, thus requiring an extra day on the water. It was late on the fourth day after departing Riversedge before they finally stepped onto the dock on the island.

"Damn, it's good to set foot on solid ground once again," Sordaak griped.

"Oh yes," said the paladin, "I forgot about your aversion to travel by boat." He smiled at the mage. "But you could have teleported here, could you not?"

Sordaak returned the smile as he grabbed the hand of the cleric. "Of course." Together, they walked down the pier toward the construction site.

A couple of hours later found the companions seated around a table in the dining hall, plates heaped with food in front of each.

Thrinndor looked across the table at the sorcerer, who was seated next to Cyrillis. "What is next?" he asked around a mouthful of stew.

There had been some discussion along these lines during the voyage back to the island, but the mage had been vague in his answers. More often than not the conversation had drifted to filling one another in on the happenings during the winter. That had suited Sordaak just fine, because he was not exactly sure *what* was next, and he was not all that excited about discussing that fact.

The sorcerer took in a deep breath. "Well," he began as the door to the hall opened, spilling cool night air into the heated room. In walked a troglodyte, one that Sordaak thought he recognized, but it was hard to tell—they all looked the same to him.

The trog recognized the sorcerer and walked over to stand next to him at the table. "I was sent here to give you a message."

"Yes?" the mage waited as he chewed a mouthful of the stew.

"Our defenses were broken on the north end," the creature spoke in very good common.

"By who?" Thrinndor spoke first.

The troglodyte turned its limpid eyes on the paladin. "That is not known. It is also not known exactly how many came ashore. Three of our sentries were slain, and we found three boats used by the attackers."

"Can you take us there?" Thrinndor asked.

The creature nodded. "Of course. However, it is on the northernmost tip of the island, across much rough terrain."

"If we leave now," Breunne said, "we'll be there before first light."

The troglodyte hesitated. "Possibly," he said. "A large party will take longer." The creature shrugged.

Sordaak scowled at the plate of hot food in front of him. "And that is one of the reasons why we all will not go." All eyes turned to look at the magicuser. "An even better second reason is that the landing on the north shore could be just a ruse to get us away from the construction site."

"A ruse for what purpose?" Cyrillis asked the obvious question.

The mage glared at the cleric. "How in the Seven Hells should I know?" he demanded. "To get us away so a main force can attack here? Or maybe just to distract us? *I don't know!*" His glare shifted to the paladin. "This development *cannot* be allowed to delay construction! We're behind already and the next leg of our quest is not obvious to me yet!"

Thrinndor raised an eyebrow but remained seated. "I do not like splitting our force, yet I fear Sordaak is correct. We cannot leave this base unprotected." He pondered for a moment as he stared down at his plate of food, which was rapidly growing cold.

When he looked up, his face was determined. Some were not going to like their assignments. "Breunne, Savinhand and I will accompany the messenger back to—"

"You're not leaving *me* behind," the barbarian said evenly, his tone low and unwavering.

The paladin stood and turned to face his old friend. "Hear me out old friend." Vorgath's brows knitted together as he crossed his arms on his chest. "We must not leave this post unprotected, nor can we ignore the intrusion into our lands." Thrinndor paused, waiting for the dwarf to continue his argument, but Vorgath just stared. The paladin cringed; a quiet dwarf was not always a good dwarf. "Your leadership will work best with the giants should the construction site be attacked while the three of us are away." He took a deep breath as he turned to face the ranger. "I will need Breunne and Savin for their tracking skills to see if we can determine how many came ashore and which way they went." The rogue and the ranger both nodded.

Thrinndor turned back to the barbarian. "The healer and sorcerer should remain in the event their services are required, and that leaves either you or me to stay and watch over them." Again he took in a deep breath. He needed to win over his friend with this next part. "My skills in tracking and the out of doors will best be served going with Breunne and Savin—besides, a decision might be required that needs my attention." It was the best he could come up with. "If this base is attacked—which I am starting to think likely—I will need you here to deal with the attackers." The paladin smiled down at the dwarf. "With you, these two," he swept an arm to indicate Sordaak and Cyrillis, "and the giants, woe be unto any that try to breach our defenses here!"

The one great eyebrow on the dwarf's head separated somewhat, and the paladin knew he had won the verbal skirmish.

Vorgath stood, took the two steps necessary to get into the paladin's face and said, "Very well," he grated as he jabbed a stubby finger into the big fighter's chest. "I'll do as you ask. But," his brows unified again, "if there is trouble on the north end, you must send for us immediately."

The paladin nodded his head. "Agreed," he said. "And the reverse is true. If you are attacked, get word to us posthaste."

The two stared at one another for a few moments more and then clasped forearms. The paladin did some mental brow-wiping. *That went better than expected.*

Thrinndor released the dwarf's arm and turned back to the room. "It is settled then." He looked over to where the ranger and rogue sat. "You have a half-hour to get what you will need. We will meet at the stables at that time." Both men nodded as they looked longingly at the lukewarm food on their plates.

They stood at the same time, each grabbing some bread and stuffing some of the meat into it. Quickly they made their way to the door and disappeared into the night. The troglodyte followed them.

"How will we stay in contact?" Cyrillis asked.

The paladin's forehead furrowed. "Good question," he said as he turned to look at the sorcerer.

Sordaak rubbed his chin. "I've been working on something in the event we must become separated," said the mage. "It will not work for great distances, but this rock is not that big." He grinned over at the paladin. "While it has become difficult for me to be away from Fahlred," at the mention of his name the familiar appeared, perched lightly on the magicuser's shoulder, "I found that I can send him away for those short distances and we can still communicate. And, if we lose communication, he can pop back and forth between places. That would allow us to stay in touch, as it were." He grinned.

The paladin nodded. "That should work. How should he travel with us?"

"You'll never know he is there," promised the mage. "If you require his presence, just call his name."

Somehow that does not seem all that reassuring, thought the paladin. He nodded, shrugged and started for the door. He turned before exiting. "I must get ready. We will return within three days unless we are detained." He looked over at the dwarf and smiled. "I would expect any action to happen here. Do not try to defeat the entire army by yourself!"

"Like you'd be of any help!" replied the dwarf through a mouthful of stew. "Just you hurry your narrow ass along and try not to get into any trouble without me."

Thrinndor briefly considered a suitable reply but could not come up with one. He turned and pushed the door open, stepping out into the cool evening air.

Vorgath continued chewing and then swallowed. He washed the savory stew down with some cold ale. "So you believe we will be attacked here?" His eyes never left the door.

"Yes," said the mage, his eyes also on the door. "Something about how the troglodytes lost three sentries, but there not being an attack doesn't make sense to me." He twisted his head around to lock eyes with the barbarian. "I feel it in my bones that was but a feint."

"But," both men turned to look at the healer, "how is it that anyone knows of this place?" Her eyes befell those of the sorcerer. "You have taken such great care to ensure none know what you are doing here."

Sordaak shook his head slowly. "Nothing this big can be kept a secret forever," he said. "That it has remained so this long is a wonder." He smiled at the healer—he couldn't help himself. "People talk, even though warnings have been given. I've been on and off this island several times in the past two years. Someone was bound to notice."

"That and the torches of the night construction crew cannot be kept hidden," Vorgath said.

The mage let out a sigh. "I know. We've tried shielding the light, but that is problematic at best. A passing ship, a flying bird that reports to a master, it's too hard to keep a secret this big for long."

"So you think Praxaar's people are coming to do something about the construction here, then." Cyrillis' eyes were a mixture of sadness and determination.

Sordaak nodded. "It's the only explanation I can come up with for an incursion onto this island, at this time, by three boatloads of men." He grimaced. "There is—and has been—nothing here of interest to such men for two thousand years. Why now?"

"Why indeed?" Vorgath said as he emptied the flagon and set it gently back on the table. Abruptly he stood and headed for the door. "I'm going to go have a word with the sentries and turn in. Good night."

"Good night," Cyrillis and Sordaak replied at once.

Chapter Six

Welcoming Committee

Two days passed without incident at the construction site. The communication via the quasit had worked well, and Thrinndor's party had been able to determine at least fifty men had come ashore in the three boats but had as of yet been unable to locate their camp.

This bothered Sordaak.

Then, on the morning of the third day, a messenger knocked politely on the door to Sordaak's chambers. Instantly the mage was awake and he swung his bare feet off of the cot he was using as a bed, swearing bitterly as they touched the cold stone floor of his room.

Quickly he jerked the door open and poked his head out through the opening. He blinked a few times as the much brighter light of the corridor beyond momentarily blinded him. "Yes. What is it?" he asked of the indistinct mass he assumed was human who stood in the passage.

"Lord Vorgath requests your presence in the west tower, sir," a voice replied.

"*Lord* Vorgath?" Sordaak blinked a few more times to clear his vision.

"Yes, my lord," replied the dwarf.

The sorcerer could now see that it was a dwarf. Why would a dwarf call the barbarian—who was also another dwarf—'lord'? Sordaak shook his head. "Tell him I'll be there shortly."

"Very well."

Sordaak slammed the door behind the man and quickly turned to change out of his night clothes. Briefly he wondered just when he had begun wearing night clothes, but shook his head as he rushed through his morning routine.

The mage took the circular steps two at a time as he hurried to join the barbarian. Therefore he was more than slightly winded when he stepped off of the last one—just over one hundred steps from the rocky shoreline below. He'd had this and the other tower on the eastern side of the harbor entrance built first so they could see anyone that might approach from the south. They also served as the first line of defense as they were both equipped with massive catapults and two large ballista, each capable of launching six-foot arrows at the rate of three per minute. He liked the catapults best, though. The buckets could be loaded with smaller, head-sized shot that could be set ablaze, and those would be devastating to any wooden vessel that tried to run the narrow opening between the two towers.

"A bit out of shape, aren't we?" the barbarian greeted him at the top.

"Yes," admitted the mage, his hands on his knees as he tried to catch his breath. "What is it you had me awakened for, *Lord* Vorgath?"

"You like that, do you?" The barbarian was beaming. "I figure we who are building this keep should be shown some respect! After all, I—we—brought the dwarves here, introduced them to the rich ores below and now they *want* to treat me like a king!" The smile on the dwarf's face went from ear to ear. "Who am I to say no?"

Sordaak straightened. One eyebrow had traversed the skin on his forehead and was mingling with his hairline. "You wanted to show me something?"

Without saying another word, Vorgath turned and pointed out through the window to the south. On the horizon were five black dots—dots that could only be ships.

"And so it begins," Sordaak said quietly.

"Yes," agreed the barbarian. "It would seem so."

"You've been watching their approach. How long until they get here?"

The barbarian hesitated as he looked out over the water, and then at the shoreline below. "With these favorable winds, they'll be here by noon."

"I'll see what I can do about the favorable winds." Sordaak smiled as he touched the collar to his new cloak.

Grimly the barbarian's eyes went back to the ships. "Those are large craft— each capable of carrying at least forty or fifty men. Perhaps we should contact the tall skinny guy."

The mage nodded and called for his familiar. Instantly Fahlred appeared. The two communicated silently for a few moments, and then the quasit blinked out again.

When the mage opened his eyes again, Vorgath could see he was worried. "They finally found the trail of the intruders. Thrinndor reports it's a group of fifty fighters, and they headed this way more than a day ago."

"That means they probably arranged to get here about the same time as those in the ships," Vorgath observed.

"Sounds like they plan on hitting us from both sides," agreed the sorcerer.

"Fahlred also reports Thrinndor can't make it here until at least early afternoon."

The barbarian looked out over the water at the approaching ships. "Then we're going to have deal with this crowd on our own." He turned and smiled at the mage. "Damn, he's gonna be pissed when he misses out on all the fun!"

Sordaak couldn't help but smile. "I'll get with Stormweaver to see if we can delay this group, somewhat."

Vorgath nodded. "That would be prudent, I believe."

"Something's bothering me," said the sorcerer as he stroked his goatee. The barbarian raised a questioning eyebrow, but said nothing. "Counting both groups, it looks like they brought somewhere between a hundred and fifty and two hundred men."

"So?"

"We have over two thousand dwarves."

Vorgath nodded his head slowly, combing his own beard with his fingers. "Perhaps they don't yet know about the Dragaar Dwarves."

"Perhaps." Sordaak was deep in thought now. "Vorgy, I want you to go to the barracks. I want about two hundred of the dwarves outfitted for battle with pitch-forks, picks and other non-standard implements of war. Bring them to man the defenses here in the harbor. I want them clearly visible to the approaching ships."

"Why not the entire Clan? And why not with their usual array of weaponry?"

"Because, in the event some of our adversaries escape to fight another day—and some of them certainly will—I don't want the strength of our full force known by our enemies."

Vorgath nodded slowly. "I like the way you think!"

"In prior conversations you mentioned that your brethren had gotten soft. Can they fight if need be?"

"I was a bit harsh on them due to their complacency," the barbarian admitted. "However, do not discount their worth in battle. They will avail themselves well when defending their home—and this is now their home."

Sordaak looked into the dwarf's eyes to determine the conviction of his words. He was convinced. "Good. I don't want them to have to fight. We need them working on the Keep."

Vorgath leaned closer to the mage. "We won't need the Keep if we don't survive this. The dwarves will fight."

"Good point," Sordaak answered. "However, it is my intention that at least on this front there will be very little fighting."

The barbarian raised an eyebrow but held his tongue.

"Worry not, o axe wielding disdainer of the arts, there will be adequate opportunity for melee along the northern front."

"There'd better be!" the dwarf grated. He started for the stairs.

Stormweaver poked his head up through the opening in the floor before he could get there. "What are those ships for?" his voice boomed into the cramped space.

"I'll let you explain," replied the barbarian as he brushed past the giant and started down the steps, going slowly at first.

Sordaak turned to point back out over the water. "Wait!"

Vorgath, on the third step down, stopped. He turned and raised an eyebrow inquisitively.

The mage nodded toward the ships.

Vorgath rolled his eyes and climbed back up to stand beside the mage and the giant, who was stooped over to look through the window.

The ships had gotten closer, but now they were taking down their sails and appeared to be coming to a halt. "What are they doing?" Vorgath asked the obvious question.

"Well," Sordaak said, scratching his head as he considered this new information, "it appears they are waiting for either their other force to attack first or they want someone to come out and talk."

The barbarian looked up at the mage's face and nodded. "I doubt it's that first option because I believe that force behind us is planning to attack while we're distracted with the ships—at least that's how I'd do it."

Sordaak looked down at the dwarf. "Makes sense." His eyes meandered back to the ships. "So I guess I've got to go talk to them."

"*We* have to go talk to them," corrected the barbarian.

The mage was about to argue, but he changed his mind. "Very well. *We've* got to go talk to them. But only you and me. If things get ugly out there, I can only bring the two of us back quickly."

Vorgath glared at the sorcerer, still miffed at being left out of the original plan.

Sordaak smiled and headed for the stairs. "Let's go, shorty. I'm not getting any younger!" he said as his head disappeared below.

Vorgath looked over at the giant. "Damn wizards! Always trying to be funny!" He followed the mage down the stairs.

"What about me?" asked the giant of a now empty room.

"Wait here," the answer wafted up from below. "We won't be long. Based on what we find, I'm sure we'll have some action for you and your brethren."

The barbarian caught up with the sorcerer as he approached the village docks. He selected a small skiff easily handled by one, but with plenty of room for several more. They boarded and the barbarian cast off the lines.

Sordaak assisted the dwarf getting a sail set and soon the small craft was skimming across the water, the distance between them and their objective diminishing rapidly. The mage pointed at one of the ships, where someone on board was using a signal light to get their attention. Vorgath adjusted their course accordingly.

Within minutes their skiff sidled up to the vessel Sordaak had pointed out. The dwarf released the rope on the sail boom, allowing it to flap noisily in the early morning breeze as their boat slowed to a halt, stopping precisely where the barbarian had wanted.

Sordaak turned and looked at the dwarf and lifted an appreciative eyebrow. Vorgath merely shrugged as he lowered the sail. The two of them grasped ropes that had been dropped from the ship above for the purpose and quickly secured their much smaller vessel to the larger.

A rope ladder was then dropped from above and Sordaak again made eye contact with the barbarian. At a slight shake of his head, the mage stood aside as Vorgath shouldered *Flinthgoor* and quickly ascended the ladder.

Sordaak waited for the barbarian to hoist himself over the rail of the ship above and, with his best air of authority, followed his friend more slowly.

The sorcerer stepped gingerly over the rail and planted both feet on deck, much happier than he'd been on the moving ladder. Vorgath stood feet shoulders' breadth apart, his greataxe dangling loosely from his right hand in front of him. He faced five armed men, each ready to deal death at a word from—whom? Sordaak could see no one obviously in charge.

The mage made sure his cowl hid his eyes and stepped around the dwarf to confront the men. "Who is in charge here?" he demanded, his voice audible above the normal creaks and groans of a vessel at sea.

"I am," said a voice that boomed loudly from the door that led below decks. A magnificent figure clad in full plate armor pushed past those blocking the door. She took two steps, and the men stepped aside for her as he passed between them. *She?*

The woman was tall—several inches taller than the sorcerer. Her armor was *white*—made of a metal that Sordaak had never seen before. She wore a cloak that covered her shoulders, denoting hierarchy of some sort. She was clearly a person of noble stature. The symbols woven into both the cloth of the cloak and etched into the shoulders of the armor the sorcerer recognized as denoting a servant of Praxaar. The young woman's stance, charisma and overall demeanor told Sordaak she was almost assuredly a Paladin in the ancient god's service. That was going to complicate matters.

"My name is Jaramiile—"

"I am Sordaak," interrupted the mage. "What is your purpose in these waters?"

The paladin's eyes only briefly registered uncertainty at the demand, but quickly she recovered and her smile revealed straight, beautiful teeth. The overall effect: beautiful. Striking, even. Freshly brushed long hair the color of corn silk flowed like a mountain stream down to her tiny waist. Her dazzling green eyes appeared to look into one's soul. Those eyes did not reflect the smile, however. "We are here to determine just what you are doing out here on the forbidden Isle of Grief."

Succinct and to the point. Sordaak could grow to like this girl—too bad she was going to have to die. Pity. "My purpose is my own," replied the sorcerer. "You will reverse course and return to the mainland, never to enter these waters again."

This time Jaramiile's eyes widened slightly. Quickly, they narrowed them to mere slits. "You are in no position to make demands!" She waved her arms to encompass the flotilla, clearly bolstered by her apparent position of power.

"Your ruse has failed." Sordaak's tone was unwavering. "The men you placed ashore have been—or will soon be—captured and neutralized." The mage paused while the surprise in the paladin's eyes flared. "Reverse course and return to the mainland or be destroyed."

Sordaak could tell his words had had the desired effect on the paladin's men, but Jaramiile didn't even flinch. "You are bluffing, of course!" Her eyes flashed again. "I will come ashore and determine for myself what purpose you seem to hold so dearly."

There was an uncomfortable silence when the mage didn't immediately reply. "I do not bluff," Sordaak said evenly. "This is my final warning; disregard it at your own peril. Turn your ships around or be destroyed."

Now the paladin looked around nervously. This sorcerer was *too* confident. Yet there was only the two of them. "Take them!" the paladin shouted as she waved her arms. Her right hand flashed, suddenly holding a really large bastard sword, its blade sheathed in ice.

Sordaak took one step back and put his left hand on the barbarian's shoulder. "You have been warned." Simultaneously he squeezed both Vorgath's massive shoulder with his left hand and *Pendromar* with his right. The mage felt the barbarian's rage tremble beneath his hand as the two winked out of existence on the ship's deck, to reappear in the tower they had so recently left. Only now all four of the giants were present. It was suddenly very crowded in the tower.

Sordaak released the barbarian's shoulder and shoved him toward the stairs. "You have your orders," he said sternly, knowing Vorgath's rage waited just below the surface. He wanted no part of that right now.

The dwarf took two steps, but then he paused as he glared briefly at the sorcerer. Unable to think of anything brilliant to say, he began his trip down the stairs, his rage dissipating with each step.

Sordaak waved the Storm Giants over and explained to them what he wanted. "I don't want a single, major storm that blows them back out to sea," he said. "Instead, I want individual, localized storms that produce lots of lightning. Damage their ships and maybe even destroy one or two of them, but I want the bulk of their force to make it to this point."

Stormweaver nodded, but his eyes held the obvious question.

"Some of them will escape back to the mainland, only to tell the tale of what they faced. We must disguise our true power so that if and when they return, they don't bring enough men for the task then, either." Sordaak smiled at the giant.

Now the giant smiled in return. "Very clever."

"Yup. I seldom get accused of being deficient up here." Sordaak tapped his head. He then also explained what he had planned for the dwarves and about the other force that would probably be attacking from inland.

"You have thought this through, I see," Stormweaver said. "Very well, we will make the sailors uncomfortable." He looked around the chamber. "Where's Thrinndor?"

"He, Savin and Breunne are on their way, but they are probably several hours out," answered the mage. He had started down the stairs.

The giant leader looked out through the window at the ships. They were once again under full sail and approaching the harbor defenses. Individual men could now be seen standing at the bulwarks. "Then they are going to miss all the fun."

"Uh, huh," Sordaak agreed as he disappeared. "Vorgath agrees with that sentiment."

After making preparations to defend the northern front—mostly by leaving that to Vorgath and a select group of dwarves outfitted for war—the magicuser decided to monitor the approach of the flotilla from the East tower. First he ensured the dwarf had selected a messenger to send for him should he be needed. This was all going too easily.

The giants were set up in the West tower and the dwarves were staged in two groups, one on either side of the entrance to the harbor in regiments of one hundred each. They looked pretty comical with their makeshift implements of war, but Sordaak hoped they would see no action. In fact, he was counting on it. If all went as planned, the so-called battle would be over in time for the dwarves' evening shift.

As the ships approached the entrance to the harbor, the winds began to swirl. Clouds formed and joined together. The skies darkened and flashes of lightning briefly chased the gloom.

Without anything to do but watch, Sordaak grew bored and decided he would try his hand at storm control, as well.

He caressed the collar of his new cloak and spoke the words of power. He had done this many times since receiving the promised cloak from the Storm Giants but had yet to test these new powers in battle. The mage felt the power course through his fingers and allowed the spell to charge his being. When he felt the power was at its peak, he reached out with *Pendromar* in his right hand and used the staff to focus that energy. As the mage watched, a cloud formed and grew. He continued to pour the energy into the cloud and the mass darkened and began to roil.

Sordaak licked his dry lips and focused his attention on a single ship, one at the back of the flotilla. The cloud moved obediently in the direction indicated. When the seething dark mass was close enough, the sorcerer released the rain.

A torrent lashed out, drenching the crew of the vessel that looked so tiny from the sorcerer's vantage point. Many of the men raised shields over their heads for protection from the elements. Sordaak smiled and then whispered another word of command and hail began to pelt the boat. This new menace sent the few still exposed scrambling for cover.

With still another word the hail increased in size, now causing large splashes all around the boat. Wood splintered under the assault from the skies. Frantically, the crew tried to maintain control of their vessel, but the swirling winds made that difficult at best.

As Sordaak watched, the commander of the boat shouted orders to turn around. That's what the mage had been waiting for. He released a lightning bolt with a pointed finger. An arc of light shot from the cloud and blasted the water off of the starboard bow of the ship. A miss. His next blast merely lit up the sky as no bolt extended to the sea. *No matter, there are many more where that came from.*

Sordaak pointed again and a bolt flashed from the boiling clouds and crashed into the stern of the vessel. The wood detonated in an explosion of splinters turned missiles and was easily heard from his perch in the tower, sending screaming and charred bodies sailing into the air only to splash into the water nearby. Some flailed about wildly, others rolled over, their unseeing eyes pointed toward the heavens, bobbing silently in the churning seas.

The flash from the bolt served to also illuminate the boat for a brief instant and the sorcerer saw an unprotected face turned toward him from her place at the single mast. *Her* place.

That brief instant was enough for him to recognize the woman as his sister Shaarna. Then the sundered wood caught fire and she was hidden from him by smoke as the vessel foundered without direction from the helm.

Sordaak made a slashing motion with his hand and the hail stopped. He poured more rain onto the burning vessel, trying to quench the flames. But that simply created more smoke as the crippled vessel listed heavily to port. It was taking on water at an alarming rate, already visibly down by the stern.

The magicuser called up a gust of wind to clear the smoke. That worked, but the decks of the boat were now listing heavily to port and no one was visible. His sister no longer stood at the mast.

Damn! He cursed under his breath. He briefly considered going back out there in another skiff but quickly discounted that as a bad idea. His sailor skills were probably just good enough to get him killed.

Wistfully, he shrugged and turned his attention back to the rest of the ships. Three of them were aflame and two of those were clearly sinking—including the one he and been toying with. The third drifted aimlessly with no one at the helm.

One of the remaining two vessels was under maximum sail, headed back to the south. The other was clearly also still under command and had multiple ladders draped over its side picking up survivors from the water.

"You want us to destroy that boat, as well?" Stormweaver asked.

Sordaak hesitated and shook his head. "No," he said. Visions of his sister's face haunted him. Should he just let her die? Wouldn't that make things easier? But, he couldn't shake the feeling that her fate was tied to his in some way. "No, allow them to collect survivors." He turned at the sound of feet coming up the stairs. "They won't be bothering us anytime soon."

Chapter Seven

by Land

Vorgath, worried that they would be attacked on the northern front first, went to the barracks and arranged for one hundred appropriately armed dwarves to meet him along the northern perimeter—the fighter-types anticipated along that perimeter would be heavily armed, and he wasn't attacking a reported fifty well-armed fighting men with a bunch of dwarves outfitted with pitch-forks and shovels! They'd be slaughtered!

That settled, he did as directed and outfitted two hundred dwarves, separating them into two regiments. Selecting a commander for each, the barbarian explained what he wanted.

Finally, he set aside ten men for the defenses on top of the towers, ensuring that those selected had been trained on the use of the ballista and the catapult. The remainder he directed to array themselves loosely along the shore at the entrance to the harbor, with instructions to fall back to their main camp should any ships make it through.

Certain his orders were understood, he ordered them into place. His last words were to make sure those on the ships saw the weapons they wielded. He had to answer the usual questions, and he got the expected disappointed looks when he explained they were for show and had little expectation of actually using the weapons.

Vorgath watched his orders carried out and then he turned and ran along what was quickly becoming the outer wall of Sordaak's keep. *Damn, this is a BIG keep*, he thought as he rounded the northwest corner and located his men milling about.

The barbarian looked the situation over and didn't like what he saw. Plaintively, he looked to the skies, wishing that damn dragon—Icy Bitch—was around for support. He needed to know where the opposing force was to get his men situated in proper defensive posture and she was good at flying recon.

No matter, he thought, *with these dwarves and Flinthgoor, this will be short work*. Scratching his jaw, he summoned his men. Again he selected two sub-commanders and told them what he wanted.

Obediently, two groups headed toward the two hills he had selected between which Vorgath figured the enemy force must pass. They got themselves into position and settled down to wait.

Vorgath had retained twenty dwarves, and they set up a camp out in the open between the hills for all to see. He even directed that they build a fire and begin a meal.

Finally, he selected two of the younger dwarves and sent them out as scouts, ensuring that they knew to report back at any sign of the enemy.

He then settled in to wait. He checked the sun and could tell it was not quite noon. *Surely the enemy had planned on a coordinated attack and would soon show themselves.*

Noon came and went and impatience began to grow in the barbarian. He could see the storms brewing off to the south and knew the wizard was engaging their foe there. He paced back and forth and everyone knew to give him space.

Vorgath looked up at the sun and saw that at least an hour had passed. "Put out that damn fire! We're going to take the fight to them!" The barbarian stalked off toward the north, heading for the valley between the hills where the bulk of his force waited. His men scurried about, trying to catch up after dousing the flames.

Without being told, Vorgath's men formed up into two columns and began to march. Initially they had planned to march four-abreast and five deep, but the grumbling from the interior dwarves about not getting to see any action got loud enough that the barbarian acquiesced and allowed them to march two abreast.

Sheesh! You'd think these dwarves were all warmongers! Or maybe even barbarians! Vorgath smiled; he was glad his brethren were excited about swinging at something other than rock. *I could get used to this, leading a group of dwarves into battle...*

As he topped a small rise between the two hills, Vorgath could sense the eyes of those waiting on either side on his back. A flurry of movement from their right turned out to be one of the scouts returning.

Vorgath spoke with him in subdue tones as the others waited.

Irritably, the barbarian motioned for the scout to go back into the field. He turned to his men. "Nothing!" he spat. "They're nowhere to be found." Vorgath glared at those gathered around him, and his anger began shifting to worry. Something about this didn't seem right.

Quickly he evaluated their position and determined it was pretty good under the circumstances. No enemy could approach from the north without going through this valley, and they had good cover from those who waited on either side. *Dammit! Where were they?*

"Wait here," he said to his second-in-command. "You're in a good position. Call for reinforcements and send for me if you're attacked." Without waiting for a reply, he broke into a run, heading back toward the keep.

As he rounded the northwest corner, he noted multiple storm clouds outside the entrance to the harbor, with lightning dancing all across the water. The dwarf shuddered briefly as he thought about how it must be to be on those boats.

Vorgath ran down the path and turned toward the construction tower—still the highest point on this part of the island. He took the steps two at a time and was mildly surprised to find himself more than lightly winded when he finally reached the top.

Quickly, he rushed over to the window overlooking the keep and, bracing his hands on the ledge, shielded his eyes against the sun as he searched the compound for movement. Seeing none other than those who were supposed to be there, he shifted his attention to outside the walls. Still not finding anything, he continued his search by selecting smaller sections of ground to cover.

He was beginning to think he had been wrong and was about to give up when he spotted movement along a ridge *east* of their position about a half-mile away. Not sure, he marked the position with landmarks, ensuring he could quickly find it again, and looked away. The dwarf counted to three and looked back. *Yes! There they are! Keeping to the shadows, but that has to be them!*

Vorgath did a quick count and was again confused. There were no more than twenty or thirty men in the group. And why from the *east?* Quickly, the dwarf surveyed the compound, trying to determine its defensibility. What he saw didn't please him. The walls to the keep had scarcely been started and could be easily breached from *any* side.

He was about to head for the stairs when a thought struck him. He focused his attention to the west, looking for anything out of the ordinary. Any sign of movement.

There! Damn! They've split and are coming at us from two sides!

Vorgath looked from one grouping to the other and back. Both groups were about a half-mile off and coming fast. This was a well-coordinated approach. What the dwarf couldn't figure out was why they hadn't attacked at night.

Ten minutes—maybe fifteen, the barbarian surmised as he turned and threw himself down the stairs, taking them two and three at a time in reckless abandon as a plan began to formulate in his mind. Reaching the bottom, he burst through the door into the sun and stopped, momentarily confused as to direction by the repeated circles of the stairs.

Spotting the bunkhouse, he launched into motion toward the door and kicked it open. "Get your asses out of bed!" he shouted. "To arms!"

Nothing. No movement at all. *Damn!* The barracks had been where he pulled men from first to build the forces out on the harbor defenses. *Shit!*

Vorgath ran back out into the bright sunlight and stopped. Briefly, he considered retrieving the force he had left up north, but knew he hadn't time. Frustrated, he looked around, knowing the bulk of the dwarves were underground in the mines and there was no way to get them to the surface in time, either.

Wait! He had seen some of his brethren still hard at work in the temple and knew there were others who had remained on shift—at Sordaak's insistence, of course.

The barbarian turned and sprinted through the half-finished outer gates of the keep. Inside, he spotted a fellow dwarf pushing a cart of mortar toward the temple. Vorgath grabbed the man by the shoulder and spun him so they were eye to eye. "Go north out of the gates. I left a crew of dwarves out there. Bring them here, *fast!*" The dwarf hesitated. "*NOW!*" The barbarian pushed the man toward the gate.

The startled dwarf stumbled for a couple of steps and then turned and broke into a dead run, not looking back.

Vorgath shoved the cart out of his way and continued toward the temple.

Once there he was able to round up twelve men. He sent two of those to gather anyone else working inside the walls. Then the rest ran to the makeshift armory, only to find it mostly picked over by the prior fighters.

As Vorgath handed out the implements of war, he was torn. This rag-tag group of ten or so stone workers armed with seldom-used swords, halberds and an axe or two was no match for a presumably well-equipped, seasoned group of fifty or so fighters. He could either set up a skirmish line to prevent the enemy from entering the keep and try to hold out until his men from up north arrived, or he could leave the keep, leading the enemy toward one of the larger forces of dwarves in the harbor.

Silently, he cursed the magicuser and his grand schemes. He couldn't lead the enemy to his poorly armed kindred; the death toll would be too high. In fact, he had to *make sure* those supporting the harbor assault were not attacked.

"I need a runner!" Vorgath demanded.

A young dwarf holding a sword stepped forward. "I-I can do that," he stammered.

Vorgath doubted the young man was out of his twenties. "Very well," grated the barbarian. "Run to the west tower and inform that damn magicuser that we are under attack and may require assistance." The boy nodded and turned to leave, but Vorgath grabbed him by the shoulder. "Tell him to bring the healer, too." It hurt to ask, but there was no help for it. Too many lives were at stake.

The boy nodded and sprinted through the gate.

Vorgath took a deep breath and turned to face his men. Rag-tag didn't begin to describe what he saw. Most of the dwarves still had their work aprons on, and several had mortar stains in various locations. Weapons were random. A rusted greatsword here, a greataxe with a huge chip missing there, a poleaxe, a couple of swords, a smattering of shields. The weaponry was a disgrace.

Vorgath made a mental note right then to ensure that this was never allowed to happen again. Sordaak was going to complain, but these men needed time to make weapons in defense of this island—their new home—if there were those out there who were going to try to take it from them.

The barbarian sighed heavily, fighting back the battle-lust building inside. There was no way he could lead this group into battle against a greater number of foes who were certainly better-equipped and better-trained.

Damn.

But, he couldn't let these men know that. Looking around, Vorgath saw faces of men eager to defend what was theirs regardless of the situation. Of course they didn't know exactly what faced them.

Quick estimates in his head informed him that time was running out. Their enemy should be here any minute, while his northern force was at least a half-hour away.

"Follow me!" he shouted as he turned and ran toward the gates.

As the barbarian approached the entrance, a man with misguided theories as to the powers of his command stepped in front of the onrushing Vorgath, raised his hand, palm-outward and said loudly, "Halt!"

Not recognizing the man, Vorgath didn't even break stride. He brought *Flinthgoor* crashing down on the man's shoulder, splitting him from the base of his neck almost to his groin.

The man's face went from confident, to surprised, to sheer terror. Then his eyes rolled back in his head as the force of the blow knocked him to the ground.

Vorgath skidded to a halt, motioning for his men to continue running. "To the dining hall!" he shouted. "We'll make a stand there!"

The dwarves thundered past, leaving Vorgath searching right and left to see where the now defunct man came from. He didn't have to look far as a grouping of six or seven men separated themselves from the shadows as arrows began chasing his men.

An arrow brought down the dwarf bringing up the rear when it lodged in his upper thigh. Vorgath took the two steps necessary, reached down and ripped the arrow free in one harsh movement. He then helped the man to his feet and shoved him after the others. "No time for lying around! Now *move*!" Obediently, the dwarf stumbled after his companions, limping badly on his damaged leg.

Vorgath didn't have time see whether the injured man made it. Instead, he screamed a battle cry and whirled to face the enemy he heard coming up behind him.

He was just in time to block a slash from a sword wielded by a tall fighter. The sword clanged harmlessly off of *Flinthgoor's* shaft as the barbarian twirled it like a much smaller axe. Catching the glint of another blade out of the corner of an eye, Vorgath dove for the ground and tumbled twice, rolling at the legs of an adversary.

As the dwarf surged back to his feet, he whipped his greataxe in a sweeping arc where he remembered those legs to be. His aim was true and the creamy white blade severed the man's right leg just above the knee. The fighter screamed as he toppled over, his hands going to his thigh to stanch the flow of blood pouring from the open wound as best they could.

Knowing he was surrounded and in deep trouble, Vorgath looked around for a way to put his back to something solid. The only thing nearby was the right side of the gate tower for the keep. The barbarian took two steps that direction, swinging at and missing another fighter who blocked his path, only to see another dozen or so fighters step between him and his chosen defensible position. *Damn!*

Vorgath spun again, swinging *Flinthgoor* blindly at arm's length and connecting with a slicing rip across an enemy's midsection, not doing much damage but forcing the man to think a little harder about following so closely.

The barbarian didn't have time to celebrate as two very capable-looking fighter-types stepped in front of him. They kept out of the reach of the dwarf's greataxe, though, having seen what it could do first-hand.

Vorgath took the brief moment that allowed to again assess his situation. It didn't look good. They had him trapped. He doubted the tumble move would work again. He felt rather than saw someone coming up behind him, so he ducked down to one knee and swung *Flinthgoor* in a wide arc, focusing behind him. The tactic worked, slicing deep across one man's thighs and burying the blade into the side of another.

Both screamed in pain and flung themselves back. Vorgath used the distraction to wrench his blade free with a nasty sound. He surged back to his feet and dove between the two injured fighters. He tumbled three times, feeling blades narrowly miss as he rolled across the hard-packed earth.

As he finished the third roll, he stood just as a sword bit deep into his upper torso—at least one of his adversaries had anticipated that third roll. The barbarian felt a second flash of pain as an arrow clawed its way deep into the fleshy tissue of his left shoulder.

Vorgath roared as he brought *Flinthgoor* crashing down on the arm that held the offending sword. The fighter stepped back, inspecting his much shorter right arm in horror as blood sprayed from the stump that had been his forearm.

The barbarian's satisfaction was only momentary as he felt another stabbing pain in his back. He spun to face this new adversary his greataxe again at the ready, but the man had dodged aside and narrowly avoided Vorgath's blade.

Hearing the commotion behind him, the dwarf injured by the arrow looked back to see if he was being pursued. Seeing the barbarian's plight, he shouted to his companions for help. Stone masons and iron smiths they were, but cowards they were not. In seconds, the group of ten men had reversed course, formed into a wedge and dove into action.

So intent on taking down the barbarian were the men that they neither heard nor saw the approach of the dwarves. And so it was with complete surprise that these ill-equipped tenders of the earth fell upon the enemy from behind.

Many men fell before that first surge, but there were many men behind that, for both parties of men had now joined together and they numbered well over the original estimate of fifty. Closer to seventy-five.

Vorgath saw his comrades and briefly considered yelling for them to run, but he knew that would be a waste of breath. Seeing they were now probably going to die together if they didn't get help fast, he felt a surge of pride that his men had returned for him. They were obviously willing to die for him, if need be. He couldn't allow that.

Damn, Sordaak's gonna be pissed!

With a broad smile on his face he howled another of his battle cries and charged through the mass of fighters between him and his men. He was concerned to see some of the damage done by his blade undone by some sort of healing spell! *They had a cleric! Maybe more than one! Dammit!*

Vorgath planted his greataxe between the shoulder blades of a fighter who had had the misfortune of turning his back on the barbarian. Vorgath shoved the dead man aside as he wrenched his axe free, feeling the sharp pain of yet another arrow, this one in his right thigh.

In that instant, he was through to his men and he could see that while they had done some major damage—at least ten men lay dead from their assault—they were not faring so well now that the enemy knew they were there. Two of the dwarves lay dead or dying, sword slashes easily visible on their unarmored bodies. A third went down with an arrow to the throat as Vorgath watched. This is what he had tried to avoid. Vorgath waved at them wildly. "To the tower!" he shouted and turned to run toward the structure.

Still another went down, slashed from behind as he turned to follow his wild-man leader. Using *Flinthgoor* like a scythe cutting through wheat, Vorgath hacked his way toward the tower, hoping the stone walls of that edifice would be able to protect them.

He was bleeding from multiple cuts to his upper torso, arms and lower body by the time he made the door to the tower, and he looked like a pincushion, with at least four arrows protruding from various places on his body. Two more of his men had fallen on their flight to this place, leaving him with only five that made it through the door, and most of them were in bad shape.

As the last man stumbled through the door, Vorgath kicked it shut and slid home the latch with a thud. There were several accompanying thuds as arrows lodged themselves into the wood from the other side.

"Break it down!" someone shouted from outside, and the barbarian knew their reprieve was limited as this tower had never been designed for defense.

Soon the sound of axes splintering the wood of the door could be heard, and Vorgath looked around at his men. Two were leaning heavily on their weapons, having suffered hits to their legs. One tried mostly unsuccessfully to stanch the flow of blood from a nearly severed arm. Others had almost as many cuts and arrows as did the barbarian.

"Up!" Vorgath hissed as quietly as he could, only speaking loud enough to ensure that he was heard over the pounding on the door.

Again the barbarian was proud of his kindred because, without complaining, they turned and quickly moved up the stairs. Vorgath took the time waiting to yank the two arrows he could easily get to out of his body. He bore the pain with clenched teeth and he had to reach for a rail to steady the spinning room. *Where was that damn cleric when you needed her?*

"You gonna live?" one of his men called down. Vorgath thought he even heard something akin to compassion in the man's voice. Or sarcasm.

"Of course," grumbled the barbarian, his vision steadying. "Takes more than a couple of measly arrows to keep *me* down."

"Whatever!" the dwarf above said as he continued his ascent with a shake of his head.

Yup. I could get used to leading these men.

Vorgath forced himself to begin climbing. That exposed more places that hurt than he cared to think about.

About halfway up, the door burst in below and the dwarf peered over the edge and made eye contact with a burly human male below.

"After them!" shouted another as he followed his leader through the door.

The burly fighter looked at the man, stuck out an arm and blocked the man's path. "No." He slowly raised his eyes to again lock eyes with those of the barbarian. "We don't have time for that." Vorgath felt a sudden chill in his core that momentarily blocked the pain. "Set fire to the steps. We'll roast them alive!"

Chapter Eight

Fireworks

The dwarf messenger was out of breath by the time he poked his head up through the opening in the floor. Spotting the sorcerer, he wearily climbed the rest of the way up and stood panting before the mage.

"The compound is under attack," the man said between gulping breaths.

Sordaak crossed his arms and waited, knowing there must be more.

"Our forces were divided," the dwarf continued. "Lord Vorgath sent me to tell you he was under attack and to tell you that you may be needed." That sinking feeling in Sordaak's stomach became full-blown concern. "He also said for you to bring the healer."

Vorgath asking for a *healer*? Involuntarily he took a step toward the dwarf. "Where?"

"I left him at the armory."

"*CYRILLIS!*" shouted the mage, startling everyone in the tower.

"Yes?" The cleric's voice came from the opening in the floor. She was about halfway up the stairs.

Sordaak shoved the dwarf out of his way to get to the stairway and began taking the steps two and three at a time. "Stormweaver, gather as many men as are in the immediate vicinity and meet me at the keep. *NOW!*"

"Yes, my liege," the giant called after the receding mage.

As Sordaak rounded a bend and spotted the healer he said quickly, "Vorgath's in trouble."

"Again?" was all Cyrillis managed to say before the sorcerer touched her and the two were instantly teleported to the armory. "What the—" the healer blurted out as she struggled to get reoriented. She hated it when Sordaak teleported her without warning.

"Shhhh!" hissed the mage, holding a finger to his lips and staring around at nothing. Suddenly he rushed out the door and stood in the alley out front while the cleric scowled at him. She didn't care for being hushed and followed more slowly.

Abruptly the mage cocked his head, clearly hearing something. Cyrillis heard nothing and was about to tell him so when the mage reached out and grabbed her hand. "C'mon!" he said, pulling her along behind him.

Sordaak's demeanor began to infect the healer, so she said nothing and did her best to keep up as he took off running toward the main gate.

As he passed the dead man ripped from shoulder to groin Sordaak said, "Vorgath's been here." He paused to listen and then headed for the commotion that could easily be heard coming from the direction of the tower.

Cyrillis looked at the grisly sight and shook her head. Briefly she wondered which god the man was standing before at this moment and what the conversation was like. Again shaking her head, she ran after the sorcerer.

*

It had been a long time since Vorgath had felt fear crawl into his heart, and he didn't like the feeling. Forcing that fear down, he bellowed in rage and leapt from his perch a full thirty feet above the ground. He held *Flinthgoor* in both hands as he fell toward this hated enemy.

The burly fighter, clearly the leader of this band of men, had turned and was issuing orders to burn the entire compound when the howl of rage came from above. He looked up just as Vorgath's boots struck the man in the chest, knocking him backward into the wall, where he slid to the ground.

His fall broken somewhat by the big man, the barbarian hit the ground hard, tumbling to his left. The majority of his wind left him, but he retained his wits and jumped to his feet, only to discover a searing pain in his right ankle. No matter, he whipped his greataxe around in a wide arc, beheading a robed figure who had bent to render aid to his leader.

Good, one cleric down. Limping badly but not caring, the barbarian waded in. *Flinthgoor* arced through the air in wide swaths, dealing pain and death wherever flesh was encountered.

His chest heaving, Vorgath stood above the stunned leader. "Burned alive? This day you will cower before your god ere I do!" With all his remaining strength the barbarian raised *Flinthgoor* and brought it down on the man's head.

The leader raised a hand to block the blow, but Vorgath's greataxe severed his hand at the wrist and continued its inexorable descent. The blade split the man at the forehead, clear down into his chest. There it halted, the weapon's momentum spent.

The dwarf raised his foot to place it on the dead man's chest and provide leverage, but a white-hot pain from the back of his head blinded him and he sank down to lie next to the dead man on the floor.

*

Sordaak, with Cyrillis behind him, peered around the end of a bunkhouse opposite the tower to see several dozen men running in all directions. Many of them held burning torches and, as he watched, a man threw one of those torches up onto the thatched roof of the bunkhouse.

Sordaak forced Cyrillis back against the wall, held his finger to his lips and quickly backed up and into the open doorway. Once inside, he waited only briefly to see if he could tell if they'd been seen. No one came their way, so he assumed they had escaped notice. For the moment.

"I'm going to create a distraction," he whispered. "Find Vorgath. Check the tower first. I saw several men come out of there."

Cyrillis nodded. Without waiting for a reply, Sordaak stepped around her and back out into the bright sunlight.

He was spotted immediately. "Hey!" a man with a sword and shield shouted. "Who are you and—"

Sordaak didn't hesitate. He raised *Pendromar* and blasted the man with a lightning bolt, knocking him backward into an alley next to the tower.

The crack of the lightning bolt was loud, and the sorcerer now had the attention of several in the street between buildings. Sordaak raised his left hand and he fanned it back and forth, spewing a sticky, sinewy web from his fingertip. He continued the spell a second time, ensuring that he had covered anything that moved in his web. He heard a whisper of movement behind him as the cleric slipped out of the building and ran along the wall in the opposite direction.

Sordaak smiled as he raised both hands and, placing both thumbs together, released a sheet of flames from his splayed fingertips. It had taken some practice to get the spell just right now that *Pendromar* always occupied one of his hands, but the effect remained the same.

The web material was extremely flammable and ignited instantly, going up in a loud *whoosh*! For good measure he launched a fireball across the street to ensure all the web material on that side burned, as well.

The resulting screams were most satisfactory, and Sordaak smiled as he stepped further out into the street and turned to the left, his staff at the ready. The men in this alley were too busy putting out fires in their clothing and hair to give any concern to the man in robes who walked silently past them.

At the intersection, he encountered too many men to count. Briefly his brow knitted in concern; there *had* to be more than fifty remaining in this street *alone*! There were way too many for the healer to be able to get past undetected.

More distraction. Fortunately, the black-robed figure with a cowl pulled down hiding his eyes wielding a black rune covered staff did a large part of that work for him. Shouts and curses caused eyes to turn toward the sorcerer. As several started toward him, Sordaak closed his eyes, raised *Pendromar* high over his head and spoke a word of power.

A blinding flash exploded from the staff, bathing the entire area for blocks around in pure, white light. Men screamed as they covered their eyes, but it was too late as most of them were blinded.

Next, the sorcerer brought the heel of the staff down hard on the ground and the earth beneath their feet began to rumble and shake. Blindly the men fell to the ground, unable to tell what was going on around them. But that only took care of about half of his adversaries. Others had been looking away or were able to withstand the earthquake.

Of immediate concern was a group of about five who took the brief lapse of spells from the sorcerer as proof that they were safe. Gathering themselves, they charged at him, thinking the mage would have no answer for a mass attack.

They were wrong. Sordaak again raised his left hand and pointed a finger at the rapidly approaching men. His spoken word was said so quietly that they never heard it.

Another lightning bolt shot from the end of his finger, but this time upon striking the lead fighter, it emerged at his back, split and went to the next two where they emerged and to the next two behind them. As Sordaak held the spell, the fighters danced uncontrollably under the electricity that coursed through their bodies. The mage held them for a few seconds longer and then released them, all five falling to the ground, their bodies smoldering in the street. They did not move. The mage made a mental note to move that particular spell up in his repertoire of useful battle spells.

Sordaak turned and pointed at another group that had had similar ideas, but those ideas fled in a hurry, soon to be followed by the men who had them.

Out of the corner of his eye, the mage saw Cyrillis cross the street and slip into the tower. There was some commotion inside, but he didn't have time to wonder whether she was all right as a group of fighters that had been caught and burned by the web had recovered sufficiently to regroup. And they were less than pleased.

Sordaak turned and blasted the ten or so who had gathered the courage to try to attack him from behind with an Ice Storm. Icy, swirling winds howled from the sorcerer's lips. Ice pellets stung exposed skin, and snow blinded the men as they leaned into the wind, hoping to fight their way through to the source on what was now treacherously slick ground.

Several looked like they might actually make it through, so Sordaak released the spell and launched a fireball into their midst. That did it. The resulting blast knocked the remaining few who stood to the ground.

Hearing footsteps behind him, Sordaak spun to see more than twenty men running at him with raised weapons. *Damn, how many had made it ashore, anyway?*

Knowing he was in trouble and that it was too close for his standard fireball, he again chose the web spell. The sticky substance shot from his finger and entrapped the men wherever it found them. But there were too many. Sordaak could see that some were going to make it through or around.

The sharp pain of an arrow in his side reminded him that there were more men to his left. A quick check showed another ten or so men running at him from that direction. *Shit!* Sordaak's right hand gripped his staff, and he felt the stabbing pain of a sword from his right as he winked out of existence.

That stabbing pain was more than enough to distract him. The teleport spell works by the magicuser picturing in his mind where he wants to go, and the magic takes him there. When distracted at the wrong time, the spell—like any other—can go awry.

This one did.

Cyrillis rushed from the brightly lit street into the gloom of the tower without regard to what she might find. What she did find caught her by surprise.

First of all, the tower was not gloomy from lack of light; the stairs leading aloft were ablaze, and it was smoke from that blaze that made it hard to see. There was a man with his back to her bent over a dwarf she was certain was Vorgath. He lay next to a man with his head clove in two. The back of the barbarian's head was a mess of twisted metal, blood and gore and she couldn't tell from where she stood whether he yet lived.

But that was not her immediate concern as another man had seen her enter the tower. He smiled the smile of a man knowing he was about feel the flesh of a woman against his skin and started toward her.

Cyrillis had other ideas. The ground shook under their feet and she used the distraction to go on the attack. She whipped *Kurril* around and clouted the man on the side of the head with the heel of the staff. That only dazed him, however, and he put his hand to the side of his head, looked at the small amount of blood in his palm and grinned insolently. "That all you got?" he said as he cast aside his sword and shield. The man who had been bent over Vorgath straightened, turned, crossed his arms on his chest and also smiled a crooked smile. More than one of this man's teeth was missing. The first lunged at her.

Cyrillis was ready for the move, however. She stood relaxed with the heel of her staff on the ground until he moved. A quick step back and she was in full defensive posture, *Kurril* held before her in both hands.

The man dove at the cleric, intending to use his much larger mass to drive her if not into the wall, then to the ground. Cyrillis planted the heel of her staff into the dirt and the head into the man's midsection. She used his momentum to raise him up and over, where he sailed past and slammed into the wall head-first. He slid down the wall and shook his head when he made it to the floor.

A glance at the second man revealed a surprised look on his face. He forced that aside and grinned wickedly. "Works for me," he said. "Now I get you all to myself." He started to cast his sword aside, but instead he looked down at the blade, obviously intending to hang onto it. "Prepare to be boarded, bitch."

Cyrillis glanced down at the man's crotch. "With that little thing?" she said sweetly.

"Huh?" Suddenly concerned, the man looked down at his groin.

With unanticipated quickness, the cleric used the distraction to whip the heel of *Kurril* up and the sharp edge clipped the fighter's forehead. He staggered back a step, raising his left hand to a slice on his forehead. When he pulled it back, the palm was covered in blood. The malevolent glare he focused on the healer caused her to step back. "You're going to pay for that, whore."

Cyrillis licked her lips, drawn tightly over her teeth, and dropped back into a defensive posture. Her opponent straightened and turned to face her. His eyes shifted slightly and she could tell he was trying hard *not* to look behind her.

Alerted, the cleric started her spin, but suddenly her arms were pinned to her side. She struggled but was unable to break free of the man's greater strength. Cyrillis screamed and slammed the heel of her staff down onto his toes.

It was his turn to howl in pain, but he did not relinquish his grip. She squirmed, slamming her head back to where she hoped her assailant's was. The healer connected, but only a grazing blow to the man's cheek. Again she screamed as she twisted in the fighter's arms.

"Hold still, damn you!" the man said through clenched teeth.

"Yeah, hold her still," said the other man as he approached, loosening his belt when he got close. "I have something here you're gonna like!"

Cyrillis aimed a kick at his groin, but her foot got tangled up in the man's pants as they fell toward his ankles. She pushed herself backward and whipped her leg toward the wall, taking the man's legs out from under him.

"I told you to hold her still, you moron!" bellowed the man from the ground.

The fighter behind the cleric loosened his grip to slap her hard on the side of her head, momentarily dazing her. "You hold her," snapped the man behind her as he shoved Cyrillis toward the man as he stood, "I saw her first, anyway." His grin indicated he had had enough of this struggle. "Firsties are *mine*!"

"*What?*"

A splintering crash was heard behind them as a section of the still burning staircase fell noisily to the floor, startling all three of them. Out of the flames rushed two dwarves, their beards and portions of their clothing ablaze. They held twisted and broken weapons high over their head as they rushed to the cleric's aid. Another dwarf leapt off of the broken stairs above their heads, not wanting to miss any of the action. He screamed in pain when he landed on an injured leg, but he charged forward anyway, ignoring his discomfort.

The two fighters were easily subdued, one of them slain outright when the greataxe in the lead dwarf's hands buried itself deep in the man's neck. The other dropped his weapon and surrendered, his eyes wide at the sight of the flaming dwarves.

Cyrillis freed herself from the remaining fighter and immediately used her cloak to smother the flames on the nearest dwarf. Others did the same and soon there was nothing left but smoldering hair and an article of clothing or two.

Next she retrieved her staff and administered to her rescuers. Two more dwarves tentatively swung down from the burning stairs, and she tended to them as well. Cyrillis smiled as she pushed back a lock of stray golden hair. "Thank you," she said and bowed low, her arms outstretched in salute. As she straightened she added, "I owe you my life."

The dwarf opposite her blushed and returned the bow. He straightened suddenly and stepped around the cleric to kneel beside a dwarf that remained on the ground. Vorgath.

A sharp intake of breath showed the cleric remembered why she had rushed into the tower in the first place. Gently she tapped the kneeling dwarf and pushed him aside. "Allow me, please."

The cleric was immediately concerned because she sensed no sign of life from the prone form of the barbarian. A quick glance showed gray matter mixed with the blood and bone splinters on the back of his head.

Vorgath was dead.

*

Sordaak dropped to his knees, confused by his surroundings. This wasn't the West Tower! Dark smoke billowed all around making it difficult to determine where he had teleported to. Wherever that was it was certainly *hot*!

Hot enough that breathing in seared his lungs. *This is the construction observation tower!* The smoke was coming from below. He could vaguely see the flames on the steps not far below his position.

My drawings! There are no copies! Sordaak struggled to his feet, temporarily ignoring the pain in his side. Briefly he looked down and his brows knitted together in concern at the size of the pool of blood that he'd left behind. *Damn.*

His hand went to his side, trying to stanch the flow of blood from the gash that had soaked his robe on there. Sordaak took two staggering steps necessary to reach the chart table, bent over and grabbed the rolled up documents below it. He straightened and almost blacked out from loss of blood. Fighting that, he pulled the collar of his robe up over his nose and mouth, trying to filter out the smoke.

He dropped the tubes onto the table and rolled the stacked documents already there around those, picked the resulting bundle up and bent to put them under his cloak. That motion caused the mage to stumble. He took a couple of steps toward his staff which was over by the window now acting as a chimney.

Sordaak fell to his knees and tried to crawl to *Pendromar.* Instead, he pitched forward, his eyes rolled back in his head and he lay still.

Chapter Nine

License to Die

A tear coursed its way down a smudged cheek, past a distended nostril, around a slightly upturned upper lip and along the cleric's jaw line to hang precariously on the tip of her pointed chin. A shudder that began deep within her body shook her form and the tear dropped to join its predecessors in a growing ring of wet dust at the cleric's knees.

Thrinndor burst into the chamber only to be waved to silence even before he could speak by a pair of dwarves who stood guard at the healer's back. Quietly, he moved over to join the vigil for his best friend. He dropped to one knee and began to pray.

Breunne, Savinhand and Stormweaver stepped through the splintered doorway and were similarly silenced before they could interrupt.

Cyrillis chanted the words to her prayers as her hands moved methodically, inspecting exposed brain regions, replacing splintered skull fragments with whole and melding them together into one as she went. Her most powerful healing spells coursed down her forearms and into her hands as she worked.

She had learned the ability to raise dead while training back at Paladinhome, but that spell would not suffice if the recipient still had life-threatening injuries or damage to the brain. Her investigations had revealed no such damage, but so little was known about the brain that she had no confidence in her ability to find any if it was there. She also had been told that the longer a person was dead, the less likely her spell would work.

Stormweaver wanted desperately to get the humans out of the tower. The staircase continued to burn above their heads, and at any moment the whole stair infrastructure could come down on their heads. But he knew that he dared not disturb the healer as she worked. Thus he stood over them so that if anything fell, he would be in place to deflect the burning wood before it could hit the cleric or her patient.

Finally finished with the reconstruction of the barbarian's skull, Cyrillis took in a ragged breath, placed both her hands on the shoulder blades of the dwarf and began to chant. At first nothing happened, but those in the chamber could feel the power build. Still the healer chanted, and still the power built.

Her chants grew louder until they were easily heard by all in the chamber over the crackle of burning wood above their heads. She continued to chant. Even the air in the room seemed to be charged with her power.

Stormweaver heard the wood shift far above and silently beseeched the cleric to hurry. His brow knotted in worry as the beads of sweat flowed freely down his face and neck.

Cyrillis raised her head and looked toward the ceiling far above. Her unseeing eyes opened wide and she released her power into the prone body of the barbarian with a single word.

Vorgath's body arched under the force of the spell, and the healer trembled as the power coursed its way down her arms and into the dwarf.

A hushed silence fell upon the chamber as the spell ran its course. No one in the chamber dared utter a sound, and indeed no one dared to even exhale. Suddenly Vorgath pulled a ragged breath into his lungs. Without waiting, Cyrillis rolled the barbarian over and poured her most powerful healing spell into him, knowing that her companion's life remained in the balance. The barbarian took another ragged breath and again the cleric cast her heal spell. Then she held her breath as she waited. After an agonizingly long stretch, the barbarian took another breath, this one less labored.

Sordaak's familiar appeared and was clearly agitated as it tried to get Cyrillis' attention. Thrinndor stepped in, and although touching the creature caused his stomach to churn, he grasped it by the shoulder and pulled him aside. The paladin could tell the creature needed to tell him something, but he motioned for silence. Fahlred spat a vile curse in his own tongue and walked slowly outside, staggering unsteadily on rubbery legs.

Cyrillis leaned over to check the barbarian's eyes, but that simple movement by the cleric was what the giant had been waiting for. He reached down, scooped both into his arms and ran for the door.

"Hey!" protested the cleric.

"Everyone out!" shouted the giant. "*NOW!*"

The volume of the giant's shout was the catalyst needed as those that remained inside burst into action and ran for the door. Within moments of their exit, a section of the stairwell collapsed, causing a cloud of smoke and dust to billow through the open door they had so recently exited.

The paladin looked around for the quasit and found him leaning against the base of the tower, clearly distressed. He walked the short distance and stood over the creature. "What?"

The creature turned its listless eyes on the paladin, and Thrinndor could tell the demon was in pain. "Master dying."

Suddenly, Fahlred had his undivided attention. "What? Where?" demanded the paladin.

The quasit turned and raised a finger toward the top of the tower.

"Sordaak is up *there?*"

The quasit nodded. "Yes," he hissed, his voice barely audible.

Thrinndor looked up to where smoke was pouring out of the upper window, his mind racing. Abruptly he turned and ran over to Breunne, grasped him by the shoulder and pulled him over to where Sordaak's familiar waited. Surprised, Breunne waited for the paladin to speak.

"Give me your boots."

"What?"

"I do not have time to explain," replied the paladin quickly. "Give me your boots."

Without further questions, the ranger dropped to the hard-packed earth and removed first one boot and then the other.

Thrinndor dropped to the dirt next to the ranger and pulled his own boots off as well. He looked at the first boot the ranger removed and instantly noted the size difference—his feet were much bigger than those of the ranger. Briefly he hoped what he had heard about magic boots was true; that they were one size fits all.

Without hesitation he slid his foot into the boot and was mildly surprised when the supple leather slid easily onto his foot. Thrinndor smiled, repeated the process for the other foot and stood up, stamping the boots into place on his feet. He did not want them to come off while in mid-flight.

He already knew the trigger word and spoke it. Instantly he rose unsteadily into the air, but the fighter's innate sense of balance served him well and within moments he was able to control his flight. He looked up at the window and the paladin rose toward it effortlessly.

"What's he doing?" Savinhand asked as he walked up behind the now bare-foot ranger, his eyes following the big fighter.

"I don't know," Breunne said shaking his head. As Thrinndor disappeared from sight through the window, he looked over at the quasit, now sitting with his back to the wall and looking distinctly pale. "But I believe it has something to do with Fahlred," he pointed over at the creature.

At the sound of his name, the quasit slowly raised its head and nodded. He licked his lips and tried to speak, but no sound came out. Breunne leaned closer and barely heard the whisper that sounded as if it rose from the depths of a deep, dark cavern. "Master dead." The demon then closed its eyes and didn't move again. Only the ragged rise and fall of the creature's chest told the ranger that he yet lived.

"*What?*" Breunne tried in vain to get the creature to speak again, but Fahlred didn't open his eyes.

"What did he say?" Savin asked, suddenly concerned.

Breunne shot a quick glance over to where the cleric continued to administer to the barbarian and lowered his voice. "He said, 'master dead'."

"*What?*" the rogue said louder than he wanted to. He also glanced over at the cleric, ensuring he hadn't disturbed her. He hadn't, although others in the vicinity were beginning to take notice of the subdued conversation.

Thrinndor ducked his head as he fought through the smoke and entered the tower. Instantly, his eyes watered in protest of the atmosphere in the upper chamber and his skin burned red from the heat. Flames were coming up through the floor where the opening was for the stairs, and also around where the floor was tied to the stone walls. He knew this chamber was soon to become an untenable position.

Slowly, he allowed himself to sink toward the floor, only to encounter something soft before his feet made contact with the planked wood. Sliding sideways he found bare wood and quickly knelt where he had met the resistance.

Feeling around blindly he found the form of what he had to assume was the magicuser. "Sordaak?" he shouted. Nothing, "*Sordaak!*" He shook the robed figure but met no resistance. A quick check revealed no pulse, either. The paladin put both hands on the sorcerer's chest and spent one of his healing abilities. Another check of the mage's pulse again revealed none.

The intense heat from the flames only feet away was becoming unbearable, so Thrinndor scooped the mage's slight body into his arms and stood. He heard the sound of the rolled parchment hit the floor as it fell from under Sordaak's robe. Instantly he knew what that sound was and he knelt, felt around for the sheaf of drawings and finding them, picked them up and tucked them under one of the sorcerer's arms.

The flames were only an arm's length away now and getting closer by the second. The paladin stood, repeated the trigger word and pointed himself toward the blurry sunshine of the window. Briefly, he hoped the boots could handle the additional weight.

They did, and Thrinndor ducked through the window into the cool, bright outside air. Quickly he lowered them both to the ground and set the magicuser down into the yard at the base of the tower.

Sensing something was amiss, Cyrillis looked up from her patient who was breathing normally now, and saw Thrinndor lay Sordaak onto the ground.

"No," she moaned as she jumped to her feet and ran the short distance over to where he lay. She dropped to her knees and skidded to a halt at the sorcerer's side, tears already welling in her eyes.

Sordaak's exposed skin was bright red and she could see he was not breathing. A quick check confirmed her fears: his heart was not beating, either. "No," she moaned again as she placed her hands in the center of his chest and began to message his heart externally. Occasionally she leaned over, pressed her lips against his and blew fresh air into his lungs. After a few moments of this, she glanced up at the paladin. "What happened?"

Quickly, Thrinndor explained as she continued to work. "What are you doing?" he asked when he was done. The cleric was still massaging Sordaak's heart.

"I must get the smoke from his lungs before I attempt to revive him," she explained. "Else he will choke and pass all over again."

Thrinndor nodded, certain he understood at least a little of what she was doing. "I have healing available if my assistance is needed."

"Thank you," replied the cleric. "But healing is not what is required at this point." She tried to smile at the paladin, but failed miserably.

Deciding she had done all she could with his lungs, Cyrillis separated her hands and placed them palm down on the mage's chest. Once again she closed her eyes and began to chant. As she worked her spell, the companions gathered in a circle around the pair.

Thrinndor, too, lowered his head and began to pray.

Breunne alone remained apart, his attention instead on the quasit. The creature had not moved since it had closed its eyes, and the ranger believed it might be dead. His concern was that he knew that if the master died, the familiar also died. And if the familiar died, then a portion of the master's vitality could never be regained. That's assuming the death of the familiar didn't also kill the master. This was known to happen, as well.

The ranger slid over and knelt beside the demon, preparing his meager healing spell should it be needed.

Again the power built around the cleric as she continued her chant.

When she raised her face to the sky and opened her eyes wide, her chanting stopped. A single tear released from the corner of her eye, made its way across her cheek and to her ear. Cyrillis looked back down at her patient and closed her eyes, releasing the energy of the spell.

Power again coursed through her arms and into the chest of the magicuser. Abruptly, Sordaak's eyes opened wide as if terror gripped his heart, and his back arched such that only the back of his head and his heels touched the ground.

The sorcerer made a sucking sound into his mouth and lungs that didn't sound right and then he fell back to the ground, his eyes again closed.

Cyrillis poured her most potent healing spell into the body of the sorcerer and bent to check for a pulse.

Breunne's eyes never left the quasit. He could tell by listening what was going on over with the healer and the creature's master. The quasit did not move. He was now certain the demon had died.

"No," Cyrillis moaned for a third time in what seemed in only as many minutes. Suddenly she raised both her hands above the prone caster, clenched them together into one ball of a fist and slammed them down onto Sordaak's chest.

"*What*—" Savinhand began, but the paladin silenced him with a quick slashing motion of his hand.

The healer bent to check for a pulse and apparently didn't find what she was looking for because she again raised her hands high into the air, formed the same ball with her fists and hammered on the mage's chest. "Come on dammit, *breathe!*" she hissed through clenched teeth.

Once again she checked for a pulse, and once again she was disappointed. She repeated the chest thump a third time, and suddenly the sorcerer's eyes flared wide open as before and he drew in a ragged breath.

Cyrillis immediately cast a healing spell on the mage and the redness left his cheeks. After a few moments his eyes regained their focus. Again the healer worked her healing art, and Sordaak improved visibly.

He tried to sit up, but the cleric pressed him back to the ground. "No, you must rest."

Breunne thought he saw movement behind the quasit's eyelids. He couldn't be sure, but it was the best he had to go on. He said the word of power for his spell, leaned forward and touched the creature on the shoulder and released the small amount of healing energy he had stored into the creature.

Fahlred's eyes fluttered open and he turned his head slightly to focus his black pools on the ranger. "Thank you," the quasit said hoarsely as he struggled to his feet. He then disappeared. Breunne smiled, assuming he had done well.

Sordaak tried to speak, but only hoarse crackling sounds came out of his mouth. He licked his lips and tried again. "Water," he finally managed to get out.

Thrinndor removed a skin from his belt, removed the stopper and handed it over to the mage as Cyrillis helped him to sit up. Sordaak took a tentative sip, immediately coughing and spitting a small amount of the liquid all over the cleric.

"Sorry," he croaked and again raised the skin to his lips.

"Slowly," the healer admonished. Sordaak nodded as he allowed a small amount of the life-giving fluid to trickle past his parched lips. Having survived, he swallowed that mouthful and tried again, this time taking a longer pull.

"Thanks," he said, handing the skin back to the paladin. "I'm good, now." Next he tried to stand.

"The hell you are!" snapped the cleric, tears of joy welling in her eyes. "You were *dead!*"

Startled, the magicuser looked at her with their eyes no more than a few inches apart. He nodded. "I know, but you brought me back." He smiled at her. "Now help me to my feet, please."

"What is the hurry?" Thrinndor asked as he extended a hand to help the mage to his feet.

Sordaak rolled his eyes as he reached out and took the proffered hand. "Because I need to pee!" Once he was on his feet, he held on to the paladin's hand and the cleric's shoulder to steady himself. "Whoa," he said as the ground and the sky seemed to circle one another rather dizzyingly.

"Please go slowly," Cyrillis said, not really expecting to be heeded.

Sordaak nodded. "Gotcha," he said as he licked his lips. "I'll be right over there should anyone need me." He pointed between the buildings next to the tower and walked unsteadily in that direction.

While the companions watched the mage disappear between buildings, Vorgath stumbled up from behind to lean on the paladin. "What's all the commotion?"

Cyrillis spun at the sound of his voice and her eyes narrowed. The healer took a step toward the barbarian and jabbed a finger in his chest. "You!" her voice was nearly a shout. "Once again I had to rescue you from death!"

Vorgath didn't move, but he did lift an eyebrow. "And I thank you for that," he said amiably. Cyrillis' scowl deepened and he went on hurriedly, "I will remind you that I called for your assistance this time!"

The cleric's eyes widened. "You most certainly did not!"

The dwarf was about to argue, but Sordaak walked back up, straightening his robe as he did. "Actually, he did. It's how I knew to come to his rescue."

"*Rescue?* You call that a *rescue?*"

It was Sordaak's turn to raise an eyebrow. "You yet live, do you not?"

"No thanks to you!" The twinkle had returned to the barbarian's eyes.

Realizing what was going on, Cyrillis decided to get in on the melodrama. "Actually," she said coyly, "Were it not for our hero's distractions—"

"Hero?" Vorgath spat into the ground at his feet.

"Distraction?" Thrinndor also decided to weigh in.

"—I would have never made it into the tower to save your sorry ass!"

"See?" Sordaak puffed out his chest and hitched both thumbs into his belt proudly. "Rescue!"

"Bah!" The dwarf spat into the same spot as before.

Suddenly both eyebrows shot up on the sorcerer's face. "You were dead, too?" Vorgath nodded. "You know what that means don't you?"

The barbarian's eyes opened wide as well. Vorgath reached out an arm which Sordaak took as they clasped. In unison they said, "We have a license to *Die!*" Both were beaming.

"WAIT!" Cyrillis shouted as she separated the two. She shoved both back a step with a hand in their chests. "Listen to me, you marble-headed morons!" Her eyes shot daggers. "Death is not a *game!*" Her breathing was coming in great gasps. "While I now indeed have the power to return what was dead to life, that power *is not* an exact science!" She was mad. "There are no *guarantees!*" Her eyes went back and forth, blistering each with their touch. "Each time that spell is cast, there is a chance that it might not work. Many factors affect those odds." She shoved them again. "And, each time a person is returned to the living from the afterlife, that chance of life returning is diminished!" Her next shove pinned both to the outside wall of the tower. "So, you *will not* treat death as any sort of a *GAME!*" She glared at both of them. *"DO YOU UNDERSTAND ME?"* Her chest was heaving.

Wide-eyed, both merely nodded.

"GOOD!" Her eyes darted between the two.

As the cleric turned to walk away, the two recalcitrant warriors turned to look at one another. Each smiled and raised a right hand to do a fist bump, but Cyrillis spun on them again. *"DO NOT!"*

Chagrined, both men nodded again and lowered the offending fists. The healer pinned them to the wall with her eyes for a moment longer before releasing them and returning to stand next to the paladin. She was trembling with emotion as Thrinndor slipped an arm across her shoulders and pulled her to him.

Cyrillis returned the embrace, but there was no warmth in her actions. Recent events were beginning to catch up with her, as were the potential ramifications if she had failed.

The cleric dropped to her knees in the street, put her face in her hands and released her emotion in great sobs. He shoulders shook as the pain of the previous few minutes was washed away.

Somberly Sordaak approached, his face a twisted mixture of concern and regret, but a warning glance from the paladin caused him to stop short of his goal. Instead, the mage walked around and stood silently in front of the healer at respectable distance and waited for her emotions to run their course.

Cyrillis' sobs slowly quieted, and the mage could hear her voice change over to the sing-song chant of prayer. Still he waited, not wanting to interrupt her communion with her god.

When she finally looked up, the cleric realized all eyes were on her—or at least had been, because most of those present suddenly found somewhere else to look. This did not fool her, of course, and she flushed at the attention. "I am sorry," she began as she used the palms of her hands to scrub the tears from her cheeks.

When she tried to rise, Sordaak took the one step necessary to help her to her feet and pulled her into his arms. He placed his lips on hers and for a moment they shared a passionate kiss. When he pushed back, his eyes lingered on hers. "It is I who am sorry," he said softly as he brushed her wheat-colored hair with his hand. "It wasn't my intention to distress you so."

Tears formed in the cleric's eyes, but she brushed them away and nodded. "I know," she said. "But, you were *dead!*" She buried her head in the soft folds of his robe at his shoulder.

"I know," Sordaak replied softly. "But you came to my rescue." Gently he pushed her back so he could peer into her eyes. "I promise you I will be more careful in the future." Even as he said it, he knew that to be a lie. For in death he had seen where it was they must go, and being careful was not going to be an option.

"Promise?" Cyrillis was almost begging.

The magicuser merely nodded as he gently pressed her head to his shoulder.

Chapter Ten

In Defense of Defense

Cleanup up from the battle took more than a week. Cyrillis insisted on bury-ing each and every creature that died that day—including the bodies of their enemies. She even held a service for those lost in the battle at sea. Sordaak couldn't help but wonder if his sister was one of those.

Deep down, however, he was pretty sure she was not.

The mage had pulled the paladin aside for an explanation as to what had happened after his and Vorgath's unfortunate deaths.

Thrinndor said that he and Breunne had raced ahead of the rest of their party, riding their mounts into the ground in their efforts to make it back in time. They had met up with Vorgath's northern contingent and gotten to the settle-ment in time to surprise the attackers while they searched for some unseen pow-erful wizard who had devastated their ranks. He, the ranger and the dwarves had made short work of those that remained when they saw the commotion over at the observation tower. They left the dwarves to handle the mop up duty as he, the ranger and the rogue went to investigate. The rest the mage knew.

Praxaar's minions had succeeded in burning three of their buildings, including one used mainly for the storage of food. The three damaged build-ings were going to take a week or so to replace, but repairs to the observation tower were going to take longer. Sordaak insisted that the steps be made of stone this time around.

The loss of supplies required the mage to send Breunne and Thrinndor to procure replacements. Savinhand was also to go, but his reason had a differ-ent purpose. The companions needed to find out the depth of the movement against them and who was behind it. Most likely Praxaar could be blamed, but unless things had changed drastically, the god surely was not in direct command of any resistance. No, it must be someone else, and Sordaak wanted to know who and how big was his or her following.

As it went without question that their ability to use Farreach as a supply port was no longer an option, it was decided that better fortune might be had in the ports of Pothgaard. It was also decided that for that reason that Vorgath should remain on the island and assist in the repairs. Savinhand, however, would go to Farreach.

That turned out to not be as tough a sell as he had at first thought because the barbarian had indeed convinced the sorcerer that arms were badly needed for defense of their new home. As such, he was allowed to work with his father and select a council to plan out the weapons they would need, what materials they wanted to make them from, and how many they could designate for enchantment. It was this last part—enchantment—that proved to be the sticking point. They had no one to *perform* these enchantments.

The amount of time required to properly enchant a weapon or article of armor made it impossible for Sordaak to attend to the task. Days, weeks, months or even years was sometimes required to get the enchantment correct. Obviously the goal was to not get too elaborate in these enchantments, but even a single day was out of the question where Sordaak was concerned. There were far too many tasks that required his attention.

So, it was with that in mind that Vorgath and his father asked for and received an audience with the sorcerer. The mere fact that such a request was even required rankled deep in the barbarian's being, but he forced that even further down as he knew his request was going to be met with resistance.

The paladin, ranger and rogue had been gone for two days when Vorgath and his father went to the tower, which is where the magicuser spent almost all of his time now. As the steps were at least a month from completion, a complex of ladders had to be used to reach the upper platform if one didn't have the ability to fly—a feat only Sordaak seemed to have.

This greatly pleased the mage, as it cut down seriously on the number of visitors willing to climb the just over one hundred feet of ladders. Sordaak had even taken to pulling the bottom-most ladder up to the first landing to further discourage visitors.

His time was precious to him, and he spent every minute either studying his spells or going over the plans for the keep with his builders. An audience with the barbarian and his father did not fit well into his schedule, but he made the allowance anyway.

When Vorgath and his father finally poked their head up through the opening in the floor, the barbarian was slightly put out. He straightened his new leather tunic and absently brushed at his beard while he caught his breath and waited for his father to join him on the landing.

Once Morroth stood beside him the two met eyes and nodded. Sordaak was seated at his desk with a massive book open in front of him. In spite of the warmth of the spring day, there was a small fire going in the hearth on the opposite side of the chamber.

Without preamble, Vorgath cleared his throat and began. "I have allocated additional men and women to finish the steps below."

Sordaak looked up from the book and raised an eyebrow. "To what purpose?" He abhorred the notion of *any* of the dwarves being removed from their duties in building the keep, and more specifically, the temple.

"It seems the lower ladder wanders off, limiting one's access to this chamber," replied the barbarian. "I don't suppose you would know anything about that?" Vorgath knew full well what was going on, but he felt the need to needle his friend, nonetheless.

Sordaak merely glared at the barbarian. "Of course," he said. "I raise it to keep the riff-raff away when I am working."

"Riff-raff present and accounted for," said Morroth with a smile.

Sordaak shifted his glare to the dwarf clan leader. "So it would seem."

Again the barbarian cleared his throat. *Why did the sorcerer's presence make him so uncomfortable? It didn't use to be that way.* "Be that as it may," he growled, a littler harsher than he'd intended, causing Sordaak's stare to shift back to him, "we requested time with you to discuss our weapons inventory." The mage blinked once but said nothing. Vorgath shifted uncomfortably. "Specifically, we need to discuss with you some proper weapon—"

"And armor," interrupted Morroth.

"—enchantment."

This caused Sordaak to remove the spectacles that had been perched on the end of his nose, fold them gently and set them on top of the open book. He then leaned back in his chair and folded his arms on his chest. "Go on."

If the barbarian had been uncomfortable before, he was positively in pain now. Sweat began to form under his suddenly too-tight collar and wind its way down his back. *What the hell? Why is this so hard?*

"It is understood that you don't have the time or energy to perform the enchantment on hundreds—"

"Or thousands," intoned Morroth again.

Vorgath turned to glare at his father. "Of items personally," he finished. He turned his head to again face the sorcerer. "It is with that in mind we would like for you to contact your mentor Rheagamon to see if he—"

"Impossible," snapped the caster before the barbarian could say more.

"Hear me out." Vorgath glared back at the magicuser, more than slightly irritated at being treated so. Sordaak sat in his chair, not moving. The dwarf took that as a sign to continue, right or not. "I understand your mentor must also be as busy as yourself," he said, using his best placating voice, "so what we propose is that he contact his kindred—"

"The Drow."

Vorgath turned to glare at his father again, trying to remember just why it was he had brought him along. He turned back to the mage. "To see if an alliance can be reached between our people." The barbarian could see he had piqued the mage's interest, so he hurried on. "We will need appropriate weapons for the defense of this rock, and it is my understanding," he again looked over at his father, who nodded, "that the Drow might be amenable to a pact that allows them access to proper weapons to enchant and at the same time return them to prominence in the land." There, he'd said it. It was his turn to fold his arms on his chest and wait.

Sordaak looked from one to the other, settling on Morroth. "Your contact with the Drow over the years leads you to believe they could be interested in such an arrangement?"

Morroth nodded, causing Vorgath to roll his eyes. "Oh sure, *now* you keep your mouth shut!" His father smiled.

Sordaak leaned forward and put both his hands on the table. "Very well, I like this idea. I will speak with Rheagamon. Wait here."

The mage disappeared.

Vorgath looked over at his father and both shrugged. "He got anything to eat up here?" Morroth asked, sniffing around tentatively.

"I don't know," Vorgath answered. "But I *do* know that he keeps a cask of wine behind his chair in this basket." He lifted the lid on the basket, reached in and lifted out a small cask.

"Kind of small," Morroth observed.

"Should do in a pinch," replied the barbarian.

"As long as he doesn't take very long," Morroth said, winking.

Vorgath shook the cask and returned the wink, "Well, at least it's almost full." The two of them walked over to where a small table with four chairs had been set up by the hearth. They sat down, and Vorgath removed the plug and he was in the process of pouring wine into a couple of small flagons the dwarf had retrieved from a shelf when the magicuser reappeared.

"That didn't take long," observed the barbarian.

"Long enough for you to find my good stuff," Sordaak replied with a smile as he walked to the shelf and picked up a third flagon and joined the dwarves.

"Well?" Vorgath asked over his raised cup.

"Deep subject, shallow mind," the mage said over his. He winked.

"Hey, I resemble that remark!" The barbarian replied, returning the wink.

Sordaak stood, raised his cup and waited for the others to do the same. When they had, he said formally, "Here's to great ideas."

"Great ideas are how kingdoms are born," Morroth added.

"Here, here!" Vorgath agreed.

The three tapped cups and raised them to their lips. Sordaak took a sip of his, Vorgath and Morroth drained theirs and reached for the cask again.

The barbarian raised an inquisitive eyebrow. "So does that mean the Drow have agreed to enchant our weapons?"

"No," the mage said as he eyed the two dwarves helping themselves to his wine. That caused Vorgath to stop mid-pour. "Relax," Sordaak smiled, "they *will* agree, but first Rheagamon has to present the plan to them at council. He will do so later today."

The sorcerer raised his glass to his lips and quaffed what remained. He held out his cup and cleared his throat. "However, I might have ad-libbed on the offer just a bit." It was Sordaak's turn to hold his breath while he waited for a reaction. He wasn't disappointed.

Vorgath was in the process of refilling the mage's cup, but stopped halfway. "Explain."

Sordaak's left cheek twitched as he inspected his half-full cup. He sampled the wine before speaking. "Good year," he said as he put his nose deep in the cup. "Great nose; hints of tobacco, deep earth and ripe, red berries." He took another sip and smacked his lips. Vorgath raised an eyebrow as Sordaak set down his cup. "I've asked Rheagamon to bring the Drow to join us."

Now two sets of eyebrows were raised. Sordaak was glad neither had wine in their mouths, as surely they would have spit it out.

"You *what?*"

Sordaak held up both hands. "Hear me out," he said as he eyed both men sternly. "I heard you through."

Both dwarves crossed their arms on their chests and glared at the mage.

"But first I want to hear why it is that you object so stridently."

The two looked at one another, and by an almost imperceptible nod Vorgath allowed the explanation to his father. Morroth returned the nod.

"Very well," the dwarven leader began.

"Wait," Sordaak interrupted. "Is this going to take a while? Because if it is, I'll have more wine brought up and perhaps lunch."

Perturbed at the interruption, Morroth first thought to decline, but then decided otherwise. He nodded his agreement to the arrangements.

Sordaak did so, using a unique set of call-down tubes he had had installed. Word went directly to the kitchens, and he had found that rather convenient of late.

That settled, the mage walked back over to the table and refilled all cups and sat back down opposite the dwarves. He looked wistfully over to the chair at his desk, as it was far more comfortable, but decided further delays might send his guests into apoplectic shock. "Please continue."

What followed was in essence a description of why the dwarves distrusted the Drow. But, since the whole damn dwarven race was hell-bent on drawing out every detail to the point no one ever remembers what the original point was, what should have taken fifteen or twenty minutes at the most, instead took nearly the rest of the afternoon.

In the end, Sordaak was able to surmise the entire dislike for the dark elves was based on the fact that the damn elves insisted on using the precious ores mined from the earth to make jewelry or other articles to wear, like crowns, bracers or some other such nonsense. And when they did make weapons, they were limited to the smaller, daintier variety: rapiers, daggers, bows and special elven arrows.

Sordaak briefly considered pointing out the absurdity of their dislike, but decided he didn't want to be thrown from the window of his own tower. Not today, anyway.

Just as the mage was about to open discussion, Rheagamon appeared. Seeing the dwarves, he motioned for Sordaak to join him on the opposite side of the room.

"Excuse me for a moment," Sordaak announced as he stood and followed the wizard over to the window. Once there they had a brief conversation and then Rheagamon disappeared. The mage walked back over to join the two who waited.

Vorgath looked up at the mage inquisitively.

"I believe I have a solution," said the mage ceremoniously as he sat down. He didn't give either dwarf an opportunity to interrupt, moving on quickly. "The Drow have agreed to come and assist you in your efforts to build a proper armory." Vorgath took in a sharp breath to interrupt, but a stern look from the mage cut him off. "However, they have agreed to occupy the undead-riddled Ardaagh. Even Rheagamon has elected to assist, agreeing to take over the chambers once held by Dahjvest."

Sordaak took a sip of his wine, making a mental note to ensure that he had obtained all of this particular vintage as was available, as it was really good. "In return for their service and the enchantment of weaponry you provide," he took a deep breath, "they require half of all ore and gems obtained from the mines below be submitted to them for the purpose—"

Vorgath jumped out of his chair. "Preposterous!"

Morroth grabbed his son by the arm and pulled him back to his chair. "Twenty-five percent," said the dwarf leader sternly, "and not a single amethyst more!" He folded his arms on his chest.

Vorgath looked at his father, his face red with indignation, but held his tongue.

The magicuser shook his head minutely. "Not acceptable." He rolled his eyes as he pondered. "Forty percent! And choice of all gemstones."

"Bah!" spat the elder dwarf. "You are mad, sir! You want my men to dig the stones from the ground and give the Drow *choice*?" Morroth pretended to take a sip from his empty cup. "Twenty-five percent, *our* choice and they must provide a workforce to assist in working the mines!"

Sordaak clucked his tongue as he shook his head. "You must be getting daft in your advanced years, o venerable one!" Sordaak admonished. "You inquire as to the availability of services to enchant your implements of war from a basically peaceful people—"

"Pfft!" Vorgath was just happy to get a word in. He had lost track of where he had lost control.

"— and offer them baubles in return." Again he clucked his tongue. "I have been empowered to negotiate on these misunderstood peoples behalf, and I assure you your offer is insulting." Morroth waved his right hand, dismissing the thought. Sordaak continued, "However, if you are willing to concede oversight of all mining operations, forty percent of all ore and a one-for-one selection process of all gemstones, I might be able to convince these grossly underappreciated people to do as you ask."

Morroth surged to his feet, his face red. "One-third of all ore produced. Subservient positions on my oversight staff and I'll grant the one-for-one selection process of all gemstones if the Drow will perform magiks as denoted in a contract!"

Sordaak jumped to his feet, as well. "Deal!" he said loudly and stuck his right hand out.

Morroth glared into the eyes of the mage for a few moments and then smiled. "Deal!" he took Sordaak's forearm and the two grasped until the sorcerer winced.

Rheagamon reappeared, unrolled several parchments on the table and said, "Morroth, if you will sign here," he handed a quill pen to the dwarf, pointing at a line on the paper, "and initial here, here and here," the wizard continued, pointing at several places for the dwarf to sign."

When the dwarf leader had done as indicated, Rheagamon rolled up the parchment and disappeared.

Vorgath stood with his mouth hanging open, having watched the entire operation. Finally he spluttered, "Aren't you going to at least *read* that before you sign?"

Morroth looked at his son as if he had asked him to wash his hands before dinner—a particularly bad no-no—and said, "Of course not! If the Drow—and/or your esteemed colleague over there—wanted to cheat us in any way, it won't be with the written word, I can assure you of that." He winked at Sordaak.

"You are indeed wise and magnanimous, Morroth, chieftain of Clan Dragaar," the magicuser said formally with a bow. "These people indeed want only the opportunity to serve and restore their once proud name."

Morroth smiled and raised an eyebrow. He winked at the sorcerer. "How low were you authorized to go?"

Sordaak returned the wink and the smile. "Forty percent," he lied. "But I had to make adjustments to that when I saw your determination." He had been in fact allowed to go to twenty-five percent—but the dwarves didn't need to know that.

Finally recovering somewhat, Vorgath scratched his chin. "How many Drow?"

Sordaak walked over and rang down for some more wine. He was in the mood to celebrate. "I'm told almost three thousand." He smiled at his friend.

"*Three thousand?* Are you trying to build an army?"

Sordaak walked back over to the table and winked at his old friend coyly. "Maybe."

Chapter Eleven

Icy Bitch

hrinndor and Breunne returned a few days later with two ships laden with supplies. Savinhand sent word that he was on his way but had been detained by Guild business. Sordaak wondered just what that meant.

The Drow delegation arrived on the island the same day as the supplies, and within a couple of days the operations both above and below ground had been streamlined. With the stone-working skills of the dwarves and the engineering mastery of the Drow, soon the walls of the keep were going up much faster than anticipated.

Sordaak held council after council with committees of delegates from both races, weighing the strictness of the plans he had gleaned from the Library of Antiquity and modifications that occasionally made more sense.

When Savinhand finally showed up almost a week later, the restlessness in the companions was beginning to show. Vorgath had discussed traveling again to Pothgaard to, he said, "hone his skills." Inactivity was making him "rusty," he'd complained on several occasions.

Sordaak immediately called together his companions; he, too, was anxious to get their quest under way. Too much time had been lost already, and there was much to be done before winter settled once again on the land.

A larger table had been brought to the tower, as the observation post was not much needed for its original intended purpose anymore. Sordaak looked around the table, satisfied at the friends he had made in—what? Less than a year? Could it be? He shook his head and raised his glass. He had imported real crystal, and each of his companions had a full one in front of him or her. Although for some reason Vorgath's kept having to be refilled.

"A toast," said the mage. "To those that a year ago knew naught of one another, and yet now," his smile beamed, but his voice cracked slightly as he continued, "now we are as one!"

"Here! Here!" his five companions said as one, each raising their glass in salute. Sordaak sipped his wine first and his friends did likewise. Except the barbarian, of course.

The mage sipped again to hide his emotion as he sat down. "I have called us together so that I can update you on progress with not only the keep, but also as to what I now know we must accomplish."

This drew several concerned looks, not the least of which came from the beautiful young cleric seated at his right hand. "The added engineering of the Drow has enhanced the abilities of our dwarven brethren such that the keep walls are far ahead of schedule. In fact, I believe by winter the outer fortifications will be complete." He beamed as he delivered this news. "The temple is progressing nicely, as well. And I believe it will be ready to serve our purposes in less than a month."

A murmur of appreciation for that surfaced and the mage waved it aside. "The Drow have set up residency in Ardaagh, clearing out the undead that remained and have rebuilt structures as necessary. In all, thirty-two hundred of the dark elves occupy that once defunct seaport, providing us needed support in many facets of our operation.

"We have also now brought in the remaining Dragaar Dwarves, and that contingent stands at twenty-four hundred and change." He smiled at Vorgath, who nodded. "I do not wish to discount our security forces—augmented by the four Storm Giants—that now consists of just over four-hundred Troglodytes."

"For those of you that are math-challenged," Sordaak again winked at the barbarian.

"What?" Vorgath said plaintively.

Thrinndor smacked the dwarf playfully on the back of the head. "You do not have enough toes, old one!"

"Ha!" the barbarian said, crossing his arms on his chest in mock indignation.

"That brings our current available force to six-thousand souls, give or take."

Breunne pursed his lips and did a low whistle. "Six thousand? That is by far the largest force currently deployed in the land, surely."

Sordaak acknowledged the statement by the ranger and turned to Savinhand for verification. The rogue nodded. "I have it on good faith that to be sooth," replied Savin formally. "There were several small sects of the servants of Praxaar that banded together for the recent incursion into the Isle of Grief, but their numbers are currently limited."

"How so?" asked the paladin.

"I'm glad you asked," replied the rogue with a smile. "I called in several informants during my time at Shardmoor, and was able to determine that the armies of Praxaar have grown lax over the years—the past thousand years, to be more accurate. Inactivity and lack of resistance has decimated their ranks to where all totaled, they would number less than two thousand."

"But the Paladinhood—" Thrinndor said.

"The Paladinhood of Praxaar is alive and well," Savin interrupted. "But their numbers too have dwindled over the years to where, if they could all be gathered in one place, they might number an additional three-hundred warriors.

"Clergy?" Cyrillis asked, working her lower lip.

"Another good question," acknowledged Savinhand. "The priests of Praxaar are far less stringent in reporting their proper numbers. Either way, my informants can only account for two hundred—maybe two hundred fifty—of the clergy that once numbered in the thousands."

"Surely those numbers cannot be correct?" Cyrillis continued to work that lower lip; it was apparent she had expected more.

As did they all. Savinhand shook his head. "Of course I can't know for sure, but I have been assured that the methods used to obtain this information are sound. There are no more than two-hundred-fifty known clerics of Praxaar in the land."

"*Known*," repeated the paladin, coming to the aid of his kindred servant of Valdaar. "Surely there can be others that are not *known* to you?"

Savin turned slightly to acknowledge the paladin. "But of course," he said amiably. "But why would a servant of Praxaar wish to hide him or herself from being known in this day and age?"

Thrinndor took in a sharp breath and arched an eyebrow. "OK, you have me there." His smile didn't reflect the puzzlement in his voice, however. "But, two hundred and fifty is hardly what I thought would be available to him."

"Nor I," admitted the rogue leader. "You might be interested to know how many servants of Valdaar are known."

Thrinndor and Cyrillis looked at the rogue, hope reflecting in their eyes.

"The Paladinhood at Khavhall is the last known remaining of your kind," Savin said slowly. He then looked over at the cleric. "And the clerics of your order–all five of them–represent the bulk of the clergy serving Valdaar." His voice remained soft. "There are only two—maybe three—others in isolated parts of the land, and that information has not been verified."

Again Thrinndor wanted to argue, but there was no conviction in his voice. "Certainly there may be others who work to keep their true service hidden?"

Savinhand turned slowly to face the paladin. "Certainly," he agreed. "However, my informants have known of you and your parents for many years." His tone remained restrained. "I do not make these statements lightly."

Grimly, the paladin nodded. "Very well," he said, looking over at Cyrillis, "we will have to assume that we are all there is." The healer continued to chew on her lip. Thrinndor turned back to Savin. "Is there any way you can get word to any of those servants of Valdaar to join us here?"

Savinhand hesitated. "Of course," he said. "I can have word sent—I must protect my informants, after all—to each of the known supporters of our god to report to the Isle of Grief." A look of worry clouded his face. "But, are you sure you want to put all of your eggs in one basket, so to speak?"

Thrinndor also hesitated. Finally he let out the breath he had been holding. "Yes," he said heavily. "It is in my heart that this will be our one and only chance at returning Valdaar to power. If we fail, then I fear there will be no more."

A heavy silence hung over the chamber.

After a few moments of that, Sordaak cleared his throat. "Ahem," he said. "I called this gathering to discuss *good* news! We have six thousand to their two! We are in the position of power now!"

Smiles returned—all except for the rogue leader. "Ahem," he cleared his own throat. Everyone at the table turned to Savin and waited. "There is one other faction that I didn't mention." Thrinndor lifted an eyebrow. "There are many thousands of men in the nomadic tribes to the south that sided with Praxaar and his armies in the battle against his brother two thousand years ago."

"What? The Sahrandhii?" scoffed the barbarian. "They're dirt farmers, ranchers and an occasional hunter."

Savinhand leveled his stare at the dwarf. "The bulk of armies are made up of such men," he said. "While the fighters and Calvary garner much of the glory in battle, those called together for their mass are generally such as you describe."

"How many are there?"

Savinhand took in a deep breath before answering. "That is not known for certain. However, it is thought that more than ten thousand men could answer the call from that region."

"*Ten thousand?*" Vorgath was incredulous. "Surely not that many would respond after all these years."

"Of course that could be true," replied the rogue. "But there are actually more than twice that number in the southern region, and my estimates of ten thousand should actually be considered conservative."

That caused some solemn faces all around.

"Damn," said the sorcerer as he sipped his wine, "that sucks."

"At least we have the keep and a defensible position on an island," Cyrillis said, hope a mere thread in her voice.

"We are extremely defensible from the seas to our south," Vorgath agreed. "But the recent incursion by our enemies that put ashore on the northern fronts showed that we are vulnerable from that direction."

A silence hung heavy in the air until Thrinndor broke it. "The good news is that building such an army by our enemies will take longer time than they have to stop us." His eyes went to each of his companions. "Sordaak believes we will have what we need in a month's time." The paladin looked to the sorcerer for confirmation.

Sordaak took in a breath to speak, opened his mouth, closed it again and shrugged. As he exhaled he said, "That's not exactly what I said." Thrinndor raised an eyebrow. "Let me begin by stating that I can make no guarantees. Bahamut will certainly do his best to stop us as he will probably have to die for us to be successful, and I have my doubts that he will do so willingly." He took a sip of his wine before continuing, his voice monotone. "He and his consort of twelve—yes *twelve*—powerful gold dragons—"

A loud clatter was heard outside the window to the tower, and a woman in white robes flew through the window to land on her feet, coming to a skidding halt a few feet behind where Thrinndor, Vorgath and Breunne sat at the table— the paladin in the middle.

Thrinndor drew his sword as he jumped to his feet, sending his chair skittering back toward the sound behind him. Vorgath cursed and dove to the floor to his left, tumbling to the wall where he had left *Flinthgoor*. He stood, turned and dropped to a crouch, the greataxe held above his head at the ready. Breunne rolled to his right and when he regained his feet, he held his longsword in his right hand, a nasty-looking kukri in his left. Savinhand simply vanished.

"Did I hear someone mention *dragon*?" the woman said.

Sordaak was the first to recover, recognizing Pantorra. "It's about time you got here," he said.

"There were matters I needed to attend to ere I answered your summons," replied the beautiful middle-aged woman, an edge of sarcasm in her voice.

"Summons?" Thrinndor blinked twice as he slowly lowered his flaming blade. He turned his head so that he could see the mage without taking his eyes off of the dragon-woman. "You *summoned* her?"

Sordaak hesitated. "Sort of," he shrugged. "*Summoned* is such a harsh word. She owes me a debt, and I sent word to her that I wanted to collect."

Vorgath lowered his weapon. "Was that dramatic entrance necessary?"

Pantorra leveled her ice-blue eyes on the dwarf. "Well, I wasn't climbing all those damn ladders and stairs!" she said haughtily. "Not when I can *fly*." A concerned look clouded her handsome face as she looked around the chamber. "You may show yourself, rogue. I assure you I mean this group no harm."

"That be as it may," replied the sorcerer, "I would prefer he stay unnoticed until we conclude our business."

"Still don't trust me, eh?" the woman said with a half-smile. "Even though I answered your *summons* and did not even slay the messenger?"

"That is indeed appreciated," Sordaak returned the half-smile. "I would have been less than pleased had Fahlred been harmed." His smile didn't touch his eyes.

The two squared off, separated by about twenty feet. Neither flinched nor even blinked.

Cyrillis broke the tension. "Why did you ask her to join us?"

Ever the statesman, Sordaak thought. "Because I happen to know that my bringing her here is not the only summons she is answering right now."

Pantorra's eyes widened slightly, and Sordaak knew he had been correct. "What are you talking about?" The dragon licked her lips nervously.

"Yes, do tell," the barbarian said, holding his position, but now he was leaning heavily on the shaft of the inverted *Flinthgoor*.

"The dragons have all been summoned," the mage said smugly. "It is the time of the gathering."

A stunned silence settled on the group as each digested that bit of information. "How could you possibly know that?" Pantorra demanded.

"I didn't." The sorcerer smiled. "Not until I saw your reaction, anyway." He held up both hands to forestall her objection. "Rest assured, however, that I was fairly certain my information to be correct. With my informants telling me of suspected dragon movement and what I have since discovered about the gathering, the time is right."

This time it was the dragon's silence that spoke volumes.

"I am calling in your debt to me," the mage said, his tone hardening. "I require you to take me to Bahamut, King of all Dragons, for an audience."

The chamber erupted as everyone began to speak at once. Neither the dragon nor the sorcerer blinked, and their eyes remained locked on one another.

When the uproar died down somewhat, Thrinndor was the first to make himself heard. "You of course mean 'us.'" He was looking at Sordaak, and it was not a question.

"I do not," replied the mage. He didn't explain.

"You do realize," Pantorra said steadily, "that what you ask is impossible."

"No, it is not." Sordaak's gaze did not waver. "I climb on your back, you flap your wings, and *voila*, we're at the gathering."

"I—we—would not be allowed in," replied the dragon, her eyes also unwavering. "We would be hunted and slain long before we even reached the region. None of mankind has ever seen the gathering, and none are permitted."

The murmur in the room had died down and the eyes of the companions alternated between Pantorra and Sordaak, depending who was talking. It was obvious this was not idle banter, and none wanted to miss anything. Only Breunne watched the opposite for reactions.

"I could remain hidden from sight until we are close, where you could then put me afoot and I will make the rest of the way on my own."

"You cannot fool the great Bahamut with *tricks*!" the dragon sneered. "He would see through your subterfuge ere we left this place! His High Court would rend the skin from your bones slowly."

"Yet his twelve escorts are diminished by five—one having fallen recently to the tide of man flowing into the land from the southern region."

The dragon-woman's eye went wide. "How can you know this?"

Sordaak shrugged. "I have informants *all* over the land." He paused. "You will take me to the gathering for an audience with Bahamut."

Pantorra licked her lips nervously and shook her head. "I will not," she said, her voice barely above a whisper. "I *can* not." Now her eyes darted around the room, lighting at last on the cleric. "My dragonlets need me, and I would be slain for my part in this."

"Not if my plan works."

Pantorra squared her shoulders. "I cannot—will not—take that chance. *You* may have no allegiances—none who depend on you; but I do! I will not abandon them nor will I forsake my kind to satisfy a debt." She held her chin high and her eyes flashed determination.

Sordaak's eyes held hers for a moment longer. Then he let out a deep sigh and allowed his shoulders to droop dejectedly and his eyes to drift to the floor at his feet. "Very well," he mumbled, "Can you take him this message, then?" The mage dug a sealed scroll tube from a pocket and held it out.

A momentary spark of triumph flashed in the dragon's eyes. Quickly she forced it aside. "What is it?" she asked suspiciously.

Sordaak looked back up, trying to regain some sense of control. "It spells out our demands for where and when he can bring *Valdaar's Fist* without incurring further ramifications."

A collective gasp escaped the lips of a couple of the companions as Thrinndor and Cyrillis glanced at one another.

"Ramifications? What ramifications?"

Sordaak blinked twice, obviously surprised at the question. "Why, if he does not surrender the sword immediately, he will preside over the eradication of his entire council and his own demise, of course." A half-smile crossed his lips. Indolently he allowed it to stay as he wiggled the scroll in the direction of the dragon woman.

Complete silence settled into the chamber, easily allowing the occupants to hear the sounds of construction wandering through the window from far below.

Again Pantorra licked her lips. "There have been rumors surfacing of late concerning your sanity. I'm beginning to believe them."

Sordaak straightened. "I assure you, my lady, that I am in full control of my faculties." He waved the tube. "It's all spelled out in here. He can surrender the sword or suffer the certain agony of death after ruling all these centuries to a band that has sworn to ensure his kind are rendered inconsequential in the land."

Vorgath nodded as he growled from deep within his chest and patted the haft of his greataxe.

"You'll *what?*"

Sordaak rolled his eyes. "I'll translate it for you: He can either give up the sword or we're going to kick his scaly old ass and take it!"

Thrinndor's eyes nearly bugged out as he fought back the urge to laugh. He brought his fist to his mouth and coughed a couple of times to cover. "Sorry."

Pantorra pressed her lips into a fine line. "I will take him no such message."

Sordaak allowed his hand to drop to his side with another sigh. "Look, lady," he said, no humor in his eyes, "you have two choices. You can either deliver this scroll," he held up the sealed tube again, "or you can take me to him so that I may deliver the message in person." Silence again held the room. Now even the construction noises were nonexistent. "What's it going to be, *Icy Bitch*?"

"Why you arrogant bastard!" Suddenly the dragon-woman was breathing hard, and she spoke more loudly than she had intended. "If I could, I would take you to him just to see your face as the Lord of Dragons rips your limbs from their sockets to pick his teeth!" Her ice-blue eyes flashed as they circled the room. "Give me that tube, and I will ensure my lord gets a good laugh from it!" Pantorra's chest was heaving as she snatched the scroll tube from the magicuser's hand.

The dragon stalked over to the window, then turned to again lock eyes with Sordaak before leaving. "You have gone too far this time, *sorcerer*! You and your friends will not live to regret your temerity."

Sordaak's eyes did not waver. "Just make sure Bahamut gets the scroll, or it will be your scales that adorn our barbarian's shield ere summer begins."

Pantorra struggled to maintain her composure, but failed. Frustrated she screamed and jumped out the window. The companions heard the results of her immediate transformation and the powerful flap of her wings as she disappeared into the night. A screech ripped the air as the dragon let all in the area know that she was displeased.

Thrinndor looked over at the mage, a semi-smile pursing his lips. "What, pray tell, was that all about?"

Sordaak, his focus still on the window said, "I'll explain after dinner." With that he walked over and signaled down for the meal to be served.

Chapter Twelve

Up in Smoke

Dinner passed quietly as the party members had thoughts and emotions of their own to deal with, and none particularly wanted to deal with any other's.

While the meal was being cleared away the companions broke up into small groups and small talk was made until the chamber was once again clear of everyone except the six. Sordaak made his way back to the head of the table and sat down, noting that the wine glasses had been refilled and a pair of full carafes stood by.

As the others followed and also took their places, the conversations naturally died away once all were seated. Sordaak got the attention of the dwarf and raised an eyebrow as his hands reached into his robes and pulled out his pipe and tobacco pouch. Vorgath nodded almost imperceptibly and reached for his own makings.

Seeing what was about to happen, the remaining companions settled in for the show and murmurs of excitement danced around the table as the two prepared to once again do battle.

The murmurs changed to those of surprise as the barbarian removed his pipe. This was clearly a new instrument, as the stem was much longer than the previous version. The bowl was larger and made of a white wood, adorned with gold and other metals in a pattern that was carved in the form of dragon that had two small rubies for eyes.

Sordaak nodded his approval as he tamped the tobacco tight into his bowl. Satisfied, he waved a hand and the rolled-up bamboo curtain that hung above the window unraveled and covered the opening. He waved the hand again and about half the lamps and candles in the chamber were extinguished, throwing the chamber into shadows.

Thrinndor looked at the mage, but said nothing.

"I have some special effects," Sordaak said, his lips pursed in a half-smile.

The paladin's eyes widened slightly, and he nodded as he looked at the now extinguished candles on the table. "He has some special effects."

Sordaak squinted his eyes at the paladin as he reached for one of the remaining lit candles—one that happened to be in front of the mage. He tilted the candle and slowly, with deliberate purpose, began to light his bowl. Soon a cloud of noxious smoke surrounded the sorcerer.

Sordaak looked over at Vorgath, raised an eyebrow and slid the candle over to the dwarf at the minute nod he received from the barbarian.

Vorgath caught the holder and proceeded to light his bowl as well. The barbarian took his time, ensuring he worked all sides of the large bowl. Satisfied, he looked up and fixed both eyes on the sorcerer.

"Shall I?" Sordaak asked, his eyes squinting to keep the acrid smoke from them.

The dwarf nodded. "Please do."

The mage returned the nod and began work in earnest on building his cloud. He followed each inhale with a tilted-back head and a long exhale. Smoke billowed, and a large cloud swirled up near the ceiling fifteen or twenty feet overhead.

As the companions watched the swirling morass of smoke, the single large cloud began to separate into smaller ones. Still they swirled and began to fan out, such that heads had to turn to watch individual apparitions as they passed overhead. Sordaak continued to blow the aromatic smoke into the air; however, now it was clear he was fine-shaping each cloud as it passed by him.

The black of the smoke began to change colors. Dark red, darker blue, an odd green, one that paled before their eyes to a light gray, and two that occasionally glinted metallic; perhaps gold and maybe silver—seven in all. The seventh remained a deep black.

Mesmerized by the clouds passing overhead, the companions began to see them take shape. Cyrillis gasped as wings protruded from the clouds, then clawed feet and finally a long, sinewy neck. The heads formed last, each with eyes that glowed the same color as their scale-covered skins.

Dragons.

A red, a blue, a green, a black, a white, one silver and the remaining one a gold.

The small dragons circled uncomfortably close overhead, occasionally craning their lithe necks to peer at the puny humans below, their eyes ablaze with hatred. Every now and then one would call out to another in the screeching language of dragons, causing the cleric to jump slightly in her chair each time.

She leaned over and whispered to Savinhand, who sat next to her on her right, after a particularly loud screech. "You would think I could get used to that." She shook her head. "But they are *so real!*"

The rogue merely nodded, his eyes focused on the gold dragon. For some reason that one bothered him more than the others.

Apparently satisfied, Sordaak took an occasional hit off of his pipe, and went into what he had described as "maintenance mode." A quick glance at the dwarf informed Vorgath that he was ready.

The barbarian had anticipated this and was working his bowl such that the tobacco began to glow a bright orange, exhaling the resulting smoke toward the window.

Although the dwarf's tobacco was far less repulsive than the sorcerer's, Cyrillis at first assumed Vorgath was directing his smoke toward the window out of consideration for the others at the table. Soon, it became clear that was not the case.

The smoke flattened out in the only space left in the room not being threatened by the dragons. As Vorgath poured more into his cloud, a wall began to take shape, followed quickly by two towers and a gate. Soon it became apparent to all that Vorgath was building a keep.

Still the dwarf built, and soon the keep solidified. Spires, temples and other structures formed behind its walls. Figures formed from the smoke atop the towers, as did massive weapons the resembled a giant crossbow—one on each gate tower.

Sordaak had waited long enough. At a wave of his hand the nearest dragon— the black—tucked its wings and dove for the keep, spraying dark acid onto the gates as it pulled out of the dive. Men could be heard screaming as the acid ate through the gate, some splashing inside the keep.

The dragon flapped its wings hard, regaining altitude as it continued past a tower. The men atop that post spun their weapon and fired as the dragon rushed past. The massive bolt launched into the air, trailed by a thin wisp of smoke that resembled a tether.

The black shrieked in pain as the bolt pierced its hide beneath the powerful wings. The companions held their breath as the dragon clawed for additional height, the tether paying out behind it. Then one of the men by the crossbow used a massive war hammer to slam a bar into place, and the line snapped taught. The black dragon immediately came to a stop and began to tumble toward the ground, having lost all momentum and air from under its wings.

As the black dragon crashed to the ground the gates to the keep were thrown open and men poured out. The injured dragon climbed unsteadily to its feet, but the companions could tell the beast's injuries were mortal. Defiantly, the dragon blasted the first wave of men with its acid breath, cutting a wide swath. But those behind stepped over their fallen comrades and attacked the creature with axes and swords.

Overhead, the remaining dragons screeched loudly, and one by one they rolled over and dove on the stricken black. First the red dragon blasted the contingent with fire, followed by the white with ice. Green came next, and clouds of noxious gas covered those close by. Blue spat lightning, and the silver and gold each chose fire for their pass. But by the time the last pass happened the black dragon was dead and the remaining men ran across the open field back to the protection of their keep.

Now ever wary of the towers, the dragons made passes at the keep itself, raining their breath weapons onto the men exposed on the rooftops. Soon the temple and spires were ablaze. However, the men fought on, pouring arrows, bolts and an occasional spear from open windows at the dragons when they passed by. The giant crossbows on the gate towers released a bolt anytime a dragon got close enough.

Men and women screamed and died in fires. Others were caught in talons or teeth; undaunted they fought on. The gold dragon got impatient and ordered an attack on the gate towers directly. The red and blue dragons dove to draw the fire of the crossbows, with the gold and silver dragon circling above, waiting for an opening.

But the blue got too close and again the bolt buried itself into the exposed breast of the beast. A scream of agony ripped the air as the injured dragon swooped to regain speed and flapped its powerful wings toward the ceiling.

Again the hammer fell and the tether snapped taught. A look of panic crossed the dragon's face as it fell toward the ground. At the last second, the blue careened over and dove on the offending tower. Lighting blasted from its open maw, and every man was knocked from the parapets to fall into the courtyard below. None moved.

But the dragon's injuries and momentum were too great for it to recover, and it crashed into the space cleared by its lightning. The blue fought to regain its feet, but dark dragon blood poured from its wounds. The leathery blue wings draped down the sides of the tower, and the creature laid its head down and was still.

The red dragon succeeded in clearing the left tower, but as the dragon flew off more men climbed the steps from inside to replace their fallen comrades.

Still Vorgath and Sordaak continued to pour clouds of smoke into their creations, apparently directing movements with flicked fingers and dancing eyebrows. Both men were sweating with effort in the cool evening air, and their eyes expressed the concern they had for their work.

With two of the dragons down, one might have thought the dwarf and his men of the keep were soon to be victorious. However, the keep was ablaze in multiple locations, and if those were not brought under control soon the entire edifice might need to be abandoned.

At a signal from the gold dragon—clearly the leader—the remaining four dragons dove simultaneously at the men struggling to regain the tower. The red dragon took the lead and lambasted those manning the crossbow with fire before they could bring their weapon to bear. White swept in from the opposite direction, blasting the weapon and nearby men with ice.

One of those men lunged at the bow, sweeping it around to aim it at the white dragon, which remained dangerously close. He whipped out a sword and sliced the holding rope with it, releasing the bolt point-blank at the creature.

The dragon tried to evade, but there was not enough time to react. The huge bolt entered through the beast's mouth, open to release another blast of ice, and exited though the back of the monster's skull, taking the dragon's brains with it.

The white dragon didn't even have time to scream before its life was extinguished and the beast crashed lifeless to the ground at the base of the tower.

This infuriated the gold dragon. It screamed and dove on the tower as yet more men scrambled to reload the bow. He first scorched the surface of the tower and then landed on the weapon. His powerful claws grasped the wood of the main shaft and the dragon's powerful wings launched him back toward the sky, the offending crossbow clutched in his grip. Once clear of the tower, he cast the bow to the ground, where it shattered into many pieces.

Now the keep was certainly doomed. With three dragons down, four still remained, and those in the keep were now weaponless.

Then more figures emerged onto the barren tower roof. Two of them bore no weapons, only staves. Both were hooded figures, clad only in robes. At least a dozen men armed with longbows and spears ringed the two, providing a defense.

Sordaak raised an eyebrow, shrugged and directed an attack.

The gold dragon responded by again leading the assault himself, intending to rid himself of these impudent souls that stood in his way to victory. As he opened his mouth to bathe them with fire, spears were thrown, arrows were released and both robed figures raised their staves and cast. One launched a fireball that exploded just as the cone of ice hit from the other sorcerer.

The combined effect stopped the gold dragon's attack, knocking it back and disrupting its flight. Stunned, the dragon plummeted toward the ground below. However, he was able to recover in time and he beat his wings furiously to regain altitude.

Arrows, spears and magic missiles from the casters hastened his retreat.

Injured but still able to fly, the gold dragon was infuriated beyond reason. He immediately ordered his remaining three dragons to sweep the tower clean of these vermin that dared to oppose them.

Obediently the green, silver and red dragons begin sweeping passes at the tower. Lightning arced toward the sky as the dragons passed, along with fireballs and an occasional magic missile. Arrows bounced harmlessly off of their scaled hides, and spears missed for the most part. The spells did damage, but nothing significant.

The attacks of the dragons, however, had their desired effect. One of the mages was down and the other had to be propped up by a companion. Still, he kept the dragons at bay with an array of deadly spells.

But it appeared the dragons again had the upper hand as the keep behind them continued to burn and was certain to soon fall. Then as the red and green dragons made another pass on the keep, a puff of smoke was launched skyward from the ramparts adjacent to the towers and both dragons were snared in giant nets!

Unable to maintain flight, both crashed to the ground, the red dragon inside the keep and the green just outside the walls. The gates once again opened and dozens of men ran to the stricken dragon, hacking and slashing with whatever they had in their hands. Similarly, another group attacked the red dragon and soon both creatures were overcome.

The men stood and cheered, raising their weapons to taunt the two remaining dragons.

Then the roof of the temple collapsed in a shower of sparks and flames, causing the figures in the vicinity to flee for safety. Nearby, the same happened to the roof covering one of the main halls. Flames leapt higher, and now the entire inner keep was an inferno. All remaining men and women ran toward the open gates to escape the fires.

Seeing an opportunity, the gold dragon signaled and both he and the silver dragon dove toward the ground, alighting just outside the gates to the keep. Once there, they used breath weapons, sharp talons and even sharper teeth, augmented with buffeted air from their wings to keep those inside from escaping.

Certain doom appeared the outcome for the men and women of the keep, for they had no answer to the dragons' blockade of their gates. Then the remaining magicuser who had disappeared from the roof of the tower appeared at the gates. He pointed his staff at the dragons and launched a barrage of missiles, fireballs and ice cones with such ferocity that the monsters were forced to retreat.

A flurry of arrows and spears rained down from the archers remaining on the towers caused the dragons to retreat further, allowing those trapped within the burning walls to sprint past the magicuser.

Fear that they would soon be surrounded, the dragons leapt into the sky, their wings beating mightily for the heavens as arrows and spells urged them on their way.

Sullenly, the dragons circled, hurting but not yet desperate, certain in their superiority with mobility and size on their side.

The pitifully few remaining men—perhaps fifty in all—gathered around the magicuser a safe distance from the cauldron that had become their home.

Abruptly the silver dragon screeched and fell from the sky, succumbing to its wounds. The dragon landed with a crash not far from the gathering of men, but this time they didn't move to attack it. Instead they looked to the skies at the one remaining dragon with trepidation on their faces. Trepidation and something else: determination.

With ever-tightening circles the gold dragon began his decent, keeping his distance from the formation of men and women who watched his approach with weapons at the ready.

The one remaining dragon alighted lightly a safe distance from his adversaries. He paced briefly before stopping and staring at the humans just out of range with their bows.

The humans stared back, their weapons bristling. But they did not advance on the injured dragon. A close look showed many of their number also leaning on spears as crutches, or limbs wrapped to hide wounds and/or burns.

The dragon began to shrink and suddenly a man stood in the monster's place. With a contrite look of determination on his face, the dragon began to walk purposefully toward the gathering of men and women.

A murmur rose from the humans, the crowd parted and the magicuser limped from their midst. Using his staff to support his right leg, he strode unsteadily toward this man who had so recently opposed them as a dragon.

As the companions held their breath, the two approached one another, stopping only an arm's length apart. There they stood, eyeing one another suspiciously. Neither spoke.

Then the dragon slowly reached out his right hand. The mage eyed it briefly, then reached out and grasped the dragon/man's forearm. The two held this stance for a moment and then the smoke from the apparitions began to lose substance and fade.

Cyrillis jumped to her feet, sending her chair skittering back a few feet, clapping her hands wildly. She was radiant with a beaming smile that touched on everyone in the chamber.

Thrinndor stood more slowly, also clapping. He nodded first to Sordaak, and then to Vorgath. "Well done."

"Indeed," Breunne said as he pushed himself to his feet, clapping as well.

"Stupendous!" Savinhand announced, clapping as wildly as the cleric.

The mage waved a hand and the chamber once again brightened as the candles and lamps that had previously been doused relit.

Sordaak and Vorgath's eyes never left the others. The barbarian stood, stepped around the chair vacated by the paladin and made his way over to stand in front of the sorcerer. Slowly he shifted his pipe to his left hand and stuck out his right.

Sordaak hesitated for a moment, but then reached out his hand and the two grasped forearms, not unlike their creations had moments before.

The mage was almost certain he saw a tear glistening in the corner of the dwarf's eye. Almost. "Well done," Sordaak said, his voice somewhat restrained due to the effort he had just put forth.

Vorgath nodded. "Indeed. That was an admirable challenge."

"*Admirable?*" Cyrillis said, clearly not amused. "That was *epic!*" The cleric moved to stand defiantly next to the mage.

With a smile on their lips, Vorgath and Sordaak both turned to look at the cleric. "Indeed," the barbarian repeated with a wink.

"New pipe?" the mage asked, turning to look at the elongated stem on the instrument in the dwarf's hand.

"What, this old thing?" Vorgath's eyes twinkled as he suppressed a smile. "Just something my father gave me when he heard of our adventures with smoke." Now he was smiling openly.

"May I see it?"

"Of course," the barbarian said, handing over the pipe with a formal bow.

The instant his fingers touched the bowl, Sordaak knew he was dealing with an enchanted pipe. That explained a lot. Briefly he considered pointing this out, but he decided against it; mostly because his pipe was enchanted as well.

After a brief inspection, he handed it back. "Very nice," he said. "Did your father happen to say where he got it?"

"He might have." Vorgath grinned and his eyes sparkled. "Something about not all past encounters with the drow being contentious."

Damn! Sordaak had gotten his pipe from Rheagamon. The sorcerer returned the grin and winked. "Game on."

"Game on, indeed." Vorgath returned the wink.

"Ahem." Both the mage and barbarian turned to look at the paladin, who stood with arms crossed. "I believe you said something about an explanation?"

The sorcerer arched an eyebrow. "Oh that," he said, pretending not to have remembered. "Sure. Let's us sit and partake of more of this fine wine and I'll enlighten you."

Some shuffling ensued as chairs were pushed back into position and the companions returned to their places. Sordaak alone remained standing as he walked around the table, topping off each of his friends' glasses before returning to his chair.

Once there he stood for a moment, looking into each pair of eyes seated around the table. "First a toast." He raised his glass.

"Another?" grumbled the dwarf as he joined the others who all climbed back to their feet.

"Yes, another!" Now the mage's eyes were twinkling. He cleared his throat noisily. "Just a few months ago I was a fledgling Sorcerer's Apprentice, trying to recruit party members to help me to obtain this," he said as he held up his staff. "I had not a care in the world, nor a real friend to come to my aid should I require it." He took in a deep, ragged breath, clearly fighting his emotions. "Had I known then what I know now—that I would meet this group of friends, companions and," his gaze paused on Cyrillis, but he quickly looked away, "friends, I would have begun that quest much sooner." The mage lowered his head and used a sleeve to wipe his eyes. "Son of a bitch!"

"You said something about a toast?" grumbled the dwarf. "I'm parched over here!" The barbarian grinned at the sorcerer and held his glass aloft.

"Silence, o grouchy one!" Sordaak raised his glass in salute, aimed at the barbarian. "The toast." He cleared his throat again. "Very well. To companions, friends and those that will traverse all that life and death has to offer for one another."

"Here, here," the companions said as one. Each put their glass to their lips and drank.

"Now," Vorgath said as he regained his seat, "quit trying to get out of telling us what's going on."

Sordaak chuckled as he pulled his chair closer to the table and sat. Once the others had done the same, he took another sip of his wine. "If it seems that way," he looked over at the barbarian, "let me assure you that was not intended. First, I had to verify that The Gathering was indeed under way or about to get under way. However, I'm certain that was cleared to everyone's satisfaction by our friend Pantorra."

"Former friend, I'm afraid," Savinhand interrupted.

"No," Sordaak replied. "Icy Bitch owes us a debt she can never repay, and she knows it." He turned to look at the dwarf and grinned. "Besides, I think she has taken a liking to our barbarian."

"Don't make me get up, come all the way over there and slap the shit outta you!" Vorgath took a sip of his own wine as everyone chuckled. The look the mage got from the dwarf over his glass told Sordaak there was more to that story.

Cyrillis also took note of the look, filing the information away for future verification.

"OK," Sordaak began, "really it wasn't much of a stretch to figure out. Super-pally here was able to determine that Bahamut is most likely in possession of his sword." Thrinndor nodded. "Then we learned about The Gathering from a couple of sources." More nods. "And now Pantorra has informed us that that is either taking place now, or will soon." He shrugged.

A brief silence settled on the chamber, broken by Thrinndor. "The scroll?"

"Ah, yes, the scroll." Sordaak smiled as he took another sip of his wine. "That is just as I described it to our friend, the white dragon. I've asked Bahamut to turn over *Valdaar's Fist* or get his ass kicked up around his ears." He shrugged again.

Thrinndor arched an eyebrow. "But why alert him that we are aware he even *has* the blade?"

Sordaak looked at his friend. "Good question. Easy answer: He already knows." That caused several sets of raised brows. "He was chosen as keeper of the blade not only because of his obvious ability to protect it, but also because of his extensive net of informants. If he didn't know before we took down Theremault, he found out then." The paladin nodded.

"But the real reason I gave Pantorra the scroll to give to the Platinum Dragon is that I wanted to make sure The Gathering was about to happen *and* to make sure she went."

"Hoping she would take you with her," finished Savinhand.

"Not really," replied the sorcerer. More raised eyebrows. "There is no way she could take me to The Gathering—as she stated, we would have both been killed before we got near the place. I only asked her to do that so I could make her feel better about taking the scroll." He shrugged again.

"OK." All eyes turned to Breunne. "That still does not explain *why* you wanted to send him the scroll in the first place."

"Finally!" Heads swiveled back to Sordaak. "There's the question I've been waiting for." He grinned. "I had to make sure she delivers the scroll to the old windbag so that Fahlred could follow her."

Chapter Thirteen

A Familiar Ending

"So he could *what?*" several voices said at once.

"He's following Pantorra," replied the mage with a shrug. He took another sip of wine. His hand shook noticeably as he set the glass back down. Quickly he pulled his right hand back and grasped it with his left.

A shocked silence settled over the chamber.

Thrinndor was the first to speak. "But, as I understand it, you cannot be away from your familiar for any length of time."

"You understand correctly." Sordaak took a nervous gulp of his wine and looked around for a carafe to refill his glass.

"I also understand that if the separation is too great, for too long, that death is possible in one or both," Thrinndor said.

"*What?*" Cyrillis grabbed the mage by the shoulder, spinning him so they were face-to-face. "You never said anything about *death!*"

"I am not going to die!" Sordaak glared at the paladin over the cleric's shoulder. "Fahlred and I are both stronger than that!"

"And if the distance is too great?" Thrinndor persisted. "Or he is gone for weeks?"

The cleric's eyes bore into those of the mage, refusing to be brushed aside. "Bring him back." Her tone left no room for argument.

The sorcerer squared his shoulders. "I will not." His eyes flashed. "We *must* know where Bahamut makes his home." His nostrils distended slightly. "And we must know *soon!*" His chest was heaving with the effort required to keep from shouting.

"There must be another way!" Cyrillis' eyes begged for his answer to change.

Realizing her plight, Sordaak shook his head slowly. "I've tried." It was his turn to beg, needing her to understand. "There *is* no other way." He reached out and gripped both her shoulders. "He'll be all right." The cleric's lip quivered. "*I'll* be all right." His right hand reached up and brushed a lock of hair away from her face. "I have you to make sure of that." He tried to smile, but that smile only twisted his lips into a grimace.

Cyrillis threw her arms around Sordaak's neck and buried her face in his shoulder. The mage looked around awkwardly, his hands unsure where to go. Finally the healer pushed back and her tear swollen eyes looked deep into those of the sorcerer. "You will not leave my side until he returns." The mage looked around again, unsure how to respond. "Say it," she demanded.

Sordaak looked down into Cyrillis' eyes and nodded.

"*SAY IT!*"

The mage swallowed hard as his eyes found hers. "I will not leave your side until Fahlred returns."

The paladin decided he had better go to the aid of his sorcerer before this conversation got even weirder. "Where is he now?"

Sordaak looked up, trying to decide whether to be pissed at his friend for getting him into this in the first place, or to be grateful for getting him out of it. He squared his shoulders. "He is with Pantorra and her dragonlets back in her lair."

"So they have not yet left?" Cyrillis asked hopefully.

Sordaak looked down at the cleric. "There is no other way." He stroked her hair gently.

Cyrillis hesitated, again chewing on her lip. Then she nodded slowly. Her face contorted as she pushed back and looked away. "I do not understand why I am so damn mushy of late!" She walked over and retrieved *Kurril* from where it was propped up against the wall and spun, her eyes flashing. "This is beginning to piss me off!" She leveled a glare at the magicuser. "You will indeed not leave *my* side until the return of your familiar. *Understand?*"

A bewildered Sordaak nodded.

"Good. I will make the necessary arrangements for another bed to be set up in your chambers."

"I don't think that's nece—" Sordaak stopped talking when he saw the look that flashed across the cleric's face. "No problem," he said quickly.

"Ahem," Thrinndor was getting good at distractions, and the sorcerer was glad he was. All eyes turned to the paladin. "What are your plans when you find out the location of The Gathering?"

"Good question." The mage's eyes conveyed a 'thank you' to the big fighter, and then he turned to the barbarian. "How goes the construction of that item I asked for?"

"The cage?" Vorgath asked.

"Shhhh!!!" the sorcerer hissed. "That is *never* to be mentioned again!"

"But—"

"*NEVER!*" The look Sordaak administered to the dwarf left no wiggle room.

Perplexed, Vorgath shrugged. "The *item* has been manufactured and is in the hands of the Drow for enchantment." Sordaak nodded approval. "The old man I turned it over to said he would need a week for the spells you requested."

"Very good," replied the mage as he turned back to the paladin, whose right eyebrow was hovering near his hairline. "*What?* Oh, that?" He smiled big. "That is all part of my plan that I will reveal only when the time comes." The sorcerer waved a negligent hand. The paladin's look changed to the standard one of distrust. "Look," the mage said, his tone disarming, "I have been working on this plan in secret for *months*. I'm not about to blab about it now!" Thrinndor's eyebrow didn't budge. "Disapprove all you want, but I will not discuss that aspect of my plans further until the time has come. Understood?" His narrowed eyes indicated there would be no negotiation.

The two glared at one another, ending with a slight nod from Thrinndor. "Very well. We have come too far *not* to trust you, I fear," growled the paladin.

"That's the spirit!" Sordaak replied with a contrived smile. The smile vanished. "Rest assured that there is nothing about knowing that will help you to do what must be done." Their eyes locked again.

The big fighter sighed. "You certainly are a secretive son of a bitch!"

Sordaak smiled. "I know. It makes me more endearing, right?"

"Hardly!" spat the barbarian. "One of these days you're going to get pasted right before you were going to reveal one of these big secrets, and then what?"

Sordaak turned his grinning face on the dwarf. "I'm sure you'll figure it out—you always do. Besides, it's *your* job to ensure I don't get pasted, right?"

"Whatever!"

"Look people," the magicuser said in his best placating tone, "there will be much to do ere we get to the point where we'll need that item."

"For instance?" Thrinndor was not convinced.

"For instance, we will need to get to where this Gathering is being held. My research indicated that The Gathering is done where Bahamut makes his lair. If what Pantorra told us a couple of months ago is correct, it could take us weeks or even months to get there."

"So should we leave now?" Vorgath asked.

"And go where?" Sordaak replied. "No, until I get word back from Fahlred, we must be content to wait."

"And prepare," Thrinndor said. "We can make some basic assumptions as to what we will need and begin preparations so that when we have a direction we are ready."

"A sound plan, I believe. If our barbarian is correct, we have at least a week for those preparations. We *cannot* leave without that item."

"I'll take care of the horses and pack mules," Breunne said. "Shall we assume we will need supplies for about a month?"

Sordaak shrugged. "As good an assumption as any. We'll never be able to move quickly with much more than that, anyway. And, if we need less, we'll leave it."

Thrinndor nodded. "Agreed. I will outfit and prepare a ship for a long voyage, should that be necessary."

"I'll help with that," Vorgath said.

"If we're going to be at least a week, I'll go back to Farreach and meld into the woodwork to see if we've pissed anyone off lately." He grinned at the mage.

"Good idea," Sordaak said. "I'd like to know how big a price has been put on our heads, and the status of any army building that might or might not be in progress."

"There's no 'might' about it," Breunne said. "The call to arms went out following that ass-whipping you guys put on your sister and her companions. Those that survived will not soon forget and are certainly plotting their revenge."

"We'll be ready," beamed the barbarian. "They'll not find our island so hospitable the next time around, that I promise."

An uneasy silence followed, each knowing that the next time their enemies would not so easily be turned away.

"And I will do my best to ensure that sparky here," Cyrillis pointed at the mage, "lives long enough to complete these super-secret plans he has been concocting inside that pea-sized brain of his."

The cleric's sudden change in attitude left Sordaak scratching his head, and that same change only served to worry the paladin even more.

*

The next few days passed without event as preparations were made for travel. The construction on the keep progressed at an astounding pace. Those setting the blocks of granite into place in the outer walls had soon used all available stone, and reinforcements were sent into the quarry to speed up the process of cutting the blocks required.

At first, Sordaak showed no outward signs that anything was untoward. But after a couple of days he began to shun his friends and allowed many questions concerning the keep to go unanswered. Cyrillis kept her promise by maintaining a watchful eye on him, checking the status of his health and mental state on a regular basis.

Health-wise all seemed to be normal. But, continued silence from his familiar was wreaking havoc on his mental faculties.

One day in sheer boredom he tried to explain what he was going through to her. "It's like having a part of your brain ripped out—the part that has a second set of eyes and a second thought process. Fahlred is a *part* of me. Even when he's not visible to you guys, I *feel* his presence. I *see* what he sees. I *know* what he knows." Sordaak's mouth clamped shut, and his eyes took on a faraway look. "But not now. Now I see nothing." He walked slowly to their chamber and lay down to take a nap—also something he never did.

Cyrillis tried to ease his pain, but it was pain of the mind, of memories never born. That part of his mind was not accessible to her. And the further along the week went, the further he—and his mind—drifted from her.

On the eighth day following the departure of Pantorra and the sorcerer's familiar, Vorgath came to their chambers to deliver a package. Sordaak merely nodded, unfolded his portable hole and shoved the covered item inside. He then refolded the opening and stuffed it into a bag and tied it at his waist.

"What? You're not going to check it?" Vorgath asked.

"Why?" the sorcerer asked, his eyes listless and unfocused.

Vorgath declined to answer. He shook his head and motioned for the cleric to follow him out to the hall. Cyrillis showed a moment of trepidation at leaving the magicuser behind, but decided he couldn't go anywhere or get himself into trouble in only a minute.

She was wrong.

Once in the hall, the barbarian turned on the cleric. "How long has he been like this?"

Cyrillis hesitated, thinking. "A couple of days now." She turned and looked back into the room. "However, he has gotten worse just this day." She shook her head. "I fear something has happened to his familiar." She spoke quietly.

"I'll get the others," Vorgath murmured as he turned on a booted heel and left.

Cyrillis wanted to stop him but decided against it. Perhaps the presence of his friends would snap the mage out of it. She pushed the door open and walked back into the room to find Sordaak lying on the floor, his eye rolled back into his head and his back arched in obvious pain.

"No!" moaned the cleric. She ran to his side, reaching out to him with her health sense even before she skidded to a halt next to the mage. This time she could see with her vision that his life was in danger from forces she could not control. As she touched his shoulder, she poured her healing power into him. Instantly, she felt his pain ease. But he was not whole, and she could sense that his mind was no longer present.

Again she worked her healing on the mage's prone body, and again his body responded. She could see that some event had almost taken his life; some recent event.

Cyrillis could see that she could do no more for him at the moment. She believed he would live, but she didn't know if he would ever be whole again. The cleric slid her arms under his slight frame and groaned as she lifted him clear of the floor. She staggered over to the mage's bed and set him gently down.

Next she did a full check of his health, and that revealed something was draining his vitality! *Damn.* She waited and when his health degenerated enough to warrant a full heal, she did so. Sure enough, as she watched he began to regress again.

This is not good—I cannot keep this up indefinitely. Furtively, she looked toward the door, hoping help would arrive, and soon.

Sordaak remained unconscious and the health drain was slow, so Cyrillis decided she could take the time to search the chamber to see if anything in the chamber caused this.

She had concluded that was not the case—at least so far as she could find—and had moved back to check on her patient when Vorgath returned with Thrinndor. Besides, she was fairly certain she already knew what was causing his distress.

Cyrillis brought the mage back to as near full strength as she could and turned to face the fighters. "After speaking with Vorgath, I found him like this." She turned to gaze upon the sorcerer's supine form. "Something is slowly draining his life force." The healer turned back the paladin, deep worry in her eyes. "I am able to keep body and soul together, but eventually my spells and prayers will no longer be sufficient to do so. We must find whatever is trying to kill him soon."

The paladin shook his head minutely, his lips pressed together in a grim expression. "I fear it is worse than that."

"Explain," she said, searching the big fighter's eyes.

The paladin tore his eyes away from the cleric's to look down at the mage, whose breathing was shallow and labored. "Fahlred must have been discovered and slain."

"No!" Cyrillis knelt at the sorcerer's side, healing him again as she did. She looked back up at the paladin with a tear forming in her eye.

"The loss of his familiar has taken Sordaak's will to live." The paladin's eyes reflected the pain he saw in those of the cleric. "I have heard of this before. It is a chance taken when so powerful a companion answers the call."

"But—"

The paladin's expression changed to one of anger. "Move, please," he said, rougher than he'd intended.

"What?" Cyrillis was confused by the change in the paladin's demeanor.

"MOVE!" Thrinndor pushed the cleric aside as if she were a rag doll and quickly knelt beside the bed.

"Hey!"

Thrinndor ignored the cleric. Instead the fighter reached out with both hands, grasped the sorcerer's tunic and easily lifted his upper torso clear of the bed.

"HEY!" Cyrillis repeated.

Still ignoring the healer, the paladin shook the mage. "Sordaak! SORDAAK! SORDAAK! Wake up!" He shook the slight figure again. "Wake up!"

"Take it easy!" Cyrillis tried to push her way back up to the bed, but the paladin again shoved her roughly aside.

When he got no response from the mage, Thrinndor shifted his grip so that his left hand held Sordaak clear of the bed and then he slapped him hard with his right. "SORDAAK! CAN YOU HEAR ME?"

"STOP THAT!" Cyrillis grabbed the paladin's arm. "You will kill him!"

The paladin looked at the cleric, anguish plain on his face. "If we do not rouse him, he will kill himself." He turned his attention back to the sorcerer and slapped him harder. Getting no response, he pressed his nose up against the mage's. "SORDAAK!"

Cyrillis watched in horror as the paladin—one of the two men she really trusted—alternated between slapping, yelling and using his healing powers to try to revive the mage.

After a full minute of this, Thrinndor lowered Sordaak back to his pillow and stepped back. He was exhausted. When he turned to look at the cleric, Cyrillis was shocked to see something in his eyes that she had never seen before: despair.

"I fear he is too far gone," the paladin's shoulders slumped weakly. "We have lost him."

"Let me try," the barbarian said as he pushed his way past the bigger fighter.

"No," commanded the healer. Both men turned to look at her—the tone in her voice demanded that they do so. "Leave us."

Neither of the fighters moved. Thrinndor was torn with trying to dissuade her from hurting herself further and hoping she had a plan. Vorgath was simply unwilling to give up so quickly. He was clearly ready to see if he could wake the mage.

"Leave us," Cyrillis repeated.

"Cyrillis—" Thrinndor began as he took a step toward her.

When the cleric looked up at her name, the paladin could see a tear coursing its way down her flushed cheek. It had not been the first, nor would it be the last.

"Leave us," she said a third time. She lifted her chin defiantly, clearly ready to argue should the need arise.

Still not ready to quit, Vorgath took another step toward the bed. Thrinndor touched the dwarf's arm lightly and shook his head. The barbarian turned his attention on the paladin and he glared at his best friend in the land for a few moments, but then allowed his shoulders to droop as he nodded and turned toward the door.

Both men left quietly, closing the door behind them.

Cyrillis squared her shoulders and wiped the tears from her eyes. Next, she stepped to the bed, knelt beside the man she loved so much and took a hand in both of hers.

Seeing that he was again weakened by the drain he was doing to himself, she first cast a full heal on him, knowing that if there was any hope it rested with her.

She then bowed her head, closed her eyes and began to pray. "Hear me, O Valdaar. Hear the cries of this, your humble servant." Her voice broke and she had to swallow twice to regain it. "This man is necessary to do what you have asked of us—without him your cause in the land is doomed. We will not be able to return you to your rightful place among us without him."

Cyrillis opened her eyes, stared down at the barely breathing man on the bed and then raised her face to the ceiling. "Yet there is more. I ask you to return him to us—to me—for selfish reasons. For I have chosen this man to father the children I would raise as followers of your greatness."

The cleric's voice fell silent as she looked down at the man she loved so much. His face was twisted in the torment he was doing to himself, but she saw past that. It was a face that she was certain was yet to do so many great things.

"I trust in your judgment, O Valdaar. I will heal this man no more. If it is your will that he survive to do that which has been spoken, then it will be your doing." Her voice hardened and her eyes narrowed in grim determination as she again raised them to the ceiling. "But, if this man dies, so too will my service to you or any other god." Her lips pressed together to form a thin line, her eyes beseeching. "Return him to me and I will raise many followers of your name."

Her face softened as she again bowed her head and closed her eyes. "Hear me O Valdaar."

She felt rather than heard a voice in her mind. "He dies because he has not the will to live. I cannot save him."

Cyrillis heard her love take in one last ragged breath and then he lay still, his chest no longer rising. She raised her head, her vision marred by tears, and stared into the face of her beloved.

She leaned forward, her voice a whisper. "Come to me, my love. Come to me that our love may last forever. If you do not, I will come to you." Cyrillis placed her lips on those of the lifeless sorcerer and kissed him passionately, baring her soul as she did not know was possible.

Chapter Fourteen

Warnings

Cyrillis stepped out of the bedchamber into the hall to find Thrinndor and Vorgath pacing impatiently. They stopped and stared when she emerged, their faces questioning her openly.

She pushed back her hair and scrubbed the tears from her face.

Thrinndor could stand it no more. "Well?"

Cyrillis looked at the pair, feigning seeing them for the first time. "He will yet live." She smiled.

"*What?*"

"*How?*"

"I gave him something to live for." The cleric winked at the two and turned to walk down the hall, her hips swaying in a most interesting fashion. "Now he is hungry."

"But—"

Vorgath flopped onto his back and began making twitching motions. "I've lost the will to live," he said.

"In your dreams, old man!" the healer said without turning.

"Yes," agreed the dwarf as he climbed back to his feet, a smirk on his face, "and I guess it'll have to stay that way." Cyrillis didn't answer as she rounded a corner and disappeared from their sight.

Thrinndor helped the barbarian to his feet. "You really must work on your delivery."

"You think that will help?" asked the dwarf, his face split in a grin.

"No."

"Me either," Vorgath said with a shrug. "Oh well. Shall we go see what she left of him?"

Thrinndor retuned the grin as he reached for the latch and opened the door.

They found Sordaak sitting up in bed, propped there by a stack of pillows. His face was pale, and he looked gaunt. But the familiar spark had returned to his eyes as he watched two of his friends approach. A wan smile played on his lips.

"All right, wiggle-fingers," Vorgath began, "spill it. What was all that about?" He squinted an eye. "And I want *details*!"

"Oh, no," Sordaak said, shaking his head. "A gentleman never discusses such matters."

"Well, you're no gentleman," replied the dwarf. "Now give it up, or I'll squeeze the information out of you." Vorgath reached for the mage, but it was obvious the barbarian was having a little fun.

"All right," the sorcerer said, swatting the dwarf's hands away. His face turned serious as he focused on the paladin. "Fahlred is dead." He choked back his emotion. "In despair I passed to the afterlife. I could see images of my past mingled with what was supposed to happen. The events were confused—impossible to tell apart. I saw my mother." He shuddered as he remembered. "But I heard Cyrillis calling me back. I resisted." Sordaak's face twisted in pain. "But she said that if I did not return, she was going to join me." His hand shot out and grasped the paladin by the tunic and pulled him closer. "That must *never* be allowed!" he hissed, surprising both fighters.

The mage glanced at the door, verifying that it remained closed. "I am but a pawn in this quest of yours," he said. "But her! She is *vital* to your success. You *need* her—the land *needs* her! I have seen it!" The wizard was suddenly breathing hard. "If I die, *do not* allow her to follow me!" His eyes took on a crazed look. "Promise me!"

Thrinndor blinked twice, not sure what answer to give.

Sordaak pulled the paladin closer until their faces were mere inches apart. "*Promise me!*"

"Very well." Thrinndor was suddenly very uncomfortable. "I promise."

Thrinndor tried to pull away, but the sorcerer held on with surprising ferocity, holding the eyes of the paladin with his own. After a few moments, Sordaak seemed satisfied and nodded slowly, releasing his grip on the fighter's cloak. "See that you keep that promise."

"That's it?" Vorgath protested. "That's all it took to return your will to live?" He shook his head. "You could have gotten more."

Sordaak glared at the dwarf, sharp words dying on his tongue. Finally, he shook his head and smiled thinly. "Yes, I believe you are correct, o venerable one. But," his voice lowered and regained some of its intensity, "*that* is not yet hers to give."

"What? Of course—"

Both were silenced when the door opened and Cyrillis came in bearing a tray of assorted fruits, nuts, cheeses and breads. There was also a flask and some cups on the tray. The rosy color in her cheeks led Sordaak to believe she might have been outside the door to hear some of that conversation.

While the three of them picked lightly at the food on the tray in silence, Sordaak ate like a man who hadn't anything to eat for days—which was at least in part true. He finished every last morsel and drank most of the wine, allowing only a small amount for each of his guests.

Satisfied her charge had eaten his fill, Cyrillis shooed the two fighters toward the door. "Sordaak needs his rest, he is not yet himself." A quick glance showed this to be true. While the mage's color was indeed better, his face was still pale and ruddy. "I will come and check on him later, but I believe the worst is past."

Sordaak said nothing as he slid farther down in his bed. The healer removed the additional pillows and tucked in the sheets around the magicuser's slight form.

"But—" Thrinndor had some questions he wanted answered.

"No," Cyrillis interrupted, "no buts. Whatever you require, it can wait until morning." Her stern eye left no room for argument, and the paladin reluctantly nodded and walked out into the hall, the dwarf in tow.

The two fighters had only a moment to wait before the cleric joined them. She closed the door behind her and ensured it was latched.

Thrinndor hesitated. "There really are some important questions that require answers."

Cyrillis put her hand on his arm. "I know," she said, steering him down the hall toward the exit, "but he has been through a lot and must get some rest. The questions will still be there ere morning."

The paladin briefly considered arguing, but it *was* late. "All right. But I fear our time is rapidly approaching, and we still know not where it is we must go."

The cleric pushed open the door at the end of the hall, allowing the cool, night air to waft over them. "I know," she repeated. "But we will go nowhere this evening. Best to let him rest. For it is in me that our journey will be a long one and we will all need to be near one hundred percent ere we begin."

*

Savinhand returned the next morning before breakfast, having sailed all night to escape prying eyes. Breunne rode up while the remaining companions were at the table; he had spent the past several days inspecting the northern defenses and worked on improving the watch system of the troglodytes.

Although pressed by his friends, Sordaak bade them to wait. He said he needed to first consult his notes and asked them to join him in the tower for lunch.

During lunch, the mage permitted only idle chatter concerning the weather or discussions involving the islands defenses.

Lunch consumed and the dining implements cleared away by his servants, Sordaak shut and bolted the door leading below. Next he walked over and lowered the bamboo window covering, adding a second covering which he tied in place with some thongs attached to the stone of the walls.

Satisfied at last, he turned and lit more lanterns, using the single candle he had prepared in advance.

The sorcerer then walked to his work table and picked up a large rolled up tube tied with a leather thong. He carried it to the dining table in silence, slipping the thong off as he walked. He set the obviously old parchment onto the table and unrolled it, using lanterns to hold the four corners in place.

The companions leaned in, each trying to get a better look at what the mage had laid out for them. It was a detailed map of the land, drawn to scale using colored inks depicting the several mountainous regions, seaports, villages, the three seas and the isle on which they sat: The Isle of Grief.

Thrinndor was first to look up. "What is it you—"

"*Shhhh!*" Sordaak hissed. "Quietly!" He raised and then slowly lowered both hands, indicating they should use subdued voices.

"Why all the secrecy?" griped the barbarian, whispering as best he could.

Sordaak rolled his eyes. "I should think that would be obvious!"

The mage looked around the chamber, checking both the window and the hatch before proceeding. "However, I will explain for those of you," he looked pointedly at the dwarf, "who require such things."

Unfazed, Vorgath grumbled, "Whatever!" quaffed half the wine in his cup, belched loudly and grinned at the mage. "Just get on with it!"

At least he kept his voice low, reasoned the mage as he again rolled his eyes. "There are spies *everywhere*! We must trust none that are not in this chamber and a select few that cannot be avoided. Only I get to say who those select few are!" He glared around the table, looking for dissenters. He could see that the paladin thought to protest this last part—as expected—but was apparently satisfied with a raised eyebrow and a sour face.

For now.

Sordaak got the feeling the topic would come up again later when they were alone.

The barbarian merely rolled his eyes, finished his wine and searched around for a refill.

"Very well," the mage continued, ignoring the dwarf. "The death of my familiar was not completely in vain, as I led each of you to believe." Now Thrinndor's other eyebrow wandered up to consort with the first. Sordaak licked his lips and swallowed the lump in his throat; Fahlred's death—and very nearly his own—was still too vivid a memory. "While the empathic ability cannot cross great distances—that was my heaviest worry when I embarked on this plan—I did get to see where they were going." The mage took a deep breath. "That, and I briefly was able to communicate with him while—while I was being transported to the afterlife." There, he'd said it. That had been hard. "He told me he had seen The Gathering, where it was, and he even showed me the location in his mind." Sordaak took in a ragged breath. "He even showed me Bahamut—"

"*What?*" several said at the same time.

"Yes," Sordaak continued, "it was Bahamut, The Platinum Dragon, that ended Fahlred's life." The mage's face took on a determined look not often seen. "For that, that damn dragon will pay with his."

A stunned silence held the companions until the barbarian broke it. "Yeah, but where *is* he?"

Sordaak looked over at the barbarian and then down at the map. He reached into his robe and pulled out a metallic figurine depicting a dragon. The mage leaned over and set the figurine down on the map. When he looked up, his face was grim.

"The *Badlands?*" Breunne said, sitting straight up in his chair.

Sordaak nodded. "And, not just any point in the Badlands," the mage's eyes drifted back to the dragon figure on the table, "The Valley of Khandihaar."

"*Khandihaar?*" Vorgath also sat upright in his chair, his feigned disinterest completely gone.

"What is Khandihaar?" Cyrillis asked, bewildered at the looks on the faces of the men.

"It loosely translates from the ancient Drow as 'Valley of the Damned,'" Thrinndor explained.

"If that is where Bahamut makes his lair," all eyes turned to Breunne, "and hundreds of dragons meet there on occasion, I should think that an adequate description."

The barbarian nodded. "That valley is reportedly deep in the heart of the Badlands, high in the Ugregardt Mountains." He licked his lips nervously. "In my twenty plus years of forays into the Badlands, I saw that mountain range only once." He looked up at the paladin. "Those are some high peaks—snow covers most of them year around. The highest points in all the land are in that range—with at least six mountains taller than any other known."

"Do you know where this Valley of Khandihaar is?" Thrinndor asked.

Vorgath shook his head. "To my knowledge, none alive have ever seen it."

"That may be the case now," everyone turned to look at the sorcerer, "but it has not always been so." He slipped a scroll tube from a hidden place in his robe and held it up for all to see. "Legend has it that it was once home to all the races of giants in an age when dragons and giants were the rulers of the land. Then, when man came to the land, there were disparate opinions among the rulers as to what to do about this invasion. Disputes became battles, and battles became wars. For a thousand years wars waged between the dragons and the giants, resulting in the expulsion of all giants from the area we now know as The Badlands."

"I've heard some of this," Vorgath said into the quiet that followed. "Many dragons and thousands of giants died in those wars. The giants were scattered to all points on in the land—and some even left the land completely." Sordaak nodded. "So few were the giants in some of the races that the settlements of man easily overcame them, eradicating entire races."

Again Sordaak nodded. "Hill giants and stone giants reportedly were among the races decimated, and are now thought to be nonexistent in the land." He rubbed his chin as he fought to remember what he had learned from the tomes in The Library of Antiquity. He'd written it down, of course, but he didn't have any of those notes currently with him. "It is said that man hunted the dragons to the point that Bahamut raised the mountains surrounding his valley so high that none may pass. The then surrounded them with an impenetrable defense." He was silent for a moment. "The last recorded incursion into that valley by man happened more than fifteen-hundred years ago, and only two of the more than one hundred fighters that entered that place lived to tell their story."

"Hence 'Valley of the Damned.'" All eyes turned to Savinhand. "You guys sure know how to paint a gloomy picture. Are you *absolutely certain* that is where we must go?"

Sordaak nodded, intrigued at the rogue's interruption. "Yes. Do you have any intel on that region?"

The rogue hesitated. "Yes and no." The mage lifted an eyebrow, certain there was more. He was right. "You are correct in that none living have been to Khandihaar and lived to tell their tale—at least not that we at Shardmoor are aware. You are also correct about the two that escaped some fifteen hundred years ago; they were known as Brakkard the Brave and Cerraunne the Silent."

Sordaak knew this already; his studies had led him to accounts of the men's journeys. What he wanted to know is how and—perhaps more important—*why* Savinhand had this information.

"That is relatively common knowledge," explained the rogue without being asked. "It has come to the surface again recently due to the amount of activity in that region." He shrugged. "In the past ten or fifteen years at least three villages along the northern sector of the Sunburnt Sea have simply vanished."

"Vanished?" Cyrillis was stunned. "How is that possible?"

"I don't know."

"What do three missing villages in a desert province have to do with Khandihaar?" Sordaak wanted to know. There was still more to this, he guessed. Again, he was right.

Savinhand locked eyes with the mage. "It is said the Fire Giants have returned to that region."

"And the two are related." It was not a question.

The rogue shrugged. "That is the assumption." He lowered his eyes. "There's more."

"I figured there was."

When Savinhand looked up, worry was plain on his face. "The rest of this has not been verified." He took a sip of his wine, the others not taking their eyes off of the rogue. "It is also said that the dragons have been active in recent years, and that they are responsible for the recent village issues."

"I figured that's where you were headed with all this." Sordaak rubbed his chin thoughtfully.

It was Breunne who spoke next however. "But the dragons have remained pretty much to themselves—at least those of the Valley—for the majority of this age. Why would they want to rouse the ire of man at this point?"

"A good question," replied the rogue. "It's part of the reason why I say this information is unverified."

Sordaak raised an eyebrow. "What's the other part?"

"Of the three scouting missions sent to this area over the past two years, only one man returned, and he has been unable to tell us what he knows."

"Why is that?"

Savinhand's eyes narrowed. "Because his mind has been blasted with idiocy and his tongue ripped out."

"What?" Cyrillis was appalled. "Who would do such a thing?"

"Who, indeed?" Sordaak stood, walked to a half-full carafe and filled his glass. "Why leave him alive at all? Unless it was to send a message."

"Our thoughts as well," replied the rogue.

Sordaak took a sip of the wine, nodded, and locked eyes with the rogue over his glass. "How long ago was this?"

"His return in that condition was one of the things that delayed me initially."

"So this happened recently?" Thrinndor mused.

Savinhand nodded. "Our man was in bad shape when he returned to us. Considerable skill was required by our surgeons just to keep body and soul together. They could do nothing for his mind."

"Perhaps I could help?" Cyrillis said tentatively.

Savin shook his head. "We, of course, thought of that. I sent for a powerful cleric we keep on retainer, but he was unable to mend the man's mind. His report said that my man had not been cursed, nor had he had a spell cast on him of any kind. His judgment was that my scout's mind had been shattered by fear, and that no spell could make him whole."

"But what could scare a man so?" the healer asked.

"Bahamut," Sordaak answered for the rogue.

"What?" Clearly, the cleric didn't believe him.

The magicuser took another casual sip of his wine, enjoying the attention. "It is said that lesser men quell in the presence of the Platinum Dragon, and that their mind will never recover." Silence greeted that revelation. Sordaak shrugged. "However, I suppose it could have been any number of things that scared the shit outta him." He grinned and walked back to his chair.

"His hair is white."

"Presumably that means it was some other color when he left for the mission?"

Savin nodded. "And he was not alone." The rogue had everyone's attention, now. "Four men were sent this last time. Four *good* men."

"That's assuming you can call those of your profession 'good,'" Vorgath said with a half-smile.

Savinhand was not amused. "I should take offense to that, but I've decided to merely consider the source." The dwarf started to protest, but the leader of Guild Shardmoor continued, dismissing him as he turned to face the sorcerer. "For everyone's information, we at the Guild have in our employ many you would not consider thieves." He looked pointedly at the barbarian. "On this mission, one rogue was sent, as well as a ranger, a spellcaster—one that could heal *and* provide some offensive firepower—"

"Nice," interrupted the mage, nodding his head appreciatively.

"—and a fighter of some renown."

"And they were all slain?" the ranger asked.

"We don't know. We may *never* know." Savinhand sighed as he shrugged. "Only the spellcaster returned."

"And he is unable to tell you what happened." Cyrillis finished the sentence for him.

The rogue nodded. "We have tried to communicate with him. Occasionally he seems almost lucid and we'll ask him to write down what happened, or maybe get him to draw a picture." His eyes found the cleric. "Once or twice he even picked up the pen, but the results are always the same. After a few strokes with the quill, he'll open his mouth in a silent scream and run from the room terrified. If we don't chase him down and bring him back, it is our fear he would leave and never return."

"Yet he returned to you in the first place." All heads turned back to Sordaak. "Pardon?"

The mage's eyes bored into those of the rogue. "Think, man! How did an idiot—a man with no mind and no voice—make it back to your encampment in the first place?"

Savinhand blinked twice before answering. "We assumed some natural instinct kicked in, bringing him back to where he felt safe. You're thinking it might be something other than that?"

Sordaak nodded. "So do you." He took another sip of his wine and sat the glass back on the table. "If you believe he will run away at the first opportunity, then it stands to reason he doesn't want to be there. So, how did he get there?"

"And why did he return in the first place?" Savinhand shook his head. "What you say certainly casts doubt on our earlier assumptions." Suddenly his eyes opened wide. "What if he was *returned* to us?"

"Now you're thinking," the mage said as he jabbed a finger at the rogue.

"Excuse me." Eyes shifted as Thrinndor spoke. "But why, pray tell, does this matter?"

Sordaak glared at the paladin for a moment and then threw his hands up into the air. "Damned if I know! *But* if this man was returned with the intent of delivering a message, then we should probably try to figure out just what that message is!"

"How hard can the message be?" Now all eyes turned to Vorgath. "It's simple: Keep out!" When no one said anything, the barbarian rolled his eyes. "As in, 'stay away!'"

Sordaak and Savinhand looked at one another. The mage shrugged. "I suppose it could be that simple."

"What *else* could it be?"

"OK!" Sordaak snapped. "I might have overthought that one just a bit!"

"Duh!"

Sordaak glared at the dwarf and then grinned, nodding deferentially at his friend. "Very well, I deserved that."

Vorgath returned the grin.

"Wait a minute!" Heads swiveled and eyes focused on the ranger. "Why was Cerraunne called the Silent?"

Sordaak, who had been silently sharing a toast with the barbarian, slammed his glass back down so hard that it broke, spilling wine onto the table top. He ignored that. "Because his tongue had been ripped out!" He looked down at his hand to discover it was bleeding. Cyrillis waved her hand, the skin knitted back together, and the bleeding stopped. "Of course!" He stood and jabbed a finger at the barbarian. "*That's* the missing message!"

"I don't get it," admitted the confused dwarf. He'd thought he'd had this figured out.

"*Duh!*"

"Touché."

Sordaak turned to once again lock eyes with the rogue. "They're telling you—us—that they know we know, and they don't care." He turned back to the barbarian. "As you so adroitly put it: Stay away."

Chapter Fifteen

A Familiar Tale

A knock on the door from below jolted Sordaak from his reverie. Irritated at the interruption, he stalked over and reached for the bolt. "Who's there?" he demanded, his hand poised over the mechanism.

"Icy Bitch," came the immediate reply, muffled by the door. "Now open up so I do not have to revert to my native form and rip this door from its hinges!"

Sordaak turned back to his friends and raised a fist. Vorgath jumped to his feet and retrieved *Flinthgoor* from where he'd left his greataxe. He took up position behind the door, his weapon at the ready. Thrinndor stood, drew his flaming sword and went to the opposite side of the door. Breunne unslung *Xenotath* from his back and notched an arrow as he stepped back toward the window. Savinhand simply vanished. Cyrillis also stood, stepping over to stand beside the magicuser, *Kurril* in her right hand.

Sordaak nodded his approval of the moves and began counting with the fingers of his raised fist. On three, he slid back the bolt and Thrinndor jerked open the door, allowing it to fall to the floor at his feet.

A moment passed, and then the beautiful white hair of the dragon woman appeared in the opening as she climbed the remaining steps. Her eyes circled the room, noting the readiness of the fighters and the absence of the rogue.

Her eyes settled on those of the mage. "A wise precaution," she said icily. "Considering your treachery almost got me *killed!*" Her eyes flashed momentarily, and Sordaak thought for a moment she might actually attack. But then her calm demeanor replaced the anger and she smiled sweetly. "However, if I had wanted to exact revenge, I would have come through your closed window in dragon form, spitting and slashing."

Sordaak noted that her smile lightly touched her eyes and he relaxed, sensing she was not here for nefarious purposes. "Why then are you here?" He lowered his fist and the fighters slowly lowered their weapons.

"I have someone I would like you to meet." Pantorra turned back to the opening in the floor and said, "Come on up Pentaath, they will not harm you."

Weapons again were brought to the ready, none trusting the dragon woman.

Slowly a male child made his way up the stairs. His tentative steps showed anxiety and something else.

Sordaak did a double-take on the boy, then he staggered back first one step and then another. After a third unseeing step, he tripped over a chair and went to the ground hard, all tangled up in the chair.

Cyrillis was instantly kneeling at his side. "Are you all right?"

The mage ignored her, his mouth agape. He fought his way clear of the chair, his eyes never leaving those of the boy. The youth was no more than five—maybe six—years old, dressed for the most part the same as Pantorra: white robes over plain sandals, tied at the waist with a rope. His hair was also the same as hers: thick and white, with tightly curled spirals adorning his head.

The others in the room watched silently—some with amusement, others with concern as the boy focused on the mage, his eyes never leaving Sordaak's.

"Hello, father," the boy said, lifting his chin proudly. His voice was clear and strong, with musical undertones.

"*What?*" several in the chamber said at once, looking from the boy to the sorcerer who remained on the floor.

"Do as we discussed," Pantorra urged, her voice silky smooth.

The boy hesitated, clearly unsure of his surroundings. After a moment, he squared his shoulders, set his jaw and strode over to stand before Sordaak. There, he dropped to one knee. "I am Pentaath," the youth said, his eyes boring into those of the mage. "And I am your servant." He bowed lightly at the waist while maintaining eye contact.

A chill washed over the room with the silence that followed those simple words. Pantorra frowned. "That is not exactly how we practiced the introduction, but it will have to do."

"What—" Sordaak struggled to find his voice. His eyes darted to the dragon woman. "What are you talking about?" His nervous gaze settled on the boy again. "Who *is* this?"

"One question at a time, please." Pantorra smiled. "First, this is Pentaath, and he is obviously not your son. However, I have discussed with him that he should think of you as his father. His sire was an ancient white of no small renown among the dragons. Following our mating, he informed me that he would pass into the great gathering of the afterlife. He also told me that me and mine would have to carry the line forward, as we are the only remaining whites in all the land." Her tone was somber as she looked at her son. "He also told me that I would bear three dragonlets, one male and two females—how he knew this, I cannot pretend to understand. Then he told me that the male would be special." She put her hand lovingly on her son's head.

"But—"

"Allow me to finish, please. All will be explained—I promise." Her smile removed any rebuke from her words. "Pentaath could not wait to tear free from his egg. His sisters—if sisters they be—remain encased and continue to develop normally. But, some three months ago now, I began to sense that this one had other ideas." She smiled down at the boy. "He impatiently kicked his egg open and emerged as you see him—a boy."

"What?" Cyrillis interrupted. "Surely you mean a male dragon?"

Pantorra's eyes flashed as she slowly turned them on the cleric. "Do not presume to speak for me, young lady." Her tone was stern. "I meant exactly what I said: Pentaath emerged from his shell as a baby boy." She looked back at her son in wonder. "In these short three months he has grown into the youth that stands before you." She shrugged. "I cannot explain it further."

Stunned, Sordaak's lips moved and the words finally tumbled out. "Is he human then? Or a dragon?"

Pantorra hesitated and then stepped back. "Pentaath, show them please."

The boy nodded and clearly his excitement grew as he closed his eyes and began to transform. Slowly at first, then with ever increasing rapidity he became a young white dragon. When he opened his eyes again they were larger, but maintained the same beautiful white—not really a lack of color, but more a sparkling like fresh powder snow when hit with first sunlight. They again fixed on the mage. "Do you prefer this form, father?"

"No! Yes!" stammered the flustered sorcerer. Quickly he looked over at the dragon woman. "Hell! I don't know what I mean!" Pantorra smiled her understanding back at the mage. "Which is his *true* form?" he asked.

Pantorra's face became somber. "That I do not know," she said with a shake of her head. "I am not sure if it matters to him. He has remained in both forms for extended periods of time—weeks even! I have never heard of anything like it!"

"Nor have I," Thrinndor said as he moved to stand beside the magicuser and in front of the dragon. "I have studied dragon lore for years and have never heard of such an occurrence—not within all the recorded boundaries of time!" He studied the dragon youth closely, but stepped back perplexed.

Sordaak stepped around the paladin and focused on the dragonlet's eyes. "There are stories from before this age of man that Bahamut was hatched/born under similar circumstances. But his youth was recorded as normal by those that did the recording. His human side was not understood and even shunned during the first thousand years of his reign." He licked his lips as he looked back over at Pantorra. "Has he shown a propensity toward the arts?"

The dragon woman nodded solemnly. "And in these short months, his abilities in the studies of magiks already exceed mine." She looked at her son, wonder and love plain in her eyes. "I do not pretend to understand how." Her eyes went quickly back to the mage. "It is why I brought him to you to study."

Sordaak walked over to the table, picked up a wine glass—not caring that it wasn't even his—and quaffed the contents in one gulp. When he turned back to face Pantorra, his gaze was steady. "You do realize that there is more to it than that?"

It was the dragon woman's turn to lick her lips. "I do not understand."

The sorcerer took in a deep breath and let it out slowly as he turned to look at the dragon youth. "I can see through his eyes."

"*What?*" several cried at once—including Pantorra.

Sordaak nodded as he turned back to the young dragon. "I cannot explain it either. But, not only can I see through his eyes, I sense his *intelligence* and *power!* He is indeed a unique creature. We are bound. I sensed it the moment his head poked through the floor." The mage reached out and stroked the dragon's head just above his eye. "He is as my familiar," he frowned. "However, I did not make the summons."

"But," Breunne said, confusion in his voice, "it is reportedly law that a sorcerer may only make the summons once."

"Agreed," said the sorcerer, his eyes not leaving the dragonlet. "But, as I said, I did not *make* the summons."

"But without the summons, there can be no bond," Thrinndor protested.

"That is because *he* made the summons." All eyes shifted back to Pantorra. "*What?*"

"Of course!" Sordaak said. "That explains what I felt. When was that?" he asked quickly.

"Two days ago."

"*Yes!*" The mage clapped his hands together. "That explains *so much!*"

"So," all eyes turned to Vorgath, who had to this point been silent, "let me see if I have this straight. As I see it, *you* are now *his* familiar?" A wry half-smile played on his lips.

"NO!" Sordaak shook his head. "YES! Aw, hell, it's *complicated!*"

Thrinndor was bewildered. "Please explain it to those of us for which this is less obvious."

"Gladly." The mage looked around for more wine but didn't see any. He shrugged. "The relationship between a familiar and his or her summoner is not as easy as saying who belongs to, or reports to whom—it's symbiotic. We can see through each other's eyes, see what is in the other's mind and feel what the other feels. If one is harmed, the other feels the pain. And that is the reason that if one dies, the other may soon follow. It is difficult, at best, to live without the other. And the longer a relationship exists, the stronger the bond, the more likely neither will survive if one dies." He took in a deep breath. "Had Fahlred and I bonded years ago, I probably would not be here today."

"So you are the boy's familiar." It was clear the dwarf was not going to let it go. "He summoned you."

Sordaak rolled his eyes. "You can certainly look at it that way." He looked at the dragon youth, and his tone softened. "Either way, we are now one."

"But," Thrinndor hesitated, uncharacteristically unsure of himself, "I have never heard tell of either a dragon making a summons, or of a human having a dragon for a familiar!"

"Nor have I," Pantorra agreed. "And I believe I would have certainly heard had such a thing—either way—occurred."

The chamber was silent as each present wrestled with the ramifications of what they had just witnessed.

"So—"

"*Shut up!*"

Vorgath happily clamped his jaws shut, having gotten what he had wanted.

Sordaak licked his dry lips. "Can he fly yet?"

"Oh yes," answered the boy dragon, startling them all. "I flew all the way here!" he said proudly.

"But it is said that dragons sometimes take a year—or longer—before they learn how to fly!" Doubt clouded the healer's voice.

"I cannot explain that, either," Pantorra answered with a shake of her head.

Suddenly the young dragon began to transform back to a human boy. Again, it took a few moments for the transformation to be complete.

"Why did you change back?" his mother asked.

"Because he asked me to," the youth answered. He didn't have to say *who* had asked him to change.

Sordaak reached out and took the boy's hand in his and then he looked up and into the eyes of his mother. "How long will The Gathering last?"

Pantorra shrugged. "That cannot be known. The length varies depending on agendas, birth announcements and the mourning of those who have passed." Her eyes flashed. "Besides, I had barely arrived before I was dismissed and told never again to return."

"Sorry about that," replied the sorcerer meekly, "but I hope you understand that it was necessary."

The dragon woman's eyes softened. "Of course." She waved a negligent hand. "I was tiring of that old windbag's pomp and ceremony every time he called us together! Sometimes he would go on for *weeks!*" She shook her head. "However, I believe this Gathering will be a short one—it may even be over as we speak."

Sordaak looked up. "I'll need to be sure."

"Why?"

Sordaak smiled. "Taking on Bahamut, The Platinum Dragon, will prove challenging enough without an army of two-hundred-plus dragons by his side!"

Pantorra's beautiful face became concerned. "You intend to go forward with that plan, then?" She looked worriedly at her son.

The sorcerer nodded. "Nothing has changed. He has the sword."

"That he does," confirmed the dragon woman. "And he now knows you want the blade."

Sordaak shrugged. "He has known for at least a year that the events have been falling into place that will require that sword to once again be part of the destiny of the land, for ill or naught. And he knows we're coming for it."

"Well said, father."

Sordaak looked down at his new companion and smiled approvingly. When he looked back up, his face did not change. "I want to give the dragons plenty of time to disperse back to their lairs." He thought for a few moments. "Yet it will take us no small amount of time to traverse the Badlands to get to the Valley of Khandihaar."

Vorgath answered without being asked, "Although I don't know for certain where this Khandihaar is, I think I can guess. With this group we should have little trouble with the journey itself." He too thought for a moment. "Perhaps a week—no more than ten days—once we depart Farreach."

"We won't be departing Farreach," Sordaak said evenly.

"Right, we won't want to alert them. So we'll have to leave from Ardaagh."

"No, not there, either."

Vorgath raised an eyebrow and folded his arms on his chest. He was smart enough to not bother guessing again.

"I am formulating a plan," Sordaak answered the unasked question. "I'll discuss it with each of you as it comes together." He smiled at the barbarian. "But for now I will require one week—minimum—for Pentaath and I to get to know one another better."

"Another week?" Vorgath was clearly less than pleased.

"Yes," the mage nodded. "You can use the extra time to shore up your defenses of *our* keep. When we do depart, we will likely be gone from here three to five weeks. I do not believe my sister will wait for us to return to make her attack on this complex. The defenses had better be ready."

"We'll be ready," the barbarian grated. He chafed at the delay, but he was actually glad for the opportunity for further preparation.

"Surely you do not plan to take my son to that place?"

"Surely I do," the mage countered. Pantorra started to protest, but Sordaak held up a hand for silence. "Rest assured, my dear lady, that I learned my lesson well from the loss of Fahlred. Your son will be the most cared for creature in the land—that I can promise you. However, where I go, he must also. We must not become separated. Ever."

"Then I am coming with you."

"That is impossible," the mage said, his eyes soft as he understood her need. "While Bahamut nor none of his minions will recognize either Pentaath or myself, they will certainly recognize—and instantly slay—you." He lifted his chin. "Besides, you will soon have two more dragonlets that require the nurturing of their mother."

Pantorra chewed her lip. Abruptly her shoulders sagged as she rushed to her son, where she bent and threw her arms around his neck. She held him there for a moment and then pushed back, her eyes wet and locked on her son's. "You must promise me that you will be careful," she said. "You must take care of your human and allow no harm to come to him."

The boy nodded, his face beaming with pride and love. "I will, mother."

Chapter Sixteen

Preparations

The week passed fast, even for Vorgath. He and his father spent much of the time overseeing the work on the outer wall, in conference with the troglodytes and in meetings with the Drow back in Ardaagh

Breunne, Thrinndor and Cyrillis traveled to Ardaagh, each with orders from Sordaak. Breunne had been instructed by the mage to travel to Farreach and covertly find out what he could about any army amassing to be used against them. He also had some very unusual instructions that required a hired group of mercenaries and an incursion into the badlands. Sordaak didn't say why, but the ranger felt he already knew the answer to that.

The cleric and the paladin were to get word to their remaining kindred to make arrangements to relocate to The Isle of Grief. Immediately.

Thrinndor knew his mother would never leave Khavhall, but the paladin had agreed to at least try.

The paladin was puzzled by a second request: He had been instructed to arrange for a large force of drow—at least a hundred strong—to press an attack into the Badlands from the Northwest. The paladin, too, felt he knew why, but the sorcerer had said he would explain when the companions met again.

For the rogue, Sordaak had a special mission: Find his sister and determine who her companions were. This was shaping up to be a holy war, and the mage didn't like it. Not one little bit. He wanted to know who—and what—they were up against.

Sordaak did as he said he would: He worked tirelessly at training his new charge—even he had trouble calling the dragon his familiar. But, that is without a doubt what he was. The wonder of that never faded. A *dragon* for a familiar! This *had* to be the first time that had happened in recorded history.

The boy was a quick study. He learned new spells at an astounding rate. Not only that, but by the third day Sordaak noticed the boy grew *physically* at an equally astounding rate. By the end of the week the youth could no longer be called a boy; he was now as tall as his master and appeared to be in his early teens. Clearly there was something unique about the young dragon—who continued to call him father, by the way—that caused him to grow at such a rate.

By the end of that same week, the young man was also starting to fill out, putting on pounds across his chest and legs. While the focus of the mage's training was primarily cerebral, it was obvious this youth had the capacity for physical training as well. Sordaak made a mental note to arrange for him to get some training from all three of the fighter-types during the upcoming journey, and maybe even some dexterity work with the rogue.

The week passed all too quickly for the pair. Sordaak learned how to properly ride a dragon, and by the fourth day he was comfortable doing so without hanging on. They even practiced diving runs on low hills with the sorcerer testing his ability to wield *Pendromar, Dragon's Breath* and cast spells from various positions.

When his companions began to trickle back to the island, Sordaak felt comfortable that he and his dragon had practiced for most possible situations that could arise. He was most happy with the dragon learning to become invisible at will—that was almost certainly going to be useful in any coming altercations. He was working on Pentaath being able to plane travel—or at least shift—so that he would be undetectable by other dragons, but as of yet the youth had not been able to master that. It was something they would have to continue to work on.

When Savinhand—last to arrive—returned, Sordaak called his friends together. They met again in the tower, this time over a heavy breakfast. Eggs, three different breakfast meats, biscuits and gravy—the mage had prevailed upon the rogue to teach the kitchen staff several of his recipes—plus trays of delectable fresh fruits.

When Vorgath had eaten his fill, he pushed his chair back, loosened his belt and belched loudly.

"Was that necessary?" Cyrillis said, wrinkling her nose in distaste.

"Of course," replied the barbarian, using his right index finger as a toothpick. "You wouldn't want me to explode, would you?" He paused in his efforts at extracting a particularly bothersome piece of bacon to flash a toothy grin at the cleric, but immediately stuck his finger back in his mouth.

"Barbarians!" Cyrillis returned the smile as she crossed her arms on her chest, shaking her head in pretended disgust.

"Yup," Vorgath said with a wink. Satisfied that he had gotten as much of the offending morsel as he was able, he leaned forward to retrieve his half-full coffee mug. He briefly considered refilling his cup from the urn at the end of the table, but as that would require him to get up, he decided against it. He leaned back again, cradling the mug in both hands. "Ahhh, now that was a repast worthy of a tale of its own!"

Thrinndor snorted as he stood. "Oh, may it please the gods *no!* We have no time for such a tale!" He winked at his friend, took the two steps to the coffee urn, picked it up, walked around the table and refilled the dwarf's outstretched mug.

"Oh, very well," grumbled the dwarf. "But this balking every time a proper tale is due is starting to make me wonder at my choice of companions!"

The paladin patted his friend on the shoulder. "Another time, old friend, another time." He turned his smile on the mage. "I believe our magnanimous magicuser is finally going to enlighten us as to what is going on inside that devious little mind of his."

Sordaak returned the smile as he held out his mug for the paladin for a refill. The big fighter walked over and did so. "I seem to remember," he said with a rueful shake of his head, "our mage relinquishing command to a more worthy leader—his words, not mine!"

"Yeah well, that was before I knew we had to cross wits with Bahamut, The Lord of all Dragons!"

"Bah!" spat the dwarf. "Dragon, shmagon! Just get me close enough and I'll wear his ass down to a nub!"

Sordaak looked at the boastful fighter, disdain plain on his face. "While that plan might seem to have merit to those with their brains in their biceps—"

"Hey!" all three fighter-types complained at once.

Sordaak smiled. "Relax! My point is: Bahamut is the smartest creature in all the land—*and* the most powerful." He shook his head. "Brute strength alone is unlikely to win the day when we cross paths with him."

"Bah," Vorgath said again.

"What, pray tell, is *your* plan, then?" Thrinndor demanded.

Sordaak told them.

He was met with plenty of resistance, at first—that, and a lot of questions. But, in the end it was decided the plan just might work.

"Make preparations," Sordaak said at last. "We sail at sunset."

*

The lines were slipped not long after the last vestiges of light had left the sky. The harbor was completely dark as the first moon was not set to rise for a couple more hours. Sordaak had ordered all fires along the waterfront extinguished a week earlier in preparation for this moment. And it was to be another week before they were allowed to be relit. Only the stars adorning the sky from horizon to horizon lit their way. That was enough for the dwarf to guide their small vessel from the safety of the harbor out into the open sea.

At Sordaak's behest, the prow of the ship was initially pointed west. He wanted to ensure there was no chance of them being seen from Farreach before making the turn to the south. The companions retired below decks to their quarters. Although the ship was relatively small, it was one outfitted for comfortable passage for the seven of them—plus a few more, if need be. There wasn't a need. Only the six companions and Pentaath in human form were aboard.

The mage returned to the deck before the first tendrils of dawn spread its fingers into the blackness of night. Only when dawn broke slowly at their stern did Sordaak give the order for the course change to the south.

When there was enough light, Sordaak pulled out a map and showed the dwarf where it was they were going and how he wanted to get there. Vorgath asked a few questions, eventually nodding his agreement with the proposed course. This was going to be a long voyage—at least a week—and that was only if the winds held and the weather cooperated.

The barbarian didn't trust anyone else at the helm when sailing by the stars, and only reluctantly surrendered control of the vessel during the daylight hours, finally admitting that even he couldn't remain awake for an entire week.

The weather held and the companions used the light of day to work on various skills—even learning new things from one another. Reluctantly, Sordaak assigned Pentaath to work for most of a day with first the paladin, then the ranger and finally the rogue. Because of his oddball sleep schedule, the sorcerer arranged for his charge to work with the barbarian during the afternoons when he returned from his sleep period.

Like his kindred, Pentaath needed to satisfy his voracious appetite while in dragon form. He could eat meals with the humans, partaking pretty much as they did, but his growing body required the sustenance only obtainable through the hunt and the kill. As such, he took to the skies at night to fly to the nearest land and forage for food. Initially his master insisted that he fly east to Pothgaard to eat, but that grew increasingly difficult as the two coastlines grew further apart. Fortunately he did not have to do this *every* night.

Occasionally Sordaak went with him, but flying at night was still a bit unnerving to the mage, so most of the time he contented himself with remaining awake and watching through the eyes of his familiar. He also found he needed to shut out when his charge actually made the kill and consumed his meal. That part— combined with the gentle roll of the vessel in the long, slow swells—turned the sorcerer green a couple of times; once even to the point of losing diner over the side.

Vorgath ribbed the mage until Sordaak explained why his normally strong stomach was more than a bit queasy. The barbarian agreed that was ample reason and decided to let it go. Besides, the damn mage's graphic description was enough to make the dwarf surprisingly happy when he stopped talking.

The weather indeed held, getting noticeably warmer the further south they sailed. Only twice did rain squalls cross their paths, and only one of those was bad enough for the dwarf to have to turn their ship into the teeth of the storm. Lightning danced in the clouds overhead and raindrops as large as pecans soaked everything not covered. But within a couple of hours the storm passed, and they were able to resume course.

Then, on the morning of the fifth day, shortly after changing course back to the north having rounded the southernmost tip of the mainland, their daily routines were interrupted. Up to this point they had seen no vessels, nor any living thing other than the occasional seabird.

But on this morning Savinhand, who had the morning duty on the helm, spotted something on the western horizon. A sail.

"Damn!" spat the mage as he trained his looking glass on the distant vessel.

"Who are they?" Cyrillis asked.

"I don't know," Sordaak admitted. "But they've seen us and have changed course to intercept." He turned to Savinhand. "Rudder hard to—" the mage paused to think, "port! Bring us around to an easterly heading."

The rogue immediately complied, spinning the big wheel to the left. Sordaak felt the rudder bite through the wooden deck and the ship heeled over. Hearing the line creak, the mage ducked just in time as the sail boom swung harmlessly over his head.

"What the hell is going on?" Vorgath demanded, rubbing the sleep from his eyes as he poked his head out of the hatch that led below. He'd felt the change in swell interaction with the hull of the vessel and that had awakened him.

Sordaak just pointed.

The barbarian jumped up the final two steps and onto the main deck. He grabbed the glass from the sorcerer and trained it on the vessel that was now astern. Cleary it was gaining on them. "Pirates." He spat a curse as he lowered the glass. He then looked aloft at their sails and rushed to make adjustments.

"You sure?" Sordaak sounded dubious.

"Yes," answered the dwarf as he strode over and shoved the rogue out of the way. "Move," he said roughly, making a minor course change to starboard. He checked the position of the vessel, noting that it was still gaining on them. "We'd better get prepared for a fight, because they're faster than us and they ain't coming out for tea!"

"Damn!" shouted the mage, startling the cleric, who was standing beside him. "How did they know we're out here?" He glared at his companions, but that only drew shrugs and shaken heads for an answer.

"Perhaps they were just patrolling the area and happened across us?" Cyrillis offered, although even she didn't sound convinced.

Sordaak shook his head as he again trained the glass on the pirate ship. "No, they're approaching from the vicinity of Karthogg. Something—or someone—alerted them to our presence! Damn!" he repeated, slamming his open palm onto the railing.

Suddenly he looked overhead and scanned the skies around their ship. "Has anyone seen any birds this morning?"

More shaking heads.

Savin alone looked confused. "I saw one shortly after I took the watch. Why?"

Sordaak looked at the rogue, squinting his eyes against the rising sun. "What kind of bird?"

Savinhand started to ask why that mattered, but then his eyes went wide as he remembered what he had seen. "A hawk, I believe. It flew lazily overhead for about an hour. I assumed it was hoping we would throw some garbage overboard. I may have assumed incorrectly."

"Yes," Breunne said, craning his neck to check the sky, "probably so; hawks seldom fly out over the open sea—certainly not this far out."

Cyrillis licked her lips. "What does that mean?"

"He means a hawk would have to have a reason to be this far out to sea," answered the magicuser. "The bird was probably sent here to search the shipping lanes by his master."

"A hawk master? I do not understand?" Pentaath, too, scanned the skies.

Sordaak shook his head. "No, not a hawk master—a sorcerer. The bird is his—or her—familiar. It's a common tactic used by pirates. Hire a mercenary sorcerer or make one a member of your crew and have them search the shipping lanes for you once or twice a day. That way, you only have to put to sea in the event something interesting happens along."

"But we are not that close to the standard shipping lanes," Thrinndor said from his perch on the mast.

"We must be close enough," the mage said. "A sharp-eyed bird such as a hawk can see for extreme distances from their vantage point high in the sky. *Damn!*" He glared at the others, daring them to say anything. "We were within a couple of days making it in undetected!" he looked at the skies again. "Kill that damn bird if it makes an appearance again." The mage turned and looked back at the pirate ship, which was by now clearly much larger than theirs. "How long?" he demanded.

"An hour, maybe two if I make them change course a few times," answered the barbarian from his place at the helm. No one had seen him go get his weapon, but *Flinthgoor* was propped against the rail within easy grasp.

"Do what you can," replied the sorcerer. "I want the encounter to occur as far away from land as possible."

"Why?" the cleric asked.

Sordaak turned to stare at Cyrillis, his lips pressed together in a grip expression. "Because none of them must survive to return to port."

The sails flapped a few times into the strained silence that followed.

"Them survive?" Savinhand asked. He pointed over the water at the rapidly approaching ship. "They will have at least fifty—probably more—men on that ship! Fighters that are trained to kill at sea!"

"And at least one sorcerer," reminded the paladin.

Sordaak looked from the rogue to the paladin. "I am not worried about scum such as them," he said with a dismissive wave of the hand. "I will be taking Pentaath aloft, and we'll attack from the air. Breunne will make life miserable for them with flaming arrows." His determined eyes spoke for him. "By the time they pull alongside to board us, they will have had second thoughts." Now he smiled—a wicked, evil smile. "That's when we'll turn lose you and Vorgath."

The barbarian nodded his approval of the plan while the paladin took another look at the larger vessel. He was less sure.

"*None* must survive," Sordaak repeated.

Thrinndor swallowed hard as he too nodded. He also wondered just when it was that he had surrendered leadership of this group back to the sorcerer.

Chapter Seventeen

Air Attack

Sordaak threw up a smoke screen and had Pentaath revert to dragon form behind that. Then both went invisible and the sorcerer felt the powerful muscles in his charge's back tense as he prepared to launch into the air. At his spoken word, the dragon leapt high, his huge wings clawing for altitude, and within seconds both were looking down on the tiny vessel below.

The mage knew that they couldn't be seen, but the wind generated from the wings of his steed had blasted his smoke screen, and anyone watching closely would have known something was amiss. However, they would have no idea just what that something was.

Once the pair had gained sufficient height, the dragon pointed his nose toward the pirate ship. To avoid making noise that might be detected, he began to soar, using existing wind currents and thermals to maintain as much height as possible. Sordaak didn't want to attack yet; instead, he wanted the ships close enough together that the pirates' attention would be elsewhere.

From high above, Sordaak could see that the enemy ship was almost twice as big as their own. The original estimation of a crew of fifty seemed a little light—probably closer to seventy-five. *Damn, this might not be as easy as I thought!*

As Pentaath glided around behind the ship and banked, the mage got a better look at the deck of the pirate's vessel. It was teeming with men scurrying around and preparing for battle. There was a curious lump in the middle of the deck just in front of the main mast that he hadn't noticed before. Sordaak instantly regretted leaving his glass behind so the barbarian could better gauge the approach.

The mage informed the dragon he wanted to get a better look via his thoughts, and soon the pair circled ever closer to the ship. Sordaak could see some aboard occasionally look up, so either they heard something or some other sense vied for their attention. But none pointed or shouted, so the sorcerer assumed they had not been seen.

However, they were getting uncomfortably close and Sordaak was about to signal Pentaath to break off the pattern and glide away so they could safely regain lost altitude when suddenly several crewmen grasped the cover they had flown lower to investigate and flipped it aside, exposing a catapult mounted to the deck on a rail system!

SHIT! It was already pointed in the general vicinity of their vessel! One of the men looked down a long sight and rotated the contraption slightly sideways. They were preparing to launch! Next a man holding a lit torch lowered it to a boulder sitting in the catapult cup where it immediately ignited.

Instantly the sorcerer knew he didn't have time to warn his friends and he made a snap decision sending Pentaath into a dive directly at the pirate vessel.

They almost made it. But, as soon as the man at the sight verified the flames held he yanked a cord and the mechanism was released. Sordaak watched in horror as the flaming boulder was sent spinning toward his friends.

Initially the arc appeared true but the boulder sailed high, missing the main deck, instead it plowed through the sheet of their sail, setting the remnants ablaze.

Sordaak saw none of this. Within a half second of the projectile's release, Pentaath roared and lambasted the pirate at the controls of the catapult and those nearby with a stinging blast of frost as the dragon sped by, unseen in his decent. Sordaak used his staff and shot a sheet of flame at the ships main sail.

To his surprise, nothing happened! The spell worked correctly and flames engulfed the sail, but the cloth didn't ignite! As he sped past, Sordaak could see that the material was *wet!* The pirates had anticipated their enemy attempting to slow them by setting fire to their sails and wetted them first!

Shit!

And then they were past. The mage noted with satisfaction first the surprise and then instant fear as several crew members spotted the dragon for the first time as Pentaath released his breath weapon. *That should keep them busy*, Sordaak reasoned as his steed again clawed for altitude and readied for another attack.

It didn't take long before the sorcerer heard arrows whizzing past his head. He was briefly concerned for his steed, but knew the arrows had little chance of penetrating the scale system that covered his dragon from head to tail. Still, a well-aimed—or worse, lucky—shot would complicate matters. Fortunately, neither happened.

A quick glance showed his friends had successfully cut the lines to the flaming sail and thrown it overboard. He knew they had spares, but that would take time and they were already slowing to a halt in the water.

A nudge and the dragon changed direction, swinging around at his master's command to attack from the stern of the pirate ship. With ever increasing speed they dove, Sordaak now worried more about an arrow hitting *him* than his charge. Just before hitting the deck, Pentaath pulled up and flew straight at the sail, blasting away with his breath weapon again as he did. Sordaak also aimed a cone of cold directly at the sail, at which they were approaching very fast.

I hope this works, the mage thought fleetingly as he and the dragon made contact with the massive sail. It did. The cloth of the sail, made hard by the now frozen water it contained, shattered and fell to the decks below as Pentaath soared triumphantly though. The triumph was short lived—actually, almost non-existent—as his right wing caught on an unseen rope on the other side of the sail. They were spun around as his wing got entangled and he lost all momentum, plummeting toward the deck below.

Pentaath collapsed the wing to his side, thereby freeing it. He rolled and dove at the deck, raking it with another icy blast as he regained speed. Pulling up at the last possible second, he grasped a pirate in his talons and beat his wings hard to regain height. Once clear of the ship the dragon released his unwilling passenger, allowing him to drop into the sea far below. It was then that he noticed that he no longer had his other passenger, either.

Sordaak had been thrown clear on first impact. He only had time to roll over and hit the water with his back. He clutched *Pendromar* to his chest with both hands so as not to lose it when he hit the water. The tactic almost didn't work.

The mage hit the water harder than expected, and the air was driven from his lungs as he plunged beneath the surface. His vision blurred as the intense pain washed over him and he sank below the surface. Sordaak's lips parted to scream, but instead his mouth and lungs filled with the salty water.

The sorcerer's eyes widened in panic as his shoulders wracked to expel the offending fluid from his lungs, only to be replaced by more of the same. A new panic coursed through his veins like lightning when he felt an object strike his foot. That's when he realized his staff had slipped from his grasp. *NO!*

Forcefully, he spat the water from his lungs as he doubled over and lunged for the staff, visible only a couple of feet below him. Wrapping his right hand around the now slippery wood he began to claw for the surface, which seemed suddenly so far away but in reality was only a few feet. A sharp pain in his right thigh reminded him why he was in the water in the first place. A quick check verified an arrow stuck out of the back of his leg.

He broke the surface suddenly with his mouth agape. His air starved lungs gulped the life-sustaining substance as another arrow splashed water into his eyes from a near-miss. *Shit!* He inhaled as much air as he could and dove back beneath the surface, hearing the splashes of more arrows all around where he had just been. He yelped as one creased his left arm, causing him to jerk to the right and thrash for more depth.

The panic returned in full force as he struggled with his cloak and robes, made incredibly heavy by the weight of the water they now held. Suddenly he felt that every bag tied at his waist and the many items in their respective pockets was conspiring to pull him ever deeper. Sordaak had to fight down the impulse to cast aside the staff and return to the surface.

His ring! *Yes!* The mage felt the increasing pressure and knew he was sinking ever deeper as he clutched the staff to his chest with both arms, allowing his hands the freedom to untie a reluctant leather thong holding a bag at his waist. He again fought down the panic as repeatedly his fingers slipped on the soggy leather and he forced his digits to move deliberately.

Finally, he jerked it free. Quickly he pulled the sack open and reached inside. Panic once again gripped him as his fingers fumbled around, unable to find what they searched for. *There!* He pulled his hand out to examine the ring and in his excitement he let go of the bag.

Sordaak removed another ring from the finger where this new one must go and slipped the plain looking replacement on in its place. Instantly, the panic washed away as he was suddenly able to draw the much-needed oxygen from the water! Water breathing! Silently, he vowed to never again remove this ring as long as their journey took them over the open waters of the sea.

Realization as to where he was and recent events snapped him back to the present. Quickly he dove after his bag, which was in danger of sinking out of sight. There were other things in there he knew he would need. Fortunately, it had only sunk a few feet.

His own panic now under control, Sordaak could feel that was not the case for his dragon. Pentaath was flying all over looking for his master. Too often, he got within range of the pirate ship and once had to dodge a well-aimed shot from the catapult.

Sordaak closed his eyes and forced himself to be calm. He then projected that to his familiar, and once he had Pentaath's attention he ordered the dragon to return to the companion's ship and await instructions. The mage sensed Pentaath's confusion, but the dragon complied anyway.

Satisfied, Sordaak opened his eyes and looked toward the surface. He could see the hull of the pirate ship not far off—perhaps fifty feet. A quick search revealed his vessel was not in sight. He could tell that the pirates must have gotten some sort of sail rigged, because the big ship was beginning to move. As he watched the rudder was put over hard to left (*port?*) and the vessel began to increase speed and come around.

Not wanting to be left behind out in the open waters of the sea, Sordaak kicked the water hard and swam toward the hull, which was now almost directly over his head. A stabbing pain in his leg elicited a bubbled curse from his lips as he was reminded of the arrow in his thigh. Dragging the injured leg along behind him, he floated toward the surface and grabbed onto the rudder as it swept by.

Once he'd ensured he had a good hand-hold, the mage twisted around and looked at the injured part of his leg. His movement through the water tugged at the feathers of the protruding arrow, which appeared to be barely hanging on just below the skin.

Sordaak felt a shudder through the hull and surmised correctly that the catapult had again launched a salvo at his friends. *I hope they, too, are moving, or they'll be sitting ducks!* The uneasy feeling wouldn't go away and he knew he needed to do something.

The sorcerer shifted the dead weight of *Pendromar* to the crook of his left arm—which was hanging onto the rudder—and twisted around to grasp the arrow with his right. Sordaak gritted his teeth together and yanked hard on the offending shaft, hoping quick movement would lessen the pain. He was wrong.

A frothy scream ripped from his lips as white-hot pain shot up his thigh and coursed through the mage's entire body. The head of the arrow had shifted under the swirling currents of the sorcerer's movement through the water and when jerked, the back of that head had ripped through a different portion of skin.

Sordaak felt his left hand slipping from the rudder and, releasing the arrow reached up to get his right hand onto another spot. Unfortunately, his thrashing fingers scraped across several barnacles before gaining a hand-hold and another curse was torn from his lips. But, he held on—just barely.

After a few moments, the pain subsided somewhat and the mage was able to open his eyes, not realizing they were shut. First he inspected his right hand, noting a couple of lacerated fingers, a nasty-looking cut in his palm and some significant bleeding. With considerable effort he shifted his grip on his staff and re-established a hold on the rudder with his left hand. Sordaak then wrapped his damaged right hand around the shaft of *Pendromar*. After verifying the blood didn't make his grip too slippery, he squeezed hard, ignoring the pain and noted with satisfaction the reduction in blood loss.

Next he twisted around to get a good look at his thigh, which still screamed for attention. What he saw immediately concerned him. Blood was pouring from the gaping hole in his leg, leaving a long curving trail behind him as the pirate ship continued its turn. At the current rate of blood loss, Sordaak knew he had only minutes before losing consciousness.

Without even realizing he had made a decision, he released his hold on the rudder and watched with mild disinterest as the ship sailed away from him. He also noted that he could see the much smaller hull of his vessel a couple of hundred yards away and he could tell that it was moving in the opposite direction, as well.

The mage briefly considered surfacing for better light but decided his continued lack of visibility better suited his immediate plans: stop the bleeding. Besides, maintaining his current depth took far less effort than trying to keep his head above water if he were on the surface.

Knowing time was short, he tore strips from a rag he kept just for the purpose. He wadded up the remainder of the cloth and tied it in place over the hole in his leg. The sorcerer took care not to tie it too tight, knowing he was going to need that leg, but tight enough to stanch the flow of blood.

He craned his neck to watch the area for a bit, noting only small tendrils of blood escaping. That looked good to him. But, damn, it still hurt! The briny water of the sea wasn't helping much with that.

Suddenly another thought came to mind, and he looked around quickly. It was said sharks could somehow sense blood in the water from great distances. Now he was decidedly uncomfortable and felt vulnerable some fifteen feet or so below the surface of the water.

Deciding he needed to put some distance between the floating blood trail and himself, he began to swim in the direction the ships had gone, slowly at first and then faster as fear of the unknown from the depths around him began to play visions in the mage's head.

Initially he kept his depth because the same memory involving the blood in the water also warned him about thrashing around on the surface like a standard meal for the aforementioned sharks. But then fear got the better of him, and he decided that being closer to the relative safety of air was more his style.

Several quick glances behind and below him showed nothing of interest until…*SHIT! That's a shark!* The fish was not fifty feet away and closing fast on the swimming magicuser.

Sordaak had come up with a rudimentary plan, hoping he wouldn't have to use it. He shouted the words to the spell while still underwater, causing large bubbles to form at his mouth. The mage continued toward the surface much faster now and broke free. He launched clear of the waves like a leaping fish but continued to gain altitude as the fly spell propelled him above the water.

Suddenly that water erupted below him and a massive shark—at least twenty feet in length—leapt skyward, its mouth open wide revealing multiple rows of razor-sharp teeth! Sordaak had been prepared for this, too. He spoke the trigger word to the fireball spell and pointed his finger down the throat of the monster.

Time almost seemed to stand still as the very small ball of flames sped across the five feet that separated the sorcerer and his attacker, disappeared into the maw of the fish and exploded deep inside.

In an instant, Sordaak could see that he had done serious harm to the monster, yet the shark's momentum carried him ever higher, gaining on the mage. In that same instant, Sordaak realized he was doomed to fail in his escape attempt. He quickly spoke the words to another spell as the rows and rows of jagged teeth clamped shut on his right ankle.

Excruciating pain shot up the sorcerer's leg as Sordaak released the contact electricity spell. Through the haze of pain the mage saw surprise register in the monster's eyes. Yet the creature did not release his grip as he reached the apex of his flight and began the tortuously slow fall back toward the surface of the water.

Sordaak swung *Pendromar* with all his remaining strength and the head of the staff hit the shark between the eyes as the two landed in the water with a tremendous splash. An explosion occurred when the ornate wood of the staff made contact with the tough skin of the shark, but Sordaak was pulled by his ankle into the frothy cloud of water and unable to gage the results of his efforts.

The mage could tell something hand changed, though. The shark was no longer trying to rip his ankle off by twisting and jerking. As the water cleared of the bubbles generated by their reentry, Sordaak could see that there was a large hole in the skin between the shark's eyes—a *very large* hole, at least a foot in diameter and half that in depth.

The mage felt a surge of elation. The shark was dead! That elation turned to sick realization as he realized the monster's massive jaws were still clamped around his ankle, which was bent over at an impossible angle. Curiously, he felt no pain.

Sordaak felt an increase of pressure in his ears and glanced toward the surface to see he and the shark had sunk at least twenty feet. They continued to sink and he only then began to understand his plight. The dead shark was sinking toward the bottom of the sea, and he was going to take the mage with him.

Panic gripped Sordaak as he realized that while he was able to breathe, the pressure from the unknown depths below would certainly crush the life from his body. Slowly.

Quickly the magicuser slid his staff behind his belt and bent to look at the gory mess that was his lower leg. He couldn't see much because the bulk of the damage was hidden by the mouth of the shark.

Briefly, Sordaak used both hands to grip the upper and lower jaws, trying in vain to pry the monster's mouth open. But he was in no way strong enough for such a feat and quickly realized it. Next he shoved *Pendromar* between the teeth and tried to pry using the leverage of the ancient staff. But he discovered there was no place to put his other foot for leverage and had to give up that attempt, as well.

The pressure in his ears was mounting, and his head was beginning to hurt. Sordaak knew he hadn't much time remaining. The mage closed his eyes and forced down the panic that threatened to engulf him. When he opened them again, he was able to survey his situation with an almost detached sense of purpose. He knew what he needed to do.

With none of the previous panic that had gripped his heart, Sordaak again slid *Pendromar* behind his belt. He quickly removed a length of rope from his waist and bent to peer at his lower leg. He tied the rope above where the shark had a death-grip on his foot and began to wrap its full length around as tightly as he could pull it. Then he tied a knot in the rope, reached to his belt and removed a long, thin dagger from its sheath.

As he put the blade to his ankle just below his rope, he hesitated, but only for a moment. Grimly and with an emotional detachment he forced on himself, Sordaak began slicing though the damaged skin. The twisting by the shark had already broken the bones in his lower leg just above the ankle such that the jagged shards of at least one of those bones already poked through the skin.

As there were no bones that required cutting, the task was surprisingly easy, and he had severed his foot in just a few seconds. Fortunately, the blade was exceedingly sharp.

Immediately the shark—and his foot—began to separate and sink faster than the sorcerer. He reached out and pulled the water toward him, kicking with his one remaining foot toward the surface, now more than a hundred feet above his head.

Sordaak knew he needed help immediately because the tourniquet on his leg was leaking blood badly. He'd already lost far too much blood from previous wounds and he was getting light-headed. As he felt himself rise toward the surface at an ever quickening pace, he calmly put the dagger back in its sheath and began blowing air out of his lungs as he felt that air expanding.

He approached the surface Sordaak again mouthed the words to the fly spell and shot up through the waves to launch skyward. A quick glance showed both vessels about a quarter mile away, maybe two hundred yards apart. The mage made for a spot behind his ship, not wanting a repeat of the arrow incident.

He almost made it.

Chapter Eighteen

Pirates

Vorgath watched the mage fly off on the dragon and felt a momentary surge of envy—not something he was accustomed to. He shook his head to clear it and focused his attention on the approaching pirate ship, glad to have the mage's eyeglass so he could study them from afar.

The much faster pirate ship was gaining, and now less than a mile separated the two. Vorgath spun the wheel, causing their ship to heel over to port. He stopped the turn almost as quickly, adjusting the sails so they would catch the maximum amount of wind.

The pirate ship adjusted their course to match, but the barbarian's move had bought the companions some additional time, perhaps even a few minutes.

The pirate vessel had closed to within a half-mile when the dwarf noted a flurry of movement on deck. He raised the glass and was startled to see a contraption on deck with a flaming ball sitting in a cup.

"*Catapult!*" Vorgath shouted. The heads of the others turned to see the threat. The barbarian handed the glass to the paladin and spun the wheel rapidly to starboard, willing his little ship to turn in time.

"Shit!" Thrinndor yelled as he trained the scope on the pirate ship. "Salvo on the way!"

The companions watched helplessly as the easily visible ball of fire arced toward them.

The shot hit the sail and Vorgath felt the mast bend as their vessel twisted slightly before the material gave way, the boulder passing through to land with a splash and a brief hiss in the water off of their starboard bow.

"Ha! Missed!" Savinhand shouted.

"That wasn't a miss," the barbarian said as he rushed to the lines holding the flaming remnants of the sail in place and cut them with a sword he pulled from his belt. The rogue gave him a confused look, but the dwarf didn't bother to acknowledge. "That shot was meant to disable us so they could board and seize the vessel." The last rope slashed, Thrinndor helped him toss the flaming sail overboard. Now he turned his impassive gaze on the thief. "They don't want to damage their prize in any way."

The barbarian glanced toward their adversary coming up fast from astern. "Run below and get the spare sail while me and Thrinndor see what—if any—options we have."

Savin nodded and disappeared below decks.

"Sordaak is in the water!" Cyrillis shouted. She'd been appointed the duty of keeping tabs on the magicuser—something that had been correctly surmised she would have done anyway.

Thrinndor had forgotten about the mage. "Where?" he yelled.

"There," the cleric answered, pointing to a spot in the water between the two vessels, but much nearer the pirate ship. "He and Pentaath went through their sail—"

"Bless him," interrupted the dwarf as Savinhand reappeared dragging a large canvas sack. He rushed to help the rogue and together with Breunne they tackled the task of getting the sail out of the bag and onto the mast.

"—but the dragon's wing got caught and Sordaak was thrown into the water. They were shooting arrows at him, and I believe he dove under their ship!" She was suddenly chewing her lower lip.

"He's smarter than I gave him credit for," muttered the dwarf as he snatched a corner of the sail from the paladin. "There's no time for that!"

"But—" Thrinndor had been trying to slide the upper yard arm through a pocket made for that.

Vorgath stole a look at the slower but still approaching pirate ship. They, too, were working on another sail. In the meantime, the pirates were chocking oars. "Just tie the corners to the arm and get the hell out of the way." His words were harsher than he'd intended, but niceties were not his strong suit during periods of inactivity, and this was certainly not one of those.

Thrinndor set his lips thinly, nodding as he did what he was told. He knew the barbarian well enough to know not to be offended.

"What about Sordaak?" Cyrillis insisted, her eyes searching the water between them and the pirate ship, willing the mage back to the surface.

Vorgath heaved on the line, raising the lower yard arm by himself. "No time for him now. He's smart, I'm sure he'll figure out a way to survive."

As the yard arm got to the top of the mast, the sail began flapping in the morning breeze and Pentaath in human form landed on an open space of deck near the stern.

"Tie the corners to anything that won't move!" Vorgath yelled as he tied the rope supporting the yard arm to a nearby stanchion. Thrinndor and Breunne rushed to do as directed.

"Where is Sordaak?" demanded the cleric.

Pentaath closed his eyes and after a moment pointed at the base of the pirate ship. "He is holding onto their rudder under their ship."

"*Under water?*" The cleric was confused.

"He has some magical device that allows him to breathe normally, I assume," the dragon said, shrugging. Cyrillis felt better with that news. "However," the young man went on, his voice grave, "he is injured. I am not sure he will be able to hang on much longer."

"*What?*" Cyrillis squared her shoulders. "Why did you leave him?" she demanded.

Pentaath looked decidedly uncomfortable under her glare. "I did not!" he protested. "He was thrown clear when my wing clipped a line! I would have gone after him—would *still be* after him—had he not sent me back here to wait!" His face was a strange mixture of pain, consternation and a desire for her to understand.

She did. Her demeanor softened somewhat as she put her hand on his arm. "How badly is he injured?"

The dragon boy started to answer, then closed his eyes and reached out to his master. "He took an arrow in his thigh and he is bleeding badly from the wound." He paused as his face contorted in pain. "He has released his hold on the rudder and is going to tend the injury. He also fears the blood in the water will attract sharks."

Suddenly the man-child gasped in pain and dropped to his knees.

"What?" Cyrillis asked. "What is it?" For the first time she noticed a gathering pool of blood at the young man's feet. "You are hurt?"

Surprised, Pentaath opened his eyes, also seeing the blood for the first time. He shook his head. "It is not mine, but his." The dragon looked up, pain in his eyes. "We are as one." He gasped again, his face contorting in agony. "He has removed the arrow and is trying to wrap the hole in his leg."

Cyrillis could not get past the feeling of helplessness that washed over her. "If I heal you, will that carry over to his body?"

Pentaath locked his pain filled eyes on hers and shook his head. "I do not believe so."

"Well, it will not hurt to try!" Cyrillis said. Quickly she said a prayer, closed her eyes and released the spell energy into Pentaath by direct touch. She then knelt to study the area where the blood came from on the boy's thigh. *Damn!* She could see no discernible effect!

Abruptly, she surged to her feet and walked to the rail. "How far away is he?" Her inability to do anything was palpable in her voice.

Pentaath struggled to his feet and limped to stand beside her. He closed his eyes and pointed at a spot behind the pirate ship, which was now again moving. "He is there. He has wrapped the wound as best he could," Cyrillis said, noting the reduced bleeding from the dragon's leg. "He is swimming this way."

"How fast?" All eyes turned to the ranger, who was looking out over the water with the mage's glass.

"Not fast," Pentaath answered. "Why?"

For an answer, Breunne merely pointed. Those same eyes followed his finger and several breaths were sucked in at once. Some distance out they could all easily see the dorsal fin of what must certainly be a very large shark.

"No!" Cyrillis moaned.

As they watched, the fin disappeared, presumably diving for the magicuser.

"WARN HIM!" the healer shrieked.

"I have," replied the dragon. "He knows and has seen the shark." His face was impassive with impending doom.

Sordaak shot out of the water like a javelin launched from some unknown platform below the surface. The companions started to cheer, but their joyous reaction was cut short when the shark also broke the surface, clearly intent on following its intended meal into the heavens, if necessary.

Still, it appeared the mage might make it as the shark began to slow. The two got closer together in mid-flight as those on the ship held their breath. Then the shark snapped at a dangling foot, and it was obvious the big fish connected.

Together the two fell back to the water with a tremendous splash and disappeared below the waves.

"Son of a dragon bitch!" Vorgath's tone was awe-stricken. "That was the biggest shark I have *ever* seen!"

"DO SOMETHING!" Cyrillis screamed.

The barbarian looked at her, an injured look on his face. "Like what?"

Cyrillis didn't have time to reply as they all heard a loud noise from the pirate ship. They turned as one to see a pair of boulders tied together with a chain sailing their way.

"DUCK!" Vorgath shouted as he dove for the deck. The others did likewise as the odd projectile passed overhead, making a strange *whoosh-whoosh* as it did because of the chain.

"Missed!" announced the rogue as he was first to recover and check out the double splash in the water alongside their port bow.

"Not by much," agreed the barbarian as he turned to look at the pirate ship, now no more than two hundred yards astern. He looked aloft and shook his head ruefully; his makeshift attempt at a sail was leaking wind all around. But there was nothing that could be done for it at the moment. "They overestimated the distance," he added as he noted the pirates reloading. "They won't make that mistake again."

"What *was* that?" Cyrillis asked, studying where the boulders had fallen.

"Mast shot," the paladin answered. "The object is for that chain to catch on our mast, whereby the rocks will spin around until they come in contact with the wood and snap it off. They are still trying to disable rather than sink us."

The healer nodded her understanding.

"Breunne," Thrinndor called to the ranger, "can you make things a bit more difficult for them?"

Without saying anything, the ranger readied his bow and stepped to the stern rail. For a second he raised the glass and studied his target. Then he handed the glass Savinhand, who stood next to him, and selected an arrow from his quiver. Breunne notched the arrow and drew it back, sighting along the arrowhead at the enemy vessel still far astern.

The ranger held that stance for a few heartbeats, not breathing as he gauged wind and distance. Then he released the arrow. He watched briefly, then turned and nodded to the paladin. "That should give them pause in their efforts."

Thrinndor returned the nod, but Savinhand, not sure whether he could believe anyone could hit anything at this distance, raised the glass and searched the deck. At first he found nothing. No one. It was as if the decks had been swept clear of all life. Wait! There! Directly behind the catapult was a man standing against the main mast. A closer look revealed the feathers of the arrow sticking out of the man's right eye socket, the back of his head pressed up against the mast. The arrow had gone through the eye, out of the back of the man's head and pinned him to the mast!

"*Holy shit!*" the rogue said with a whistle.

"What?"

Savinhand shook his head in wonder. "The arrow went through the eye of the man trying to aim that catapult, out the back of his head and *pinned him to the mast!* Everyone else dove for cover!"

Vorgath looked at Breunne, a new respect in his eyes. "Nice shootin'."

The ranger just nodded. "I'll try to keep them ducking for cover, but they'll have to get closer before I can use flaming arrows to keep them busy." He smiled.

Thrinndor turned to inspect the approaching vessel. "Perhaps it is time for us to quit running."

Vorgath's face was impassive as he spun the wheel. "I was beginning to think you were *never* going to give that order!"

The paladin smiled and turned to the cleric. The smile vanished when he saw the worried look on her face. "Keep an eye on where Sordaak went under. We will make for that spot first."

Cyrillis nodded, chewing on her lip.

"My master yet lives." All eyes turned to Pentaath, who was on his knees and in obvious pain. "He has slain the monster but cannot free himself from the locked jaws of the beast." He opened his eyes and all could see the pain through the boy's tears. "The shark is slowly sinking, taking Sordaak with him to the bottom."

"But he's able to breathe, right?" Cyrillis said, hopefully.

Vorgath answered as the young dragon only nodded. "But the pressure of deep water will soon crush him."

"He would already be dead were it not for our bond," Pentaath shuddered. "My vitality is given to him and his to me." His eyes were begging for help. "But he will not be able to withstand much more. The pressure is crushing his mind."

Thrinndor quickly began to strip off his armor. "How deep?"

Pentaath shook his head, his eyes laden with sorrow. The paladin stopped mid-strap on his breastplate. "Too deep."

The *thrum* of Breunne's bow suddenly reminded everyone what they were up against. The ranger made sure that any pirate that showed his head regretted doing so. At least until he noted a blockade of shields going up in front of the canopy.

"Ugh-oh," the ranger said, "it appears this is not our friend's first time dealing with resistance."

"What?" Vorgath asked. He'd been busy trying to get some air in the sail so they didn't stop dead in the water.

His first answer was a single arrow that sailed across the open water to stick into the very sail he was working on. The arrow carried flames.

The second answer was another salvo of mast shot from the catapult. This time the pirate's aim was true. The *whooshing* sound came first, followed immediately by a loud splintering of their mast as the chain passed completely through it about ten feet above the deck.

The balance of the mast toppled over, bringing down the upper spar and all the lines. Fortunately, the flames had not had much of a chance to spread so Thrinndor and Vorgath had little trouble stomping out what fire that remained.

"Now they've gone and done it," growled the barbarian. "Now I'm *pissed!*" He glared out over the water at the enemy ship, physically trying to will the gap to close. The pirates were now less than a hundred yards distant.

Breunne switched to flaming arrows but quickly discovered that his opponents had again wetted their sail. He nodded to the experience of the pirates and changed tactics: He put two flaming arrows into the main mast well above their heads. The dry wood caught immediately, and soon the whole mast was ablaze. To keep them busy, he found soft spots in the hull near the waterline that also began to burn with some help from the not-so-friendly ranger. Occasionally a face would show and Breunne buried one of the flaming arrows in his forehead. But those became fewer and fewer.

Still the gap closed. Vorgath and Thrinndor readied their weapons, knowing a battle would soon be at hand.

"Wait!" Pentaath suddenly called out, hope edging its way into his voice. Only Cyrillis was paying attention to him at this point; the others were too busy. "My master is freeing himself!"

The healer knelt next to the young man. "How?"

Pentaath's eyes found hers, but it was clear he did not see her. "He is cutting off his *foot!*" The youth straightened his back, jumped to his feet and rushed to the rail and pointed.

The water erupted about a hundred yards behind the pirate ship as Sordaak broke the waves. There was a brief pause as he got his bearing and then he began to fly toward them!

Pentaath's face contorted in pain. "He remains in grave danger." The dragon's voice was barely above a whisper.

"What? *Why?*" Cyrillis asked, her elation at seeing the mage alive suddenly crushed by the boy's words.

The youth didn't have time to answer. Sordaak sped toward them, but clearly he was not well. He was sinking slowly toward the water, unable to maintain altitude.

The cleric readied a spell in the event he got close enough for her healing to work, but it was soon apparent that was not going to happen.

Sordaak splashed into the water about fifty yards ahead of and to the opposite side of the pirate ship.

Thrinndor took one glance at the enemy ship and shouted to Breunne. "Cover me!" he said, and quickly stripped off his armor.

"I have this," Pentaath said through gritted teeth as he jumped skyward, transforming into his dragon form as he did.

Thrinndor briefly considered trying to stop him, but by the time he had opened his mouth, the dragon was beating its wings and well on his way to the magicuser, who lay motionless, face down in the water. As the paladin watched, Pentaath folded his wings and dove for the body bobbing in the waves. At the last second he again spread them to slow his descent to a near halt, and reached out with both clawed feet to gingerly scoop Sordaak from the water. The dragon's massive wings again began to claw for height as the pair began their return journey.

Cyrillis reached out with her senses as they approached and could tell the sorcerer's heart still beat, but it was weak. At the very edge of her spell range she cast a full heal on the mage, just hoping to stabilize him so she could begin the real work of putting him back together.

"Catch!" the dragon roared at Thrinndor as he approached. It was then that the paladin realized how big the white dragon had become—far too big to land on their little ship. Far bigger even than his mother.

Pentaath slowed and released the mage who tumbled the few remaining feet to be easily snatched out of the air by the paladin. The healer moved in and helped Thrinndor ease Sordaak to the deck.

The paladin's head whipped around at a scream from the dragon, who had been both watching anxiously the actions on the ship and trying to gain height. The pirates had taken advantage of the distraction and launched a point-blank shot from their catapult, hitting the dragon in his right wing.

"Repel boarders!" Thrinndor bellowed, seeing that the pirates were slinging grappling hooks across the narrowing gap—currently at twenty feet and narrowing rapidly.

Although the projectile from the catapult passed cleanly through his wing, Pentaath plummeted from the sky to fall into the water on the other side of the companion's ship with a huge splash.

Thrinndor stood, drew his flaming sword and attacked the lines attached to the grappling hooks, severing two before a near miss from an arrow got his attention. "Breunne, do something about those archers!"

The ranger nodded and let fly a volley of arrows and the rain of arrows from the enemy ceased.

Having cut the lines nearest him and seeing the gap between ships was now ten feet, Thrinndor looked around for Vorgath. He was mildly surprised to see the barbarian running along the deck, holding onto a rope. But, just as Thrinndor was about ask, the barbarian yelled to build a rage and jumped into the air, using the rope to swing across the splashing waves between the ships. When the dwarf released the rope he quickly unslung *Flinthgoor* and landed feet first among a slew of pirates, all with cutlass's and various other swords waiting.

The paladin smiled and shook his head. *Damned barbarian was unwilling to wait the thirty or forty seconds for the ships to come together.* A quick glance showed Vorgath had already cut a wide swath to the mast and was standing there, laying waste to any that came close.

Knowing he was about to be too busy to concern himself with others, the paladin did a quick check. Vorgath, he knew about. Breunne was switching weapons to a longsword and shield, Savinhand was nowhere to be seen—as expected. Cyrillis had moved the mage over near the hatch leading below and was busy tending wounds. *Yep, all accounted for.*

He smiled. Somehow it didn't seem fair to the pirates.

And then he was too busy defending his territory to keep track of what the others were doing. However, he placed the cleric and her charge at his back, making sure that any enemy had to go through him to get to them.

As the ship's hulls came together, Thrinndor cut the legs out from under the first who tried to cross and used his shield to block a blow from the second. Breunne stepped up next to the paladin and stabbed the third through the heart with his sword. Side by side the pair fought, sometimes giving ground and then taking it back.

The duo took some cuts and scrapes, but were for the most part unscathed by the assault. Vorgath, the paladin could see, was dealing far more damage than receiving, but still the barbarian bled from several wounds, some that appeared serious.

Thrinndor was about to call to the healer for help, but sensed her presence on his right shoulder. "On it," she said through gritted teeth. "Stupid barbarians!"

The paladin grinned as he fended off another furious flurry aimed at getting to the relatively unprotected cleric.

Cyrillis was in a bad mood, though, and took care of herself the one time a pirate got close enough. The heel of *Kurri* almost removed the head of that one.

Vorgath waved his thanks for the healing as he cut loose with another roar of rage and renewed his assault on the rapidly thinning crowd of pirates.

Thrinndor briefly considered cutting the ropes that lashed the two ships together, but ultimately decided he didn't want to get separated from the barbarian and he didn't know where Savinhand was. Instead, he hooked an eye over at the ranger. "Shall we?"

Breunne nodded and was about to step up on the rail when he heard the beat of monstrous wings behind him. A glance over his shoulder showed the dragon rising out of the water. "Pentaath?"

Something in his voice caused the others to also look. It was Pentaath, all right, but this dragon was bigger—much bigger. And mad. His normally ice-blue eyes were now blood red, and they were fixed on the pirate ship.

"Vorgath," Thrinndor shouted over the din of battle, "get out of there!"

The barbarian glanced their direction and his eyes widened as the dragon rose above the broken mast, opened his mouth and roared so loud it hurt the ears. The dwarf, realizing he didn't have time to get back to his own ship before the dragon sprayed the pirates with ice, turned, took the two steps necessary to get him to the rail and jumped into the water.

The next time Pentaath opened his mouth the expected blast of ice came. This blast lasted much longer than expected, however. The dragon continued to spew ice from his maw as his massive wings beat the air and he gained height. When it finally ended, the deck of the pirate ship was covered in ice and several pirates were frozen in place.

Pentaath rolled over and dove at the ship from the opposite side and blasted it with his icy breath from there as well. The companions stood and watched in awe, mesmerized by the transformation of the dragon. The second breath weapon expended, Pentaath rose high into the air to survey any further threat.

Thrinndor could see that the thick ice on the deck of the frozen pirate ship made it top-heavy. "Cut the lines!" he shouted and began slashing at the ropes lashing the ships together. Breunne jumped forward to help him and the two pushed the two ships apart with bent legs and arched backs.

As the companions watched, the pirate ship moved away slowly and began to list to port. Then, in one sudden motion it capsized revealing an ugly, barnacle encrusted bottom.

"Think any will survive?" Breunne asked the paladin as the two watched Vorgath swim around the upside-down hull and toward them.

Then a sheet of flame started near the water line and made its way aft. Thrinndor turned to see Sordaak standing behind him, using his staff as a crutch and pointing at the pirate ship. Another sheet of flame started near the stern and worked its way forward.

"No," the mage said as the two blazes met. Soon the entire portion ship above the water was on fire, sending thick, black smoke into the azure sky.

Thrinndor raised an eyebrow, his eyes following the mage's tortured limp toward the hatch leading below. Looking around, the other eyebrow went up. "Has anyone seen Savin?" Silence.

"Savinhand?" Breunne shouted.

Suddenly, a head poked through the waves next to the swimming barbarian. "What?"

The paladin shook his head and threw the pair a rope.

When the two were standing dripping on the deck, Thrinndor looked the rogue over. He appeared undamaged. "Where were you?"

Savinhand slid his hands along the leather of his shirt, wringing water from it. "I was below decks taking care of the oarsmen who were about to join the fight."

Sordaak, who stood on the steps leading below, stopped and glared at the rogue. "Any remain alive?"

Savin looked over at the mage. "No."

"Good." The mage nodded as he turned, leaned on the cleric and made his way below.

"What's with him?" the rogue asked.

Vorgath looked at Savin, his eyes shaded by wet eyebrows. "You know he lost a foot, don't you?"

Savinhand shook his head.

"I would give him some room for the time being," Thrinndor said.

A commotion from above caused the four to look up, only to see the dragon become a man and that man to land deftly on his feet near the opposite rail. This man only vaguely resembled the boy who had stood there not long before. "Where is he?" Pentaath said, his voice deeper than before, too.

Thrinndor pointed toward the hatch.

After the dragon/man had gone below decks, Savinhand looked over at Thrinndor. "What in the hell was *that*?"

The paladin shook his head. "*That* was a four-month-old dragon."

Chapter Nineteen

Delays, Delays

The four men reluctantly began the task of cleaning up the mess topside. Without ceremony, Thrinndor and Breunne threw overboard the bodies of the few pirates who had managed to set foot on their ship, albeit briefly. Vorgath and the rogue set about removing the spare mast components from storage.

The dwarf began by lashing the largest remaining piece of wood—originally meant as a lower yard arm—to the stump that was all that remained of the main mast. He fixed the last of the spars in place to form arms for two separate sails. Under his begrudgingly approving eyes, Thrinndor, Breunne and Savinhand all worked with needle and thread to patch or repair what was left of the two previous main sails. Fortunately, their foresail and jib had suffered little damage from the fires—just some incidental rips and tears due to the destruction of the mast.

While the work progressed on the sails, Vorgath began sorting out what rigging he would need for the now smaller sails. He made several trips up the new mast, fixing blocks and tackle into place at the correct locations.

He stood back, admiring his work, and grimaced in satisfaction as Savinhand brought him the first sail. It was the sail for the top section on the main mast. Sighing, he threw the sail over his shoulder, slung a length of smaller rope over the other and again climbed to the lower arm for the upper sail. There he took his time and lashed the lower hem of the sail to the arm, making sure the corners were in the proper location, first. Next he attached the upper hem to the top yard arm, this time making sure to use every eyelet available, and lashed the sail securely. He didn't want to have to come back up here.

Satisfied, he shimmied down the mast to the deck below to find Thrinndor standing there with the other main sail. "Let me get this one set first," grunted the barbarian. "Savin, man that line over there and help me to hoist the topsail." The rogue nodded and moved to the indicated line. "On my count: One, two, three and *pull*." Together they pulled like amounts of rope, raising the top yard arm evenly to the tip of the mast.

Vorgath eyed his work with a critical eye, noting that the sail was slightly larger on the starboard side than port. However, that would affect little and was just going to have to do, because he wasn't going back up to tie that little bit off now.

The sail filled with the light afternoon breeze and popped a couple of times due to how it was set. The barbarian walked to the stern and spun the wheel until it was hard to starboard and then eased the rudder somewhat until some speed could be gained. He motioned for Savinhand to relieve him. "Hold it here until she comes around and then point her due north." He pointed in the direction he meant.

Savinhand grasped the wheel and nodded, but Vorgath's attention was already on the sail in the paladin's hands. This sail was the larger of the two, and the barbarian took an appropriately longer period of time lashing it into place.

Finished, he stood on the deck surveying his work and scratching his beard. Satisfied, he motioned the paladin to the correct halyard and repeated, "On my count: One, two, three and *pull*." Together they hauled the top yard for the lower sail up until it almost came in contact with the lower arm of the upper sail. The sail immediately filled and bowed out more than the dwarf liked. "One more," he said, his eyes not leaving the sail. Together, he and Thrinndor pulled their lines again and the top arm inched higher until it was against the other arm. This pulled in some of the slack, and the dwarf nodded approvingly. He could feel the wind power from the additional square footage transferred to the hull and their vessel picked up speed appreciatively.

"Give me the foresail," Vorgath grumbled at the ranger who stood holding the two remaining sails. Breunne pulled the sail off of his right shoulder and held it out for the barbarian to inspect.

The dwarf half-expected the wrong one to be handed over, but the ranger got it correct. He mumbled a 'thanks' and walked back up to the bowsprit, which had taken damage during the attack and was now a few feet shorter than before. No matter; it would have to do as is. He climbed up on the jagged wood where he had previously fixed the control lines and tied the sail one eyelet at a time to the ringlets he'd put in place. Somehow he was left with one extra ringlet on the line but decided that wouldn't matter. He must have miscounted when reworking the number on the sail.

The dwarf jumped back to the deck and went to the correct halyard next to the mast, released the rope coil and began to haul the sail up the foresail line. It went up easily until the top ring was against the mast. He looped the line around its hook and pegged it in place. Satisfied, he went to the sail that was flapping lightly in the breeze, grasped the rope at the base of the sail and walked it over to a cinch point. There, the dwarf looped the rope through a block and began to pull it tight. He checked to make sure they were on course and finished trimming the sail.

He walked back to the mast and looked all three sails over. Nodding his satisfaction, he held his hand out for the final sail. He repeated the process with the jib, and soon their little ship had the maximum sail she was going to get on her set. Their speed had increased until they were making good steerageway north, with maybe a couple of knots to spare. She was not going to break any speed records, but it was the best that could be done with the sail and mast availability at hand.

With a smile, Vorgath crossed his arms on his chest, planted his feet on the deck and took in a deep breath of salt air. *Damn, I could get used to this seagoing life!*

With Pentaath's help and using *Pendromar* for support, Sordaak, Cyrillis and the dragon came up to the main deck. They all stood silently for a while, each with his or her thoughts and each enjoying the silence the sea offered. Only the occasional flap of a sail and the whisper of the hull passing through the swells broke that silence.

Typically, Sordaak was the first to speak. "How much time will that encounter and the subsequent loss of sail cost us?"

Vorgath had mulled that question before it was asked, but he checked the sails just the same. "Three-fourths of a day for the encounter and resulting course changes," he scratched his beard for the umpteenth time that day, "and we've lost perhaps a fourth of our speed—but of course that will vary with wind speed and direction. But, say a fourth of a day lost for every day we sail from here on."

Sordaak did some mental calculation. He wanted his charts from below but didn't want to go get them. Nor did he want to bother anyone else to go get them because of his condition. *Damn!* By his best guess they were now three days from his landing site, and they must approach that at night. They were falling behind. *No matter, Bahamut will still be home when we get there…*

Thrinndor cleared his throat. "Perhaps we should discuss your situation, our ability to continue and," he looked nervously at Pentaath standing next to his master, "him."

"Is this going to take long?" protested the dwarf. "I'd like to go check my eyelids for holes for a time before I'm required for the night shift at the helm."

Irritated, the paladin waved a negligent hand. "No, this should not take long! But, do as you wish. Breunne, will you take the helm, please?"

Vorgath smiled. "I'll stick around." He loved needling his friend. "As long as you don't go and get longwinded on me!"

Realizing he was being teased, Thrinndor rubbed his hand on his face, effectively wiping the frown from it. "Sit down, shut up and this will go much quicker!"

Vorgath stretched and smacked his lips together. "That little skirmish made me hungry. I'll be right back!" he announced as he disappeared below.

Thrinndor rolled his eyes but they settled again on the mage. He hesitated. "Perhaps Pentaath should give us some space to discuss this?"

Pentaath scowled, and Sordaak shook his head. "It would serve no purpose." He turned and looked up into the eyes of this young man who had come to serve him. "Our bond is complete—more so than Fahlred and I ever had. I could send him back to be with his mother and we would still know one another's thoughts." Pentaath nodded, and the mage looked back around at the paladin. "I could no more keep my thoughts from him than I could myself."

Thrinndor was taken aback. "I have never heard of such a bond. This is indeed remarkable."

"It has been rumored to have happened only once before," the mage said, causing the paladin to lift an eyebrow. "It was written in an ancient tome in the Library that Praxaar was so bonded to Bahamut in the age before man."

"*WHAT?*"

Sordaak nodded. "I found reference to it while researching your damn sword." He tried to smile, but it came off more as a half-grimace. Vorgath stumbled back up the steps just then, his arms laden with a cask of ale and two baskets stuffed with food. Savin stepped in to relieve him of some of the burden, and the two cleared space for a late—very late—lunch. Thrinndor suddenly realized he hadn't eaten since breakfast, now some eight hours ago!

As the companions took in the meal, each also worked to digest what the mage had said.

Thrinndor was the first to speak. "It is my understanding that Praxaar and Valdaar were born to their father Wyundaar *after* the age of man had begun. Yet you said the dragon and Praxaar bonded *before* the age of man."

"I'm glad you caught that. It allows me to," Sordaak glanced Vorgath's way, "*briefly* bring something you clearly do not know about your god to light."

Vorgath set his ale mug down and belched.

"Go on," Thrinndor said, always interested in hearing tales concerning his god—or even other gods.

Sordaak nodded. "Your legends spell it out that Wyundaar came to the land to find a wife to bear him sons who would eventually rule the land." The paladin nodded. "What they *don't* spell out is that Wyundaar and his two sons were gods long *before* he placed them among us to live and grow as men." The mage nodded at the excited confusion growing in the paladin's face. "The rivalry between the two brothers had been going on for countless millennia before they ever built their armies in the land."

Sordaak paused and held his mug out to be refilled. He'd recently discovered that his taste for wine had far outgrown that for ale, but still the cool, pale drink felt good on the palette today. He nodded his thanks to Savinhand for the refilling of his mug.

"Now where was I?" he asked as he settled back against the steps to the covering leading below. "Oh yes, gods, sons and dragons." He sipped at his ale. "It is written that when the dragons first came to the land the gods were intrigued by them. Never had such majestic creatures been encountered before! The many colors, scale patterns and abilities were a wonder to even the gods. Over the centuries Praxaar befriended one with scales appearing as the purest of platinum—the dragon now known as Bahamut. Valdaar likewise befriended a similarly powerful creature, one that became known as Tiamat. But, as Tiamat was the goddess mother of all Chaos, the two never bonded—not as Praxaar and Bahamut had anyway."

The mage sighed as he set his mug down, rolled to one side and pressed his hands against the step to rise. Suddenly everyone but Vorgath and Breunne was up trying to offer him a hand. He swatted them aside. "Look," the sorcerer said, his dark eyebrows knitted together in consternation, "this is going to take some getting used to—for all of us!" He glowered at everyone. "I heard it in our fearless leader's voice earlier he means to question our ability to proceed, me with my handicap." His eyes darted from one to another. "I will be fine! Count on it! I was never good at running into or from a fight. I only walked where I couldn't ride, and I'm working on a wooden stump replacement that will give me some semblance of normal mobility." His eyes settled on the paladin. "So let me work this out on my own or you will be helping me everywhere the rest of my life!"

Thrinndor stepped back. "Well said."

"Besides," Sordaak said with a smile, "I just need to take a piss!" It was the first smile Cyrillis had seen on him since the morning. "And I don't need any help with that!"

Suddenly everyone's eyes needed to be somewhere else and hands covered smiles and half-smiles as the mage stumbled his way forward. When he returned, he was sweating from the effort it now took to get from one end of their little vessel to the other. But he was still smiling as he plopped down unceremoniously next to the cleric.

"Are you about through, micro-bladder?" Vorgath demanded with half-lidded eyes. "Because if you're not, I'm going below."

Sordaak glared at the barbarian. "Yes, you overstuffed vassal of noxious gasses, I'm about through."

The dwarf merely lifted an ass-cheek and a rumble could both be heard and felt through the planks of the deck by nearby companions. "Whatever!"

"Vorgath!" several said at once, fanning their hands in front of their noses.

"What?" protested the dwarf. "I'm downwind of you!" Indeed he was, as he was nearest the mast.

Sordaak laughed openly, as did several of the others. They had needed that release. The mage waited for the laughter to die down before continuing.

"Praxaar and Bahamut's bond became so great that soon they could use one another's abilities and powers. Then one day the brothers were recalled to the realm of the gods. Bahamut reigned supreme in a land governed by law, at least until man entered the picture. That's pretty much when all hell broke loose."

Sordaak took a gulp of his ale—it tasted better the more he drank, he decided. "You know most of the rest of the story: Wyundaar returned centuries later to attempt to settle the rift between man and beast, but reintroducing his sons into the mix only complicated matters. Some rifts were partially healed, others irreparably deepened. The bond between the dragon and god had been severed by time, but their friendship endured. When I read that the last words from Praxaar's mouth was that he would give *Valdaar's Fist* to one he trusted and that no man would ever be able to take it from, I knew to whom he meant."

"Bahamut," the paladin answered for him. Sordaak nodded.

"Thank you for that tale," Thrinndor said, immensely pleased. "It fills in more than one gap in my knowledge."

"And mine," Cyrillis agreed.

Vorgath farted again. "Whatever."

More laughing ensued, and this time even the barbarian joined in. "OK, if that's it, I'm headed for my bunkie!" He started to roll over, but words from the paladin stopped him.

"One more question I would like to settle," Thrinndor began. The barbarian started to protest, but instead rolled back over and got comfortable. "It concerns Pentaath."

"Go on," Sordaak urged.

Clearly, the paladin was uncomfortable talking about the dragon with the creature sitting across from him. Deciding that was silly, he forced down that discomfort and spoke with confidence. "Pentaath as we know him is no more than four months old." At this, the dragon-man sat up even straighter, further emphasizing his recent growth. Thrinndor went on. "Yet he is already grown to full age as a man." He took a breath as he pondered how to say what he wanted to. "I do not believe you saw him as he was after his injury from the catapult." The mage shook his head. "He—Pentaath—grew *visibly* following that. He grew so large that his wingspan was almost as large as our ship!"

Astonished, Sordaak turned to look at the young man who had become his familiar, for lack of a better term. He knew better than to ask if this was true, but almost did anyway. Instead he turned back to the paladin. "What is it you would ask?"

Thrinndor swallowed hard before continuing. "What magic is it that allows a dragon that should not even be able to fly for several more months to not only fly, but to use spells—even casting the spell of summoning to bring the two of you together?" He paused, but was not through. "Also, how is it that he can shape-shift at so young an age, when that ability is for only the most powerful of dragons with *several hundred years* behind them?"

Vorgath's eyes, which had wandered shut, were now wide open and he sat up on an elbow, wanting to see the sorcerer's face as he answered these questions.

He was disappointed.

Sordaak took a pull from his ale, looked into the eyes of the paladin and shrugged. "Hell if I know."

Thrinndor blinked twice. "But—"

"No! No buts!" the mage snapped, harsher than he'd intended. "I *don't know* what's going on with that! There's no reference to anything like it that I have ever read or heard about! And if you think that doesn't bother me, you're not thinking straight! Because it does!" Sordaak had unconsciously leaned forward during the exchange, but now he leaned back. "The only possible explanation that doesn't even begin to cover this is what Pantorra said when she brought him to us." Several eyebrows went up at once. "She said that her sire told her the one male dragon of the litter would be special."

"That's it?" Vorgath spat as he pushed himself to his feet. "That's all you've got? His daddy said he was going to be special?" He shook his head. "All this on no sleep makes my head hurt. I'm turning in." He turned and looked at the ranger, who remained at the helm. "Wake me when the sun sets."

Breunne nodded as the head of the barbarian disappeared down the steps.

Sordaak, too, watched him depart. "I understand his—all of your—concern," the sorcerer said quietly. "But I'm afraid that's all I have at the moment."

"So," all eyes turned to Savinhand, who had been to this point silent, "what we—you—seem to have is a dragon that at four months is not only far larger than his mother, but larger than any dragon any of us have ever seen, correct?" He got several nods for his answer. "And, we have a boy who has grown into a man before our eyes in the space of two, maybe three, weeks?" More nods. He shrugged. "Beats me! I've not heard of such a thing, either."

Sordaak stroked the hairs on his chin. "There have been reported cases of advanced or rapid aging experimentation among practitioners of the arcane and/or sometimes clerical studies, but I don't recall much in the way of success reported along those lines."

"Wait!" Now all eyes shifted to Cyrillis. "According to Pantorra, it was rumored that the Minions of Set at the University in Ice Homme were working on a rapid aging technique so they could prepare possible hosts for that old soul they were trying to reincarnate." She looked over at Pentaath. "Perhaps they succeeded."

Sordaak nodded, remembering the dragon woman's words. "And they had their hands on her eggs for several months." His face showed a grim expression. "Perhaps they tried some of their magiks on one—or more—of her eggs."

All eyes shifted onto the new young man in the group. He lifted his chin defiantly but his feet shifted nervously on the deck.

"Meaning we could have the Minions of Set to thank for his rapid growth?" Savinhand voiced the fears for all.

"And *Pendromar*," Sordaak said, slowly rotating the staff in his hands. "I have yet to unlock all of its secrets, but control over length of life is purported to be one of them."

Chapter Twenty

More Trouble

Sordaak soared high above the ground on Pentaath's back on a clear, cloudless night well lit by one full and one partial moon. The mage was still not completely over his fear of night flying, but he was working on it. He no longer had to hang on with both hands. In fact, he pretty much trusted the dragon enough to use only his legs and one remaining foot to hang on with. They had been working on this the past couple of nights.

The sorcerer still found it a bit unnerving to be so connected with another living being. When he thought where he wanted to go, the dragon went there. So when Sordaak applied a slight pressure with his right knee and leaned forward, it was more or less unnecessary as Pentaath was already banking to the right and descending so the mage could get a better look at the promising alcove he'd spotted below.

It was farther north than he'd liked, but that was not to be helped. He and the dragon had been investigating promising alcoves for three nights now, and none to date had proved to be sufficient for their needs. First criterion: The selected alcove had to be unoccupied. That alone had resulted in several rejections. Sordaak had been mildly surprised to see so many unmapped villages attached to several promising candidates. The rest of the criteria were almost as important but could not be investigated unless the first one was met. Those were: a wide and deep enough opening for their ship to make it safely through and big enough that their vessel could easily be hidden among plentiful trees.

The width of the opening he could easily guesstimate for the most part. It was the depth that proved to be troublesome. Their little ship drew about twelve feet of draft at its deepest. That had caused the rejection of two he thought were going to be perfect. To measure that depth he had to dive the warm waters and use his staff as an indicator, knowing it was about six feet in length. Diving was the tricky part. He'd tried a couple of different leg attachments to replace his missing foot, and both had worked adequately—with practice—while walking. But neither had been of any use in the water. In fact, the preferred walking foot had been so light that he'd had a hard time that first night just getting five feet down in the water. His foot kept pulling him back to the surface! Never a strong swimmer in the first place, Sordaak found that the replacement foot had made it almost impossible! He'd had to take that foot off and had left it on the shore while he dove that night.

Sordaak was starting to get concerned that they might have to go back and use one of the previously rejected alcoves, because he knew from his maps that the arm of the badlands that reached out to this sea was not much further north— possibly no more than ten miles. And that was getting too close. But his hopes were buoyed by the thought process that the closer to the badlands they got, the less civilization there would be. So, by that reasoning, this alcove should not be occupied.

It wasn't. It took several silent passes along all of the beach front property to verify this, but that proved to be no problem. The mage noted that this particular alcove had an additional bonus in that it appeared to be fed by a freshwater river that ran—coincidently enough—down from the mountains for which they must ultimately head. He could see deep into the badlands to the north and west. *Interesting.*

Therefore his heart was racing with excitement when he signaled for Pentaath to set him down on the tree-covered sand bar not far from the opening their ship would be required to traverse. The mage jumped to the sand and cringed as his fake foot took its share of the impact. Fortunately, the sand was soft and he had no problem with the landing. Cyrillis had done her usual great job of healing the skin and severed bone that was the stump of his right leg, but his mind was a different thing. He still *expected* it to hurt when he landed awkwardly on it, despite have done so dozens of times without it doing so.

Satisfied with his footing, he sent the dragon on its way to try to locate some farm where he could poach a cow for dinner while he set about taking his measurements. The sorcerer shuddered at the thought and remained glad when his charge closed his eyes for the feasting.

The alcove opening looked wide enough; it was going to be a tight fit, however. He waded into the water and measured the deepest part at about ten feet wide, with another five feet or so of shallower water on either side of that. In all, the opening was just over twenty feet wide. Their ship had just over a fifteen-foot beam at its widest point. Tight, but with some guidance ashore with ropes, it should be manageable.

Next he set about checking out the depth. He waded to the center of the channel, put on his ring and from a pocket in his robe removed a coin enchanted with his light spell. He was careful to keep the coin underwater, as he knew light could travel enormous distances out where it was darkest. He rolled over and kicked hard for the depths, careful to keep his eyes open and the light ahead of him in the event the bottom was shallower than expected. He'd made that mistake on one occasion and still sported a knot on his head to show for it.

By the time he reached the bottom, he could tell by the pressure in his ears that he was down at least fifteen feet. He spent some time swimming slowly through the opening finding one rocky point that was shallower than the rest by a few feet. Further investigation revealed that to be the shallowest point of the transit and he stood his staff up from the bottom there. It was going to be close. Holding *Pendromar* against the bottom, he allowed himself to drift up until only his left hand remained on the staff. He stretched his right toward the surface and felt the fingertips of his hand break the surface.

Damn! This is going to be close! He twisted himself around and again dove to the bottom, checking to make sure he was checking at the shallowest point. Satisfied he was, he again checked the depth. Again he measured one staff plus the full spread of his arms minus an inch or so. He knew that his arms were fairly long for his torso, but not quite as long as his staff. The minimum depth here was slightly less than the desired twelve feet.

Sordaak scooped up his staff and kicked hard for the surface. He needed to check for status of the tide. Experience—and the dwarf—told him that a freshwater river feeding the alcove would make it less susceptible to tide, but there would still be an effect. He made his way to the inner beach where Pentaath had dropped him off and slogged his way out of the water.

His damn cloak and robes sure absorbed a lot of water! He'd forgotten to take the cloak off this time and instantly regretted it. Knowing he had time, he shook his head and stripped down to his underthings and wrung all the water he could from them. And knowing he was alone bolstered his next decision as he found some low branches on a pair of adjoining spruces and hung both his cloak and robe from them, hoping they would have some time to drip dry before he climbed again on the back of that frosty dragon. He'd had to use his spell energy on more than one occasion to keep from freezing to death from the combined cold of Pentaath's body and the chill absorbed by flying through the air while wet. Sordaak shivered just thinking about it.

The mage checked his time and realized he had been out longer than expected already. It was only two or three hours until the sun made its presence known to the east. *Damn!* He sloshed his way around the water of the alcove, not wanting to leave any more tracks than necessary in the event this haven too proved unworthy.

First he checked the tide and could see that the river must indeed have a strong influence on this spot—he could find no spots that showed more than an eighteen- or twenty-inch variation. That was good. And it seemed to be about halfway between the two now. He'd have to get with the dwarf when he returned to the ship so they could pick a time that would provide the best benefit from high tide nearest to the wee hours of the morning.

Deciding he still had some time remaining as Sordaak could tell his familiar was happily munching on a couple of farm animals, he sloshed his way over to the river opening. In this particular inlet the opening was curiously on the opposite end of the inlet from the opening out to the sea. Immediately he felt the water get colder, indicating the river probably had its beginning high up in the snow-covered peaks and that it was relatively fast moving, because water did not stay all that cool at these warmer climates this late in the summer.

There was plenty of growth along the riverbank, so he decided to risk the use of his makeshift light, but carefully cupped his hand so that most of the light shone down toward the water or onto the riverbank.

Splash! *What the hell was that?* "Who goes there?" he found he was whispering unnecessarily. Sordaak's eyes darted right and left, following his dancing light. *Nothing!*

Shit! Visions of alligators, crocodiles, snakes and several other possible denizens of this locale danced in his head. *Pentaath, get back here! NOW!*

On my way, came the immediate reply.

Sordaak surmised that whatever it was, it was in the water with him and below the surface, since his light showed nothing on the surface. A quick decision took him toward the bank that would lead him both back to his clothing, but also to where Pentaath would be looking for him. It looked like the farthest route, but he doubted a few feet would make or break him at this point.

He was wrong.

Not wanting to make a big splash himself, he strode with strong strides toward the beach now only a few feet away. A sixth sense warned him to look around and he did so just in time to see a massive set of teeth extending up out of the water and approaching fast.

Sordaak yelled in fright as he lunged out of the water, trying to jump to the relative safety of the sand. At the same time he whipped the heel of *Pendromar* around in a blind attempt to fend off the attack.

He almost made it.

The powerful jaws slammed shut on the sorcerer's feet. The hard wood of the dwarf's second iteration of the prosthetic foot saved the mage's left foot— allowing him to jerk it free with a few cuts and scrapes across some very sharp teeth. The blind swing had also hit its mark, catching the creature—Sordaak had decided it was an enormous crocodile—at the base of its skull. Immediately his staff lit up and flames ignited the length of the visible body of the beast. With a jerk the straps holding the fake foot to his right leg came free and Sordaak dove toward the sand.

This time he made it. He hit the sand rolling awkwardly toward the tree line he knew to be not far away. He came up hard against the base of a small tree and used it to climb unsteadily to his feet. Sordaak stood there for a moment, *Pendromar* held above his head, ready for a quick strike as his eyes scanned for any movement. He'd dropped the coin/light during the melee and could see it shining up from the bottom about six feet from the edge of the water. That turned out to be a blessing however, as it plainly showed the ripples in the surface of the water as the monster swam toward him.

As such he was ready when the monster jumped at him, its maw again wide, anticipating soft flesh and hard bone. What he got was a fireball down his throat followed by the heel of *Pendromar* slamming down on his now closed mouth and the discharge of Sordaak's most powerful electricity spell running down the entire length of its body and into the surrounding water.

When Pentaath finally arrived—and he had indeed hurried back—he found his master fully dressed sitting on top of the monster holding both his wooden foot and the shiny coin. His staff lay in the crook of his right arm.

"About damn time you got here," the mage said with a smile.

The dragon folded his wings and surveyed the situation. "It appears I cannot leave you anywhere anymore. Especially where toothy, water-based denizens of the deep tend to reside."

"Yeah, we'll go with that one." The mage shifted his grip on the staff and used it to help him stand. "Now help me onto your back and we'll call this little project done."

"This alcove will work, then?" Pentaath said hopefully.

"Yes, I'm pretty sure it will—assuming we can get here at somewhere close to high tide."

"Great."

Once he was settled onto the back of the dragon Sordaak asked, "Do you think you could carry whatever that is back to the ship?"

Pentaath spent a few seconds checking over the monster. "Yes, that should be doable," he replied. "Why? Are you feeling a sudden urge to stock a trophy case?"

The mage tried to stifle a smile. "No, but I'm pretty sure Savinhand has a recipe or two that includes fresh crocodile—or alligator—whichever our recently deceased bad boy is."

Pentaath took the required two or three steps over to the animal, jumped up onto its back, spread his wings and began beating them madly. With no small effort the three of them were soon airborne and on their way to the ship.

The dragon's sense of direction was true and the sun was just breaking the horizon when their unusual sail pattern could be seen less than a mile away. Pentaath began his descent and soon buzzed his way past the stern of the vessel, making sure the beam was clear so he could dump his cargo on the deck without crushing anyone. Seeing that both sides were available, the dragon selected the forward, starboard, side and made his approach. The dragon sailed in, slowed his descent and at the last second dumped his load next to the barbarian, who stood silently at the wheel.

Sordaak and Pentaath had worked out a routine by now, but this time it was complicated by a fake-footless mage. However, not wanting to be an unnecessary burden, Sordaak slid down the shoulder of the huge dragon and landed semi-deftly on his one good foot. Barely catching himself with the staff, he narrowly averted a face plant onto the deck.

Pentaath reverted to human form and landed easily on the balls of his feet next to the mage. "Nice landing, hero!"

"Hero?" Vorgath chided. "Don't tell me stumpy here killed another toothy monster from the deep?"

"Ha, ha," answered the mage. He tossed the fake-foot, version two to the barbarian. "Swamp reject over there tried to take a bite out of that. My remaining foot owes you a big debt of gratitude, and that one is going to need some repair." He turned and limped toward the hatch leading below. He was getting pretty good at using his staff as a crutch.

The commotion topside had roused those sleeping below and they began to make their appearance as the mage got to the hatch. Cyrillis was the first to appear. Her healing senses were diminished somewhat from a good night of slumber, but not so much as to miss the mage's bloody good foot and missing his not-as-good foot substitute.

"What in the hell happened to you?" She was known to wake up on the wrong side of the cot now and again. Apparently this was one of those mornings.

Sordaak was not in the most cheerful of moods, either. This feeling of becoming the next snack for every creature he met that crawled and/or swam was starting to piss him off. "Go ask that overstuffed set of luggage over there," he snapped as he stepped over the cowl and stumped down the steps.

Thrinndor was right behind the cleric. "What is eating him?"

"Damned if I know," answered the healer as she shoved her disheveled hair out of her face. "What the hell was all that racket up here? And, has anyone got coffee on yet?"

"Working on it," the rogue called from below. "Keep your robes on!"

Sordaak was in the process of telling the thief about the fresh meat up on the main deck when a shrill scream split the air. Savin shoved his way past the mage and took the steps two at a time until he stood blinking in the bright morning sun on deck.

Sordaak was pretty sure he knew what the commotion was all about, but rolled his eyes and hobbled his way back up the steps, anyway. He sighed loudly as he put his one semi-good foot on the hard planks and leaned heavily on *Pendromar*. "Now what?"

Cyrillis, who had been standing in front of the enormous crocodile with her hand to her mouth, lowered her hand to march with a stiff back to stand in front of the mage. Her mouth worked, but nothing came out.

Sordaak cringed, certain he knew what was coming.

"You will take me with you on future sojourns." It was not a request.

Tiredly, the sorcerer raised his eyes and looked into those of his beloved. "You know that is impossible." He took in a deep breath and prepared for the blast to come by speaking before she could. "Look, I have a job to do. You have a job to do—we *all* have jobs to do! I happen to have a dragon to aid me to do my job, and that means there are extra things that only I can do." He glanced over at the crocodile. "The big toothy guy over there took exception to my swimming in his front yard and made the mistake of deciding to do something about it. We had words and he lost. He shouldn't have crossed me before I had my morning coffee." He smiled at the beautiful woman who stood in front him and loved him for reasons he would probably never understand.

"You can't protect me *all* the time! I did a pretty good job at that before you came along, and I can't afford to get lazy in that regard." He smiled again so she understood he was teasing. The cleric chewed her lower lip but nodded slowly. He leaned forward and kissed her on the forehead. "Now, if you don't mind I need to go clean up and change my undergarments." Another smile with a wink added for good measure. "I'll join you for a light breakfast in a few minutes and we can discuss this further, if you like."

Before she could say anything more—he was glad she had not had her coffee yet—he turned and made the arduous trek below. Again.

When Sordaak reemerged on deck he felt much better, as did his companions—they were all at least one cup of coffee in by that point. Cyrillis met him at the top of the stairs with a kiss and a cup of coffee. He wasn't sure which one he needed more at that point, but he knew which he *liked* better.

Together, they walked over to join the others at a table that had been set up in the sun near the bowsprit. Sordaak liked it up here—the only smells were those coming in off of the open sea. Unlike the strange concoction of aromas that came from people, various food items, wet wood, wet leather and dried barnacles roasting under the relentless rays of the sun. No, this was his favorite part of the ship without a doubt.

Knowing he was going to need some sleep, he went light on the coffee—although that was tough. Fresh bread, semi-fresh fruit, several cheeses, some strange-looking nuts and an urn of butter; all of that made for a scrumptious breakfast.

Savinhand was anxious to dress out the croc; although he warned there was not much edible meat on such an old beast, but promised a couple of delectable meals at a minimum from the tail. That was the best eating from these swamp creatures, he assured them. The rest he would have to throw overboard.

Breakfast done, Vorgath handed Sordaak the refurbished fake foot. "I reworked the straps—these should hold much better."

"Just so we're clear," the mage interrupted, "I didn't *mind* it coming off *this* time!" He added a wink.

"Noted," the barbarian said. "Still, you won't want it falling off at an inopportune moment." The sorcerer nodded. "I had to dig a couple of teeth out of the ankle here," the dwarf pointed to some deep indentations in the side, "and sand down the rough spots. Should be as good as new."

"Thanks," Sordaak said as he lifted his robe and began putting the wooden foot in place. Vorgath rolled his eyes and knelt to help him. Once the foot was properly strapped on, the barbarian helped the mage to his feet and the two took a walk toward the stern.

The wood of the foot made a loud *clunk, clunk* as it made contact with the wood of the deck. "As we make it more useful, I'll glue some leather to the bottom to quiet it down some."

Sordaak nodded. "That would be appreciated." He led the dwarf over to the chart table.

"You find an acceptable place to make port?"

"Yes," the magicuser said as he sorted through the charts. Finding the one he wanted, he pulled it out and spread it on the table. Next he pulled a charcoal pencil and a measuring stick from the drawer and began tracing the distances he figured he had traveled north from the last recognizable point on the map—a major river that had been seventy-five or eighty miles south. He pulled out a magnifying glass and searched the map closely. These precise coastal maps had cost him a lot of plat back in Farreach.

There! Finding what he was looking for, he marked the alcove with an "X" and added what he had been able to tell of the river once he and Pentaath had taken flight. Then he pulled out a fresh sheet of parchment and drew the alcove in complete detail, including the measurements he had taken.

The job complete, he stepped back and allowed Vorgath to take a look. The barbarian nodded. "It will be a bit tight over this shallow spot, but we can lighten her up some if need be." He looked up at the mage. "You plan on hiding her alongside the lee of the sand bar here?" He pointed to the spot on Sordaak's map.

"That was my first thought. However, I think we'll remove the mast and haul her up the river here," he pointed, "as far as we can and leave her there. That way, there'll be no chance of spotting her from the sea *or* air—the trees cover that river as far up as I could see with my light."

Vorgath nodded again. "Sounds good." He looked up at the rising sun.

Sordaak again rolled out the first map and put another "X" at a spot due east of the "X" he had placed on the shore indicating the alcove. "I don't want to turn west until we reach this point." The barbarian nodded. "And I don't want to reach the alcove until two hours before dawn."

"That will be cutting it close," the dwarf said. He took the measuring stick. "But I think we can do it." It was his turn to flip through the charts. He pulled out the one they were currently using and slid it over next to the one Sordaak had removed. They overlapped only slightly. Vorgath took the charcoal and made an "X" on his map. "Here is where we are currently." Sordaak could see the two X's were still quite a bit distant.

Vorgath scratched his chin and slid the measuring stick across the intervening distance. "Almost two hundred miles." He looked up at the tell-tale flag on top of the mast. "I think we can get to this point," he pointed to Sordaak's second "X", "before midnight tomorrow if the winds hold up."

Sordaak looked up from the map and put a hand on the barbarian's shoulder. "That's what I hoped you would say." He looked over at the sun, now well off of the horizon. "We're already a couple of days behind, and that alcove is further north than I wanted to go but..." He hesitated. "That also puts us closer to the valley than I had anticipated. That means less walking." He smiled up at the barbarian as he stomped the wooden foot on the deck.

"By the time we get that far," Vorgath said, "I'll have that foot perfected!"

"I knew we brought you along for a reason!"

They both turned when they heard the sound of Breunne's bowstring. Together, they walked over to where the ranger stood at the wheel.

"What did you see?" Sordaak asked as they approached.

Breunne pointed to the wheel, indicating Vorgath should take the wheel. He did so and the ranger strode quickly forward. When he returned, he was holding an arrow out in front of him with a large, dead bird dangling from it.

"Yeah, so?" demanded the mage. He didn't understand.

"This is the bird I saw early on the morning we were attacked by the pirates."

Sordaak had been up too long; he still didn't understand. He shook his head.

"This bird is a common black hawk," the ranger said evenly. "It shouldn't be this far out to sea."

Sordaak blinked a couple of times, realization coming to him at last. "The familiar!" His eyes darted around the horizon. Nothing. He looked at the paladin who had just walked up.

"What is it?"

"That's the familiar that warned the pirates we were in the area," Sordaak pointed to the hawk.

"But certainly his master is dead!" Thrinndor insisted; making the assumption as they all had that the birds master had been aboard the pirate ship.

"Not if he teleported." The mage shook his head. "*Damn!* I underestimated them!" He glared into the paladin's eyes. "It's a safe bet they know where we are." He cursed vehemently.

Chapter Twenty-One

Solid Ground

Sordaak stood on the beach, shielding his eyes against the moonlight, trying to penetrate the darkness out over the open water to the east. Frustrated, he wished for the fourth or fifth time that he'd brought his spyglass. But he knew that Vorgath was going to need it more than he. So he sat there flashing his coin light, which he had recharged only moments before, once a minute out over the open waters of the sea. Although it was early, the mage had expected—or at least hoped—his companions would be early. They had much to do before the sun came up.

He and the barbarian had gone over the plan many times, ensuring each knew where the other was going to be and when. The winds had stayed favorable, and Vorgath had their ship in position a few hours in advance and had crawled in his bunk to get some sleep before the coming all-nighter. Pentaath and the sorcerer had left the ship as soon as it was dark and verified the inlet was where he'd left it and that it remained unoccupied.

After reporting as such to the companions—the dwarf remained snoring in his bunk—he and the dragon had returned to the alcove to wait while Breunne changed course to due west and began the trek toward the coast. Vorgath had left strict orders to be awakened if anything untoward was encountered, but no later than midnight regardless.

After much discussion it was decided that they must proceed as planned, and it didn't matter whether a pirate-controlled sorcerer knew of their whereabouts. Sordaak didn't like it—he'd gone to great effort and expense to throw off any pursuit or advance knowledge of their plans. There was some small solace in the hope that the killing of the hawk also put the opposing magicuser out of commission. Sordaak didn't really put much stock in that, however, as a mage capable of teleporting would probably be able to withstand the loss of a relatively benign familiar such as a hawk—even a large hawk like this one had been. But, he didn't like the possibility that they were being tracked.

The one part in it that allowed him to breathe a little easier was the fact that they were far enough out to sea that the bird was more than likely out of range of his master when Breunne had killed it. So unless the bird had first reported what he'd seen and then gone to investigate, his master might not even know his familiar had spotted their ship.

He was wrong.

He was also wrong in his assumption as to why they had been searched for in the first place.

*

Irritated, Sordaak checked the stars again. He knew it was well after midnight—probably after two in the morning. He sent Pentaath aloft for the third time to see what the holdup was.

It's dark, he told himself. *The ship might hit me before I see it!* He slammed his hand down hard on the piece of driftwood where he sat. *That helped.* He raised the coin and flashed it a couple of times, holding it out longer than usual, just in case.

As he covered the coin, Pentaath pushed his thoughts into the mage's head. *They are a bit behind because they were blown further north than expected by a large storm brewing to the south.*

Storm? What storm? Show me.

Sordaak waited for the dragon to get into position. *A storm to the south affecting traffic to the north? That's pretty unusual for this time of year.* According to Vorgath, his mentor on all things weather-related, weather patterns this time of year typically followed the northwest to southeast trek.

For a storm to affect their path from the south, they should have had to sail through or around this weather system. Unless...

Hurry up! Vorgath had warned him of massive storms that occasionally hammered the east coast of the land; storms known as hurricanes. They were infrequent—maybe one every few years, and most of those were not dangerous.

Except to ships caught at sea.

These storms, the dwarf had said, tended to blow out of the east—sometimes from the southeast.

This could pose a problem.

Sordaak closed his eyes and focused on what Pentaath was seeing, regardless of whether he was in position. *Higher*, he commanded. Obediently, the dragon pounded his massive wings to gain altitude. The mage could see an occasional flash of lightning, but that seemed to be some distance off. The dragon slowly panned his view and a bright flash much closer illuminated the surroundings.

It was a wall! A massive wall of rain and wind! Sordaak could see the wind whipping the clouds and rain *horizontally* across his field of view. It was still some distance off, but the mage could see it was *huge!* He was not completely adjusted to the vision of the dragon; they could see things humans couldn't. For instance,

heat showed up in different shades of red and yellow for the higher tempera-
tures, and dark blues and blacks for the lower. Flashes of lighting really confused
the picture as did the walls of water and clouds as they swirled by. The dragon's
eyes saw things much differently than Fahlred's had, which was vastly different
from his own vision. He was getting used to it and could make out the different
colors, but Sordaak sometimes was unsure just what he was looking at.

Higher! Can you get above it?

No, came back the thoughts of the dragon. *The top of the storm is easily two or
three times higher than where I am currently.*

Shit! That's a BIG storm. Looks like a hurricane.

What's a hurricane?

*We'll talk later. Show me the relative position of our friends to the storm. These storms
can move fast.*

Sordaak's stomach did a flip as Pentaath extended his wings, banked hard and
began a rapid descent. Soon their ship came into view far below. The dragon had
excellent vision and the sorcerer had no problem picking up the white sails of
their vessel and the wake left by its movement against the almost pitch-black ink
through which it moved. He could see she was running hard before the wind and
thus making good time. Vorgath must be aware by now of what was behind him.

Of course he was. He was the weather forecaster, after all. He could smell a
storm on the other side of the land!

Sordaak hoped.

As Pentaath came up behind the ship, Sordaak could see the treed shoreline
in the distance. Suddenly realizing he hadn't flashed the coin in a while, he picked
it up off the seat next to him and slipped the leather cover off, flashing it twice
out toward where he knew his friends to be.

There! It was a bit unnerving to see the flashes he just made with the coin
through the dragon's eyes. Another less-than-pleasing sight was that the north-
south component of the winds must have increased, because he could tell they
were off-course. The barbarian must have realized the same thing, because as he
watched the dwarf spun the wheel over to port. The winds had carried them too
far south, and now they were going to have to struggle against a building wind
shear to the north.

Get around in front of the ship and look back. I want to see how far back that storm is.

Pentaath acknowledged by pumping his wings harder and easily passed the
vessel as he strained for altitude. However, the exercise was made unnecessary
when an exceptionally bright flash of lightning lit up the horizon and suddenly
Sordaak could see the ship clearly.

Quickly he picked up the coin and began to spin it in his fingers, creating a
strobe effect. He already knew they had seen him, but he wanted the barbarian
to understand the urgency.

That was not the problem. The problem was that the winds out of the north were making passage back toward Sordaak and the inlet very difficult. He checked the progress of the storm by watching the lighting, and Sordaak was not so sure they were going to make it. And even if they did make the inlet, there was not much of a chance that even the barbarian could run their ship through the narrow opening with the swirling winds that were already beginning to pick up on shore.

Not good.

As he watched through the eyes of the dragon that now stood beside him, the mage could clearly see the barbarian shouting orders to his crew, with Savin, Thrinndor and Breunne doing their best to carry them out. Vorgath tried to anticipate wind movement and had the sails adjusted accordingly, but the gusting, twisting winds were acting almost as a living, breathing being in their refusal to be tamed.

The masts and spars continued to hold and the patchwork sails remained in one piece. For now.

Still the vessel crawled north along the coast, buoyed somewhat by the movement of the storm but fighting the clockwise direction of wind flow around its center. Most men would have fought the wheel of the ship, but Vorgath's hands almost seemed to caress the wood lovingly. A slow turn here, a twist there and occasionally a quick spin in one direction or the other. The ship trudged forward through the mounting swells as if on a rail, pounding through the surf with a ferocity that Sordaak was certain would soon tear the bow off.

And then they were past the inlet, still moving north. "Where are you going?" the mage shouted into the wind, knowing there was no way the dwarf could hear him, still a quarter-mile off shore. He waved the coin frantically over his head, hoping to get the barbarian's attention. Vorgath didn't even look his way. "Where are they going?" he screamed.

Sordaak sensed the confusion of his familiar and briefly considered trying to fly out to the ship, but he knew in his heart that the dragon—and he, for that matter—could be in serious trouble were they to try to go aloft in these winds.

He looked around furtively as an idea struck him. He broke into a stumbling run to his left along the beach to a large rock that bordered the passage through to the protected area beyond. He shouted the words to his light spell and touched the rock when he got close enough. The whole boulder—about two feet in diameter—lit up like a small sun, momentarily blinding the magicuser.

A glance showed that the storm surge was pushing water through the channel into the usually protected bay, but he decided he had to try to get across and waded in. His wooden foot made swimming difficult, but somehow, soaked and spitting briny water, he made it to the other side. There, he repeated the light spell on a similar rock and turned to check on his friends.

They were well past the opening now and the dwarf gave no indication that he had seen the mages efforts. Frustrated, Sordaak raised his hand, pointed a finger and launched a fireball toward the ship. He knew the spell didn't have the distance: he just wanted to get their attention.

After a second and a third fireball, Sordaak got what he wanted. Sort of. Thrinndor turned and pointed, but the dwarf merely waved without looking over at the mage and kept the prow of the vessel pointed north.

By now the sorcerer had figured out that the barbarian was waiting for something, but he was damned if he knew what that was. He decided he didn't like being over on this side of the inlet and fought his way back to stand soaked from head to foot next to the dragon.

And then the rains began.

Sideways rain.

Great.

Suddenly the mage noticed he had a lot more beachfront property—a whole lot more. The waterline had receded more than fifty feet, and it was still moving away. *What the—?*

Sordaak looked over at the channel leading to the alcove and saw that it was almost dry! The lagoon was emptying into the sea! There was no way their ship could make it through now!

Stunned, the mage turned back as a close-by flash of lightning briefly illuminated the boat, beach and the wall of water headed his way. Sordaak was stunned at how close it was to his ship. The storm was moving *fast!*

The lightning flashes were almost constant now as the wall of the storm neared the mage's position, illuminating the entire horizon. As Sordaak watched, the ship finally began to turn. But his concern grew as the stern began to rise. Soon the deck was at a steep angle and the vessel began to pick up speed. The mage could see figures scrambling around the deck, releasing the sails before they snapped what was left of the spars.

What in the hell was the dwarf doing?

And then it was obvious: Vorgath was going to try to shoot the gap riding the storm surge. *Is he NUTS?*

Storm surge? A memory was piqued, and both of Sordaak's eyes opened wide. A quick glance showed the ship as it continued to gather speed. It had also risen even higher. Sordaak reached out and grabbed the shoulder of the dragon that stood next to him. "*FLY!*" he shouted as he leapt onto the beast's back. Past thoughts involving flight as a bad idea were washed away by the wall of water that was headed their way. *Best to take our chances aloft.*

Sordaak landed awkwardly due to his missing foot, but he quickly recovered and settled in for a wild ride. Pentaath wasted about half a second trying to figure out what was wrong, but the urgency his master conveyed by the unspoken word was enough to overcome that. The dragon turned into the wind and leapt high into the air using his powerful legs. By the time his wings were fully spread and the first thrust complete, they were twenty feet up and climbing.

Sordaak watched the wall of water approach, now less than a hundred feet away. It was clear he and the dragon were going to make it clear. He was not so sure his friends were going to do as well, however. The now almost continuous lightning showed the dwarf remained at the wheel, his legs and feet seemingly part of the wood of the deck, so unmoving was he. The mage could clearly see Vorgath's grim expression as he attempted to will the vessel to where he wanted it to go.

Sordaak couldn't take his eyes off of the spectacle that raged below as the dragon frantically fought the ever-increasing wind and rain to maintain altitude and control.

Water rushed in ahead of what seemed such a small ship and the monster wave it rode, easily refilling the lagoon and channel well past where it had been before the approach of the storm. Too close to the northern side of the channel—where Sordaak had so recently stood—the vessel clipped a tree and the bowsprit ropes got twisted in the branches. The bow jerked to a halt, with the huge tree bending under the assault and the stern swinging wildly toward the lagoon.

"Hang on!" Sordaak thought he heard the barbarian shout, but he couldn't be sure over the screaming of the winds. The last thing the sorcerer saw was Vorgath throwing both huge arms around the wheel base and bracing for what was to come. Then the wall of water caught up with them and everything disappeared.

Sordaak twisted in his perch as Pentaath banked into a particularly violent gust of wind, trying to see what would come out of the wave. When the water subsided somewhat behind the bulk of the surge, only a stump of the tree where the ship had been caught remained. The vessel itself was nowhere to be seen.

And then Sordaak's entire concentration was required just to maintain his place on his charge's back. Pentaath clearly was struggling to maintain control in the ferocious winds, all while ensuring he didn't lose his passenger.

Turn and fly with the wind, Sordaak projected. Pentaath did as told, banking slowly to the right. *Now, slowly try to continue your right turn. Keep the wind always on your right flank and we should be able to get out of this.* The mage sensed the apprehension of the dragon, which seemed to stem from not being able to tell how high they were. The clouds and rain blinded them from seeing more than a few feet in front of them. The force of the wind also made it difficult to tell whether their altitude was stable. *Slowly try to work our way higher as you go, that should keep us from any nasty encounter with the ground.* Sordaak tried to project a smile, but that didn't work.

He did sense the tension in the dragon ease a bit as he fought and clawed for additional altitude. *Not too much. A little going up is all it takes to make sure we aren't going down.* Now he sensed Pentaath's understanding.

After a few minutes, the dragon got the hang of keeping the wind on his right quarter and the ride got much less bumpy. Sordaak could feel the dragon begin to relax slightly.

What about our friends? Pentaath projected.

Sordaak thought about that for a moment before answering. He struggled with being blunt or reassuring. *I don't really know. I'm sure Vorgath found a way to lead them to safety.* He wasn't really all that sure but decided it would do no good to say so at this point. The mage was also not sure whether this uncertainty was projected to the dragon. There was still so much to learn about this bond.

It was.

After what seemed like hours, but probably was only minutes, Sordaak could feel the powerful muscles in the back of the dragon begin to tire. The constant drain of fighting of gusts, rain and the tension of not knowing was just ahead of them was taking its toll on the beast. Likewise, Sordaak was exhausted. The battle just to hang on never let up. The mage sensed they were slowly losing altitude.

Sordaak was about to instruct his charge to reverse direction and turn into the wind so he could use his massive wingspan to soar some and thereby rest, but suddenly they burst through the edge of a cloud bank and into a lull between bands on the outer reaches of the storm. The sudden reduction in wind speed coupled with a lack of stinging rain momentarily confused the dragon, and he began to tumble downward at an ever increasing rate.

Sordaak felt panic rise up in his throat, but the lapse was only momentary and Pentaath banked hard into what wind there was, stopping their descent. It gave him a chance to soar and both an opportunity to catch their breath in the relative calm beyond.

Sordaak looked around, trying to get his bearings. There was light in the sky from a pre-dawn sun off to their right, so that was east. Far below—much farther than he'd anticipated—he could see white-capped waves. They had been pushed out to sea. How far? He could discern nothing else in the gloom before sunrise as he twisted around in his seat. He was surprised to see stars over their heads.

Once his eyes adjusted to the low light, Sordaak could see the hard edge of the storm through which they had emerged. In the opposite direction he could make out the back side of a different band of the same storm. He'd heard the big hurricanes had squall lines that extended from the main storm at regular intervals, and that must have been what he was seeing.

The sorcerer directed his charge toward the open sky to the west, imploring him to avoid the squall lines. Pentaath was only too happy to comply as he banked and flew toward the relative safety of the brightening horizon.

Sordaak scanned the seas below looking for anything other than water as the dragon banked north once clear of the band of rain. *Nothing.* He yawned idly as he realized he'd managed to pull another all-nighter. Those had been too frequent of late.

How are you doing? Sordaak asked. He could feel the dragon get stronger, but fighting the storm had taken a lot out of him.

Better, now. I'll be fine.

The sorcerer didn't know whether he could believe that. But in the end it really didn't matter. *I don't know how far out to sea the storm carried us, but we're going to have to try to make it back to land, soon. You won't be able to fly all day.*

I'll be fine, the dragon repeated.

The storm was moving ashore very fast. Perhaps we can follow the edge of this band that is now to our right back toward the coast and by the time we catch up to the main part of the storm, we'll be over land.

Pentaath seemed to ponder this for a moment. *Sounds reasonable.*

The sun cracked the horizon behind them, shooting rays of blood-red sunlight through the broken clouds to eerily light up the saturated air ahead of them. Below those rays the sea remained dark.

You're going to have to fly lower if we're going to see the coastline when we pass over it.

I will see it. I don't want to chance that we are further north than anticipated. I seem to remember you mentioning cliffs and mountains right up to the water's edge not all that far north of where we were.

Got it. Sordaak stretched and scratched his head. It had been a while since he'd bathed properly, too. *Tell me how this night vision thing of yours works.*

What? Oh, it is not really night vision. It is more a component of my sight that registers varying levels of heat reflected from whatever I am looking at. So if we were to pass over a beach line below, I would see a difference in temperature between the water and the sand. I would not really see the sand, but based on how I perceive the thermal variation I would know it was there.

Got it. I think. Sordaak grinned. *Just keep an eye on whatever is below. I don't want to miss the coast.*

Understood. It will not be long before it is full light, anyway.

The pair flew for what again seemed like hours. The sun made its inexorable climb up the eastern sky, and now Sordaak could see the mass of the storm ahead of them. The two bands began to close in from both sides as they got closer to the storm.

Slow down, Sordaak commanded as the bright flash of lighting split the air only a few miles ahead. The blast from the thunder shook the mage to his core. *We don't need to go into that mess again.*

Agreed. However, I do not believe that will not be necessary. Look below.

The sorcerer peered over the dragon's massive shoulder. They had dropped in altitude somewhat, making the sandy beach even more easily visible below. Without being told, Pentaath began a slow spiral down toward the strip of sand.

Although both were anxious to get their feet on the ground, the dragon pulled up and flew along the coast no more than a hundred feet off of the ground. He started where the southern edge of the land disappeared into a band of clouds and worked his way north. He flew slowly, soaring most of the time, with just enough airspeed to maintain control. Sometimes it seemed to the mage as if they were merely floating. Both scoured the shoreline below looking for any signs of their friends.

When after a few minutes they reached the squall line on the northern limit of what they could do, Pentaath turned back to the south and slowly descended until he alighted on the beach in a clear spot.

Unsteadily, Sordaak climbed to the ground. He stood and stretched his long unused muscles.

The dragon allowed his head to droop toward the sand and his wings to hang loosely at his side. He was more tired than he would have admitted. "Any idea where we are?"

The dragon's deep voice in the common tongue startled the mage. "No," Sordaak replied when he found his voice. "But in the several miles we were able to search the coast, I didn't see the alcove where we were supposed to be."

Pentaath nodded. "Nor did I." He reverted to human form and lay down on the wet sand. When he noticed the mage looking at him curiously he said, "It is easier for me to rest like this." This voice sounded much more normal, although tired.

It was the mage's turn to nod. His eyes turned toward the north. "If we use the alcove where we took to the air as a starting point, figure out how far we were driven inland by the movement of the storm, allow for the force of the winds pushing us to the south and adjust for your fighting the winds so that we could work our way east and out of the storm, we should be able to calculate within some reasonable margin of error where we are."

Pentaath, who had closed his eyes, slowly opened one. That single eye spoke volumes. "Go ahead" was all he said.

Sordaak mumbled something about his charge not being much help as he picked up a stick and began to draw in the sand. After a few minutes and several restarts, he was finally satisfied with the results. He started to say so, but noticed the even breathing of his companion. He looked back down at his drawing and then over at the receding storm to the north. By his reckoning, they had been blown about fifty miles to the south.

He looked over at Pentaath curled up on the sand and sighed. The boy needed the rest, as did he. The morning sun was beginning to heat the sand and the humidity from everything being soaked was already making him sweat in his robes. That's when the mage looked around where they had landed to try to find some shelter for the first time.

Holy shit! There's nothing left! There was no green left attached to any tree. Most all the trees were snapped off a few feet above the base. Even those that had somehow kept branches had no leaves. The devastation was complete.

Wow! Sordaak again looked over at the dragon, suddenly feeling the need to be moving. He needed to find Cyrillis. He fought the urge to wake the boy, knowing that one of two things would be true: Either they were alive and someplace safe—because if they had been hurt and the healer yet lived, then they were fine—or they were not. There was nothing he could do for them at the moment.

With another sigh he peeled off his cloak and scouted about the beach for some sticks that would suffice for poles. He had to go farther inland than he wanted to find any, but there was enough scattered around from the storm that he had little trouble finding what he needed once there.

He returned to the beach to find Pentaath still out. Sordaak set up his cloak to block as much sun as possible for the both of them. He then crawled into the stark shade, closed his eyes and did his best Vorgath impersonation.

Chapter Twenty-Two

Aftermath

Vorgath opened his eyes, but that didn't seem to help. Either he was blind or his surroundings were pitch black. He couldn't remember anything that would have blinded him, so he decided it must be his surroundings. Knowing his eyes were as adjusted as they were going to get, he turned his head slightly to see if there was anything to see elsewhere.

That turned out to be a big mistake as blinding flashes of pain began in his neck and shot up into his the back of his head. "Ow," he grunted.

"Vorgath?" A hopeful voice called tentatively into the darkness.

"What?"

"Can you move?" It was Savinhand's voice. "I'm trapped under the cask rack and can't free myself."

"Gimme a minute," Vorgath replied. "Something's wrong with my neck." He realized he was sweating heavily in a sweltering heat. He tried to move his head again, getting the same shooting pain into his skull as before. He gritted his teeth and checked movement of each of his extremities. They all worked, so his neck wasn't broken, he reasoned.

Since moving his arms didn't hurt, he raised his right and felt around, trying to gauge his surroundings. That's when he discovered there was something lying across his chest. It wasn't heavy, but whatever it was had his left arm pinned. It was kind of soft and smelled good. "Cyrillis?"

"Hmmm?" came the muffled reply.

Vorgath nudged her gently. "Are you all right?" The dwarf felt her weight shift, followed by an immediate intake of breath and a curse. Apparently not.

"I fear my left arm is broken," she said. More cursing. "And you can add a severely twisted left ankle to this goose-egg sized knot on my head."

"Can you get us some light?"

"With my staff, I can."

"Shield your eyes." Thrinndor's voice came from some distance away. When everyone opened their eyes, the paladin stood with his fist held high. The bracer on his wrist glowed bright, illuminating his surroundings. Blood ran from a gash on his temple, and he was favoring his right leg.

"A little help," Savinhand's voice came from behind the barrel rack. Thrinndor limped over to the rack, checked on the rogue and began lifting barrels of ale and water clear of the rack. The rogue helped him push the rack aside and took the proffered hand of the paladin, who pulled him to his feet. He stood there shakily, checking his body and extremities for damage. He was mildly surprised to find nothing serious.

Meanwhile, Cyrillis disentangled herself from the barbarian and they helped each other to their feet. Vorgath held his neck at an odd angle, causing the cleric to touch him on the shoulder. Healing energy poured into the dwarf. He immediately straightened and bowed lightly at the waist. "Thank you."

The healer nodded and glanced around. A smile appeared on her face and she hobbled over to where she spotted her staff lying beneath a pile of foodstuffs.

"What in the hell happened?" Savin asked, rubbing a small knot on his head.

Vorgath shook his head and cursed bitterly. "I misjudged the sweep currents and we clipped a tree on the way in. Our lines got tangled in the branches, and we were spun around backward. When the tree finally snapped, we were launched into the forest by the rising waters." He lowered his head. "I couldn't regain control and we hit several trees. That's when I sent everyone below. Unfortunately, our little boat had a hard time of it, flipping several times. It looks like we landed upside down."

"Breunne!" The paladin said, looking around suddenly. "Has anyone seen the ranger?"

His answer was mute shaking of heads.

"Breunne!" the paladin repeated, louder this time.

Cyrillis whispered the words of healing, taking care of her own ails first. She knew that she needed to be whole to more ably help her companions. Next she lit the gem on her staff, throwing a pale blue hue over her surroundings, which blended oddly with the yellowish light from Thrinndor's bracer. She then went to each of her companions as they searched the disheveled ship, tending to their injuries as only she could.

After a few minutes the crew felt as good as they were likely to and had discovered that Breunne was nowhere to be found.

"The last time I saw him," the dwarf said as he sat on a cask he selected for the purpose, "he had cut the lines to the sails and stood at the stern rail, waiting for the wall of water to catch up with us. We both headed for the hatch below at the same time, but things happened pretty fast after that. I don't remember seeing him come down the steps."

Suddenly there was a pounding of metal on wood and a muffled voice could be heard from outside their confinement. "Hello? Is anyone in there?"

"Found him!" Savinhand grinned. He walked closer to where he'd heard the voice. "Breunne? Some bumps and bruises but, yes, we survived."

"Good," came the muffled reply. "How the hell are we going to get you out of there?"

"I don't know yet," the rogue answered. "But it's getting pretty warm in here." He looked over at the paladin, who shrugged.

"I'll get us out," the barbarian said as he pushed to his feet. He walked over, picked up *Flinthgoor* and grinned at his companions. "Axes have other uses than splitting skulls. Gimme some room."

The dwarf then walked over to where the hull tied to the deck under his feet, balanced the greataxe in his hands and then spun in a circle, the axe held at arm's length. The blade bit deep into the wood about chest height, and Vorgath grumbled as he worked it free. "Damn boat is sturdily built. This might take a while!" He repeated the maneuver, getting the same results.

After a few hacks with little results, Vorgath leaned on the haft of his weapon and surveyed the results. "Going to get noisy in here," he announced. The barbarian stood to his full height, raised his blade, yelled one of his battle cries and attacked the side of the ship with renewed vigor.

"Apparently the barbarian rage has other uses than splitting skulls as well," Thrinndor said with a grin. He unhooked the greatsword at his back and tested its weight, waiting his turn. He knew his friend would need relief shortly.

Splinters and chunks of wood flew as Vorgath pounded the hull with a fury. After a couple of minutes of that he stepped back, his chest heaving as he again leaned on the haft of his greataxe.

"My turn," the paladin said as he pushed his way past the barbarian. "Step aside, o diminutive one, and let me show you how this is done."

Vorgath raised an eyebrow but was too exhausted from his rage to argue. He stepped back and bowed with a flourish. "By all means." He briefly considered pointing out that the sword was not well-suited for this type of work, but decided he didn't feel like arguing. Besides, he was certain the paladin didn't carry an axe and he wasn't going to surrender *Flinthgoor* to anyone.

Although the greatsword was indeed ill-suited for the task, the paladin's strength made up for some of that and pieces of wood again began to fly. After a few minutes of this, he, too, began to tire and stepped back, leaning on his sword. "Damn! That is some *tough* wood," he panted.

Now there was some pounding on the hull from outside as apparently Breunne attacked the same area.

"Move aside, pretty boy." Vorgath pushed his way past the paladin, clearly feeling better. The downtime following a rage usually lasted only a few minutes.

"*Flinthgoor* and I will show *you* how it's done." He tilted his head back and his eyes glazed over as he bellowed another of his battle cries. His first swing saw the greataxe bury deep into the wood, clearly breaking through to the outside for the first time. The dwarf had to plant his foot on the hull to gain enough leverage to pull his weapon free. With a grunt of satisfaction he attacked the side of the vessel with a renewed sense of purpose.

He and Thrinndor continued to alternate, with Cyrillis casting a restore spell now and again when the barbarian's recuperative skills proved insufficient. Light spilled in through a small opening at first, but soon it opened wider as the duo continued to work the wood.

After perhaps half an hour, the hole was big enough for Savinhand to wiggle through, which he did during a brief respite for the pair. Cyrillis briefly considered doing the same to check on Breunne, but she surmised he was probably OK as he continued to hack at the wood from the outside.

It wasn't long before the opening was big enough to step through, which they all did, each anxious to be free of the stifling heat felt inside the hull of the ship. The companions blinked away tears as their eyes adjusted to a late morning sun.

What they emerged to was utter devastation.

Thrinndor and Vorgath joined the rogue as they climbed on top of the ship's hull to gain a vantage point for viewing the surrounding country. It was no better from up there. There was no green remaining. None. Anything green had been stripped from tree branches and brush alike. About half the trees were toppled over at various angles, their root systems unable to withstand the forces to which they had been subjected. Of those that still stood, about half were snapped off ten to twenty feet from their base, leaving the visible surroundings bleak and inhospitable.

"Where are we?" Cyrillis asked, shielding her eyes against the brightness of the sun. It was then she noticed that Breunne hadn't joined the other men atop the hull and that he was favoring his left arm, which was in a makeshift sling. "You are hurt!"

The ranger tried to shrug but winced. "I think I separated my shoulder when the wall of water slammed into us and I was thrown into the mast. It's either that or it's broken."

The cleric walked the few steps necessary to be at his side and touched his arm. She sent her percipience into him to investigate—she wanted to know which she was dealing with before using her power to heal. A separated shoulder required setting before her arts could be applied.

Worry crossed her face as she looked into his eyes. "It is separated. We will have to put it back in place before I can heal the damage done."

Breunne nodded. "I was afraid of that. I've had to deal with this before." He turned and stalked over to a tree. The ranger removed the sling and gritted his teeth. Then he crouched down and slammed his shoulder into the trunk of the tree. A brief gasp escaped his lips as he held his position, his jaw flexing. Straightening his legs, he turned and walked over to the cleric.

Cyrillis felt the pain coursing through his body as she again touched his shoulder. However, the shoulder was back in its socket. She poured her healing into him, watching through her mind's eye as the ligaments and muscles realigned and tightened.

The ranger's pain eased markedly. "Thank you."

Cyrillis nodded, her mind already elsewhere. "What happened to you?"

Breunne shrugged, was prepared to wince, but flexed his shoulder instead. "After I bounced off of the mast, another surge threw me clear of the ship. I landed in the water and was fortunate to find a tree big enough that the storm didn't topple it. I rode out the remainder of the storm on the lee side of that tree, about twenty feet off of the ground."

"You climbed a tree with that shoulder?" The cleric sounded dubious.

"With one-hundred-mile-an-hour winds trying to rip the clothing from your back, it's amazing what one can do."

Vorgath jumped off of the hull to land next to the ranger, followed by Thrinndor and Savinhand.

"Were you able to figure out where we are?" Cyrillis asked. Her eyes scanned the skies.

"Yes," replied the paladin.

"We're only a few hundred yards inland, with the coast being that way." Vorgath pointed to the east.

Cyrillis turned to look at the paladin. "What about Sordaak?"

The paladin hesitated. He had wondered the same thing. "Vorgath said he saw he and the dragon take flight before the storm surge hit. We have to assume they managed to make it clear of the storm and will be looking for us." He put a reassuring hand on the healer's shoulder. "We are not far from where we are supposed to be. From the air, the overturned hull of the ship will be easily seen for miles. We will wait here for him to join us. Meanwhile, we will salvage what we can from the ship and set up camp."

*

Sordaak woke alone on the beach to his stomach grumbling. He checked the sun and could see it was late afternoon. The humidity was almost unbearable, and the heat beneath his tent was stifling. With a sigh he rolled out into the bright sunlight and looked for Pentaath. Not seeing him, he closed his eyes and made the connection. He quickly wished he hadn't. The dragon had found some unfortunate creature for lunch and was about halfway through his meal.

The mage quickly shut down the visual component of the link. *Just checking on where you were.*

You were sleeping and I did not feel it necessary to wake you. I will return shortly.

No problem. I'm going to scout around for a bit myself. However, I'd like to head back to where our friends are supposed to be before dark.

Sordaak got the acknowledgement he wanted and pushed the dragon from his mind. He then stretched and scratched, hoping idly that he had thought to pack some emergency rations before he left, but knowing he hadn't. It was going to be a long day. The mage retrieved his cloak, shook the sand from it and slung it over his shoulders.

With another sigh he glared back at the sun and walked between two tree stumps that had probably been massive, living trees at this time yesterday. He unslung his pack as he walked, and was mildly surprised to find some dried meat, cheese and the remains of a loaf of bread. The bread had of course gotten wet and was mostly inedible, but he quickly wolfed down the remainder and made a mental note to thank the cleric, because it was certain she was behind this most welcome snack.

He found a log to sit on in the shade of one of the taller stumps. He plopped down to wait for his steed.

He didn't have long to wait. Within a few minutes he saw Pentaath's shadow flicker by. The mage pushed himself to his feet and walked back out into the sun toward the beach.

Pentaath landed next to him amid much blowing sand and debris. *Damn this dragon is getting big!* Sordaak thought as he crawled up the right foreleg of the dragon and up onto his shoulders. Quickly they were airborne, and Sordaak directed the dragon north. *Let's follow the beach. I believe we were taken around fifty miles south by the storm. They should be within a few hundred yards of the beach where we started this adventure, and therefor easily seen from a few hundred feet up.*

Pentaath just nodded his huge head as he pointed his nose in the indicated direction and worked his wings to gain the requested altitude.

Sordaak looked over at the sun and estimated three or four hours of sunlight remaining—plenty of time to cover the distance necessary.

*

Cyrillis looked skyward for perhaps the hundredth time. It was getting late, and as each hour passed her worry grew. *They should have been here by now*, she reasoned. *Where could they be?*

The men had salvaged most of the undamaged supplies and stacked them neatly next to the hull so they could properly inventory what remained. It had been decided that the bunks could remain inside and that they would open up another hole for cross-ventilation on the other side of the hull. Vorgath was working steadily on that project, apparently happy just to be swinging his axe.

The cleric took the thick wood removed by the barbarian's actions and stacked it neatly. She also walked around in ever increasing circuits, gathering what little wood that had not been swept away by the storm. Soon she had an appreciable stack and began building a fire-ring as she had seen Vorgath do. Long before the sun set she had a small fire blazing not far from the opening into the ship, but far enough away so that smoke would not be a problem.

Savinhand had removed the small wood stove from the wreck—it could not be used inside any more due to the lack of a chimney—and set it up near the fire. Once he had it going again, he began preparing a meal. The smell of food reminded them all that they hadn't eaten since the evening before, and soon all were gathered around the fire, eagerly awaiting whatever their chef had prepared.

Thrinndor had just sat down with his filled plate when Sordaak and Pentaath walked up to the fire. "I thought I smelled that damn thief's rancid attempt at cooking!"

"Rogue."

Cyrillis jumped to her feet and rushed to throw her arms around the sorcerer's neck, knocking him back a step. "Hey! Easy!" he chided gently. "I haven't learned to walk on this thing very well yet." He returned her embraced tightly, however.

The healer pushed back to arm's length and her face clouded. "Where have you been?"

"Around," the mage said. Before Cyrillis could respond, he leaned in and kissed her lightly on the lips. "That was for packing me a lunch." He then walked around her and up to the stove, filled a plate and sat down. "Smells good."

The companions ate in silence, each with their own thoughts, and each with their own questions.

Thrinndor sat his plate aside with a clang. "What, pray tell, took you so long to find us?"

Six pairs of eyes shifted from the paladin to the sorcerer. Sordaak finished chewing a mouthful of stew and washed it down with a swig of the water from his cup before answering. "The storm blew us much further south than I had thought. That was a very powerful hurricane."

Vorgath grunted as he got up and walked over to the casks. "Yes, it was—too powerful. I tasted the taint of magic on its winds." He selected a cask of ale, removed the seal, jammed the wood spigot into the hole and filled his mug.

"As did I," agreed the magicuser.

"No being short of a god could have built and maintained a storm like that," protested Breunne.

"I agree with that, too." All eyes shifted back to the sorcerer. "However, I understand storms like that start small and build slowly over time. Enhancement at the proper stages of development would be all that's required to cause the magic I detected. He walked over and filled his cup from the cask, took a long pull and turned to face his friends. "Or, the magic detected was used to *steer* the storm toward us." He shrugged. "Or both."

"Horseshit!" spat the rogue. "There is none in the land powerful enough to steer a storm of that size!"

"No?" Sordaak paused with the cup halfway to his lips, fixing Savinhand with a stare. "Bahamut can."

That caused a hush to fall over the camp. The fire popped loudly a couple of times before Thrinndor spoke. "So you think our presence is known."

The mage nodded. "I no longer believe in coincidences." He drank the rest of what was in his cup and stared into the eyes of the paladin over the fire. "The pirates. The storm. Where the storm hit." He refilled his cup and resumed eye contact with the big fighter. "No, he knows we're here, and he knows why."

Chapter Twenty-Three

Journey to the Valley of the Damned

awn found the companions on the move after a sparse breakfast. Sordaak held to his original plan of using the river to take them as far as it would into the mountains. He was certain one of the tributaries originated in the valley to which they were headed.

Only one of the smaller boats had survived the storm, and it was going to be tight with the six of them inside a twelve-foot skiff with all their gear and food. So the men threw together a small raft for as many of their supplies as they could safely load. This they towed behind their boat.

The massive amounts of rain dumped on the region by the storm meant the river was high in its banks and running hard. Vorgath kept the boat as close to one shoreline or the other as possible as the currents there were less. But that meant contending with multiple downed trees and other obstacles as they rowed against the relentless waters. From the air Pentaath had been able to determine that the storm spun toward the southeast once it made landfall. That was fortunate because their path lay north by northeast. The river should settle down soon, the mage figured.

He was right. Within a few hours the river turned lazy and the current slacked. In several wide parts, they could ease up to the point that only one of them had to man the oars to keep them moving, allowing the others to rest. Cyrillis insisted on taking her turn, and she held her own very well against the men. Sordaak suspected she cast the occasional Restore spell on herself when she lagged, because every now and then her spine would straighten and she would dig deeper with the oar. But he would never say anything about those suspicions. Never.

The sorcerer alone eschewed a turn at the oars, only relieving one of the others for a brief rest period whenever needed, such as at mealtime. Manual labor was not his forte, and he didn't mind that the others knew it. Besides,

blisters and sore hands did not mix well with the dexterity required by his fingers
to form some of the more intricate symbols necessary to cast some of his spells.

"Where's Pentaath?" Breunne asked, looking skyward.

"I sent him far ahead to scout."

Cyrillis licked her lips. "Is that wise?"

Sordaak shrugged. "Probably not." He held up his hands to ward off the
remainder of her protest. "But hanging around with us has certainly not been
good for his health, either. So I've asked him to keep his distance and forage far
afield." The cleric didn't look convinced. "Look, he promised to check in peri-
odically, and I can always check in on him any time I like."

"Will not a dragon of his size be easily noticed?"

The sorcerer turned to address the paladin. "Pentaath has become adept at
disguising himself. He can remain invisible for extended periods of time and
knows how to use his surroundings to stay out of sight." He winked at the
rogue. "In that, our illustrious Leader of Guild Shardmoor has proven a mas-
terful teacher." Savin dipped his head in return, an easy smile on his face. "Of
course, another dragon would easily see through the subterfuge."

"If, as you have suggested, Bahamut knows where we are, wouldn't he send
out scouts to keep tabs on our progress?"

Sordaak turned back to the ranger, the smile disappearing from his face.
"I believe he has." The mage paused as he struggled with how much to reveal
of what he only suspected. "One: I believe the pirates—and specifically their
mage—were sent more to spy on us than to stop us." He shrugged again. "But
who's going to put the reins on a pirate once he's locked his sights on what
appears to be an easy prey?"

"Clearly they were not warned that the ship they were sent to spy on had
teeth," Vorgath said with a sly grin on his face.

"Clearly," Sordaak agreed. He took a deep breath. "Two: I think that he—
Bahamut—has not had to strain hard to know where we are. It is my belief that
dragons are somehow connected. *All* of them. Meaning Bahamut knows where
Pentaath is at all times."

"But—" Cyrillis began.

"Are you saying Pentaath was *sent* to us by The Platinum Dragon to spy on
us?" Thrinndor sounded dubious.

"No," Sordaak said. "That's not at all what I'm saying. Bear in mind this
is just a theory I have. The dragons all know to come when it's time for The
Gathering, right?" He got several nods. "Yet Pantorra never said they were sent
for, just that she knew it was time. They were summoned." He paused as he
scratched his head. "I came across a reference to an ability the dragons have to
network their minds, but it was just a brief mention in an obscure tome related
to Bahamut. However, it all fits."

Thrinndor nodded solemnly. "Thus you are keeping him far from us so that we can approach in secrecy."

"Yes and no." The paladin's eyes widened slightly but he waited for the explanation. "Yes, I fear that my new familiar's presence allows Bahamut to track our movement. No, I believe the king of all dragons already knows where we are and how we plan on getting to his domain."

"Are they not one and the same?"

Sordaak rolled his eyes. "No! I want the king of all dragons to *think* they are one and the same!" The mage noticed the light go on in the paladin's eyes. "That's right! We are going to follow this river as expected, take the appropriate feeder tributary toward the Valley—as expected—and Pentaath is going to lead the way, also as expected."

"You know of another way into the Valley?" It was Breunne who voiced the question on all their minds.

Sordaak hesitated and then reached into the top of his tunic and withdrew a small scroll tube affixed to a leather thong around his neck. He waved his hand over it, casting a spell. The end popped off into his hand, and then he tapped it gently, sliding the contents from the tube.

"He has a map." It was the barbarian's turn to roll his eyes. "Why does this not surprise me?" Vorgath glanced around quickly and decided there were no immediate obstacles that required his attention, pulled the oars in and moved closer so he could get a better look at what was in the sorcerer's hands.

Sordaak unfurled the delicate document, which was no bigger than the breadth of the paladin's hand, with great care. When it was open at last, the companions leaned in for a better look.

The dwarf stepped back, grunted and went back to the oars. "That's it?" he grumbled. "That's your map?"

The sorcerer glared at the dwarf. "This map is fifteen hundred years old, and was made by Cerraunne the Silent!"

Vorgath, who had sat back down, looked up at this news, his eyes widening. He sighed heavily, pushed himself back to his feet and stomped back over to look at the map again, rocking the boat as he did.

"Sit down, old man," teased the paladin, "you are rocking the boat!"

The barbarian didn't bother to turn around. "I'd make a rude gesture at this point, but we'll assume it's understood that it's a given." Thrinndor smiled. "Now, let me take a better look at that." Vorgath reached for the map.

Sordaak pulled it back. "Look with your eyes, not your hands!"

Color climbed its way up the barbarian's neck as he glared at the sorcerer. Visibly the dwarf forced down the reply that hung on his lips. "Do you want me to look at it, or not?" He grated.

Thrinndor held his breath as Sordaak teetered on the edge of making a snappy reply. Slowly, without saying anything, the mage gripped the edges of the map with both hands and held it out for the barbarian to inspect.

Vorgath hesitated, teetering on an edge of his own, and then leaned in. He placed his nose mere inches from the ancient parchment. When he sat back, the grimace on his face was gone. "Where did you get this?"

Now it was Sordaak's turn to hesitate. The fact was, he had obtained it only recently. And it had not been easy. "I found it on a dead man."

"There's a surprise!" the thief said, drawing a stare from Sordaak. "I sometimes wonder about you. It seems that most that encounter you end up in the hereafter."

The mage grunted an unintelligible reply and began to roll the map.

"Wait!" the dwarf stopped him. "I have some questions, if you don't mind." Sordaak stopped, trying to decide whether to listen. "Presumably you've had time to study this map?" The mage nodded. Vorgath waited for the map to again be unfurled. Sordaak did so reluctantly. "If these," the dwarf pointed to some points drawn toward the bottom of the map, "are the southern rim mountains of the Valley of the Damned and this," he indicated a wiggly line through the points, "is the river you mentioned that has its headwaters in the valley..." Sordaak nodded, waiting for the question he knew was coming. "Then what's this?" the dwarf finished.

The sorcerer looked where the dwarf was pointing and smiled. It really wasn't that hard. "That's the pass Cerraunne and Brakkard used to escape The Valley of Khandihaar all those years ago."

"But, there is no pass through the mountains there!" spluttered the barbarian.

"You know this?" Sordaak pressed, leaning toward the dwarf such that their noses were only inches apart.

"Yes! No!" The dwarf growled deep in his chest. "None alive has seen this Valley! But, as it is reported that this is where the giant lizards hide, I have done extensive research on this Khandihaar, and I assure you no such pass exists!" Vorgath crossed his arms on his chest, daring the mage to continue the argument.

Thrinndor, seeing the boat was picking up speed back the way they had come, stood with a sigh and made his way over to the seat at the oars and got them back on course, all the while keeping an ear on the conversation. That wasn't all that hard in a twelve-foot boat. He took care not to slap the water with the paddles and to not rattle the wood in the chocks. The barbarian frowned but said nothing.

Sordaak was silent for a moment. "How did the two escape then?"

Vorgath was ready for that question. "They *didn't escape!* They were delivered as a warning. Same as Savin's mute wizard!"

Silently, the sorcerer removed a leather bag from his waist, opened it and pulled out what appeared to be a folded piece of leather. He unfolded it, revealing his enchanted storage device; the portable hole. He reached inside as the others watched silently, felt around and when his hand emerged, it held a small book, also wrapped in leather. Sordaak set the storage device aside and carefully unwrapped the book. Again the companions found themselves unconsciously leaning forward as the layers came off. The mage removed a very old-looking, leather-bound book.

"What's that?" Vorgath demanded.

"This is the journal kept by Cerraunne the Silent."

"*BULLSHIT!*" The dwarf slammed an open hand onto the bench where he sat, startling everyone. "No such journal exists!"

Sordaak held the tome up for all to see. "Your argument makes no sense, old one, as I assure you this book is just that."

"But," the barbarian said, licking his lips, his eyes never leaving the bound leather book in the sorcerer's hand, "I searched for *years* assuming such a journal had to have been kept, and never found even a *mention* of it!" He was less sure, now.

"Then you were looking in the wrong place."

"Wait." All eyes turned to the rogue. "You didn't take that from The Library of Antiquity, did you?"

Sordaak's eyes narrowed. "You know that I didn't, as your precious Library still exists, does it not?" Savin nodded slowly. "While others may not understand the magiks required to maintain its existence, I assure you that *I* do. None appreciated more than I the time allowed within those hallowed walls. And, know this, none alive—save for possibly yourself—would fight to protect its secrets harder than I."

Savinhand held the mage's stare with one of his own. After a moment he again nodded slowly. "I apologize. As unexpected curator of that austere edifice, I sometimes get lost in that protection you mentioned. Of course that did not come from The Library—*nothing* may be removed from within those walls."

"Correct," agreed the mage. He turned back to the dwarf, whose eyes had never left the journal. "Now, where were we?"

Vorgath's eyes hardened as he focused them on the mage. "You were about to explain where you got that journal."

"I was?" The sorcerer looked at the decrepit-looking book in his hand. "I would have thought you'd be more interested in what's *inside* this book. But," he glanced at the sun, "we have plenty of time. I'll tell you where I got it." A twisted smile appeared on his lips. "Pothgaard."

"*What?*" The dwarf sat back, stunned.

"More specifically, I got it from your friend Arrahaft."

Vorgath's mouth worked, but no sound came out. It was Thrinndor, still at the oars, who bailed his friend out. "Please explain."

Sordaak smiled and then shrugged. "Not much to explain, really. I discovered the journal quite by accident. I have a habit of perusing any library or collection of written works whenever the opportunity arises. It turns out that your barbarian friend Arrahaft had a nice little collection sequestered away in his keep. He allowed me to peruse it while you all were partying the night away." He looked down at the book in his hand. "I found this hidden inside a cutout in an old book titled, 'Pothgaard, Then and Now.' I too would have missed it, had I not noticed the magiks concealing the tome and locking it closed. I was unable to open it there, so I piled it in with a few other books that interested me and traded the drunk barbarian leader those books for the promise to train some of his people in the arts."

"What does it say?" Cyrillis asked the obvious question.

Sordaak took another deep breath. "I'll shorten it up as best I can. It seems our old friend Cerraunne was somewhat verbose."

"He was a magicuser, all right," muttered the dwarf.

Sordaak threw a withering glance the direction of the barbarian but ended up smiling. "I suppose I deserved that." Vorgath nodded and waited, not smiling.

The sorcerer continued. "Cerraunne and Brakkard were indeed part of the one-hundred-plus warrior task force sent to eradicate the dragon scourge from the land—his words, not mine. Initially they were fairly successful, slaying several of the monsters on their way to the valley. But they also lost men and women in those battles. At first their casualties were light, mostly due to the prowess of the clerical group assigned to the mission. But the more of their number that fell, the harder their task became and consequently even more of their numbers were lost. By the time they entered the Valley of Khandihaar, they were down to forty or so.

"However, upon gaining the Valley, their confidence soared. They were certain that they had slain the majority of the dragons and there would only be mop-up duty from that point forward." Sordaak leveled his eyes on the dwarf. "They were wrong. Initially the party marched through the valley unimpeded. Only when they approached the east end did they meet resistance. This attack was led by the largest dragon they had encountered to date, an enormous dragon with gleaming platinum scales that led more than a dozen huge dragons, among them at least ten mammoth gold dragons. The battle was over almost before it began. Death was instantaneous for many in the group. Cerraunne and Brakkard had been lagging behind and therefore missed the initial onslaught. They tried to run but were captured.

"The pair was imprisoned with seven other survivors and were told they would never again leave the valley. Bahamut was furious as the portable ballista brought by the warriors had done their damage, killing five of the golds and four other dragons before they had been rendered unusable. The king of all dragons had wanted to slay them all and go after the settlements of man that dared attack him in his home, but he was dissuaded by the remaining gold dragons of his council. They wanted to first interrogate the prisoners to determine the strength of the remaining men of the land. Only then would they advocate an all-out assault on the humans if so warranted.

"The one remaining priest and Cerraunne the sorcerer had their tongues cut out so they could not cast spells." Sordaak shook his head in rue. "Most of the prisoners did not survive the interrogation, and soon only four remained—Brakkard and Cerraunne among them. The four decided that a change in tactics was required if they were to survive, so they gave the dragons what they wanted: information. Of course, most of it was false—or at the least, greatly exaggerated. Cerraunne could tell the dragons suspected this, and knew the remaining captives had to make the attempt to escape soon.

"So it was that one day, when they were escorted out for some fresh air along the southern edge of the valley where Brakkard had noticed rock formations he knew to be conducive to caverns and natural tunnels, the four of them made a break for it. A distraction for their guard had been prearranged, and therefore they almost made it. The priest and the other fighter turned to battle their dragon guard, thereby guaranteeing the escape of Cerraunne and Brakkard. A brief search of the hillside indeed revealed an opening hidden in some overgrowth. It was small, however, and they had to crawl in on their hands and knees.

"They hadn't gone far when they could no longer see. The mage was ready for this. Not all spells have a verbal component, and the light spell we like to use is one of them. He used it to turn an ordinary stone into a torch and with that in hand, they were able to continue. The deeper they went into the mountain, the larger the tunnel became. Soon they were able to stand and thereby make better progress. The pair could hear the rants and ravings of the dragons echo along the walls behind them as they were searched for. Their elation at having escaped soon was dulled by the realization that their path was unknown to them. And also by the sobering realization that they had no food, water or weapons.

"Not far into the mountain they began to encounter branch tunnels. At some intersections there were as many as three other choices. Cerraunne began to despair, but Brakkard never faltered, selecting an opening each time, appearing to do so without much in the way of thought." Sordaak paused. "He was of the race of dwarf." Vorgath snorted at what he considered the obvious. "Each opening they went through Brakkard made a mark in the stone walls with a stone he had picked up to use as a weapon. As such they made their way ever deeper into the mountain knowing each step was not one they'd already made."

Vorgath grunted and pushed himself to his feet. "I thought you said you were going to keep this short."

"I thought you said you wanted to hear this story?" the sorcerer said to the dwarf's back as he moved away.

Vorgath walked over to relieve the paladin. It was supposed to be the dwarf's turn at the oars, anyway. Thrinndor nodded his appreciation and stood. The two exchanged places with the paladin sitting in the spot the barbarian had recently vacated.

"Brakkard led the way at a relentless pace, stopping only when they found a pool of stagnant water. Occasionally they heard the distant rumblings of some pissed-off dragon, but never encountered any. There were no signs of previous occupants, and as best they could tell no one had ever passed that way before. Cerraunne had become hopelessly lost within minutes, but the dwarf continued as if he knew exactly where he was going.

"Cerraunne also lost all track of time. Only when he was unable to take another step would Brakkard halt for a break. Sometimes the dwarf would carry the slight frame of the magicuser—made more so by recent captivity and lack of food. When they slept, they did so fitfully, certain the dragons were closing in on them.

"Cerraunne was certain they had been walking for minimum of a week when they rounded a bend in the tunnel and ran into a large brush blocking their path. Brakkard dropped to his hands and knees and forced his way through with the sorcerer following closely. Abruptly the dwarf stopped, turned and held a finger to his lips. If Cerraunne hadn't been so tired and hungry, he might have found the gesture funny, as without a tongue he was unlikely to make a sound. But it was clear the dwarf wanted no sound of any kind.

"The dwarf motioned for the mage to back up, which he did. Back in the cave the dwarf leaned close and whispered in Cerraunne's ear that they must spend the night in the cavern because he feared dragons were nearby, and they were known to be able to see in the dark. They would only leave the cave when they could in turn see any nearby dragons.

"Once clear of the caves, Brakkard recognized where they had emerged, and the pair made their way to civilization, only traveling under the cover of forests and brush whenever possible. They survived on berries, nuts and occasionally a wild animal that wandered within range of the warrior's rocks or the sorcerer's spells. The pair encountered three recently burned out villages before finally meeting up with a live person.

"They were led to the village cleric who tended to their needs, which mostly stemmed from lack of food. But the healer was in a hurry, as the village was in the process of evacuating. Dragons had been seen nearby, and he was certain their town was slated as next to be destroyed. Most had already evacuated. The cleric didn't know why the dragons were so active, and Brakkard wisely didn't shed any light on the subject.

"The dwarf borrowed a couple of horses and joined the evacuation, staying with the train of people as they were going the way they wanted to go. After a couple days of this, Brakkard deemed it safe to break from the evacuees and the pair set off on their own. Back in Lorithom, Brakkard remained silent and kept Cerraunne close at hand. Eventually, he purchased passage on a freighter bound for Farreach, and from there to Pothgaard where they lived out their years."

Sordaak stopped talking and looked around for a waterskin. Finding one, he removed the stopper and took a healthy pull.

"And the journal?" Breunne asked.

Sordaak put down the waterskin and wiped his mouth with the back of his hand. He picked up the journal and waved it at the ranger. "Cerraunne started this journal when they began building the army that marched into the valley. He continued to write in it every day—sometimes several times a day—until he settled down in Pothgaard. There the entries became more sporadic. His last entry talks about poor health and that he was going to disguise the book and give it to Brakkard for safekeeping before he died." He took another pull from the skin. "I believe the dwarf could not read and that he hid the book over the years until he too passed. I don't know how Arrahaft got his hands on the disguised journal, but somehow it ended up in his meager library."

"Yes, but is there a better map in the journal?" Vorgath asked as he stroked the oars, pushing the boat upriver at a good clip.

Sordaak shook his head. "Alas, no. Cerraunne was terrible at maps. However, he did describe the cavern they exited in very good detail."

"All we have to do is find the correct mountain," Thrinndor said, his tone dripping with sarcasm as he looked down at the open map. He then turned to look ahead. The mountains were easily visible in the distance when breaks in the overhanging trees allowed. They blocked the horizon east to west with imposing height and breadth.

Sordaak shrugged. "How hard can it be?"

Of course, that proved to be an ill-advised statement. In fifteen hundred years a lot can change—including the entire landscape.

*

The remainder of the journey upriver was uneventful—relaxing even to those required to pull on the oars. Of course, as the terrain got more broken, they were required to traverse an occasional set of shallow rapids or even a waterfall now and again. This required them to leave the river and carry first the boat and then the raft to a place where they could safely be put back into the water.

One afternoon six days after they had left the coast the companions came upon yet another branch in the river. This tributary appeared to be identical to the previous three or four, but Sordaak directed their boats to make the course change and into the mouth of this new fork.

The mountains in the distance dominated the skyline to the north, casting a pall over the companions that diminished speech.

Sordaak refused to elaborate how he knew this was the tributary they sought until after their boats were safely a mile up the branch.

"I counted," the magicuser said, finally answering the dwarf's question the third time around.

"Counted what?" asked the paladin, his interest piqued.

"This was the fourth tributary entering the main river channel from the north since we began this journey upriver."

"I didn't see that on the map!" protested the barbarian.

Sordaak shrugged. "You didn't look hard enough." The mage turned his attention back to the water. This branch was much smaller than the main river channel they had just left, and with it being late summer, there was no small concern that they would soon run out of navigable waterway. Making the remainder of this expedition on foot had not been part of his plans. He arched an eye up to the mountains towering above them. There remained another twenty or twenty-five miles to their next waypoint, as best he could determine.

Sordaak glanced over to where the barbarian worked the oars. He hadn't told them about that part of his plans.

Chapter Twenty-Four

The Search

Despite Sordaak's concerns, the tributary remained passable for the most part. Occasionally the water got too shallow or a waterfall blocked their path and they again had to carry their craft. But the companions continued to make good progress.

That held true until mid-morning of the eighth day—the second since leaving the main river. Sordaak ordered the dwarf to beach their craft on a grassy shore on the south side of the river. The waterway had just made a lazy turn to the east, leaving the mountains blocking the terrain to the north.

Once ashore, the companions gathered around the magicuser. "Unload the raft," he commanded. "From here, we continue on foot.

Several of the companions began to speak at once. The mage stood and waited for the questions to subside. When they did, he continued. "I will put the bulk of the smaller supplies into my almost empty portable hole. The rest we must carry. Leave any empty barrels and containers on the raft." He held up his hands. "No questions for now. Just do it." Flies could be heard buzzing along the riverbank in the silence that followed.

Thrinndor was first to head for the raft to follow the sorcerer's commands, the others taking up step behind him. The remaining supplies were sorted into piles. Sordaak walked among them, selecting what he deemed possible to put in his device and shoving them into the black opening he held in his left hand.

There remained several bags of foodstuffs and all of the bigger casks.

"Fill your water bags from the large casks. We will only carry the small casks and the rest of this food."

Vorgath opened his mouth to protest. "There will be no discussion in the matter," Sordaak said. "We should encounter water aplenty during this march, so fill your bags with whatever else you want to carry. The rest stays behind." His eyes searched the skyline, clearly looking for something. "Put everything we can't carry back on the raft."

Amid much grumbling—most of it from the barbarian—the companions complied. When the raft was reloaded with what they weren't taking, they again gathered around the sorcerer, who continued to scan the skies.

Finally his eyes widened slightly when he spotted what he was looking for far to the east. Soon what had started as a speck on the horizon turned into Pentaath as he banked over the river, alighting by their boat. Quickly he changed to human form and approached the party.

It had been several days since anyone but Sordaak had seen the dragon. He'd remained away from them at the mage's request, checking in only occasionally, and then only late at night.

Savinhand leaned over and whispered to the ranger who was standing next to him. "Is it me, or does Pentaath look even bigger than before?"

Breunne nodded but said nothing, not wanting to miss any of what was about to happen. Or at least what he assumed was about to happen.

He was disappointed. Sordaak motioned to his familiar, and the two stepped out of earshot of the others where they spoke for a few moments. When the magicuser returned to the gathering, Pentaath walked over to the raft, shoved it out into the river and stepped over to the small boat. He shoved that into the river as well and jumped into the craft. Then he stepped carefully over to the main bench, stepped the oars and sat down. With smooth but powerful strokes he soon had both vessels headed up the river to the east.

Sordaak watched his companion until he disappeared from sight around the bend in the river. Then he turned to face the others.

"What in the seven hells is going on?" demanded the barbarian.

The mage lifted an aloof eyebrow, turned away from the river and stepped off at a brisk pace. "I'll explain as we march."

Thrinndor, Breunne, Savinhand, Vorgath and Cyrillis all traded glances. The paladin shrugged, knowing he had relinquished command long ago but he was unsure as to exactly when, and started after the mage. "Marching formation, please. Breunne, you are at point."

The ranger nodded as he shouldered his pack and began jogging after the sorcerer. Soon he was past him and out of sight ahead of the group. Savinhand melded into the trees and drifted back to cover their flank. Vorgath shouldered his way past the mage and took up the lead position for the remaining party, immediately followed by Thrinndor. Cyrillis hustled until she was next to Sordaak, where together they brought up the rear.

Satisfied, the mage shifted the pack on his back and began to speak. "I'll talk loud enough for all to hear if you haven't strayed too far." He shifted the pack to his other shoulder. Perhaps he should have put more in his device. "Pentaath will continue up the river with our craft until he is unable to go farther, maintaining the guise that we will approach the valley using the riverhead." He paused as he shifted the pack again.

Thrinndor, who had noticed the mage's discomfort, dropped back and without a word took the pack from Sordaak and returned to his place in line. The sorcerer considered complaining, but he was too relieved to do so. Instead, he mouthed his silent thanks to the paladin and resumed his march, much lighter now. "We are, of course, headed for the pass beneath the mountains that will lead us to Khandihaar."

They marched in silence for a few moments before Cyrillis said, "Is it wise to allow Pentaath to continue without us?"

Sordaak snorted. "Wise? I'm not sure any of this would be classified as *wise!*" He marched forward, stealing a glance at the cleric, who marched at his side. She looked neither right nor left as she trudged along next to him. "Taking on the Platinum Dragon in the effort to return a dead god to the land? No, I doubt that will ever be listed in the annals of wisdom."

The companions marched in silence for a while before Sordaak continued. "Pentaath will be fine. I don't want him traversing the confines of the caverns beneath the mountains. Were he to be required to revert to dragon form in one of the tunnels we must enter, he would be killed instantly." He paused as he had to crawl over a felled tree that crossed their path. "He will rejoin us once we gain entrance to the Valley."

"Assuming that entrance was not closed off by the dragons thousands of years ago!" Vorgath called over his shoulder.

"Let's hope not," replied the mage. He, too, had thought of that. Many times. If the dragons had found where Cerraunne and Brakkard had exited the valley and closed it off, that would spell an end to their little sojourn, posthaste. However, during his research he had discovered that it was not true that dragons were like bloodhounds and could track a prey by scent. That was an old wives' tale, apparently.

Spying a patch of wild blackberries, the mage paused to pick as many of the ripe berries as he could reach. "We must augment our remaining food supplies with what we can kill, pick and dig if we are to traverse three, maybe four days beneath the mountains without going hungry."

"Noted," came the sound of the ranger's voice from some distance ahead. "We won't starve."

"That's good to hear," mumbled the caster as he shoved another handful of the berries into his mouth and began to chew.

The companions continued their trek toward the massive, looming peaks for two more days. This mountain range was not like a normal range with foothills and weather-worn mounds leading up to them. Rather, they thrust out of the ground with little or no preamble. A few valleys and ravines, then the towering peaks that loomed more than ten thousand feet above their heads! And in some cases, twice that.

Sordaak angled the party toward the highest peak in the visible skyline, never wavering in his approach. When the companions gathered by necessity at the base of a thousand-foot cliff, they all looked to the mage. They could go no farther along the path he had set.

Sordaak looked north, then south, scratched his unruly mop of hair and pulled out the journal he now kept tucked behind the sash at his waist. While the others watched, he opened the old book and flipped through the pages, obviously looking for something in particular.

Finding the page he sought, he stopped, scratched his head some more and again looked north and south along the cliff face. He lifted the journal and turned it around in his hands a couple of times and dropped his hands in exasperation.

"Let me see that," said the dwarf, stretching out his hand.

Sordaak hesitated and then handed the journal over. "Be careful with that!" he said when the barbarian snatched the book from his hands.

Vorgath glanced askance at the mage while eyeing the pages the mage had open. "You obviously don't recollect the innate dwarven reverence for all things ancient." Sordaak didn't immediately respond. "Rest assured this journal is in better hands than before." The dwarf deliberately left off just what he meant by "before."

"Whatever," replied the mage. "Just don't damage it!"

Ignoring any further comments from the wiggle-finger, Vorgath turned his attention to the drawing that covered both pages of the open journal in his hands. He, too, looked north and south and spun the book in several directions. "What makes you think we are anywhere near what is shown on these two pages?" He glowered at the mage over the top of the journal.

Sordaak jutted his chin out defiantly. "Because we were to travel slightly east of true north from the bend in the fourth river from the coast to the cliffs at the base of Mount Gharrindorr." He folded his arms on his chest.

"Mount Gharrindorr?"

The mage rolled his eyes, turned and pointed to the peak looming thousands of feet above the cliff blocking their path. "Mount Gharrindorr," he said. "The highest peak along the southern rim of Bahamut's Crown."

"Bahamut's Crown?"

Sordaak took the two steps necessary to take him to the barbarian's side, where he snatched the journal from the dwarf's hands. The flipped through the pages until he found the one he wanted and handed it back to Vorgath. "Bahamut's Crown," he said, pointing to a drawing on the left hand page. "The ring of peaks that surround Khandihaar, Valley of the Damned."

Vorgath looked down at the page, his eyes scrutinizing the new drawing, and then looked up at the peak. "Bahamut's Crown," he repeated reverently. "I had heard tell of that fable, but it was assumed that the tale referred to an actual crown." He looked up at the peak that blocked their path north. "Mount Gharrindorr." He closed the journal and handed it back to the mage. "It appears the wiggle-finger may actually know what he is talking about." He grinned at the mage. "Go figure."

"So what are we looking for?" asked the ranger, breaking the levity.

Sordaak turned to acknowledge the ranger. "Not a cliff."

"That's unfortunate," Savinhand said. The sorcerer glared at the thief, who continued quickly, "Because the cliff seems to continue in both directions for a considerable distance."

Sordaak continued to glare at the rogue. "There is no mention of a cliff. But Gharrindorr is a big mountain. We could be miles off course." He looked again north and south before looking at the paladin. "To conserve time and resources, I recommend we split up and investigate. There must be a canyon or ravine that leads toward the mountain on one or both sides of the cliff."

Thrinndor nodded. "Cyrillis and Savinhand, you are with me. We will search west. Breunne and Vorgath, you search east with Sordaak." He looked up at the sun; it was shortly before noon. "We meet back here before sunset." It felt good to give directions again. "Any questions?"

Breunne cleared his throat. "What exactly are we looking for?"

Sordaak's eyes widened slightly, realizing he hadn't divulged that tidbit. He flipped through the journal until he found the page he sought. "It says here that the opening to the cavern is hidden behind a large amount of overgrowth at the end of a ravine at the foot of Mount Gharrindorr."

The party was silent for a few moments. "That's not much to go on," Breunne said finally.

The mage shrugged. "It's all we've got." He took in a deep breath. "Look, while this mountain is indeed a big one, I believe we are in the right area—we followed what directions were given to the letter. I doubt there will be that many ravines at the foot of this big rock. We must simply find the right one."

"Very well," agreed the paladin. "You have your assignments. We meet back here at dusk."

Cyrillis looked longingly at Sordaak, but she knew the party had been divided correctly. Still, she loathed being apart from him—he had a way of getting in trouble without her. Reluctantly, she turned to follow the paladin as he set off to the west.

"Wait!" Vorgath said, causing the others to stop and wait. The dwarf's eyes were suspicious as he glared at the mage. "You said back on the boat that there were no maps in that journal."

"I did?" Sordaak said as he turned his head in apparent thought. "I guess I did, at that." He smiled at the barbarian and shrugged. "I lied." He then started walking east along the cliff.

As it turned out, Sordaak was at least partially correct: There were not many ravines or cul-de-sacs at the foot of the mountain. However, some of those they encountered ran back toward the peak for several miles.

As such, the sun had set and darkness was rapidly approaching when Thrinndor, Cyrillis and Savinhand heard the others clearly as they approached from a distance. The barbarian and sorcerer were arguing loudly.

The paladin stifled his annoyance at the clatter they created and asked, "You find anything?"

Vorgath threw his hands in the air. "Hell no! That damn wiggle-finger wanted to search beneath every bush, tree and clump of grass we encountered! We were only able to cover two short cul-de-sacs before we had to turn back!"

Sordaak crossed his arms on his chest. "Well, that damn pompous windbag wanted to skip over entire side branches of those same cul-de-sacs! We had to be certain we didn't pass the entrance by!"

The barbarian's eyes bugged out he was so mad. "Windbag?" He shifted his glare to the paladin. "You're going to have to assign me to a different group or, so help me god I'm going to *kill him*!"

"You can try," shouted the mage, "but I wouldn't recommend it!"

Vorgath spun to again confront the magicuser and jabbed a stubby finger at his adversary. "I don't *try*! I finish what I begin!"

"Whatever!"

"*Gentlemen*!" the cleric interrupted.

"What!" both men shouted at once.

"Easy," Thrinndor warned, his voice low but conveying conviction.

"We have all clearly had a frustrating day," Cyrillis said, ignoring the outburst. "Here, have something to eat and you will both feel better." She held out a plate for each of them.

Sordaak accepted his with a nod. "Thanks," he said as he sat down next to her. Vorgath eyed the plate distastefully before hunger got the better of him. He grabbed it, marched over to a rock away from the others and sat down.

Thrinndor watched the barbarian shovel mounds of the tuber mixture into his mouth for a few moments and then turned to look at the caster, who silently picked at his food. "Has this argument been going on all day?"

The mage looked up at the paladin, his spoon halfway to his mouth. "No. Just since you assigned me to search with that *moron*!"

"Moron?" Vorgath stood and waved his spoon. "If you'd listened to me, we would have been able to at least double our search area!" He took a step toward the magicuser.

"*Stop it*!" Cyrillis shouted. "Your petty bickering is getting old." Her glare went from Vorgath to Sordaak and back to the barbarian. "I, for one, have listened to all I am going to! Either the two of you make amends or, so help me Valdaar, I will knock the two of your heads together!"

Embarrassed silence settled over the companions as the subjects of the cleric's ire turned red. The remainder of the party found somewhere else to look. "Well?" she said.

The dwarf and the sorcerer glared at one another. Abruptly Sordaak stood, shifted his plate to his left hand and strode purposefully toward the barbarian. He stuck out his right arm.

Vorgath continued to glare at him, ignoring the proffered arm.

"Grasp my arm," Sordaak hissed loud enough for only the barbarian to be able to hear, "or so help me I'll turn you into a *real* jackass!"

Vorgath's eyes widened slightly, but then he grinned. He reached out and locked forearms with the mage. "I don't fancy myself as a mule." He winked at the mage as he also whispered. His smile disappeared. "Just make sure we don't get assigned to the same search party again."

Sordaak bobbed his head slightly and turned back to the party, a beaming smile plastered on his face. "See? We're good now."

Breunne scratched his head while Savinhand paused with his spoon halfway to his mouth, as well. *Damn, this is getting weird.*

"Thank you," Cyrillis said. She blushed slightly, not sure if she was being made fun of. Either way, at least the arguing had ceased.

Thrinndor edged closer to the barbarian as the mage returned to his seat. He leaned over and whispered to the dwarf. "What was all that about?"

Vorgath spun so his back was to the sorcerer and returned the whisper. "Like I said, he insisted on looking under every living branch."

"So?"

"So?" Vorgath fought down the urge to shout. "Most of those canyons and arroyos were shaped by the ground moving." He looked up to see a blank stare on the paladin's face and rolled his eyes. "What we're looking for is a cavern or tunnel made by wind or water. Only certain types of rock are susceptible to such wear, and what I saw up the ravines in question would not have worked!"

"Why didn't you say so?" demanded the sorcerer civilly, once again seated beside the cleric.

The barbarian spun and jabbed a finger at the mage. "I *did* say so! You just didn't *listen!*"

The caster waved a piece of bread negligently. "I must have misunderstood." He winked at the barbarian. "Please explain your theories so that we can speed up the search."

"*Theories?*" The barbarians eyes were bugging out again. With visible effort he looked down at his toes as he fought back his rage. When he looked up he was again calm. "Very well," he said. "Those that have ears, let them hear."

"Ha, ha," Sordaak laughed. "Very funny."

The barbarian ignored him, always glad to share his knowledge—especially when asked. "From what we know of the tunnel Cerraunne and Brakkard emerged from, it was not manmade. That means it was made by one of several possible ways. One, volcanic activity sometimes will leave lava tubes which can easily be connected to form tunnels. But," he glanced at the dimly lit nearby peaks, "there are no volcanos in the region. Two, by wind. Over the course of thousands of millennia the relentless power of the wind has been known to hollow out softer rock to make miles and miles of tunnels and caverns. Three, by water. Water is quicker to hollow out the softer stones and force its way through entire mountains to make its escape. Last, wind and water can work together to speed up the process and forge tunnels. But, again, different types of stones are more or less susceptible."

The barbarian looked around for something to drink. Sensing his plight, Thrinndor handed him his cup, which he had filled with water from the nearby stream. Vorgath nodded gratefully and quaffed its contents. His face twisted when he realized it was not strong drink, but he forced the tepid fluid down his throat anyway. The dwarf handed the cup back to the paladin. "Thanks."

"Now, where was I?" the dwarf resumed. "Oh, yes, wind and water. With this knowledge, it is easy to rule out certain types of stone as being too hard. Both the power of wind and water will work through the softer stones first. The harder rock will only form canyons, ravines and arroyos if the ground shifts." He looked over at the mage. "Knowing this, we can eliminate the jagged, harder rocks that were not hollowed out by wind and/or water." He grinned at the sorcerer. "Such as at least two of those that we searched in futility today."

Sordaak raised an indolent eyebrow and rubbed his chin. "That would have been good knowledge ere we started."

The barbarian's hands flexed into fists and his right eye began to twitch. Seeing his distress, the paladin put a hand on his friend's shoulder and squeezed. This had the desired effect, and the dwarf's tension eased as he took in a ragged breath. "That's why I'm sharing this now so we don't repeat our mistakes," he said.

Sordaak bobbed his head a couple of times. "Thank you."

The next morning, before the sun appeared, the companions broke their dry camp after a cold breakfast. *A fire would have been nice*, thought the rogue as he rubbed his hands. There was a definite bite to the air, but both the paladin and the sorcerer had expressed concern as to the nearness to the valley of dragons. The coffee was also missed by more than one of the companions.

To keep the peace, Thrinndor had Vorgath and Savinhand trade places. He didn't like it because the front-line fighters, the casters and the tertiary fighters had been appropriately apportioned before. But they had met no resistance, nor had they seen anything that would indicate that resistance was imminent, so the he felt reasonably assured that both groups would be safe.

Before they separated, Sordaak reminded both parties to stay under cover as much as possible so as to mitigate the chance of being spotted by an airborne patrol. Agreeing to once again meet back at this place before sunset, Thrinndor and Sordaak led their respective teams in opposite directions.

The second day of searching revealed no path such as they sought, and the sorcerer was secretly beginning to get worried that he might have tried to get too cute with his approach to the Valley of the Damned.

However, when on the third day Thrinndor's party didn't return to camp before the light from the sun had long since disappeared from the sky, the sorcerer's hopes made a rebound as he assumed the paladin had found something interesting.

Once again, he was at least partially correct.

It didn't take much coercion to get the ranger and rogue to agree that they needed to go find their companions. Thrinndor would never willingly be late to a rendezvous.

Within minutes of this decision, the three were on their feet and traveling west. Sordaak deemed it prudent that they should follow the cliff face as close as possible in case their friends were simply late in returning.

They traveled as fast as they dared, the mage being the limiting factor. Both the ranger and rogue were accustomed to travel at night, and accordingly had developed excellent night vision. Only one-quarter of one moon was visible overhead this night, and it didn't provide much in the way of illumination.

Quickly they came to their first decision as the terrain opened to the north, indicating a canyon. Savinhand didn't break stride. "They would not be up there. We found nothing up there or in the next such opening."

Sordaak bobbed his head. "Agreed." His breathing was labored, as he had struggled to maintain the pace the ranger set. "We can reasonably assume the next few such openings are bereft of interest. How many canyons or ravines were you able to search on that first day?"

"Two," replied the rogue. "We had come upon a third, but we decided it was too late in the day to begin a new search."

"Very well," the mage said. He fought down the fear crawling its way up his spine. "We'll stay the course and follow the base of Gharrindorr west." He set his jaw as the ranger nodded and resumed their original pace, a brisk jog that was not much short of an all-out run. The growing fear for the healer kept the sorcerer from complaining. The only thing that kept the fear from burgeoning into all out panic was that she was with the two he trusted most other than himself to keep her safe.

"Wait!" Sordaak said as loud as he dared, hoping his two companions heard him. They did. As the mage staggered to a halt, the ranger and rogue materialized next to him. "I...have...a...spell...that—"

The mage was interrupted by a shrill scream that ripped the air.

Sordaak straightened and held his breath, ignoring his starving lungs for the time being as he waited for another scream.

"Was that Cyrillis?" Savinhand asked looking to the northwest, the direction the scream had come from.

Not hearing what he had hoped for, the mage gave in to his lungs and gulped air. "No," he said, his hands on his knees. Breunne and Savin turned to stare at the magicuser. "That was a dragon."

Chapter Twenty-Five

Three Golden Canaries

"A dragon?"

"Silence!" commanded the sorcerer. "I'm going to cast a spell that will hasten our speed, while at the same time allowing me to run with less effort. Haste will not last long, so when you feel yourselves slowing, gather on me and I'll refresh it." The two men nodded. Sordaak looked at the ranger. "Take us to where that scream occurred; we'll follow." More nods.

The mage raised both hands above his head, spoke the word of power and abruptly dropped his hands to his side. He hesitated a moment, and then, "*Go!*"

Sordaak had to trust Breunne not to lead him over a cliff or into a tree, because he could see nothing but the broad shoulders of the ranger as the two sped across the terrain. He knew not where Savin had gone to, but he was certain the rogue was somewhere in the vicinity.

The sorcerer felt his wind return as the spell's energy was expended. Thus, when he felt the spell's energy cease, he was ready. A glance showed both of his companions within the range of his spell, and he quickly cast it again. And again they were off and running.

The wind rushing past his ears prevented him from hearing what he hoped he would. Yet once he thought he heard another scream from off to his right. Dragon? This time he wasn't so sure.

Breunne didn't alter his primary direction, instead running as if he knew exactly where he was going. He dodged right and left to avoid an occasional tree and leapt over a stream or two. Sordaak followed in his footsteps, doing exactly as the ranger did, trusting him implicitly.

So when the ranger stopped abruptly, Sordaak had to dodge hard to his right or plow into the fighter's back. He skidded to a halt a short distance off. "What?" His spell hadn't expired.

Breunne held up his right hand, asking for silence.

"Sordaak?"

It was Thrinndor's voice from not far ahead.

"Yes," the mage replied cautiously. He wasn't sure what to expect, but he knew a dragon, or dragons, were nearby.

There was a shuffling of feet, clearly designed to warn the newly arrived group they were being approached. The paladin stepped into the mage's vision, his face illuminated only by the sliver of moonlight.

"About damn time you got here," grumbled the dwarf as he stepped around the paladin, who had stopped not far off.

Sordaak ignored the barb, his eyes instead remaining on the dark pools of shadow that hid the eyes of the big fighter. "What happened?"

"We found where an avalanche had blocked access to the head of a dry streambed and were investigating when we were ambushed."

"Ambushed." Sordaak wasn't surprised. "Where's Cyrillis?" He already knew.

Thrinndor held the eyeless gaze of mage. He then let his shoulders slump and looked down at his feet. "She was taken."

The sorcerer clenched his teeth so tight the muscles in his jaw twitched in protest. Abruptly, he spun and walked away from the four men.

Surprised, Thrinndor called after the receding magicuser, "Where are you going?"

"Change of plans. Build a fire and set up camp. No sense trying to hide from them any longer; they know where we are."

"Yes," the paladin persisted, "but where are you going?"

"To summon Pentaath."

"Are you sure that is wise?"

Sordaak whirled around and jabbed a finger at the paladin. "Of course I'm not sure that's wise!" he shouted. "I'm not supposed to be the *wise* one! My job is supposed to be the hot-headed spell-slinger! *Your* job is to be the wise one!" He paused, his breaths coming in ragged gasps, and it wasn't from the recent run. "I've tried to be *wise* and *sneak* into the valley. *That* didn't work! Now I'm going to take the fight directly to him." The mage started to turn, but he stopped himself. "Correction, I'm going to have them bring the fight here to us." He finished his turn and disappeared into the trees.

"You're going to do *what?*" the barbarian shouted after the receding mage. Getting no response, Vorgath looked up at his leader. "Now I *know* he's off his rocker!"

"Perhaps," muttered Thrinndor, his eyes never leaving the point where the magicuser disappeared from sight. He raised his voice. "You want to fight them here? Without a healer?"

A few moments of silence were all it took for Sordaak to reappear. He was outwardly calmer. His tone did not match that calmness, however. "*You* were given charge of her safety." He was seething. "*You* failed."

Sordaak's words hit the paladin hard. Thrinndor swallowed twice before he was able to reply. "You were not here, so you cannot know what transpired. Maximum effort was expended to prevent her abduction."

"Yet you live," Sordaak's said, his tone biting, "and appear unharmed."

The paladin's jaw muscles took their turn at twitching in frustration. "It was not so a few short minutes ago. I have had time to work my limited healing on both the barbarian and myself, ere one or possibly both of us might not have survived to have this conversation!"

"Does she live?"

The abrupt change in focus caught Thrinndor by surprise. "What?"

"Does she yet live?"

"I cannot say for certain, but she was alive when she was snatched from my side." The paladin jutted his jaw forward. "We were beset by not one, but *two* dragons."

"Color?"

"What?"

Sordaak rolled his eyes. "What color were the scales on the dragons?"

Thrinndor looked over at the dwarf. "Gold." Vorgath nodded.

"Both of them?" Thrinndor nodded, as did the barbarian. The mage tugged at his goatee. "Damn," he muttered as he turned to survey their surroundings as best he could with the limited light available. "It is indeed a wonder you both survived."

"Bah!" spat the dwarf. "The cowards turned tail and ran!" His eyes flashed. "Both were wounded, one of which I believe to be mortal!" He crossed his arms on his chest, daring any to say otherwise.

"Very well," said the mage, his tone somewhat softer, "I'll grant you that I might have been hasty in my judgment of the situation." The paladin's eyes delivered the thanks he felt. "However, that changes nothing of *our* situation. They now know where we are, and I believe they will attack before dawn."

Vorgath glanced at the stars. "Dawn is about five or six hours away."

Sordaak shifted his eyes to the dwarf. "Do you have the cage?"

The barbarian rolled his eyes. "You put it in your storage device."

As the mage sighed and reached for the bag at his belt Thrinndor asked, "Cage?"

"It's a long story," answered the mage as he pulled an ornately embroidered bag from his portable hole. "But one I will tell as we make preparations. Vorgath, build a fire pit and carefully place this at its center." He extracted what indeed appeared as a small bird cage from the bag. "Build the fire over the top of it." He looked around. "And put the fire as much out in the open as you can."

The barbarian accepted the cage and muttered under his breath as he laid *Flinthgoor* on the ground and sat the cage on top of it as a marker. As the men scoured the ground to find stones big enough for the fire ring, yet small enough to move, Sordaak explained.

"The original Council of Dragons included Bahamut as its leader, twelve massive gold dragons and the biggest, most powerful dragons from each of the main orders. But Bahamut and his twelve golds were the principals in the ruling of dragon kind. According to the ancient texts I scoured in the Library of Antiquity, I found that the ancient golds often appear as twelve canaries when they are not directly threatened.

"Armed with that knowledge, I began to devise a plan where the gold dragons would be caught in an anti-magic trap."

"That cage isn't even big enough for *one* canary, let alone twelve," protested Savinhand as he dropped another large rock into an opening in the growing ring.

"It doesn't have to be—not for twelve anyway. Through attrition and losses in various battles over the centuries, at last count only seven of the golds remain. But," he held up a hand to stave off the protest he knew was coming, "I can make the cage bigger." He smiled. "A *lot* bigger."

"Good," said the dwarf as he dropped a rock into place.

Thrinndor also dropped a rock with a thud and wiped his hands on the front of his leggings. "Just how do you plan on persuading seven dragons—presumably fairly intelligent—to get inside this cage of yours?"

"Not *fairly* intelligent. These gold dragons are *exceptionally* intelligent."

"Smarter than you?" Vorgath grinned at the mage.

"You had better hope not!" Sordaak shot back. "Because if they are, you're going to have to fight all seven of them!"

The smile left the barbarian's face in a hurry. "That would suck."

"Yes, it would," Thrinndor stood with his hands on his hips.

Sordaak scowled at them both. "Wood?"

"Huh?" the barbarian asked.

"Fire." The mage pointed at the circle of rocks. "We need wood for the fire."

"Right," Vorgath and Thrinndor said at the same time. All four men returned to the trees to gather what was needed.

"My plan," continued the sorcerer, "is to lure as many of the dragons to the fire as possible. Only when I am assured I have all I am going to get will I trigger the trap."

The paladin set an armload of wood down next to the ring. "How do you plan on leading them to this point?"

"Bait."

"Bait?" Breunne had also walked up with a load of wood.

The mage turned to face the ranger. "Yes."

"Explain," Thrinndor said, crossing his arms on his chest. He figured he already knew the answer, and he was right.

"Each of you," Sordaak said after the other two had walked up to the conversation, "must get the attention of one—or more—dragons and bring them to this point."

Thrinndor hadn't moved, his eyes unapproachable in the shadow of his eyebrows. "Without a healer."

Sordaak shrugged. "It's not how I had it planned." He, too, crossed his arms on his chest. "Plans have changed."

"Indeed," Vorgath said.

The spellcaster turned slowly to face the barbarian, letting his arms drop to his side as he did. "As such, not getting mortally wounded will have to be each of your primary focus once you have their attention."

The dwarf glowered at the mage, whose feet shifted uncomfortably under Sordaak's gaze. "But—"

"No. No buts. We do not have a healer. You are going to have to shake the dust off of that defensive training you mentioned not so long ago." When the barbarian squirmed again, Sordaak continued, "You're going to have to put your need to kill a dragon second to the needs of your comrades. If you," he shifted his eyes so that they fell on each of the fighters and the rogue, "if *any of you* fall, it will likely spell the end of the rest of us." He turned slowly back to face the dwarf. "None of us has the luxury of taking the coward's way out and dying at this point." He winked at the barbarian and smiled.

Vorgath returned the glare for a moment. "Whatever!" he growled. He then stomped off to get more wood.

"What happens when we get the dragons here?" Savinhand asked.

"I shrink the cage." Silence greeted that reply. "The dragons will not be able to escape. And once they figure out what is happening, it will be too late."

"But you said they have the ability to change to canaries. Surely they will do so and escape then?" Thrinndor was dubious.

"They will try. But, like Pentaath's similar ability, that transformation takes time. It will fall on me to make sure they don't have that time."

"Won't we also be trapped?" Breunne asked.

"Good lord, I hope not!" Sordaak smiled nervously. "Good question, though. I'll shout a warning to leave when it's time."

"And if we can't hear you?" persisted the ranger. When Sordaak looked over at him, a blank look on his face, Breunne added, "There will be multiple dragons in close quarters. We might not hear you shout."

"I'll be loud," promised the mage.

"Why not just launch one of those sun-like thingies?" Savinhand asked.

"Good question," replied the mage as he turned to face the rogue. "One: I will have already lit up the sky with those thingies. And two: magic will not work from inside the cage. Mine nor theirs." He let that sink in.

"What?" more than one of the men asked.

"You heard correctly. That cage," he pointed to the small structure still sitting on the blade of *Flinthgoor*, "will block *any* attempt at magic use once inside."

"Oh," Savin said.

"That's not all," Sordaak said, suddenly studying the shadows at his feet. "Enchanted weapons will become mundane."

"*What?*"

The sorcerer bobbed his head slowly as he looked up at the paladin. "Flaming swords will not flame. Weapons enchanted to make them lighter will seem suddenly much heavier. Wands will just be wooden sticks. And," he paused for a melodramatic moment, "of course spells will be just words."

A stunned silence settled on the gathering until Vorgath dumped the load of wood onto the pile, causing the others to jump at the sudden sound. "You mean *Flinthgoor* will be just a greataxe?"

"A very heavy greataxe." Sordaak nodded. "Now you're getting it. Special alloy weapons will maintain their properties and whatever sharpness bestowed upon them prior to their enchantment. But any enchantments to make the weapon *sharper* will suddenly be nullified. A sharp sword enchanted to make it sharper will revert back to just a sharp sword."

"Damn." The barbarian looked down at his prized greataxe.

"Keep in mind you will be in defensive posture," the mage warned, "and will therefore need your lightest weapon."

"And a shield," added the paladin.

"Damn," repeated the dwarf.

"Wait!" All eyes shifted to the rogue as he spoke. "Will the dragons be able to change form once inside the cage?"

Sordaak bobbed his head. "Yes. I've verified with Pentaath that shape-shifting for them is an ability, not an enchantment."

"Good," Savinhand said. "Otherwise it's going to get *real* crowded in there." His eyes locked on the cage in its present form.

"Right," agreed the sorcerer. "Now can we *please* get a fire going?"

"Where will you be if your spells are useless?" Thrinndor asked.

Sordaak pointed toward a rock near the fire. "The incantation that will allow me to shrink the cage is not a spell, merely a trigger." His eye shifted to the staff in his hands. "*Pendromar* is not affected by the anti-magic of the cage, and with it in my hands I will be able to do what is necessary." He smiled and winked. "I hope."

Vorgath half-buried a flat rock under Sordaak's watchful eye and set the cage upon it. "Make sure it is perfectly level," warned the mage.

The barbarian bit off a sharp reply, contenting himself with merely rolling his eyes instead. He dribbled water from his skin onto the rock and watched the results. Satisfied, he surrounded the cage with roughly identical pieces of wood. Then he added vertical support and began building the base in earnest. The dwarf knew what alloy the cage was made of and was not concerned that heat from a mundane fire could damage it.

As the others stood and watched, Vorgath got the requested large fire going. Mesmerized by the flames Savinhand asked, "Do you think Bahamut will be among the attackers?"

"No," Sordaak said. "He will not risk an all-out assault at his point." He hoped he sounded more confident that he really was. "At least one must remain in their haven to guard against a surprise attack. He will be that one."

Thrinndor nodded slowly. "Makes sense."

The mage looked over at the paladin and stroked the hairs on his chin thoughtfully. "Yes, it does."

The paladin turned at the tone in the spellcaster's voice. Sordaak ignored him while the big fighter's eyebrow elevated slightly.

Sordaak gave a few more instructions and the men moved away from the fire, each in a different direction, and made their beds.

Pentaath arrived shortly thereafter and changed to human form. Sordaak was possibly the only one who didn't notice that the dragon had grown again. As a dragon, his wingspan was now well over forty feet, and in human form he towered head and shoulders over the sorcerer. The mage was perhaps too preoccupied to notice.

Together, they walked out of the clearing and into the darkness of the night.

*

The sky had just begun to lighten to the east when the attack came.

Deafening screams rent the air as the dragons alighted as one before their chosen foe, who remained wrapped in their blankets.

Or so they thought.

The battle cries of the dragons turned to hails of confusion as shredded blankets revealed nothing but stones beneath. And then their confusion turned to screams of pain as the men jumped from their hiding places beneath trees and bushes, weapons raised and slashing at whatever dragon part presented itself.

Vorgath was on his dragon before the beast suspected anything was amiss. He howled his battle rage just as he swung *Flinthgoor* in a vicious arc and buried the blade to the haft into the flank of his foe.

A horrific scream ripped through the air as the surprised monster twisted slowly—hampered by the damage done to his hind leg—to see what had hit so hard from that quarter.

Just then a round of six flares lit up the sky, blinding the dragons as their eyes were in full night vision mode.

Vorgath ripped the greataxe free and used that momentum to assist his next swing, a whipping motion that he put every ounce of muscle into. This time the barbarian was surprised to feel the weapon hum in his grip as the blade sliced through the hardened gold scales at the base of the dragon's neck as if they were butter.

He was even more surprised when the severed neck fell to the ground next to him with a thud and the dragon collapsed, writhing in mindless pain. The dwarf had to dodge several close calls as the monster's life slowly ebbed like the blood gushing from the gaping hole where its head had been attached.

He was wondering how he was going to follow the mage's direction to bring a dragon to the fire when another landed with a crash in front of him, claws and fangs extended in a most unappealing manner. Vorgath smiled as he raised *Flinthgoor* and charged in swinging.

Thrinndor was not quite as lucky as his barbarian friend, but nonetheless he was able to get in two separate attacks before the dragon turned to face his adversary. The monster's eyes watered due to the brightness of the orbs of light illuminating the countryside around them.

The paladin's first thrust also did considerable damage to the flank of the creature, his flaming sword buried to the hilt. As the dragon spun, the sword was ripped from his grip and he switched to his two-handed sword, regretfully dropping his shield in the process. His second swing slashed a deep gouge across the beast's chest, dislodging several scales in the process. The paladin raised an eyebrow; that was not supposed to happen!

The dragon howled and then attacked with a blast of flames from its open maw. Thrinndor had been prepared for that and tumbled hard to the right, causing the brunt of the blast to miss. When he surged to his feet he swung wildly, again surprised when he connected solidly with the creature's right foreleg, severing the limb about three-quarters of the way up.

The big fighter again tumbled, this time to the left, when another blast of flames blasted the air where he had been. He continued the rotation, extended his huge arms and whipped the massive sword around, aiming for the area bared by his first thrust. The blade bit deep, its momentum carrying it through the previously damaged area, this time exposing muscles and even bone in places as Thrinndor dodged a feeble counterattack from the remaining foreleg.

That was when he heard the amplified shout from the magicuser. He slashed again with the blade as he tumbled toward the raging bonfire a hundred feet way. Again he connected, knocking more scales from the flank of the beast when his sword cut deep into the muscles there.

Breunne loosed a volley of his special dragon arrows from *Xenotath* into the back of a dragon's head that had had the misfortune to land directly beneath him. Quickly he slung the bow over a shoulder, pulled a longsword from his waist with his right hand, a kukri with his left and leapt from his perch. Briefly the ranger noted that all three of his arrows had found their mark as the dragon turned to lambaste this unseen foe with flames.

The ranger passed through the fiery blast on his way to the target, feeling the heat of what felt like a thousand suns as he dropped. He blessed the foresight of the magicuser as the companions had prepared for this contingency. Thus the majority of the breath weapon blew harmlessly past.

Still, he was more than a little singed when he landed feet first on the beast's shoulders and plunged both weapons to the hilt into the base of the creature's neck.

The dragon screamed and then launched itself into the air, clearly intending to shake this painful pest from its back by scraping him against tree branches and/or rock.

But Breunne has seen this act before. He threw himself flat on the monster's back, his hands locked onto the grips of his weapons. As such, he was able to maintain his advantage as branches whipped at his skin and crushing blows from rocky surfaces hammered all around him. During lulls in the action, he would rip first one weapon from the body of the beast and slam it home again, and then the other, working his way further down the dragon's spine. He was surprised at how easily he was able to find openings between the scales, and even more surprised when entire scale sections were torn away by his thrusts.

The dragon twisted and writhed in agony as he beat his wings and clawed for precious altitude. Occasionally the monster would turn and blast away with another round of fire, but Breunne saw the attacks coming and was able to shield himself behind a scale or shoulder.

The fighter could sense the dragon was weakening as his weapons found their mark without fail. The damage was obviously taking its toll on the beast. Abruptly, the dragon changed tactics. He folded his wings and dove for the ground.

Breunne had expected this long before now and prepared himself. At the last possible second, he ripped both weapons free and said the activation word for his boots. The ranger felt the power surge around his feet, and he used all his might to push clear of the dragon as the beast crashed into the ground. The creature spun at the last so he landed on his back, intending to crush the fighter with the mass of his body.

Instead, the air was knocked from the dragon's lungs, and he struggled ineptly to rise. With an ease that belied what the situation should have been, Breunne landed at the base of the monster's neck and raised both weapons.

The two adversaries locked eyes, and the ranger felt compassion for the once regal beast as he again thrust both his sword and dagger to the hilt in the creature's neck. Breunne twisted the blades and slashed sideways with all his might, nearly severing the monster's head.

The dragon nodded slowly as its eyes glazed over and the massive head fell to the earth at the ranger's feet.

Somewhat stunned by the ease at which he had dispatched the beast, Breunne turned to see how his companions had fared. That was when he heard the magicuser's cry for them to bring the dragons to him. A quick glance at his chosen opponent showed that this dragon would not be going anywhere.

The ranger ran the short distance, sheathing his weapons and pulling his bow as he did, to where Savinhand was doing his best ranger impersonation. The rogue was flailing about wildly with his vorpal blade and a dagger in a losing effort to keep one of the dragon's claws and teeth at bay.

Breunne loosed a volley as he ran, his dragon arrows burying themselves to the feathers in the back of the monster's skull. One of them must have pierced the creature's tiny brain because the head collapsed to the ground and the body writhed without a brain to guide it.

Savin dodged aside as the head whipped by, the beast's sightless eyes still open, staring at nothing. When he regained his feet, the vorpal weapon flashed in the light of the bonfire. The blade's keen edge hummed in Savin's hand, and the sword passed cleanly through the exposed neck with no more resistance than if he were slicing a soft gourd.

Breunne and Savin locked eyes, the thief lifting his right eyebrow. The ranger shrugged as the two turned at the second shout from their mage.

"Do not kill them all!" Sordaak shrieked. "I must have prisoners for my plan to work! Bring those that remain to me!"

Startled, Breunne glanced around. His eyes found two dead dragons other than the one he and the rogue had recently dispatched. Vorgath was slowly backing in toward the fire, clearly annoyed at being in a defensive mode, doing his best to not slay the monster he was having trouble keeping at bay. Thrinndor also was leading his dragon to the fire. That made five— there was supposed to be seven. Where were the other two?

The ranger's eyes were drawn skyward as a shriek pierced the air high overhead, but he could discern no threat from that direction as the huge fire they had built rendered his night vision useless.

Breunne was about to complain when he was shoved hard to the ground by the thief, who also tumbled his way past.

A horrendous crash erupted where he had recently stood as another of the gold dragons fell to earth and lay still. The creature was bleeding from dozens of places, and one of its wings was shredded such that it would never again hold air. The other was pinned beneath the beast, which did not move. Another dragon was dead.

The ranger was about to investigate further when Sordaak screamed again. "No! Bring it to me!"

Breunne thought at first the mage was yelling at him, but another shriek from up high revealed that Pentaath must be in combat with the remaining dragon up there.

The fighter helped the thief to his feet and the two turned and ran toward the bonfire. Once there, they turned toward Pentaath as the dragon landed lightly next to them, his massive wings fanning the flames of the fire.

A badly damaged gold dragon landed with much less control twenty feet from the trio, sending a column of flames their direction. Pentaath stuck out a wing and absorbed much of the energy. He howled in pain as some of the webbing in the appendage was burnt away.

The white dragon recoiled and opened his maw to deal his icy blast weapon, but the sorcerer yelled "Do not!" before he could release it. Pentaath clamped his mouth shut, and the massive muscles in the dragon's neck bulged as he fought back his weapon.

"Now!" shouted the mage as he raised *Pendromar* over his head and began to chant.

Barely audible at first, the sorcerer's chants gained in volume as he continued. His eyes remained closed as he turned slowly to his right, making a full circle as worked his incantation. He didn't stop there, instead continuing to rotate and recite his spell.

Pentaath nodded and began the change to human form. The dragon opposite him saw an opportunity to attack and jumped at the shrinking creature in front of him.

Only a quick reaction from both Breunne and Savin kept the gold dragon from making good his intention, because Pentaath was indeed vulnerable in this state. Both men positioned themselves between the two dragons, swords raised, but they did not swing. They could see the gold was seriously hurt, and further attacks from either of their blades would surely finish the diminished creature.

The gold dragon's eyes opened wide in surprise as it paused in its attack, mistaking the men's hesitation as weakness and fear. "Get out of my way puny humans so that I may finish this," the dragon growled.

Breunne was considering an appropriate reply when the mage paused in his chanting long enough to shout, "Run!" He then returned to his chanting, but now the incantation was going much faster.

Having discussed this previously, Vorgath and Thrinndor broke away from the dragons they were holding at bay and ran past them, away from the fire.

Breunne traded a glance with Savinhand and then checked on Pentaath. He was still changing to human form but was almost done. The ranger briefly considered waiting, but he saw one of the wires of the cage closing in fast. He turned and sprinted through the narrowing gaps between the almost invisible wires, Savin right behind him.

Pentaath began to move slowly toward a gap in the wire, but the confused gold dragon stepped in front of him, blocking his path. "Move, old one!" the white dragon said, now completely in human form.

Hearing the altercation, Breunne skidded to a halt and unslung *Xenotath*, notched a single arrow and loosed it. The arrow sped true and clanged off of a scale at the base of the old dragon's skull with enough force to cause the monster's head to bob. It was all the distraction Pentaath needed as he bolted around the much slower dragon and shot between two of the bars before they closed in.

Sordaak stepped down from the rock on which he'd been standing, his eyes remaining closed and the tone to his enchantment unchanged. As his second foot hit the ground the mage slammed the heel of *Pendromar* to the ground. The metal-shod heel of his staff hit the metal of the bottom of the cage, and a blast of sound rang out with such force that it blew out the fire and scattered its glowing embers. The sorcerer continued his march until he was clear of the wires, where he turned and faced the way he had come. All the while he continued to chant.

One of the dragons roared a warning, and the three remaining gold dragons began to change form. Slowly they began to shrink, sprouting feathers from their previously skin covered wings as they did.

Breunne readied an arrow as it was beginning to look like the gold dragons might be able to change form fast enough to escape. But once clear of the cage, the mage quickened the pace of his incantation, causing the wires to close in even faster.

When Sordaak finally ceased chanting, the cage had shrunk to where it was only a couple of feet tall. Inside were three golden canaries.

Chapter Twenty-Six

Water Dragon

"Nicely done!" Savinhand exclaimed, clapping his hands slowly.

Sordaak spun on the thief, slamming the heel of his staff to the ground in frustration. "I wanted *six*!"

"Six?" The paladin's eyes widened in obvious surprise. "Why in the name of Valdaar would you want even one?"

The sorcerer turned his glare onto the big fighter. "Bargaining chips," he said through clenched teeth.

"Bargaining chips?" Savinhand said. "For what?"

Sordaak allowed his shoulders to droop while a sigh escaped his lips. When he spoke his voice was barely above a whisper. "Never mind." He waved a hand negligently. "I had hoped to prevent what I know must occur: Direct battle with Bahamut, the King of all Dragons."

"You wanted to trade them for the sword?" Thrinndor was skeptical.

Sordaak nodded.

"Maybe we can use them instead to barter for our cleric." All eyes turned to the ranger, a seed of hope burgeoning in those of the sorcerer.

"Maybe," mused the mage as he stroked the hairs on his chin. "Just maybe." He turned back to the cage and picked it up, peering inside in the fading light of the last of his orbs. "Such a scrawny lot." Indeed, the birds inside had feathers that were flecked with blood. One had an obviously broken wing, and another limped badly on a severed claw.

"You've got that right!" snarled the barbarian as he leaned on the haft of *Flinthgoor.* "Four *gold* dragons dead, and only the insistence of our mage kept the remaining three from the same fate!"

"What are you saying, old one?" the paladin asked.

"Don't you get it?" snapped the barbarian. "*Four* gold dragons—*ancient* gold dragons! Reportedly powerful beyond belief! Yet we bested them with just the four of us and without the aid of our cleric!"

"Indeed," the mage mused, his eyes still on the three canaries in the cage. "It is clear that these dragons had—have—grown fat and lazy."

"Perhaps they have had no cause for worry or training these past fifteen hundred years." Thrinndor continued the thought.

"Perhaps," the mage agreed as he turned slowly to face the others in the party. "I have heard tell of no forays into Khandihaar since Brakkard and Cerraunne made their escape."

"Nor I," agreed the ranger.

"Damn!" muttered the mage as he dropped to a rock, removed the wooden foot Vorgath had carved for him and scratched hard at the bare skin.

"Father," Pentaath said, his tone one of wonder, "look." The young man pointed at the stump that was the bottom of the mage's leg.

Sordaak looked where Pentaath pointed but could see nothing in the shadows. He spat a curse, waved his hand and *Pendromar* began to glow. In the light of the staff the mage could see that something was growing from beneath that stump. It was a *small foot!* That was what itched so much!

"What in the name of the Seven Hells is that?" exclaimed the dwarf.

"A foot!" Sordaak whispered. "*My* foot!"

"How is that possible?" Savinhand asked.

Sordaak looked at the new appendage—damn it itched—and then up at the young man who called himself his son. "It is said that given time, dragons can regrow a severed appendage. Tails, claws and so forth. Is that true?"

Pentaath turned his head slightly to the right, clearly searching his head for memories he didn't yet have. "I do not know."

"I do," the ranger answered for him. "They do have that ability. And now it seems that it has been granted to you, as well."

"Damn," repeated the mage, staring at that which protruded from the stump on his leg. Had it grown larger while he sat? Was this even possible? Hell! The proof was before his eyes! Sordaak tossed the wooden appendage to the dwarf. "You're going to have to clear out the top of that to make room for this!" He pointed to his new growth.

Vorgath deftly caught the boot and considered several withering replies. "Whatever!" he snapped as he looked for a rock on which to sit so he could get to work. Finding a suitable such rock, he sat, pulled a dagger from behind his belt and began carving on the wooden contraption, hollowing out the top. The dwarf glanced over at the sorcerer's stump several times as he worked, deciding to dig out additional wood in the event the foot grew back quicker than anticipated.

Grew back? What the hell was going on here? He shook his head as he carved.

As Vorgath worked, Thrinndor assessed the party's condition. A few scratches and bruises were all he found. The paladin shook his head in wonder at the good fortune they had experienced. He tended the wounds as best he could with mundane wraps and poultices while they waited.

"We must rest," Thrinndor announced.

"No," Sordaak replied, his eyes never leaving the workings of the dwarf. "We can rest once we are inside the caverns." His eyes scanned the stars, knowing there was nothing he could see there. "Bahamut will believe his council dead, and he may come looking for them."

"But we don't even know if the entrance is near," protested the thief.

"Yes, we do." Sordaak's eyes found those of the paladin. "Those dragons were guarding this place. I'm certain that pile of rocks you found will reveal the entrance we seek."

"Very well," began the paladin.

"I *knew* you were going to say that!" Vorgath shook his head as he tossed the boot back to the sorcerer, who fumbled to catch it with his one available hand. After bouncing it around in that hand a couple of times, he managed to grab and hold it. "Let's go, pretty boy." The dwarf glared at the paladin. "Looks like we have work to do before we can get something to eat!" The dwarf pushed to his feet, shouldered his greataxe and padded silently over the rise that had brought he and the paladin to this spot in the first place.

"What about Cyrillis?" Thrinndor asked solemnly. "Should we not attempt to recover her?"

Sordaak ignored the question. Instead, he reaffixed the wooden appendage to the stump of his leg and stood to test the fit. Finally, he allowed his shoulders to slump as he raised his eyes to meet those of the paladin. "Of course *I* should. But I can't face Bahamut alone and Pentaath—strong though he is—cannot carry more than one or two of us at a time." It was Thrinndor's turn to allow his shoulders to slump. Sordaak continued. "We stay together."

The paladin nodded meekly and turned to follow the barbarian.

"He won't kill her," Sordaak said, his voice low but laden with conviction.

The paladin turned to peer through the darkness at the mage, hope welling in his eyes. "You know this?"

"Of course not," spat the sorcerer. "There is *no way* I could know that. But if she is dead, then you, your sword and this quest will cease to have meaning. So therefore we *have* to believe that she yet lives."

Thrinndor stood to his full height and seemed to reach out with every fiber of his being, testing the very air with his authority.

Sordaak found that he was holding his breath while he waited.

Abruptly the paladin let out a deep breath he had been holding of his own, looked at the sorcerer and smiled. "You are correct. She yet lives."

"Now how in the hell do you know that?"

"If she were dead and our quest were for naught, I would be able to *feel* that." The paladin smiled, turned and followed the barbarian. "I do not, so she yet lives."

Savinhand and Breunne walked past the stunned sorcerer, following the other two. "Damn, that's good news," the mage whispered as he followed more slowly.

Working through the night the five men and one dragon youth managed to clear an opening large enough for even the paladin to get through. On the other side was indeed a cave opening.

As first light began to show on the horizon, Sordaak stepped through and turned to face Pentaath who was to be last. "No," the mage said, sorrow in his eyes. "You must fly ahead and wait for us on the other side." The dragon youth opened his mouth to protest. "No," the sorcerer repeated. "The journal says these caverns shrink in places where we will have to crawl through. We still don't know how long you can maintain human form. If you were to have to revert to dragon form while in such a place…" Sordaak's voice trailed off.

The youth who was now taller and stronger than any of them lowered his eyes and nodded. "Fare thee well, father. I will await you on the other side."

The mage reached up and placed a hand on the young man's shoulder. "Stay out of sight and give us three days. Do not enter the valley before then."

Pentaath nodded and stepped back. Abruptly, he spun and sprinted back the way they had come.

Thrinndor stepped up behind the mage and put a hand on his shoulder. "That was indeed wise. He will be fine."

Sordaak turned slowly, called forth light from his staff and said. "Of course he will. It's us I'm worried about. The journal said Brakkard and Cerraunne spent five or six days beneath the mountain. We now have only three." With that, he pushed his way past the paladin and began the trek down the corridor they had discovered. The wood of his boot made a hollow thumping sound as he moved quickly down the passage.

"Damn, there goes that breakfast and the snooze time I was promised," muttered the barbarian as he shouldered *Flinthgoor*.

Quickly the paladin recovered and rushed to catch up. "Savin, you and Breunne take point. Vorgath, you're next, but stay within the circle of light provided by Sordaak's staff. I'll bring up the rear." Everyone nodded.

Savin moved ahead, speaking as he did. "Give me a few minutes up ahead to allow my eyes to adjust to the darkness."

"Me, too," said the ranger.

"Very well," agreed the paladin. "But do not move so far ahead that you cannot see our light. We must stay together in this labyrinth."

Both men nodded as they moved out.

Vorgath dropped to the floor and pulled a sack off of his belt and he rummaged around inside for something to eat. Plenty of food remained, but nothing seemed even remotely appealing. He leaned back against the cool wall of the cavern, munched on a dried biscuit and imagined that he was eating one of

Savinhand's special biscuits covered in his savory sausage gravy. As such he was able to make a palatable meal of what he had, washing it down with stale water from his skin.

The others did the same.

At the prearranged signal from Breunne, the remainder of the party got wearily back to their feet and started after their scouts.

They moved quickly and slowed only when an intersection was reached and those ahead were not sure which direction to take.

Sordaak showed the men the journal, explaining how the passages were marked fifteen hundred years ago by the two escapees. He hoped that the markings had not faded with time, but he didn't mention that to his friends.

They had not, at least most of them. Where there were no markings, Vorgath provided the direction. He was wrong only once, and that almost cost them their lives.

They had gone about a half mile down such a passage chosen by the dwarf from the last intersection when they began to descend. The air also grew cooler and became more damp.

Presently the tunnel opened into a cavern, and a pool of mirror-surfaced water blocked their path.

"I don't recall any mention of an underground lake," Savinhand said as the others caught up to where he had stopped.

"Actually," replied the sorcerer as he pulled the journal from its pouch, "there are several references to pools of water that kept them alive." He thumbed through the journal to just such a place. He was about to read from the page when Savinhand spoke first.

"Yes, but was there a place where they had to *swim* across a vast lake where the other side was not discernible?"

Sordaak looked up from the journal, raised an eyebrow and then his staff. He called forth more brightness from *Pendromar* as he strained to penetrate the darkness on the outer limits of the light.

He could see nothing but more water. And the water followed the edges of the cavern such that there was no way around—at least not without getting wet.

"No, I don't believe they encountered such a lake." The mage turned to the dwarf. "How certain are you that this is the correct passage?"

Vorgath shrugged. "As sure as I can be with the information available to me."

"Is it possible that this lake formed *after* Brakkard and Cerraunne passed this way?" All eyes shifted to Breunne amid his question.

"I *suppose* it's possible," the dwarf said. He bent over and dipped a hand into the water, stood upright and put his hand to his mouth. He quickly spat the water back out. "Very brackish," he said. "While I can't say for certain how long it's been here, but I would think several centuries at a minimum."

Sordaak pulled at the hairs on his chin, clearly working hard to not be snide. "I'd love to ask just how it is you know that, but I'm not sure we have time for the answer."

Vorgath grinned. "Minerals. Over time the water dissolves whatever it is sitting on; stone, ores, anything. Those minerals are then part of the water." He winked at the rogue who grinned. "A discerning palate can sometimes tell what minerals and how much has been dissolved."

"Wow, aren't you a wealth of useful knowledge," Sordaak said, surprising himself that he was able to do so with a straight face.

"Damn straight," snapped the barbarian. "I've been trying to—"

Suddenly, the surface of the water erupted and the silence of the deep underground was shattered as a scream bounced around the walls of the cavern.

Momentarily stunned, Thrinndor faced this new foe as he tried to wrap his brain around just what it was. "Water dragon!" he shouted. "Fall back and regroup!"

But the hesitation cost them. The dragon attacked with a blast of pressurized water, knocking all but the barbarian from his feet. Vorgath was able to bring the flat of *Flinthgoor's* blade up and deflect most of the water away from him. Still, he was forced back a few steps by the sheer ferocity of the attack. *Why didn't I taste the damn dragon?*

The barbarian shouted a battle cry and was about to charge in when the paladin stopped him with a shout. "NO! I said to fall back!"

Sordaak shook his head as he got to his hands and knees. He'd hit his head hard on the stone floor when he'd been knocked down. The dragon was sloshing his way ashore when the mage stood and raised *Pendromar*. He shouted the word of power and released the staff's most powerful spell: Meteor Storm.

Six small orbs raced toward the dragon, growing in size as they traversed the distance. Abruptly they ignited and then slammed into the creature, which was still rising out of the water. *Damn this is a big one!* The meteors hit the dragon square in the chest, knocking it back a step. The monster screamed and turned loose another jet of water when it was able to regain its feet.

But this time the companions were ready. Thrinndor brought his shield up and braced himself. Sordaak cast a shield spell and did the same, expanding it to protect those behind him, which now included everyone but the paladin and the barbarian. Vorgath again used his greataxe to deflect what he could of the jet of water.

When the blast ended, the paladin shouted, "Fall back to that last bend!" As one the companions turned and sprinted the hundred or so feet to comply. The dragon again screamed its displeasure at having been denied at least one tasty snack after having been so rudely awakened.

Once out of sight of the dragon, the party stopped.

"I do not believe the creature can squeeze its bulk up this passage. Not from what I was able to see," Thrinndor said.

"Damn! That's a *big* one!" agreed the rogue.

"I've not heard of one getting that big," said the sorcerer.

"We can take him," snarled the barbarian, shaking *Flinthgoor* for emphasis. "Just cover me and I'll go in and whack the monster with this!" More shaking.

Sordaak rolled his eyes. "Not without a healer, we can't."

"What?" Clearly the dwarf was still under the effects of his battle rage. "We just took out four *gold* dragons—each of them bigger than that oversized minnow. Surely we can handle this scrawny excuse for a dragon? Who's with me?" He glared around, daring any to contradict.

"Scrawny minnow?" The booming voice came from around the bend. "Just you step your midget ass back out where I can see you and we will see just who is the scrawny one!"

"Midget?" bellowed the dwarf. He took a step toward the opening, but Thrinndor grabbed his arm and held tight. "Why, you sorry excuse for a waterborne rat! It's lucky for you my companions are holding me back!"

The paladin smiled in spite of the situation.

"Waterborne rat? You are the lucky one. You go ahead and run away; scared like cockroaches in a baker's pantry!"

"Cockroach?" howled the barbarian. He glared at the paladin. "Let me go so I can teach that bottom-sucking scavenger some manners!"

"Yeah, let him go so this bottom-sucking scavenger can have one unhealthy snack this century! All that fat on the dwarf's bones would surely be the death of me!"

"FAT?" Vorgath's eyes were bugging out. "I'm not the one whose ass is too fat to fit down the passage!"

"Zing! Ouch, that one hurt. But I would not be so fat where I not to dine so often on the blubbery dwarves of the Silver Hills!"

"That does it!" Vorgath shouted. "Let me go!" The dwarf struggled in vain against the vise grip of the paladin. "Besmirching the good name of the Dragaar Clan is the last straw! I must defend their honor!"

"Honor?" This time the voice was much closer, not as loud and certainly more feminine. "What does a dwarf know about honor?" Suddenly a beautiful, shapely woman rounded the corner, resplendent in a shimmering blue gown that flowed like a waterfall from her graceful neck to just above her unadorned feet. "A dwarf knows only greed. They are fraught with it from the time they are brought into this world kicking and screaming until they leave it the same way!" Her voice was musical—almost mesmerizing.

Thrinndor shoved the barbarian aside and drew his sword. He heard the hiss of steel against leather as others behind him did the same. He also heard the almost silent popping noise as an arrow was notched and a bowstring pulled taut.

The woman smiled such that her face lit up, making her even more beautiful than before. Her bright blue eyes glistened in amusement. "You may lower your weapons. I no longer mean you any harm. I cannot hold this form long, nor can I do battle with those such as you while I walk on two legs." She laughed. "No, I just wanted to meet face to face the first dwarf I have encountered that I was able to hold a meaningful conversation with." Her smile grew even broader, causing even the most hardened of the men to unconsciously return the smile and lower their weapons slightly.

Vorgath was twitching he was so mad and yet so taken aback by the dragon woman's beauty that he was unable to raise his axe.

Silence held the moment until Breunne broke the ice. "That was a meaningful conversation?"

Again the dragon woman laughed her melodious laugh, and the weapons lowered the rest of the way. All except for *Pendromar*—Sordaak held his staff at the ready. While her smile and laugh were infectious, he was already smitten by a different bug. This one had no hold on him.

"Well, truth be told," the woman continued, "I have not had *any* conversation with those in human form in many centuries, let alone a meaningful one."

Her smile included her eyes, Savinhand noticed. *Damn, she's beautiful.*

The barbarian stepped forward and cleared his throat noisily. "You'll find *this* dwarf has little or no fat on his bones!"

"But plenty between the ears!" Sordaak muttered sotto-voce.

"I heard that," the barbarian said without turning. He couldn't take his eyes off of the dragon woman.

Again she laughed, her eyes flirting with every man in the passage as she made her way among them. "Well, I am sure you will agree there is not much fat on these old bones, either." She did a slow turn, showing off her shapely figure.

"Ummm, nope," agreed the dwarf. "You have clearly maintained yourself well over the centuries."

The dragon woman's eyes settled on the dwarf and she backed off on her smile somewhat. "Thank you," she said as she bobbed her head demurely. "This is indeed a rare occasion for me. I do not wander from my watery home all that often. When I do, I seldom get to have a conversation such as this." Her smile returned. "For that I owe each of you a debt of gratitude."

"Just how often do you encounter humans down here?" Sordaak asked. He remained wary despite the growing ease of his companions. Something about her presence among them bothered him.

The dragon woman's smile disappeared as she turned slowly to face the sorcerer. "So it was you that blasted me with that spell? I see you have *Pendromar, Dragon's Breath* at your command. Very nice." She bowed slightly at the waist. "But to answer your question: almost never. Occasionally an orc or troglodyte gets lost and wanders near my home. Most, if not all, of my encounters with humans have been outside the confines of these caves."

"So there is another way out?" Sordaak continued, probing. Gently. Something about this woman made him uneasy. Still, she could not shape-change back to the dragon in this narrow passageway without crushing herself.

And them...

"Of course," the woman acknowledged. "But not one such as you would easily find." Suddenly her smile returned, but this one didn't touch her eyes.

It was all or nothing at this point. "Will this passage take us through to the Valley of Khandihaar?"

The woman hesitated, clearly not expecting the question. She also just as clearly hid something in her answer. The dragon took in a shallow breath. "No, not such as the one you seek." Suddenly she was speaking in riddles, Sordaak noted. "Why do you seek the Valley of the Damned?"

"We have business there," the sorcerer explained. He too could dance around the truth when required. He smiled at her sudden unease. Apparently he was the only one to notice, however.

"What possible business can a well-armed band of humans have in the home of Bahamut?"

"We mean to slay him and take back what is rightfully ours." There was no point in dodging that issue, the sorcerer reasoned. What other purpose could they have in the Valley after all?

The woman's face turned solemn as her eyes shifted to the paladin. "*Valdaar's Fist?*"

The paladin was floored. "How could you possibly—"

Sordaak cut him off, "Of course we seek the sword of our master." His eyes bored into those of the woman. "What can you tell us of it?"

The dragon was taken aback by the reversal. "I can tell you nothing! None have seen the blade since it was brought here more than four centuries ago for safekeeping."

"So it *is* here, then," Thrinndor said, his eyes aglow with the confirmation of what they had only assumed to this point.

"What? Of course it is here!" Her eyes narrowed to slits. "Damn you! Damn you all to crawl The Seven Hells for the remainder of eternity!" Her voice rose to a shout as she voiced the curse.

Is she getting bigger? Sordaak alone seemed to notice. Her skin also was showing signs of the scales that they had seen before. "*RUN!*" he shouted as he hobbled further back the way they had come as fast as his wooden foot would allow.

"What?" Vorgath asked, shaking his head to clear the reverie that was the beautiful woman who stood just a few feet away. And then he saw the scales too—those hadn't been there a moment ago.

The barbarian made a feeble swing with his greataxe, which had somehow ended up head down on the stone floor of the passage, but he missed badly and was thrown off balance by his thrust.

Thrinndor had heard the concern in the sorcerer's voice and had been a bit more wary. However, as he brought his flaming sword to bear, he raked it across the rapidly growing dragon's scales without damaging them in the slightest. He tried to bring the sword back around, but found he no longer had room: the rapidly expanding bulk of the dragon had him pinned uncomfortably against the wall of the cave! He realized fleetingly that he should have listened to the mage when he had had the chance.

Savinhand had been the closest to the woman, but the wizard's shout had startled him into action. He tumbled his way clear, but his unthinking reaction had taken him closer to the underground lake! The opposite direction of his friends!

Although Breunne had succumbed like the others to the womanly wiles of the dragon, he had maintained his distance as rangers typically are wont to do. He stepped back even further, bringing *Xenotath* up to firing position and releasing a volley of arrows. In his haste two of the arrows—mundane type were the quickest to hand—clanged harmlessly off of her scales, but the third found a niche and buried itself to the feathers in her neck.

She screamed, twisted her head and shot a torrent of water in the direction of the ranger, who had stopped just behind the magicuser. The blast hit Breunne hard in the chest, knocking him back just as he was notching one of his special dragon-bane arrows.

Sordaak, who was in the process of turning to face his adversary, was again knocked to the stone floor by the combination of pressurized water and the bulk of the ranger. The fighter then tripped over the flattened sorcerer, and both were painfully washed back down the passage by the continued onslaught of water. Knees, elbows and hands scraped uselessly across uneven floors and walls in an effort to halt their slide. But the dragon was relentless in her attack, pouring even more water than seemed possible after them.

Savinhand skidded to a halt and spun to confront the monster, his vorpal weapon in his right hand, a dagger enchanted specially for use against dragon scales in his left. What he encountered was the massive bulk of the dragon completely blocking the passage, with the tail on his end. He could see one of the paladin's legs struggling to his right, but the dragon continued to grow so even that was just a fleeting glimpse.

Knowing his friends had little time remaining, and not knowing how many of them were trapped by the bulk of the dragon, he immediately rushed back in. After all, with no teeth or claws on this end; all he had to be wary of was the tail. That was formidable enough, with his having been already knocked to the ground by it once.

However, with the dragon pinned against the walls, she couldn't move, either. That made target selection between gaps in her scales easy. But, the rogue quickly realized there was not much major damage he could do from this end—there was no neck for his vorpal weapon to focus its energy on. Instead he attacked where he had last seen the paladin, slashing and hacking away in gaps between the scales. He had to be careful, though; he didn't want to cut through to his friend underneath.

I might not be able to damage major organs, but I can sure make myself a pain in the ass! The rogue grinned as he attacked the monster's backside with abandon, easily dodging the tail whenever it whipped his direction.

Vorgath found himself pinned against the wall of the corridor, his right arm across his chest and maintaining his grip on *Flinthgoor*. He tried to twist the head of the axe so he could do some damage as he brought his arm back across his body, but he was unable to get the blade to turn. Reluctantly, he let go of his prized weapon and worked his way to his belt. The only weapon in reach there was a longsword he kept as a backup. He grasped the hilt as he felt the air being forced from his lungs by the dragon's continued expansion and used every ounce of remaining strength to drag the sword across her scales.

Unfortunately that meant the sword's back edge also faced him and, despite his straining against doing so, the blade cut through his armor in more than one place and he felt blinding pain as it cut through the muscles in his chest. He didn't hesitate, however; instead, he continued to draw the blade to arm's length in the hope the dragon would feel enough pain to cease her death crush.

Although Vorgath felt the muscles in her side tense, she continued to expand so as to crush her victims against the walls. The last thing the dwarf remembered before blacking out was that he had been done in by yet another pretty face.

Thrinndor was in a similar situation, but he had managed to bring his shield up to protect his head and chest from the crushing pressure by its curved shape. However, the metal rim across the bottom cut painfully into his midsection, slowly squeezing the air out of his body. His last thoughts before blacking out were that he was failing his friends and his god. As such, he mumbled a short prayer of apology to Valdaar before blackness overtook him.

The dragon's water weapon expended, Breunne climbed painfully to his feet and stepped behind the protection that a small alcove in the wall provided in the event she followed that attack with another. He didn't know that unless she was able to replenish the water she could do no more. He used the cover to ready his entire supply of dragon-bane arrows, and stepped out to release them at the exposed head of the beast one at a time.

Screams of pain and rage told him he was hitting the mark with each of them. However, the damage from even these specialized arrows was slight in comparison to the life force a dragon this size could command. He knew that if he was going to have any hope of saving his friends, he was going to have to abandon this tactic for one that involved direct attacks with his blades. Thus, after he had loosed his last arrow, he dropped his bow without hesitation, drew his longsword and kukri and charged out of his hiding place shouting at the top of his lungs in his best Vorgath impersonation.

Blinded by pain and the loss of one eye to an arrow, the dragon didn't see him coming until he was on her. The ranger slid under her massive jaws, surging to his feet to bring both weapons to bear on the hopefully softer tissue at her throat.

Sordaak likewise got first to his hands and knees, then he used his staff to push his scraped and bruised body painfully to his feet. *Why didn't I listen to my instincts?* He cursed himself as he turned to face the dragon. A blinding darkness welled up from deep inside and he unleashed the frustrations of the past few days on his foe.

The magicuser used the pain in that frustration to blast away with the most powerful spells from both his repertoire and that of *Pendromar*. He walked slowly toward his foe, releasing lightning bolts, fireballs, meteor swarms and every other spell he figured could do maximum damage to the creature that he knew blocked his path.

Sordaak! Through the haze of rage, frustration and pain the mage thought he heard someone shout his name.

Sordaak!

That time he knew he heard someone. The magicuser hesitated only slightly, but it was enough for Breunne to wrap both arms around the sorcerer, pinning the mage's scrawny arms to his body, thereby preventing him from casting further.

"*Release me!*" Sordaak fought against his captor.

"Sordaak!" the ranger shouted at close range. He relaxed his grip long enough to slap the mage hard on his right cheek, and then wrapped his arms tightly around the man again against the fury he knew to come.

But the blinding effects of his rage slowly faded and the mage shook his head to clear the rest. "What?" he mumbled through foam-flecked lips.

"She's dead," Breunne said, relieved but still wary. He maintained his grip on the sorcerer's arms in the event his friend's anger returned. What he had just witnessed was power from a man he not only hadn't seen before, he hadn't even *heard* of such power from a human. A power that worried the ranger. How could a man hope to control such power?

When the mage stopped struggling and focus returned to his eyes, Breunne warily released his grip. "If you are up to it, we must try to get to our friends to determine if they yet live."

Sordaak nodded mutely and stumbled without the support of the ranger. Breunne caught the mage, steadying him until he was able to stand on his own. After he determined that he could, he released the mage, drew his weapons and began hacking at the right shoulder of the massive monster that blocked their path.

The mage, partially recovered from his rage but still weak, stepped to the left side and began cutting away the scales on that side. Realizing this was going to take far too long, he threw down the dagger in disgust, held his staff in front of him with both hands and called forth its power. The sorcerer focused the energy on the head of the staff and when he applied that to the body of the dragon, was able to use it like a surgical saw and slice away huge chunks at a time.

Even still he feared he was too late when he finally saw the black armor of the paladin behind a layer of scales and skin. Carefully Sordaak cut him free, grabbed an arm and summoned enough strength to drag the limp body of his friend through the blood and piles of dragon remains to a clear spot on the floor. A quick glance showed that the paladin had a pale bluish tint to his skin and that he wasn't breathing.

"*Breunne!*" shouted the sorcerer.

"What?" came the immediate reply. The ranger hadn't seen the success the mage had had using his power to cut through the dragon's body.

"Come help me revive Thrinndor!"

Breunne stumbled to the mage's voice, nearly exhausted from his efforts to free the barbarian. A quick glance was all it took for him to assess the situation. As he knelt at the paladin's side he said, "Go use your power to free Vorgath. I'll take care of this."

Knowing his skills were useless with the paladin, the mage pushed to his feet and stumbled over to where the ranger had been working. By now in death the dragon was doing as all creatures do: she was shrinking. Air exhausted from her lungs and waste flowed from other places. As such, Sordaak's work went very quickly, especially with Savinhand working from the other side.

Together they freed the barbarian, whose face was a pasty and bluish white. They then dragged him over to where Breunne had the paladin sitting up. Sordaak was about to ask as to his status, but he was shoved roughly aside by Thrinndor.

"You should have searched for him first," the big fighter admonished.

Sordaak sat down and put his head in his hands. He was exhausted. "I had no idea where either of you were, moron!" He didn't bother even to look up. "And you're welcome for saving your miserable life!" The mage looked up suddenly. "Is he—?"

"Dead?" Thrinndor finished for him. "No, but unless I can restore his heart to beating and air to his lungs, he soon will be."

While the paladin and ranger worked on the barbarian, Savinhand plopped down next to the mage. He, too, was spent. "Correct my misconceptions, please," he muttered, watching the paladin intently, "I thought when the heart stopped beating and one stopped breathing, you *were* dead."

Sordaak looked up, opened mouth to speak but then shook his head wearily. "It's complicated." He put his face back in his hands. Savin did the same.

After a few moments both looked up when they heard the barbarian coughing, gagging and then cursing. He, too, would live it seemed. For some reason the mage had never doubted it.

Once the barbarian was back on his feet, the five men looked around at the mess. "I must rest," Sordaak announced suddenly.

"We must all rest," agreed the paladin. "But not here. Carrion crawlers and the like will sense the death in this place from miles away. I deem it wise to not be here when they arrive to clean this up."

Silence followed that announcement until Savinhand, feeling somewhat better, asked, "Right. Which direction, then?"

Thrinndor thought about it for a minute and said, "We must return back to that last intersection and choose another path."

"No." All eyes pivoted to the caster. "It is my belief that she," he pointed at what remained of the bulk of the dragon, "was put here as a guard. I am reasonably certain we are on the correct path."

Inevitably the paladin lifted an eyebrow. When the explanation wasn't immediately forthcoming, he asked, "On what do you base that belief?"

Sordaak's eyes went from the dead dragon to the very much alive paladin. He shrugged. "In part by the fact that our guide," he nodded in the direction of the barbarian, "has been correct to this point." Vorgath returned the nod. "In some part because of what that dragon bitch told us." He hesitated. "And in part on a hunch." The mage shrugged again and used his staff to push himself to his feet.

"Shall we?"

Chapter Twenty-Seven

Labyrinth

The five men gathered again at the edge of the lake that blocked their path. Sordaak was tired beyond belief, but he agreed with the paladin that resting here was out of the question. With a sigh, he began stripping off excess baggage and heavy items.

"What are you doing?" Thrinndor asked.

"I've got a ring that will allow me to search the depths without requiring air. With that I should be able to find the exit much quicker."

The paladin shook his head. "You are in no shape for such a swim." He held out his hand. "Give me the ring, and I will be able to search much faster."

The mage hesitated only slightly, then removed the ring from the middle finger on his left hand and handed it to the paladin.

"I, too, have such an enchanted item, however mine is this pendant I wear around my neck," Breunne said, pulling a blue stone affixed to a simple leather thong from under his tunic. "Together we can search much quicker."

"I'll wait right here," said the dwarf as he walked over to the wall, sat down and closed his eyes. "I'll thank you to keep the light from that staff dim, please." He then pulled his dented helm down over his eyes and was snoring within a couple of breaths.

Sordaak shook his head as he turned back to face the paladin, a smile playing on his lips.

Savinhand rummaged around in a bag at his waist. "I used to have an item that would allow me to breathe underwater, as well. But I haven't worn it in some time, and I'm not sure I even brought it."

While he continued his search, Sordaak enchanted three coins so that they glowed brightly and gave them to each of the men going swimming.

Savin found what he was looking for: a pair of bracers. He put them on and accepted the coin. "These aren't as effective as what the other two have," he explained. "Their use is limited. With them I can cast a limited use spell up to three times in a day that will allow me to breathe underwater for a few minutes at a time." He shrugged. "They'll have to do."

Without preamble, the men took to the water. Savinhand went left, Breunne right, and Thrinndor angled such that he swam straight out into the middle.

Sordaak watched them go, the makeshift lights bobbing eerily underwater this way and that as the three spread out and eventually disappeared. He turned and ambled over to the wall opposite the snoring barbarian and sat down. He wanted to remain awake just because someone needed to, he reasoned. Idly, he reminisced about Fahlred and how good his familiar had been at keeping watch.

He was startled awake by the sound of sloshing water coming from the direction of the lake. He hurriedly raised the light of his staff and swung it around that direction. "Thrinndor?" He knew he would have never have been awakened by the approach of either the rogue or the ranger. Hence it had to be the paladin—well, he *hoped* it had to be the paladin.

"How did you know it was me?"

"I'll explain later," replied the relieved sorcerer. "Did you find the exit?"

Thrinndor hesitated. "I found *an* exit." He slung a large, heavy-looking bag that he'd been dragging behind him up into the light. "And this." He let the bag fall open, and the light from Sordaak's staff glittered off of several items inside.

Suddenly Vorgath was standing next to the paladin. No one had heard him approach. "Hello. What have we here?" He reached into the bag and withdrew a simple-looking helm, much nicer that the one he was wearing. He reached up, flipped aside the one on his head and immediately donned the one from the bag. "Do I look smarter?" he smiled up at his friends.

"No," the paladin replied. "And you should not don items until we have had a chance to determine their value, use or enchantment." A half-smile appeared on his lips. "That could have been a Helm of Idiocy."

"That would have been an upgrade," the mage noted wryly as he watched the ranger approach the group followed by the rogue.

"Hey! I resemble that remark!" the barbarian said good-naturedly. "Nevertheless, I claim this helm. It would be of no use to any of you." His eyes glowed in admiration as he removed it and looked it over more closely. "And it's made of the purest mithral I have ever laid eyes on!"

"He's right," acknowledged the ranger. "That should keep him from getting his brains scrambled on such a regular basis." He grinned at the dwarf.

"Ha ha, very funny!" Vorgath grinned back.

"What else is in there?" Savinhand asked as he reached for the bag.

"We'll find out once we get to a place where we can rest," snapped the caster. He reached out, closed the bag and attempted to lift it. As it turned out, the bag was *very* heavy. He looked up at the paladin and snorted. "You carry it!"

Thrinndor stifled a grin and took the bag from the mage.

"Anyone find the passage we seek?" Sordaak asked the three dripping men.

The three looked at one another and shrugged. The paladin pointed to the rogue, indicating he should go first.

Savinhand shook his head, his eyes remaining on the bag. "Nothing to the left. I followed the wall until I reached where the path apparently continues on the far side. I saw Thrinndor's wet footprints there, turned around and came back."

"That's pretty much my story as well," Breunne said.

"I found a passage directly across from us," the paladin said when it was his turn. "This lake is not that big—perhaps four- or five-hundred feet across. I do not believe it was originally that deep, either. However, in the center I found where a cavern opens up. In that cavern I found this," he shook the bag, "as well as a large amount of coin, some gems and a few other things I was unable to bring back with me. I selected that which I deemed useful and came back."

"Were there any exits from that cavern?" Sordaak asked.

The paladin shook his head. "I was unable to find anything. It almost appears as if that cavern was carved out to be the dragon's lair some years ago."

The mage tugged at the hairs on his chin. "It makes no sense," he said, not looking at anyone. Instead, he was staring out over the water.

"What makes no sense?" the rogue asked.

Sordaak shook his head as his eyes refocused on the group. "Well, if I am correct and this is the path we need to take, then this lake was not here fifteen hundred years ago—I'm certain Cerraunne would have mentioned something of this size were they to have encountered it." His hand moved up and scratched the side of his head. *Damn, a bath would sure feel good!*

"So?" demanded the dwarf.

"So how did the water get here?" When no one answered, the sorcerer continued. "Again, if I'm correct and Bahamut put that damn dragon here as a guardian, then he—they—flooded this chamber so she could survive. The water had to come from somewhere!"

"Not only that," all eyes shifted to Breunne who spoke softly, "she had to have had the ability to leave this place—at least if we are going to believe anything she told us."

"She could have left in human form?" Savinhand offered.

"Doubtful," replied the sorcerer. "The woman we saw could not carry much in the way of loot this far under the mountain. *And* she said that her ability to remain in human form was limited, at best." He shook his head. "No, there must be another way out of this cavern."

"I saw no such entrance or exit," protested the paladin. "And, rest assured I would have found an opening if it were large enough for a dragon to pass!" He was mildly perturbed at his scouting skills being questioned.

"I'm certain you would," agreed the sorcerer. "At least you would have *if* you had been looking in the right place!"

Those who had begun to lose interest in the conversation—and there was more than one—suddenly had their attention snapped back into place.

"What?" the men said in unison.

Sordaak grinned and without saying a word, pointed to the ceiling above the lake with his staff. Or rather, where the ceiling *should* be.

"Can water dragons fly?" Savinhand asked, his eyes trying in vain to penetrate the blackness above the still water.

An elongated pause greeted that question. Vorgath was the one that finally answered. "It is my understanding that flight is what makes a dragon a dragon. Without flight, a dragon would be merely an oversized, mundane lizard without much to attract interest. Dragons fly."

"While I never noticed wings on our most recent adversary, I do not doubt the esteemed dwarf in his knowledge of dragons," Thrinndor said formally. "Dragons *must* be able to fly."

"I'll check out your theory," Breunne stated. He held his light ahead of him and spoke the power word for his boots. Instantly he lifted off of the ground and sailed slowly toward the area above the water.

"Take care," cautioned the paladin, "and remember the limitations of your boots. Please allow yourself flight time for a return trip."

"Understood," replied the ranger as he sailed out of sight. "Either way, I'll be back in a few minutes."

The four remaining men stood silently at the edge of the pool for a few moments. Finally Vorgath broke that silence. "You sure you got everything of value from that dragon's horde?" He eyed the paladin suspiciously.

"Of course not," replied the fighter. "I did not take time to dig deep into the piles of coin, nor did I inspect every gem."

"Give me the ring."

Thrinndor rolled his eyes, removed the ring and handed it over. "Do not take long, old one. When Breunne returns we must continue on to our destination."

"And find a place to rest," Sordaak added.

"I'll be back before you finish that dried biscuit," Vorgath replied smugly as he placed the ring on a finger and waded into the water.

As it turned out, Vorgath and Breunne returned within moments of one another. The dwarf dragging two large bags behind him and the ranger had nothing to hide but a smile. The dwarf handed the ring back to Thrinndor.

Sordaak ignored the barbarian. "Well?" he demanded, his eyes on the ranger.

"There is a large, more or less vertical shaft that goes as far as I was able to travel with my boots."

"You never saw the end?"

Breunne shook his head. "I believe this might be an old volcano shaft. As such, it could end up among the highest peaks in the region. I had to take care not to hit any outcropping, but I nonetheless was able to travel very fast. I would say I went about a mile almost straight up before I had to turn around and return."

"Vorgath," the mage said without turning to look at him, "what time of day is it on the surface?"

The barbarian scratched his head, mildly miffed that no one concerned themselves with the bounty he had returned. "Early evening."

"We have been here a couple of hours at least," pondered the mage, "and yet we saw no hint of light from there." He pointed to where the ranger had gone.

"I said *mostly* vertical," Breunne corrected. "Actually, the shaft switches directions in multiple places. No light would penetrate the depths of this shaft even if it were a volcano and the sun passed directly overhead."

The mage nodded but said nothing. Clearly his brain was working hard.

Vorgath had finally had enough waiting. "What's going on inside that nasty little mind of yours?"

"We're not getting out that way," the sorcerer answered at last. "We continue as before." He looked at the edge of the water. "But first we must all get to the other side of this lake." He was again scratching his head.

"We're not going up?" Savinhand asked. He was confused.

"Of course not," Sordaak answered as if he had been expecting the question—which of course he had. "It could take us weeks to scale the vertical shaft of this old volcano. We don't have weeks, we have two days." He took in a deep breath. "So we continue on the way we were going."

"But—"

"No buts!" snapped the sorcerer. "We don't have time to debate, either!" He turned to glare at the paladin. "How are we going to get across?"

Thrinndor took in a deep breath and a puzzled look appeared on his face. Clearly he had not considered that option.

"Not the right answer!" Sordaak answered for him. "You said it was four or five hundred feet across, right?" The paladin nodded. "Very well, we swim." The mage looked around until he found where the paladin has set his shield against the wall. "Pile everything heavy on this and our two muscle-bound types with water breathing rings can drag it across while the rest of us simply swim."

When no one moved, he startled the others by yelling, "That wasn't a suggestion. *LET'S MOVE!*" He then dropped his bag of food and his weapons onto the back of the shield. *Pendromar* he hung on to. He could swim with that, he knew.

The others did as directed without further discussion. The sorcerer was grouchy from lack of sleep, lack of food—or both—and they didn't want to provoke him. In the end, there proved too much for the one shield, so Vorgath turned his over and they filled it as well.

As they prepared for the trip across the lake, the barbarian held out his hand to the ranger. "Your amulet, if you please."

"I can handle one of the loads," Breunne protested.

"Of course you can," agreed the dwarf, his hand unwavering, "but I would prefer not to have to swim across wearing my armor."

Breunne smiled and his eyes twinkled as he untied the thong that held the amulet to his chest and handed it over.

Vorgath put it around his neck and turned to take up one of the ropes attached to his shield. "Thank you," he muttered as he took the first few steps into the water.

"Wait!" The barbarian stopped, turned and all turned to eye the rogue. "Something's been bothering me. Bahamut and his dragons knew of the exit from this labyrinth, blocked it and were watching in the event someone showed up and tried to use it. And, if what you believe is true and that water dragon was put here as a deterrent, then why is it we think the entrance to these caverns in Khandihaar will be not guarded as well?"

Sordaak blinked twice as he stared at the thief. He was flippant with his answer. "Because there are no more dragons—only Bahamut remains, and he doesn't guard entrances."

It was the paladin's turn to scratch his head. "You know this?"

The mage shrugged as he turned to look over the water. "I've done the math." He flipped the cover off of the bird cage. He was mildly surprised to see that the three birds now appeared to be healthy. "These are the last three gold dragons of the council. No other dragons remain in the valley—they all have to be summoned for The Gathering. Only Bahamut remains."

"And if they have blocked the entrance into these caverns as they did the exit?" Savinhand persisted.

"Then we'll unblock it."

An uncomfortable silence settled on the group. "Up is not an option?" Breunne asked.

Sordaak shook his head. "No. Too many uncertainties, and we'd have to use my fly spell on repeated occasions. I'm exhausted and we just don't have time to rest and explore that possible out."

"We move on?" the dwarf asked hopefully. He was getting hungry. When the mage answered with a nod, Vorgath turned and sloshed into the underground lake, his shield in tow behind him.

Breunne rushed to catch up. "Here, you'd better take this, too." He held out the enchanted coin given to him by Sordaak. "We wouldn't want you to tumble into the dragon's lair."

Vorgath nodded his thanks, accepted the coin from the ranger and resumed his trek into the water where he soon disappeared.

Thrinndor hurried to follow before the light of the barbarian's coin faded from view. He wanted them to stay together.

Within a few minutes the party was gathered on the other side of the lake, dripping water on the stone floor of the cavern. Sordaak was shivering—the water had been cold, and the temperature in the caverns had never been that warm in the first place. Now they were positively *freezing*—or almost. He gathered everyone around him and called forth heat from his staff. Soon the shivering stopped and they all felt better—tired, but better. The mage wanted to call a rest period, but the paladin's words about scavengers rang in his ears. They were in no shape for a prolonged battle—even one against carrion crawlers, rust monsters and the like. No, they must move on.

Yet they must also rest, and soon.

And rest they did in the next side cavern. Although it was barely enough rest to restore the magicuser, he felt better now that his energy was back and he had eaten.

As such the men made good time. They stopped for brief rests only when one or more of them could go no further—usually Sordaak.

By the barbarian's proclamation they were nearing the end of their third day in the caverns when the passage narrowed and shrank. Breunne and Savin returned to the party to announce the way forward was indeed blocked.

Sordaak wanted to see for himself. He crawled forward until he came up against a seamless end to the tunnel. No rocks. No cave-in. The tunnel just stopped. The mage tested the walls with his spells but could discern no weakness. *Damn!*

He crawled his way back to the others and rubbed his elbows to soothe the abrasions he had just inflicted on them. The sorcerer avoided the eyes of the rogue, lest some of that 'I told you so' stuff be thrown his way.

"There *must* be another way!" Sordaak turned his hope upon the barbarian. "You said these caverns were carved by wind and water, right?" Vorgath nodded. "Well, we've passed several intersections recently." His words began to rush as a barely formed idea tried to push its way clear of his mind. "If wind and water carved these tunnels, then there had to be someplace for either to escape!" The barbarian returned his stare without speaking. "Those intersections could lead to other openings somewhere in the valley!"

"It's certainly possible—maybe even likely," Vorgath said at last. "But what makes you think they will not have been also sealed?"

Sordaak glared at the dwarf. After a few moments he threw his hands up. "Hell, I don't know! But, we must *try!*"

Back they traipsed to the most recent intersection. One by one they investigated each possible path. Some went the right way. Others wandered back into the mountain. Those they left alone. All ended the same way: sealed or otherwise ended like the first. None ended with an opening into the valley.

It looked like Bahamut had indeed been thorough.

The companions gathered back in yet another intersection that had not panned out. Frustration levels were high, and lack of rest for the previous four days laid like a wet blanket over the party.

"What's—" Savinhand began tentatively.

"*Goddamn it!*" Sordaak slammed the heel of *Pendromar* to the ground and the earth shook beneath their feet.

Vorgath eyed the walls suspiciously. "I don't think that's a good idea when there is an entire mountain above our heads."

The mage was on the brink of exploding in rage, but visibly fought back the urge. He looked down at the rock at his feet and after a few deep breaths control returned and calmness descended upon him. When he looked up, his eyes were normal and the determination they had become accustomed to had returned.

"Bahamut knows we're here. There is no longer any reason for subterfuge. I am going to summon Pentaath and have him find the opening to that underwater pool we found. We will meet him there."

"What then?" Thrinndor asked.

"Between Pentaath, boots and my spells, we will fly out of there to meet our fate on our own terms."

"Now *that* sounds like a plan I can wrap my hands around," declared the dwarf.

"Let us make haste back to the pool, then."

"I can help with that." Sordaak smiled and cast the spell.

With Sordaak's judicious use of his speed boost spell, the men made it back to the pool in less than half the time it had taken to get from there to the sealed entrances. Pentaath was already there, waiting impatiently by the side of the lake.

Sordaak checked his charge over carefully, noting that the dragon had grown yet again. He was not only the biggest dragon he had ever seen, but the largest he had even heard tell of. A close inspection also revealed that Pentaath's white scales were taking on a metallic tint.

The dragon informed the companions that he had not only found where the volcano opening was, he had found where a side tube opened into the valley. This opening would shave several thousand feet off of their required ascent and subsequent descent.

Plans made, the men took only what they determined would help them in the upcoming battle and a few days' supply of food.

"Will not Bahamut try to stop us?" Thrinndor asked.

"I hope he does," Sordaak replied, his lower jaw set. "That means he will be out of his element, and that will give us an advantage." His smile did not touch his eyes. "But, I doubt he'll chance that. No, he'll wait for us to approach him in his home."

"You are certain of this?"

"You keep asking that," the sorcerer answered. "I am certain of *nothing*. However, he is *supposed* to be the smartest creature in the land! Waiting for us to attack him in his home is what I would do in his place." He shrugged.

The paladin's eyes held those of the mage for a moment longer. Finally, he too nodded. "Very well, what then is your plan once we get to the valley?"

"Finally a question worthy of an answer." He winked at the big fighter. "We rest." That drew raised eyebrows from several of his companions. "We will gather at the east end of the valley, set up camp and make preparations for what is to come."

"You assume we will be undisturbed?"

"I do."

Chapter Twenty-Eight

Khandihaar

The plan went as anticipated, and the companions minus the cleric set up a camp next to a bubbling stream in soft, deep, green grass.

While Savinhand prepared a meal in the late-afternoon sun, Sordaak took time to empty his pockets, bags and portable hole onto the grass. He also removed his robe and made several repairs. Finally he sorted through his scrolls, wands and potions, placing each in a way that those he deemed he would need first were closest to hand.

Evening meal complete, the mage called the group together as the sun dipped below the mountains rimming the valley. "I have been working on this plan of attack for months," he began. They were all tired, but each now gave him undivided attention. His face grew grim. "The plan has had to change with the loss of our cleric. However, my new plan has a remedy for even that." Thrinndor started to speak, but Sordaak raised his hand, blocking him. "No interruptions, please; it will go quicker this way." He got a reluctant nod.

He turned to the rogue. "Savinhand, following this briefing, you will immediately get what rest you can." The rogue's eyes narrowed, waiting for what he knew not. "You are going to rise well ahead of the rest of us. Your task will be to get in undetected, find Cyrillis and release her once I have Bahamut's full attention. Get her back to where we are doing battle as quickly as you can." The sorcerer hesitated for a moment. "I cannot stress this enough: there is no plan that will work without the aid of our cleric. Do you understand?" Savin nodded, his mind whirling with the possibilities.

"Good." The sorcerer turned so that he could look into the eyes of each of the three fighter types. "I will go in first. Alone." The paladin started to protest, but Sordaak ignored him. "When I give the signal—you'll know what it is—you two," he pointed to Vorgath and Breunne, "charge in and attack with everything you've got. I will hold his attention, so you should meet little, if any, opposition. Bahamut's scales are of platinum—duh. Only the most powerful, highly enchanted weapons can harm him. Vorgath has *Flinthgoor*; Breunne, do you have such a weapon?"

"I do," replied the ranger. "My first attacks will be with *Xenotath* and some special arrows I have set aside just for this purpose." Sordaak started to protest, but the ranger continued before he could. "Rest assured that these arrows will do far more harm to the great beast than anything else we have." The mage hesitated and then nodded slowly. "Once I have exhausted those arrows, I will switch to a sword I seldom use, but one that has special characteristics that will also prove useful."

"Good," Sordaak repeated. He turned at last to the paladin. "You, old friend, are going to have the most important job of all." Thrinndor's right eyebrow twitched slightly, but he didn't say a word. "You must keep me alive until our cleric arrives." The mage's eyes narrowed. "Because if I fall, you will all soon follow. Is that understood?"

Vorgath grunted something unintelligible. Sordaak spun on him. "No, I see that you don't. Bahamut is the most powerful creature in all the land by far. The dragons we have battled to this point were his *minions*. None of them had *one-tenth* the abilities of the Lord of Dragons—*One-tenth!*" he repeated. "He knows every spell in the books—both clerical and arcane, and he will use them for both his defense and as weapons. I intend to make sure he aims that energy at *me*. I will be prepared for that. However, if I go down and he directs that energy at any of you," he slung is arm around, encompassing all four of the men seated around the fire, "you will not survive. Of that I can promise you!" The sorcerer returned his attention to the barbarian. "Do I make myself clear enough for you?"

Vorgath's jaw muscles were working hard. "Yes," he whispered through clenched teeth.

"I didn't hear you," the mage persisted.

Vorgath raised his head and looked into the eyes of the sorcerer. "Yes," he repeated evenly. "I understand that if you fall, the rest will soon follow. So you must not fall."

"Exactly," Sordaak said, his head bobbing as he did. "Not only that, but if any of you get the dragon's attention at any time during the battle, you must go into defensive posture until I can regain his attention. *Flinthgoor* is a mighty weapon, and in your hands it will undoubtedly deal massive amounts of damage to whatever flank you attack. Bahamut's attention will be to whoever he sees as the greatest threat. I intend for that threat to be me. But again, if one of you attracts his attention, you must go into defensive mode. Is that clear?" Sordaak locked eyes with each of the fighters, ensuring they understood.

"What about me?" Pentaath asked from the edge of the fire. As a white dragon he remained uncomfortable around fire, but he'd been able to overcome that somewhat of late, particularly while in human form as he was now.

Sordaak turned slowly to face his self-proclaimed son. "You must remain alive at all costs. If we are to defeat the King of Dragons, I will need to draw on both your abilities and your stamina. If you fall, I fall. You must not put yourself in a position where Bahamut would turn on you. While you would now provide a serious threat to any living being in this realm, you would prove no match for this dragon were he to focus his attention on you. That must not happen." Sordaak took a breath and gulped. This next part was going to be hard. "In dragon form I fear you would be able to take Bahamut's attention from me; your size and power would certainly distract him. I will need you to remain in human form until I give you the signal to go into full attack. I believe Vorgath has a suitable weapon for you to use."

The barbarian nodded. He removed a longsword from his belt, stood and walked over to the youth. Pentaath took the weapon, but it was clear he was not happy about it.

Sordaak's voice grew stern. "You will remain in human form and attack with the barbarian and ranger, is that understood?"

The youth swallowed hard and then nodded. "Yes, father."

"Good," replied the mage with a sigh. That had gone better than expected. "I can't be worrying about you during the course of this battle."

Sordaak removed an amulet from a pouch. He then walked over and handed it to his son. "Before you attack the dragon, I need you to affix this to him somewhere. Anywhere will do."

"What is it?"

The sorcerer took in a deep breath. "At some point in the battle I believe Bahamut will sense he is in trouble and will travel to another plane of existence so that he can heal himself. That must not be allowed. He may even travel from one plane to another, hoping to shake me because I will be following him. That amulet will allow me to do so without having to guess which plane he went to."

Pentaath nodded and tucked the amulet behind his belt, verifying it was secure before looking back up.

"What do we do when that happens?" Thrinndor asked.

"You heal up as best you can and wait for our return. We *will* return—he has no option. The sword he is trying to prevent from falling into our hands is in this plane—it is bound here, and cannot be removed from it. He will therefore return here to protect it."

"Any questions so far?" Sordaak had hit his companions fast and hard, giving them little time to think of any questions. So far. "Good," he continued. "Once Bahamut runs low on spell energy, I will signal for an all-out attack." He turned to face the dragon youth. "Pentaath, that will be your signal to revert to dragon form and maximize the damage you can do. And Thrinndor, that will be your signal to jump into the fray if you are not there already." He got nods from both.

"Good. Thrinndor, at some point you will need to break away and find your sword." That caused some raised eyebrows. "I found a reference in one of the tomes back in the Library of Antiquity that said, 'The King of all Dragons can only be slain by the sword of a god'. There are only two of those known to exist, and one of them remains in the Library. That leaves *Valdaar's Fist* as the only viable weapon capable of finishing him off. I believe he will have the sword close at hand; he'll not chance that we have scouts out looking for it while we do battle with him. Find it."

The paladin's determined expression said it all. He nodded. "It will be so."

Sordaak took in another deep breath and exhaled slowly. "Good. Everyone here has a vital role in making this happen. If one fails, then it is likely we will all fail. Is that clear enough for everyone?"

He got nods from everyone.

"Very well. It is imperative that all get a good rest. We—each of us—must be at our maximum potential when we face this our strongest test to date. While I'm counting on Bahamut to also have lost some of his prowess in battle in the millennia-and-a-half since last he was required to do so, a slightly less ready King of Dragons will still prove more of a test to us than all of the other dragons we have faced to date even if we had faced them all at once. We must be at our peak. Yet, in my heart I know this foe can be defeated *if* we each do our part." He looked into each pair of eyes, one pair at a time. "Can I count on each of you to do your job?"

The four seated men and one youth got to their feet.

"Yes," they said quietly.

The mage nodded, satisfied. They would do their best, and he could ask for no more from them. At least, not yet.

"Savin, when you release Cyrillis, tell her that her sole task will be to keep me alive. At all costs. She can heal others in the party only if time permits. She must keep me alive."

"Yes, boss. She will be informed."

"Thank you. Now get some sleep. You will need to sneak in unnoticed under the cover of darkness. Know that Bahamut has many forms of vision and his eyes will be able to see what others can't. You will have to take extreme precautions to remain undetected."

Savinhand smiled. "Rest assured he will never see me. I have some tricks up my sleeve that I have yet to use. If all goes well I may even have the healer back here so she can also get some rest before the battle begins!"

Sordaak shook his head. "Where does he get this arrogance from?" When the barbarian opened his mouth, the mage cut him off. "Don't answer that!" Vorgath clamped his mouth shut, satisfied his message had been received.

"One more thing," Sordaak called after the rogue, who was rolling his bed out on the thick carpet of grass. Savin looked up at the mage. "You must also find Cyrillis' staff. She must have it in hand when she returns to heal us."

"Of course," Savin said, and then he went back to making his bed.

"All right," the sorcerer announced, "Pentaath will keep watch. The rest of us must sleep."

"I guess this means we won't get some of the thief's barely palatable biscuits and gravy in the morning?" Vorgath had already climbed into his blankets, but he poked his head back out to speak.

"Afraid not old one," Savin said with a laugh.

"Damn!"

*

Morning dawned gray and gloomy with a cold wind blowing across the peaks to the north. Vorgath had announced that he could smell snow on the air. Wonderful.

However, it did allow for a quick modification to the sorcerer's announced plans. Luring the King of Dragon's outside would allow him to use the powers bestowed upon him by the Storm Giants' cloak he now wore. Any damage done without the use of actual spell energy could only lend a hand toward their success.

After a light breakfast, Sordaak looked around in the unreasonable hope that the rogue's boast had somehow proved possible. But neither the rogue nor the cleric was anywhere to be seen. *Sigh.*

The mage gathered his troupe—now two short—around the fire and again went over his plan and making sure that each knew his role and informing them of his small revision.

Together, they extinguished the fire and began the march to the west. The temperature continued to drop and the first few snowflakes twisted down to alight on whatever crossed their path. The snow thickened and it was some time before the west end of the valley loomed into view through the veil of white.

From what he had read, Sordaak knew what he was looking for. Still, even he was surprised by the scale of what they found as they approached the Platinum Dragon's home.

A pair of massive stone doors stretched between columns that were carved from the base of the mountain that stood guard over the west end of the valley. The magnificent doors were hewn from the purest white granite, adorned with runes, and inlaid with what Sordaak was certain was platinum. They were also more than one hundred feet wide and at least half again that in height.

They were imposing. And closed.

"Will your—" Thrinndor began.

Sordaak didn't wait for him to finish. "Prepare yourselves for battle and give me room," he said through clenched teeth. His companions drew their weapons and took a few steps back, crossed their arms and waited.

The mage stood facing the doors with his feet shoulder-width apart and raised *Pendromar.* His forehead wrinkled with strain as he focused his concentration on the enormous portals. The earth began to rumble beneath their feet as the doors fought the power of the sorcerer. Beads of sweat formed on Sordaak's brow, and the veins bulged in his neck.

Just when it seemed certain his efforts were to be for naught, the mage slammed the heel of his staff onto the stone path. Power surged and suddenly the doors burst inward with a thunderous crash. The door on the right hung awkwardly from a shattered hinge.

"Knock, knock," Vorgath said loudly.

Sordaak didn't turn around. "Heed the plan." Without waiting for a reply, he strode through the doors, his steps unwavering. He limped slightly from the wooden foot—it wasn't fitting correctly again. But he wasn't going to take time to fix that now.

"Should we consider waiting—" Thrinndor began again, but the sorcerer was already deep into the chamber beyond the doors. "I guess not," he mumbled. While he didn't have a better plan in mind, he was not fond of the mage going in alone. Nor the plan to start this battle without their cleric.

Sordaak had explained that if Savinhand had not managed to free Cyrillis by the time he was inside, then it was likely that they would not be joining the foray. The paladin kept getting hung up on the mage's admonition that none of this was going to work without her.

Once the mage was deep inside, Thrinndor waved for the others to come with him. He was ad-libbing by moving inside before they got the signal, but he rationalized it was going to be hard to see or hear the signal if he could not see the mage.

Sordaak continued deeper into the chamber, deciding he was probably not going to get to use his cloak after all. *Well, it had been a long shot anyway.* Part of him noticed that the King of Dragon's foyer was very impressive. The entrance hall was more than two hundred feet wide and stretched deep under the mountain— at least five hundred feet, the mage guessed. The walls had regularly placed flaming sconces, providing illumination there. The ceiling—far overhead—was lit by some sort of indirect lighting that had a blue hue, making the massive room look almost as if it were outdoors.

Almost, the mage thought, *but the clouds are missing. Maybe they don't get much in the way of clouds up here.*

Elaborate tapestries adorned the walls, polished suits of armor complete with weapons stood on labeled daises, and opulent carpets covered the gleaming marble floor at regular intervals.

Impressive. Sordaak never even slowed as he approached another set of massive doors at the end of what he believed to be merely the entryway to this under-mountain palace. He raised his staff with his left hand and made an almost negligent waving motion with his right, which also held the covered cage.

The doors crashed into the walls behind them, sending splinters in all directions. Sordaak strode through the open doorway into the even larger chamber beyond. The room approximated a square, perhaps five hundred feet to a side. There were regularly spaced columns surrounding a raised platform that supported thirteen elaborately carved throne-like chairs, six to either side of one massive, gilded throne. This throne was well lit, as were three of the side chairs. The others were dark. Sordaak was fairly certain he knew why.

Sordaak came to a stop twenty or so feet from the platform and briefly searched the chamber with his eyes. There were two more huge doors in the wall behind the platform and smaller sets of doors in the walls to his right and left. The mage was beginning to get mad. He didn't want to have to search the entire palace.

"Show yourself!" the sorcerer shouted, his voice reverberating off of the walls as he had enhanced it by magic. "Quit hiding behind closed doors!"

Sordaak alternately searched the doors for movement and was slightly startled when a voice spoke right in front of him.

"I am not hiding." Sordaak's head spun to see a stately elder male sitting with his legs crossed in the largest of the chairs. "What is it you seek, young man?"

The sorcerer glared at Bahamut and fought down the urge to scream at the old man. "You know the answer to that," he said with more calm than he felt.

"Yes, I suppose that I do. It however seemed more appropriate—and certainly more dramatic—to ask." The old man smiled, but just as quickly the smile disappeared. "The girl is dead, and you will never put your hands on the sword."

"Tsk, tsk," Sordaak shook his head. "I thought those such as yourself—few though they are in the realm of late—were incapable of lying." Bahamut's eyes widened. "Yet you sat there and did just that."

The old man sighed and allowed his shoulders to slump slightly. "Desperate measures called for by desperate times. How did you know?"

Sordaak hiked a thumb over his shoulder. "Super-Pally back there says he can sense that she yet lives." He shrugged. "So she yet lives." It was his turn to smile. "He's another of you annoying unable-to-lie types."

Bahamut's eyes narrowed. "I was unaware they had that type of bond. Very well, the cleric yet lives. However, that changes nothing. She is where you cannot reach her, and you still will never lay hands on the sword."

The sorcerer eyed the elder human for a few moments. Finally he put the heel of *Pendromar* on the marble floor, rested its head against his shoulder and shifted his grip on the cage to his other hand.

Curiosity got the better of the dragon lord. "What do you have there?"

Sordaak stifled a smile. It was what he had been pushing for. "What? This?" The mage lifted the cage until it was at eye level. Slowly he raised his other hand and whipped the cover clear, exposing the three birds inside.

Bahamut's eyes widened in surprise. "I knew they were not dead, yet I have not been able to commune with them. What type of cage is that?"

"Just a special alloy of Mithral, Adamantine and a couple of ores I would prefer not to divulge at this time."

"Stargold," the old man stated flatly. This time Sordaak's eyes widened slightly. "The formula for that enchantment opposing alloy has not been used in two millennia. How did you find it?"

The sorcerer shrugged. "Again, I'd rather not say."

"The Library of Antiquity." The old man shook his head as he studied a fingernail. "I should have destroyed that foul edifice when I had the chance." Slowly he raised his eyes to meet those of the mage. "Release them."

Sordaak chucked. "Surely you jest. Release them? After I had so much trouble keeping my men from killing them all before I could capture these three?" The sorcerer shook his head. "I think not."

The old dragon seemed to age a few more years. "What is it you want in return for their release?"

"The sword and the girl."

Bahamut's back stiffened, and his eyes flared. "Now it is you who are the jester. Surely you know that I cannot—will not—agree to those terms?"

"Cannot? Will not?" Sordaak shrugged. "Then you have sealed their fate. None but I can open this cage. Even if I fall in battle this day, what remains of your council is destined to spend the remainder of their miserable lives within the confines of these wires." The mage's face twisted into an evil grimace. "Unless," he waved *Pendromar* near the wires of the cage and it began to shrink.

Bahamut stood and jabbed a finger at the mage. "Stop! You cannot do this!"

Sordaak looked up and his eyes locked with those of his elder. "Cannot? Or will not? *Give me what I want!*" Sordaak shouted.

Unable to tear his eyes from the shrinking cage, the elder male shook his head slowly. "I cannot."

"So be it," the mage hissed. Abruptly he dropped the cage and, gripping *Pendromar* with both hands, he swung it like a club and smacked the three canaries such that the cage skittered across the slick floor and slammed into a wall.

The old man shook with rage. With an enormous effort he fought that down. "Do you feel better?"

Sordaak shrugged. "Somewhat."

"You insolent little twerp! I have had enough of your—"

"Silence!" The sorcerer shouted. "I have had enough of *your* stalling." He lowered his voice slightly. "I can see in your eyes that you know of the prophesy. My troupe and I are *destined* to raise Valdaar. We can do this one of two ways, old man: You can give me what I want, or I can pry them from your cold, dead talons!" Sordaak was mad. "Your choice." Sordaak forced down the knot growing in his throat. "Now which will it be?"

Chapter Twenty-Nine

Bahamut, The Platinum Dragon

Bahamut stood to his full height, his eyes turned reptilian, and his skin took on a metallic sheen. "You have tested my patience beyond what I can endure. Bear the wrath of your words, puny human!"

Finally! Sordaak knew he had a finite period of time while the dragon changed form to get prepared. With no wasted motion he went through a well-planned sequence, casting enhancements on himself to maximize both his protection and the damage his spells would do. It was a process he had taken to calling "buffing."

The mage looked up just in time to see the dragon lunge at him. He managed to squeeze his staff, activating the powerful shield he had recently unlocked therein.

Bahamut's talons and teeth drew lightning-like bolts from the shield when they made contact, but they could not penetrate the invisible barrier protecting the mage.

Sordaak's knees buckled under the strain of keeping the mass of the dragon at bay, but he clenched his teeth, and as the muscles in this neck bulged, the mage fought back to his full height.

The ferocity of the dragon's onslaught forced Sordaak back one step and then a second, but none of the attacks made even a scratch on the wizard. Unfortunately, the shield had a drawback: While it kept the dragon at arm's length, Sordaak couldn't cast spells while it protected him.

The dragon fought the shield ferociously for several moments but soon he realized these attacks were having no effect. Bahamut screamed and exhaled a stream of fire that also parted at the shield, leaving the magicuser singed but otherwise unharmed. The beast howled in frustration, moved a few feet away and began casting spells. Chain Lightning was first, followed by Cone of Cold and then Meteor Swarm in rapid succession.

All were turned away by his protective shield, although Sordaak was beginning to worry; the shield's duration was limited.

Again the dragon screamed in frustration, but this time the sorcerer anticipated the lull. He dropped the shield, gripped the staff with both hands and swung it with all his might and hit the surprised dragon on the end of his nose. While normally this would have had little or no effect, the Storm Giant cloak augmented the mage's strength to that of a giant and *Pendromar* had some special effects attuned just for dragons, as well.

The resulting contact lit up the dragon with an explosion of sound and light, and the force of the swing knocked the beast's head around, his eyes watering to the point where he couldn't see. Without hesitation Sordaak shouted the words to the chain lightning spell he had prepared, causing bolts of electricity to dance all along Bahamut's metallic scales looking for and finding gaps in the armor to penetrate the skin beneath.

The dragon screamed again, this time in excruciating pain, writhing as the magicuser noted the success of that particular spell. He followed it with another and then another for good measure. But Bahamut leapt into the air, beating his massive wings in an effort to escape this human that was causing him so much misery.

It was what Sordaak had been expecting, however. He eschewed a fourth lightning spell, instead changing it up with a Meteor Storm. The dragon had not had much time to gain altitude, and at close range damage done by the meteors was devastating. The balls of fire blew holes in the membrane of the dragon's wings, and Bahamut flailed helplessly as he began to lose height and control. The Lord of Dragons bellowed in pain and frustration, but then he rolled over, turning his free fall into a dive pointed directly at the source of his pain.

But Sordaak was ready for that, too. He squeezed *Pendromar* hard and again the protective shield formed around him. This time he extended the base of the shield such that it rooted itself on the polished marble of the floor. The mage planted the staff at his feet and braced for impact.

Bahamut slammed into the globe, talons and teeth extended to rip flesh from bone, only to be brushed aside as if he'd hit an obelisk of solid rock.

Even with the protection of the Globe of Invulnerability, the sheer mass of the dragon knocked the mage to his knees. Seeing the dragon was stunned, Sordaak pushed to his feet, dropped the shield and again swung his staff with all his might. This time the metal head of the staff slammed the dragon on the side of his head, snapping it around as if it were a marble attached to a string.

Under the force of the blow Bahamut rolled to his right, his claws and wings flailing uncontrollably. Then the dragon seemed to pull it together, continuing the roll to gain distance from this pesky human. Finishing the second roll, the Lord of Dragons regained his footing and shook his head to clear the ringing.

Relentless, Sordaak stepped after the monster and cast another spell, this time going with Ice Storm, hoping to blind the dragon while doing at least some damage. The dragon screamed and flailed around, clearly unable to see. The mage stepped in and followed the Ice spell with another Chain Lightning.

But Bahamut had been feigning blindness! Anticipating the mage would step in if he thought his foe was blind, the dragon lunged at the unsuspecting human.

Sordaak saw the blow coming, but he couldn't react in time before contact was made. He only managed to bring his staff up in a feeble attempt to block the oncoming talons. While this action probably kept the sorcerer from being raked from head to toe by the razor-sharp claws of the beast, it did nothing to absorb the energy of the thrust itself and the sorcerer was knocked backward toward the wall. The wooden foot failed the mage at this point and he tripped and fell hard to the stone floor.

Bahamut, sensing that victory was at hand, followed the physical attack with another blast from his maw, this time an icy blast in place of the fire he had used previously.

Only his pre-battle preparations kept Sordaak from serious harm as the resistance spell absorbed the majority of the energy from the dragon's breath weapon. However, he had been trying to regain his feet when the full force from the dragon caught him square in the chest, knocking him back closer to the wall. *I wish I'd paid more attention in my tumbling classes*, he thought as both knees and elbows scraped painfully across the floor.

Sordaak hit the wall with enough force to knock the wind from him. Blindly, he brought his free hand up to wipe the frost from his face, only to see the dragon charging at him, claws and teeth bared to finish the mage.

The spellcaster quickly threw down a wall of fire a few feet out, hoping the spell's lingering effects would continue to draw the monster's attention toward him, because it was now time to get some help. At the last possible second he squeezed *Pendromar* and brought the last Globe of Invulnerability the staff had up for his protection.

He felt the ferocity of the incensed dragon' attack and hoped his companions heard his cry for them to begin their assault through all the noise.

They did. Vorgath had been cheating closer to the action, and with his ears tuned to the voice of the magicuser he was the first to react. The barbarian raised *Flinthgoor* high over his head and shouted a cry of battle, running at full speed to engage the enemy.

He was followed immediately by Pentaath, who had a sword and shield in his hands—both given to him by the barbarian, who reasoned he would need neither. Remembering the task he'd been assigned, he pulled the amulet given to him by his father from his belt and slid it beneath a scale on the dragon's leg, trusting in the gooey substance Sordaak had covered the device with to hold it in place. Briefly he hoped it would work as planned. Then he stabbed beneath another scale with the sword and promptly forgot about the amulet.

Breunne immediately loosed a volley of the special dragon bane arrows, noting with satisfaction that each sank to the feathers in the beast's neck. He followed the barbarian more slowly, loosing arrows with each step, knowing the damage done by each was more than he could do with his sword. But, alas, he soon ran out of those precious arrows and had to toss *Xenotath* aside and draw his sword and dagger. These in hand, he waded in and began work on the flank opposite the dwarf.

Thrinndor had been less sure he'd heard the call to arms, but ultimately he decided the charging dwarf must have, so he charged in. As he did, the paladin reached out to the sorcerer with his health-sense, knowing he could do nothing for him as long as the shield was up. But he wanted to know whether his ministrations would be necessary when he could. The mage's injuries were to this point slight, however, and the paladin turned his attention to doing what damage he could as he stepped up to fight next to Breunne.

The dragon's attention was indeed locked on the sorcerer. The four men—or, rather, three men and a dragon in human form—had free rein on the monster's flanks. Vorgath with *Flinthgoor* was in particular doing incredible damage to the King of all Dragons, and Thrinndor wondered idly just how long the beast's attention would be on the mage.

It didn't take long to find out the answer.

Bahamut shrieked as he clawed ineffectively at the Globe that protected the mage and then spun to deal with the pesky creatures causing him so much pain from behind. He'd tried brushing them away with his tail, but all he had to show for that effort was a shorter tail.

The dragon brushed aside an unarmored human he didn't recognize to focus his attention on the dwarf he did know wielding a greataxe he knew from centuries past. *Damn, that hurt!* Bahamut first cut loose with his fiery breath before raking the impudent dwarf with both claws. This seemed to have little effect on the puny human, so he snapped at the dwarf with his jagged teeth.

Sordaak saw that he was losing the dragon's attention and dropped the globe. Noting that direct contact with his staff had done the most damage to this point, he took the two steps necessary and bounded up onto the monster's back. Balance was tricky with his wooden appendage and a moving dragon, but the mage fought for control and swung *Pendromar* with everything he had, adding a Shocking Grasp spell for good measure.

When the head of the sorcerer's staff made contact the usual explosion occurred, this time with several scales becoming dislodged. Bahamut's howl of pain was so loud that it hurt the humans' ears. Still the dragon's attention remained focused on the dwarf.

Vorgath felt searing agony as the dragon's razor sharp talons shredded his skin from shoulder to hip along his left side even through the rage he had developed. This caused him to turn and thus see the jaws of impending death racing toward him. *Flinthgoor* was too far into the dwarf's current swing to be of any use in blocking the attack, so the barbarian dove toward the floor, rolling quickly to his left. This put him directly under the chin of the monster, where he launched himself back to his feet and swung his greataxe with all his might.

Bahamut's jaws snapped shut where the dwarf had been only a split-second before. And then a blinding flash of pain obscured everything else as *Flinthgoor* penetrated deep into his lower jaw. The resulting roar momentarily deafened the companions as the dragon writhed in agony while he attempted to clear his mind to make his escape.

Sordaak swung his staff again, and again he was able to knock a patch of scales free, exposing the silvery-pinkish skin beneath. He used the impetus to launch his way clear of the heaving back of the dragon. The mage landed awkwardly on his wooden foot, severely twisting his ankle, which dropped him to his knees. He reached down and quickly released the thongs holding it in place, surprised to see his own foot had grown significantly larger than before. Seeing that the manufactured appendage was no longer needed, he cast it aside and used *Pendromar* to help him to his feet. He was going to have to limp until the foot grew back fully, but this was going to be far better than that which had been made for him.

Feeling better, the sorcerer turned back to confront the dragon in time to see the monster wink out of sight. *Shit!*

"I'll be back with the damn dragon shortly!" Sordaak shouted. "Heal up and remain prepared!" He looked over at the paladin. "Find that bumbling rogue and—more importantly—that healer!" The mage then reached up and grasped the gold chain wrapped around his left wrist. Briefly he hoped this worked as he too winked out of the others' sight.

"Status report!" Thrinndor bellowed into the suddenly empty and completely quiet chamber.

"Good," replied the ranger. He hadn't been harmed in any way during the encounter.

"Also good," Pentaath said.

"Not good—" began the barbarian. His eyes rolled back into his head and he fell backwards to the polished marble floor and lay still.

"Damn!" spat the paladin as he rushed to his friend's side. Breunne and Pentaath did likewise. A quick glance was all that was required to see what ailed the dwarf, as much of his lifeblood lay spilled in a pool beneath him.

For about half a heartbeat Thrinndor hesitated, remembering he was to keep his healing powers in reserve to keep Sordaak alive. But also remembering the mage saying that they must all survive if any were to do so, he placed his hands on the dwarf's chest and whispered a prayer to Valdaar as he released his healing powers.

The shredded skin melded together, and the bleeding mostly stopped. Vorgath's eyes fluttered open, and a confused look crossed his face as he struggled to identify his surroundings. Abruptly he sat up, but a large hand on his shoulder prevented him from rising further.

"Easy, old friend," the paladin said soothingly. "You have lost a lot of blood."

Vorgath scowled at his friend, reached down and loosed the thong on a skin of wine and raised it to his lips. The barbarian drank deeply from the contents, quaffing fully half of it before removing it from his lips. A loud sigh was next, followed by, "Said bodily fluids replaced—the important ones, anyway." He smiled at the big fighter and took Breunne's proffered hand and climbed unsteadily to his feet. The dwarf then cocked an eye at Thrinndor. "Shouldn't one—or more—of us be looking for that damn thief?"

"Damn!" the paladin said for the second time. He had forgotten the directive from the sorcerer. It was something he should have thought of as well. "Pentaath, you and Breunne go find them. Start there," he said as he pointed to a small door opposite the much larger ones they had come through into the chamber.

Both nodded and made their way around the raised platform that held the chairs. Neither wanted to go directly across the raised dais.

"If you do not find them quickly, meet us back here in ten minutes." Again the ranger nodded.

*

Sordaak felt the icy fingers of transition claw at his inner being as he made the leap from the Material Plane to wherever it was the dragon had gone. He hoped.

Scorching heat from walls made of fire threatened to sear the skin from his body, but the mage knew his protective spells would keep that from happening for a time. Fire. The dragon had chosen fire for his first foray into Plane Walking. He had expected that. So far his plan was going pretty much as he'd expected.

There! Sordaak spotted the dragon through the flames not far off. While in a different plane of existence, the two maintained their distance as if they remained back in the Material Plane. Only in the Plane of Fire solid objects were flame-based.

Bahamut had beaten him here and was trying to move away to lick his wounds—or heal them. *That cannot be allowed to happen!* The sorcerer raised *Pendromar* and blasted the dragon with a single bolt of lightning. He hoped the concentrated effect of a single bolt would penetrate deeper into the Lord of Dragon's body.

But the bolt skimmed harmlessly along the surface of Bahamut's scales and then disappeared into a wall of flame beyond the giant creature. *Damn! He has cast spells making him resistive to my lightning attacks!* "Very well," Sordaak muttered as he called forth an Ice Storm, using the powers bestowed upon him by the giant's cloak. He hoped the contrast between fire and ice would cause more damage than normal in this plane.

It did.

Bahamut roared in pain and frustration as he spun to face his tormentor. The spell of massive healing he'd been trying to cast on himself was interrupted by the sleet pelting his hide with ice. He focused on the magicuser some twenty feet away. *How had he followed me here so quickly? That matters not! He will surely die here without his allies!* The dragon opened his maw and cut loose with his own icy breath weapon at close range. *Two can play that game!*

Sordaak saw the icy blast coming, and having anticipated this attack he was able to deflect much of it with his staff. The mage smiled and took a step toward the dragon. "Is that all you've got?" he shouted. Pointing *Pendromar* at his adversary, he launched a volley of meteors at the creature.

Bahamut's eyes widened in surprise at the use of this very exclusive spell and braced for impact as the fiery orbs grew and slammed unerringly into his body. He was knocked back a few steps, and now dragon blood oozed from more than one deep wound. The dragon began to feel the first nudge of fear grasp at his heart.

The Lord of Dragons brushed that fear aside and coiled his mighty legs, launching himself upward. His damaged wings clawed at the air, and he was able to pull himself aloft only with great effort. He prepared another healing spell.

Again anticipating the move, Sordaak spread the fingers of his right hand. Sticky bands of an ultra-strong substance shot from his fingertips and sped toward the dragon trying to escape. Web—but not your father's web. These strands had the strength of spun adamantine.

Bahamut tried to spin away, all thoughts of healing brushed aside for the moment. However, the strands quickly spread out and covered him with their sticky surface. His wings fouled, the dragon plummeted to the floor of the chamber, where he landed with a crash that shook the floor underneath.

Stunned by the impact, the Lord of Dragons again felt the icy vestiges of fear tug at his heart. *Ice.*

Sordaak watched as the dragon again winked out of his perceivable vision. Quickly, he snatched two vials tied together from the quick-release thongs at his belt, ripped the seals from them and downed the contents. As he felt the power of the pneumonic enhancer flow through his veins and thereby restoring a portion of his spell energy, the mage flipped the empty vials aside, wrapped his fingers around the gold chain on his wrist and squeezed.

Immediately the transition took him, and he fought the panic that always seemed to arise when traversing the planes.

Ice. This dragon is too predictable! And that was beginning to scare the mage. Sordaak pointed his staff and shot a prepared series of fireballs at his opponent who remained constrained by the web spell.

Bahamut fought the web pinning his wings to his body. The blasts from the fireball, while they did their usual harm, actually helped free him from the bindings. The dragon roared as he sprang at the mage.

This Sordaak hadn't expected. The dragon was most powerful when he was using his spells on offense. Claws, talons and teeth were usually relegated to the lesser dragons. With the Invulnerability spells exhausted from his staff, the sorcerer had to trust in the normally much less useful Shield spell he had in his repertoire. He barely had time to call it up before the dragon was on him.

The magicuser felt the monster's claws rake his skin, easily bypassing the shield and completely unaffected by his protective cloak. White-hot pain flashed up and down his body as he tried to dive beneath the enormous tooth-filled mouth arcing toward him. But the dragon had seen this move before and adjusted his attack. The result was that the mage was trapped neatly between the teeth of Bahamut's upper and lower jaws.

Why the dragon didn't immediately try to crush the life out of his foe Sordaak would probably never know, but the hesitation worked to the sorcerer's advantage. He fought the excruciating pain in his side and twisted his body so that he could wedge *Pendromar* between the upper and lower plates of the beast's maw. Then he squeezed hard on the polished wooden shaft, sending tendrils of electricity along its length, combining both his spell power and that of the staff in the hope he could prompt the monster to spit him out.

Not exactly. The electric shock involuntarily caused the dragon's jaw muscles to clench, trying ever harder to snap shut. Sordaak could feel the tension in the jaw grow, and he hoped the staff could handle the additional pressure put on it, but he needn't have worried—*Pendromar* was constructed to withstand far worse.

Sordaak felt the dragon's head whip from side to side, trying to dislodge or otherwise stop the pain wracking his mouth. The mage continued to pour energy into the spell, and he could smell the burning flesh from where the electricity made connection with the damp skin. Suddenly the jaws opened wide and the magicuser and his staff were flung at a wall of ice not far away.

Sordaak only had time to brace himself before slamming into the wall every bit as hard as its stone counterpart in the Material Plane. Once again the air left his lungs in an explosive rush as he slid down the wall and crumpled into a heap on the floor, his chest heaving in an effort to draw in oxygen.

As his vision cleared, Sordaak briefly wondered why the dragon had not moved in for the kill; the mage was doubtful he could have stopped him in his current state. Then he saw why. Bahamut had left this domain. The sorcerer grasped the chain on his wrist and squeezed, bracing for the even colder feeling of being in transition, but nothing happened!

His eyes went to his wrist to verify the chain hadn't been knocked loose. It hadn't. *What the—?* He searched the icy floor for what he hoped he would not find, yet was fairly certain he would. He did.

His mind racing, Sordaak surged to his feet and ran over to the amulet, scooped it up and stood upright. *Where would that damn dragon go next? To yet another plane—perhaps even back to fire—to heal? Or would his fear of the sword being found take him back to the Material Plane?*

Sordaak couldn't use the device on his wrist any longer to follow the Lord of Dragons, so he recited the brief incantation required. *Fire.* Surely Bahamut would be secure in his knowledge that he had hidden the sword well enough and his need for healing would override any concern as to its vulnerability. It also seemed reasonable to assume the dragon would not be expected to backtrack to a realm he'd already been to.

The icy tendrils of being in between planes were indeed making themselves felt as he burst into the same chamber as before, and again the walls were flame-based.

The magicuser could feel energy being drawn from the surroundings in preparation to cast a spell and knew he had surmised correctly. He quickly glanced right and left. *There!* The abbreviated tail of the dragon was just disappearing through a massive doorway to his left.

The distance between them was too great for any of his uber-powerful spells, so he flipped a series of force darts after the retreating monster. The tail of the dragon was gone by the time the darts got to the doorway, but Sordaak knew that spell never missed its target—another reason he'd selected it—and they bent around the corner in pursuit. However, he also knew they didn't do much in the way of harm.

The howl of pure frustration that made its way back to the mage as he sprinted toward the door told him all he needed to know: His darts had hit their mark and again disrupted any spell of healing that was in progress. He was also pretty sure the dragon was confused that he had somehow been followed again.

Sordaak rounded the corner in pursuit of the dragon only to be knocked into the wall behind him by a huge bolt of lightning. The resulting pain from both the electricity and the flames of the wall was excruciating, and he nearly lost consciousness. Only the buff spells he had performed earlier kept him alive. *Damn! I've grown too confident!* The mage ignored the debilitating agony in his chest and rolled back into the throne chamber just as another bolt of electricity split the air he'd just vacated.

Sordaak knew this time he'd been seriously injured, but he also knew he didn't have time to do anything about it. The dragon was probably renewing his health during the short time the sorcerer had lain there trying to regain his breath.

The mage triggered an amulet around his neck to cast the Fly spell, pushed himself clear of the floor and flew around the corner of the doorway, his speed ever increasing as he went. Sordaak spat the words to his Cone of Cold spell and blindly blasted away at where the dragon had been.

He's not there! Shit! The flames on a wall sizzled and were briefly extinguished from the power of the mage's icy blast. Yet within moments the fires burned hotly again. A brief search of the enormous chamber he'd entered showed no sign of his quarry. *Dammit!*

Pentaath, is Bahamut there? He asked his linked dragon.

His response was a confused, *No.*

Find the sword! He fired back at his young understudy. Sordaak again sensed the confusion of the young dragon but he didn't have time to explain.

Dammit! Without thinking, the mage uttered the words to the Plane Travel spell and he went instantly from the searing heat of the Plane of Fire into the frozen nothingness of being in between. Sordaak knew he needed to find Bahamut fast. He also knew he needed to somehow re-attach the amulet to the beast. He couldn't travel fast enough through the five main planes to catch the dragon.

Not only that, but Sordaak also knew he was at a distinct disadvantage because he didn't know the layout of the Lord of Dragons' lair. *This is not going as planned…*

Without warning, the sorcerer burst through into yet another plane, this time the Ethereal plane of existence. While the mage had done considerable travel among the Planes in preparation for this battle, the Ethereal plane upset his senses the most. The walls in the dragon's lair while in the Material plane were here, they just didn't mean much—they were more of a *suggestion*.

It was Sordaak's turn to be frustrated. He had just about completed a cursory search of his surroundings when his excited familiar spoke again. *Bahamut is here!*

Hold him. That didn't even make sense to the magicuser as he quickly recited the words to his Plane Travel spell. The tentacles of ice gnawed at his psyche during what seemed a prolonged trip through the netherworld, but he finally crashed through to *his* plane.

Relief washed over him as he could once again breathe normally. Realizing he was alone in the chamber, he stretched out his senses looking for his adversary.

There! Sordaak sensed the power being drawn to a point through the doors on the opposite side of the chamber from him. *Follow him if you can. He'll lead you to the sword.*

Fear gripped his heart when he got no response, but the knowledge that Bahamut could do no harm to his charge without Sordaak knowing it calmed the mage somewhat. The flying spell was still active so he aimed for the doors and flew at top speed through them into yet another massive chamber. *That damn dragon must have carved out the entire base of this mountain!* During the flight he took time to down two more of the Pneumonic Enhancer potions.

As he emerged into the chamber he saw Bahamut on the far side where he and his friends were doing battle. He could also see the battle was not going well. The dragon had managed to heal most of his wounds—including a new tail—and looked reinvigorated as he brought tooth, claws and tail barbs to bear with stunning results.

Thrinndor was the current focus of the Lord of Dragons' attention, and as such he was bleeding badly from several gashes on his arms and upper torso. He'd lost his shield somewhere along the way and was using both hands on his flaming bastard sword to both attack and defend—neither with much success. His strength was waning rapidly

Vorgath, too, was bloodied from head to foot, but as he was in the throes of yet another rage, he was oblivious to his wounds. He waded in with *Flinthgoor* flailing right and left, each time tearing off another chunk of the dragon's armor or burying itself deep in his flank.

Breunne stood by Thrinndor's side, blocking multiple thrusts at once with one or both of his blades. Steel clanged on talons and teeth as he fought to allow the paladin a moment to get his breath and possibly do some healing.

Pentaath hacked ineffectually with the weapons he'd been given—he simply didn't have the proficiency with what he had in his hands to do much damage.

Sordaak could see that his friends were not going to live long unless something drastic happened. *Go to dragon form, NOW!* The mage prepared a spell as he flew as fast as he could toward the erupting scene playing out before his eyes.

Once in range, he released another series of comets, aiming them at the bulk of the monster's body, not daring to try finesse in a head shot this time around. As the flaming balls of rock sped toward the dragon, Vorgath must have hit a nerve because Bahamut abruptly spun and snapped at the dwarf.

Sordaak watched in horror as the giant maw of the beast engulfed the top half of the barbarian. The muscles in Bahamut's mouth then contracted as his jaws snapped shut. The comets hit at that point and the scene erupted in fire, smoke and confusion as the dragon writhed for a few seconds. Then Bahamut winked out of existence and was gone.

The sorcerer landed and skidded to a halt where he had last seen Vorgath, Thrinndor arriving a split-second later. The smoke cleared, and Sordaak took a step back, his face ashen.

"What?" the paladin began, then he saw what the mage was staring at. On the hard marble floor at their feet was the lower half of the dwarf—just the part from the waist down. Blood was everywhere.

Chapter Thirty

Dragon Bites

Breunne walked up and stood beside the stunned paladin. Pentaath, now in full dragon form, stood silently behind them all.

The muscles in the sorcerer's jaw worked as he ground his teeth. His brows knitted together as he turned to the paladin. "Can you wield *Flinthgoor*?" Now was not the time for mourning.

The paladin blinked twice, forcing back the tears that threatened to betray him. "I do not know."

"Find out," Sordaak said as he pointed to the greataxe left lying next to the barbarian's remains. "It seems to have a power to hurt the dragon like nothing else we have. It must continue to be used in battle."

Thrinndor nodded mutely, his jaw set in obvious resolution. He took the two steps necessary to reach the weapon, hesitating only slightly before bending to pick it up. The paladin disdained to wipe the blood from it; he wanted the dragon to know from whence the pain would come. He tested the balance of the head before whipping it both left and right, up and down. Turning back to the mage he nodded. "I will wield this in Vorgath's honor." A single tear twinkled in the big fighter's left eye before slowly making its way down his cheek.

"See that you do," grated the mage. There was much to be done, yet he was loathe to get started.

"Is the battle not lost?" the ranger asked politely.

Sordaak looked down at his new toes, wiggled them and briefly noted that the marble floor was very cold on his bare foot. "No." He looked up. "While Bahamut has most certainly healed himself back to full strength by this time, he cannot restore his spell energy thus." He swallowed hard, forcing back the bile trying to make its way up into his throat. "We will continue. He has lost many scales, and that makes him vulnerable." The sorcerer removed the amulet from

behind his belt and tossed it to the ranger. "Find a way to affix that to the monster so that I can follow him."

Breunne caught the gold locket and nodded.

Sordaak eyed the paladin. "You must find the sword. It's the only reason the
Lord of Dragons has not left his home. It's here, and he is sworn to protect it.
He will not leave as long as we search for it." The paladin nodded grimly. "The
closer we get to it, the more he will have to visit this plane."

Next he turned to Pentaath. "You must inflict as much damage on him during that time as is possible. Rip a wing from his body, if possible. His flight is
keeping me… busy. I need him to stay earthbound." The mage swallowed hard.
"But ward yourself." Suddenly he jutted his chin forward and narrowed his eyes.
"If you fall, I fall. That must not happen."

The dragon nodded.

Was he even larger than before? Sordaak shook his head in wonder. *Surely his scales
are more metallic than they had been the previous night?* He shook his head again to clear
his mind. *No time for that now.*

"What happened?" It was Cyrillis' voice. She and Savinhand had walked up
on them while they spoke. "Where is Vorgath?"

Sordaak positioned his body between the cleric and the barbarian's legs. It
did no good, there was too much blood. "Oh, no," she moaned. She shoved the
mage aside and knelt beside the grisly remains.

Thrinndor put a hand on her shoulder. "There was nothing that could have
been done, sister."

The healer looked up, a single tear forming in the corner of one eye. "Perhaps
if we had gotten here sooner."

"No." Now it was the mage's turn to attempt comfort. He put a hand
beneath her left arm and pulled her to her feet. ""Nothing could have been done.
Bahamut bit him in two with a single bite—our attention had been elsewhere."

Savinhand's grim voice belied his expressionless visage. "Is there nothing
that can be done for him?"

Cyrillis, who had been studying the eyes of the magicuser, looked down at
the bloody corpse and shook her head. "No." Her emotions threatened to break
the dam she had built. "I could perhaps raise him if he were whole." She shook
her head slowly. "But like this? There is nothing to raise." Her eyes found those
of the paladin. "I am truly sorry."

Thrinndor shook his head in return. "There is nothing you could have
done," he repeated. Placing both hands on the haft of *Flinthgoor* he set his jaw. "I
will deal the death blow to that monster in his honor." Both eyes glistened as the
moisture behind his eyes pushed forward.

Sordaak tapped the heel of *Pendromar* lightly on the cold, hard stone. All eyes
turned to him. The mage sought those of the healer. "Has Savin briefed you

on our plan?" She brushed back a tear with her free hand and nodded. "Good. Those plans remain intact. What is the status of your healing powers?"

The cleric lifted her chin slightly, but her gaze fell to what was left of the dwarf. "I am ready to heal as necessary with my full complement of power."

"Good," the mage repeated. He shifted his gaze so that it encompassed those that remained. "Find the sword. Bahamut will have to come to you then. Until that time," he loosed a thong on his belt holding two more of the spell energy potions, "I'll annoy him." He downed both pots at once, smiled at the healer and disappeared.

"Be careful, my love," the cleric whispered after him.

The sorcerer again entered the space in between planes. *I feel the effects of this damn cold compound each time I pass through!* He thought as the needles of ice stabbed ever deeper into his muscles. *It seems to take longer, too. But that could just be the result of thinking it's colder...*

Abruptly he burst through into the Ethereal Plane again. Closing his eyes, he reached out with all of his senses, trying to pick up on the use of spell energy while he rubbed his arms vigorously. Nothing. In the back of his mind he idly wished he'd gone to the Plane of Fire first. He was certain the dragon wouldn't allow that bit of comfort, though. He barked the incantation and ended with "*Ice!*"

I must find him soon! This Plane Walk spell uses far too much energy. His hand went to his belt and loosed yet another pair of flasks of the precious energy potion. As he popped through into the realm of ice, he simultaneously reached out with his senses and ripped the seal from both flasks. As he downed the fluid, he felt the sudden release of energy nearby.

Trap!

Sordaak dropped the flasks and steeled himself for whatever spell was to come as his left hand dove beneath his cloak, coming out with a scroll. First one comet and then at least four more hammered into him, knocking him onto his backside.

Again, only the buffs he had done prior to battle, and redone after the death of his friend, saved him from certain death. His slight frame was not built to withstand the force of such an attack. However, even with his enhancement spells he was seriously hurt.

As he fumbled for the scroll that had been knocked from his hand, he felt the dragon move nearer.

"Here to reclaim the other half of that measly dwarf?" The Lord of Dragons chuckled. "You waste your energy." He laughed openly now.

Sordaak's nearly numb hands grasped the scroll at last. Without showing what he had in mind, he unfurled it and formed the words written there silently with blue lips.

"You will have to carve what remains of his fat torso from my—"

The sorcerer lunged to his feet and pointing the index finger of his left hand at the monstrous dragon not twenty feet away and shouted the trigger word. Comets sped from his finger at the beast; two could play that game! "Very well," he shouted. "If you *insist*!"

The dragon's chuckle became a full-throated laugh as the comets bounced harmlessly off of an invisible shield three feet before coming into contact with the beast.

Dammit! The dragon had used the mage's own tactic against him. Well, he was *supposed* to be the smartest creature in the land, after all. Sordaak dove to the ground and rolled quickly to his left as Bahamut jumped at him, clearly intending to crush the sorcerer between the ice of the floor and his shield.

Sordaak hoped the shield was the one that only protected from spell energy, not physical attacks, as he rolled to his feet and sprinted past the surprised creature. Next he did more of the unexpected by leaping onto the monster's back. Once there, he slammed the head of his staff home with both hands to devastating effect. Three scales were knocked loose and the skin beneath bloodied from the force of the blow. *Damn! I'm liking this Storm Giant Strength!*

The dragon bellowed and leapt into action before the mage could get in another blow. Sordaak dove at the dragon's neck, grasped a couple of scales and slid around as Bahamut flipped over, intending to smash the magicuser into the floor with his sheer mass.

"You're getting slow in your old age!" shouted the mage as he swung his staff again with both hands, this time connecting with the jaw of the dragon as his head came around. He was trying to see where the human had gone. Sordaak didn't know how much damage he had done this time, but if the sudden numbness in his hands was any indication, it must surely have been considerable.

Indeed. The force of the blow hammered the dragon's jaws shut, cutting him off mid-screech and knocking his head around like a ball on a string where it slammed into a wall of ice with a thunderous boom. Momentarily stunned, the dragon shook his head side to side in an effort to clear it.

Sordaak gave him no quarter, however, as he stepped in behind the blow and whipped the staff around for another. This time the head was out of reach, so he decided to see what he could do at the base of his neck where the monster's massive chest muscles contracted to draw in air. Sordaak decided to sweeten the pot by applying his Shocking Grasp spell, as well.

At the point of contact, fingers of electricity exploded along the shaft and weaved their way among the scales of the beast, disappearing beneath them to find the soft skin beneath as before. The results were even more devastating. Too many scales to count were sent flying as the mage continued to pour energy from his spell into the shaft of his staff. Quickly the skin blackened and became charred under the assault.

Bahamut roared in pain and instinctively jumped backward, causing the mage's next blow to narrowly miss the mark. Sordaak was thrown off-balance by the impetus of his swing.

Reflex took over and the dragon spun, whipping his barbed tail around in an effort to block this more than pesky human who dared combat him solo.

Too late Sordaak saw the end of the tail flashing toward his neck like a scythe. The mage arched his back and threw himself toward the icy floor at his feet, but the barb adjusted its trajectory to compensate. The razor-sharp barb easily sliced through the mage's robe and deep into the skin of his left side. The sorcerer felt white-hot pain as the barb continued its path, ripping a deep furrow from his lower front side diagonally up until it broke free just under his arm.

Through the pain, Sordaak gritted his teeth, stepped after the retreating dragon and blindly swung *Pendromar* with both hands. He hadn't time for another spell, hoping his continued assault would force the dragon to retreat. Again the staff hit home, this time on the monster's right foreleg, snapping the smaller bone there and rendering that leg useless.

But the sorcerer was injured more than he would admit to even himself. A new tactic was required. "Surrender, and I will allow you to live," he shouted as he whirled the staff around his head to gain momentum. The move caused his eyes to water as his side screamed at him in torment. The staff connected mid-thigh on the beast, knocking that leg out from under the dragon and sending several more scales skittering across the floor

"*Surrender?* I think not!"

"Very well," the sorcerer said through the searing pain in his side. "Please remember that I offered when you cross over." Sordaak slammed his staff onto a nearby claw that Bahamut was using to try to push back to his feet. Sordaak felt bones crush beneath the clad heel of the staff, and Bahamut bellowed in pain. "Surely you realize," the sorcerer shouted as he cracked the staff full force across a nearby knee joint, "that I am but the diversion. My friends certainly have located the sword by now and your death would be meaningless."

Sordaak saw the tail barb coming in time to duck as it whipped by harmlessly.

"You lie!" the dragon screamed, backpedaling and trying to regain his feet at the same time—difficult at best when on a sheet of ice with four good appendages. But with only two, he was fighting a losing battle and knew it. What he didn't know was that Sordaak was about to fall over from lack of blood himself.

"Do I?" the mage threw back. He barely had time to bring the staff up to block a flame breath attack, knowing he had to or go down for the last time. Somehow the flames buoyed his spirit, however. "Think about it. Why would I follow you alone?" He was stalling, but in so doing he was losing too much blood. Sordaak swung off-balance, yet still managed to knock a couple of scales from the lower abdomen of the creature. *He, too, must have been inactive for centuries!*

There is no way I should be able to knock the scales from any dragon with this ease, let alone the King of all Dragons! The sorcerer gritted his teeth to keep from crying out.

Yet somehow the mage maintained his feet, using *Pendromar* as a crutch when required. Whenever he got close enough, Sordaak would swing with whatever strength he could muster, sometimes knocking more scales from the beast, still others knocking a supporting leg out from under him.

And then suddenly the dragon was gone.

Finally!

Sordaak cleared his mind. *He's on the way and he's badly hurt. Finish him, and we'll find the sword together!*

Aye, father.

The mage pushed himself upright and reached over to squeeze the gold chain on his wrist. He knew he was about to fall and didn't have the strength to cast the spell. *I will need hea—*" He was unable to finish the sentence as the frosty tentacles of between the planes sucked his remaining consciousness from him. He felt himself falling and wondered briefly what would happen if he failed to reappear in his own plane? Blackness then took him.

Sordaak actually came through first, falling at the feet of the ranger. Hearing the clatter as *Pendromar* fell to the stone floor, Cyrillis turned and screamed. She rushed to his side, reaching out with her percipience even before kneeling at his side. The healer brushed aside the pain that washed over her once she established a connection and immediately said a prayer of healing. She poured her power into the sorcerer as her hands glided gently across the nasty gash in his side. The skin knitted together as she watched and she turned her attention elsewhere, looking for more injuries. Finding none, she probed his mind with hers. *Awaken, my love.*

The sorcerer's eyes fluttered open and he gazed in wonder at this beautiful woman that hovered over him. *Just how lucky am I?* Reality came flooding back and he shoved her roughly aside.

"Hey!"

Sordaak grasped his staff, used it to push himself to his feet and steady himself once he got there. Suddenly the room was swimming—he had lost too much blood.

Breunne stepped up and grabbed an elbow, further steadying the mage. "Take it easy there, sparky!" He smiled. "You've lost a lot of blood."

"Too much blood," snapped the cleric. "Let me—"

"Where's Bahamut?" the mage demanded, ignoring them. When all he got was blank stares in return, he shouted, "*DAMMIT! Where's that dragon!*"

"What?" demanded the paladin, taken somewhat aback by the sorcerer's reaction. "We have not seen him."

I was tricked! That damn dragon went to another plane to heal! DAMMIT!

The mage's hand went to his belt and came away empty. He had a concerned look on his face as his hands patted several locations on his body. At each spot he got the same results. He was out of spell energy pots. Quickly he removed a bag from his waist, opened it and slid out his folded up portable hole. The sorcerer was in the process of unfolding it when Bahamut burst into the chamber screaming at the top of his voice.

The companions scrambled—all but Sordaak. "Keep him off me," he said as he reached into his device.

Pentaath was the first to go into action. He had been circling high overhead, waiting for what his master had said would come to pass. It did. Almost lazily he folded his wings and dove silently at the back of his adversary.

Bahamut wasted no time engaging his enemy. The paladin was first in his path. The dragon brushed him aside with an almost negligent wave of his newly repaired fore claw. This slightly less puny human stood between him and the mage, who had his back to the action.

Not to be brushed aside with such ease, Thrinndor brought *Flinthgoor* down with both hands onto the tail of the dragon as he passed by, severing it a few feet from where it extended from the body. *Nice axe,* the paladin thought as he turned to give chase.

"Not again!" roared the dragon as he felt his tail once again ripped from his body. He ignored the pain, however; his focus on a familiar cloak kneeling only a few feet away. Bahamut opened his maw and sprayed acid all over the prone mage just as a tremendous weight slammed into him from above. *What the—*

Pentaath, his lower talons extended for battle, hit the Platinum Dragon on his right side, taking great care that he didn't knock the older dragon into his master.

Sordaak, having downed as many of the pneumonic pots as he could and having again tied those that remained to his belt, brushed aside the acid attack and stood slowly to his full height.

The mage then turned to face the dragon, his expression impassive. He watched as the bigger—but only slightly now, the sorcerer was amazed to see—dragon threw his familiar aside. The sorcerer grinned as he stood to his full height.

"Remember," Sordaak said as if he were lecturing a class in the school he was soon to open, "I gave you the opportunity to surrender. Now bear the wrath of Pentaath, Adamantine Dragon and soon to be Lord of all Dragons!" Stunned silence filled the chamber as all eyes—Bahamut's included—turned to see who or what the mage was talking about.

"Over my dead body!" shouted the current King of all Dragons.

"As you wish," Sordaak replied, his voice just barely audible as he used both hands to bring *Pendromar* up to eye height. "Let's finish this," he said through clenched teeth and stepped toward the dragon.

As one the companions followed suit and hammered away at their adversary. Pentaath was in glorious full fury, lashing out with talon and tooth, driving the

Platinum Dragon farther back into the chamber. Sordaak alternated blasting away with whatever spell came to his lips and knocking scales from the beast with his staff. Breunne secured the amulet where it would not work its way free and stepped far enough back that his bow was again of use. Savinhand leapt onto the back of the dragon and worked his way ever higher, stabbing and hacking as he went. Thrinndor hacked away at whichever flank presented itself, doing what appeared to be enormous damage. Cyrillis did as directed, staying out of the action, instead throwing a heal spell as required to whomever required it. The determination in her face said that no one else would die this day. And that was that.

Sordaak worked his way over to fight beside the paladin since his protégé was now in full command of this fight—at least he had Bahamut's full attention. "Go find *Valdaar's Fist*."

Thrinndor shook his head resolutely. "I am needed here."

Sordaak paused and put a hand on the big fighter's shoulder. "Remember what I said: Only the sword of a god may slay the King of all Dragons."

The paladin took yet another swing, hacking off a chunk of the dragon's thigh. Winded, he allowed his shoulders to droop. "Very well, it will be as you say." Without another word, he turned and sprinted toward the door they had intended to go through when interrupted by the mage's reappearance.

Sordaak then turned and got Savinhand's attention. The sorcerer motioned for the thief to follow the paladin. The rogue nodded and reluctantly slid down the dragon's back and immediately disappeared.

Damn, I wish I could do that! Sordaak thought as he turned back to the dragon. Still weakened by his recent ordeal, he contented himself to doing what damage he could with *Pendromar*, deciding to hold onto his spell energy should that again be needed. He quaffed two more of his potions during a lull in the action just to be sure. There was no sense in saving them at this point. It was now or never.

And then the dragon was gone! Pentaath had been fighting a mostly defensive battle, heeding his master's words concerning his health. Breunne had peppered the beast with arrows in all the places bare of scales and Sordaak had taken to launching an occasional spell as his arms had tired of swinging his staff.

The mage stood upright, checked his spell energy status and reached for his gold wristlet. "Find Thrinndor and stay together!" he shouted. "We'll be right back."

The cold didn't seem so bad this time around. Maybe the cleric's buff spells were better than his own. Frankly, he hoped so. He popped out into the Ethereal Plane again, knowing that Bahamut had preceded him here.

He was greeted by a fiery blast that singed the eyebrows off of his head. "Dammit!" he shouted. "I just got those back!" He raised *Pendromar* and returned fire with fire. Fireballs and gouts of flame shot alternately from the spell storage on the staff and his own supply of energy. *He's low on spell energy! I've got to stay on him. He must not be permitted to use what little he has left to heal himself again.*

The mage walked in behind his spells, moving ever closer to his adversary. He had some devastating spells if he could get close enough. Suddenly he felt good. *This was happening! They were going to finish this dragon! Cyrillis must've cast a spell to invigorate me, because I can't remember ever feeling this GOOD!*

And then the dragon was gone! Again. Sordaak rolled his eyes, knowing they were getting close. *Why prolong it?* He reached up and grasped the wristlet. Nothing happened! Quickly he rushed over to where the dragon had been. *Dammit!* The amulet was again lying on the ground.

But this time he knew where the dragon was going without the aid of the amulet. Thrinndor must be getting close to the sword, and Bahamut could feel it.

Sordaak recited the words to the Plane Travel spell. "Material," he said when he finished.

When he stepped through the portal into his world, leaving behind the cold of transition, he found himself in an empty chamber. Of course, everyone had followed the paladin. He cast his speed spell and took off at a full sprint through the door he had seen the big fighter pass through, his pace augmented by his magic.

The mage had not gone far when he saw his friends not far ahead, standing just inside a massive door at the other end of the hall. He slowed and then skidded to a stop not far from them. The sorcerer was about to ask the obvious question when his eyes caught sight of what they were looking at.

The chamber was one of the largest yet—at least five hundred feet square, with no ceiling in sight. There appeared to be only the doors they had passed through, no others. There were columns interspersed at what appeared to be random intervals with four sconces on each, providing illumination.

But even those impressive features were not what held the companion's attention. Instead, the mounds of gold, platinum and silver coins, interspersed with diamonds, rubies, sapphires and emeralds in piles as far as the eye could see. Suits of armor, highly decorated shields and jewelry littered the floor in between the piles. Treasure was *everywhere*.

But, that still was not what had the paladin's attention. A single ornate throne adorned a raised dais on the other side of the chamber. Behind that throne were a dozen or so swords, each sheathed and each mounted to the wall at about eye height.

Sordaak asked the obvious question. "Can you find your sword in that?" *Where was that damn dragon?*

Thrinndor, his reverie broken, replied, "I know not. There are *so many*!" His voice was barely audible above the mage's pounding heart.

"Surely the sword would speak to you were you to grasp it and pull it from its sheath?"

The paladin shrugged. "That may be so, but as I have never held it, I cannot speak to such as certainty." His eyes never left the row of swords.

"Well, you'd better get on with figuring out which of those is yours, because when Bahamut gets here, he's going to want to have a say in this." His eyes found the ranger. "He was able to again shed the amulet, so I fear he will return once again at full strength."

"Good. This time we will finish him. He cannot possibly have much spell energy remaining." With that, Pentaath stretched his wings and leapt into the air, kicking up a huge cloud of dust and sending many coins skittering across the floor as he did.

"I'm glad one of us is confident," muttered the mage. "I, too, am low on spell energy." He removed the last pair of pots from his belt. He shook his head as he tore the seals from them and dumped them into his mouth. The amount of energy restored by a pneumonic pot was always somewhat random, based loosely on whoever bottled it and the type of ingredients used. Generally, the more expensive the ingredients and the more powerful the alchemist who brewed the potion, the more energy restored to the recipient.

Generally. These last two seemed to barely give the mage a boost at all! Dammit. He turned to the cleric. "Do you have any pneumonic pots?"

She shook her head. "No. *Someone* has been going around buying up everyone's stock!" The glare she leveled at the mage said that she already knew who that someone was. "However," she added, her tone backing off a bit, "I *do* have a few of those enhancements that allow me to boost your spell energy.

Damn, I forgot about those! "Those would be great, if you don't mind," Sordaak said.

"Of course," Cyrillis said. She raised her arms and chanted a brief prayer, and when she lowered her arms Sordaak felt some additional energy coursing through his veins. The cleric repeated this ten times and then announced, "That is it—all I have."

"That will do nicely," Sordaak said. *I hope. Those were certainly appreciated, but still left me only slightly over half.* He shrugged.

The sorcerer sighed. "All right, spread out." He waved his arms for emphasis. "I don't want to be caught as a group when that damn dragon finally decides to make an appearance."

"Perhaps I should check for traps," Savinhand suggested.

Sordaak hesitated, but then shook his head. "I don't think that's necessary. It doesn't fit with what we've encountered so far." He shook his head again. "Go ahead and check where you walk, if you like. Let us doubters know if you find any, though." He winked at the rogue.

Savin smiled. "Will do." He reached out, touched the bracer on his wrist and moved out slowly, casting from side to side, looking for anything unusual.

"Thrinndor, go find your sword. The rest of us will kind of sit back and wait." When the paladin hesitated, the mage said sternly, "Now!" Sordaak then winked at the paladin.

Thrinndor was not amused. He rolled his eyes, shouldered Vorgath's greataxe and weaved his way through the piles of coins toward the throne.

"Not so fast." It was Bahamut in human form, sitting on his throne.

When had he gotten here?

The King of all Dragons looked more the worse for wear than when the sorcerer had last seen him as a human. His raiment was tattered and soaked though with blood in many places. His eyes were haggard and withdrawn. His skin seemed to hang on is body, rather than support the vitality within. "You have gone far enough. Turn, leave and vow to never return to this place and I will allow you to live."

Sordaak's right eyebrow twitched as his jaw dropped. "*You* will allow *us* to live?" He chuckled. "I don't see that as being even remotely funny." The sorcerer put his hands on his hips. "Get out of *our* way, and we *may* yet allow *you* to live!" He folded his arms across his chest and waited.

Bahamut glared at this impudent human for a few moments. And then he began to chuckle. The chuckle grew to a laugh, and the laugh turned to a deep, hacking cough. When the King of Dragons was finally able to control the cough, he wiped his sleeve across his lips, noting briefly that the sleeve was now tainted with blood.

"Well said, young mage," he said weakly. "But then again, I would expect nothing less from Sordaak, the only son of Lord Faantlaw."

Sordaak knew he was supposed to be surprised by this revelation, but he was too tired for surprises. "So, you keep tabs on the mundane world beyond your demesne?" He shrugged. "That doesn't surprise me. You would, of course, want to know of any possible threats to the current reign of power: Praxaar's."

Bahamut's eyes widened slightly. "You are, of course, correct. For thousands of years I have kept my eye on the goings on of man, knowing that one day this day must come."

The mage nodded. "So you're conceding."

Again the dragon laughed, again with the same result. "I must stop doing that," Bahamut said as he drug the cloth of his tattered sleeve across his mouth. "No," he said, his eyes sad. "No I will not concede. I have made too many promises to too many people. And one god." His eyes brightened, and his shoulders squared. "No, if you want the Sword of Valdaar, you are going to have to kill me to get it."

A silence fell upon the chamber that lasted for several moments. Sordaak was the one who finally broke it. "As you wish, old one. But if I may first ask of you one thing?"

"Ask."

"Would you please try to at least put up a fight worthy of passing along in a story to our children?"

That drew a silence that made the previous one loud by comparison. Savinhand was pretty sure he heard the nearby ranger's heart beating over even his own.

Bahamut jumped to his feet. "Why, you arrogant bastard!" He began the process of changing back to dragon form. "For that I will make certain you will have no children with which to pass!"

Savinhand leaned toward the mage. "Now you've done it! You've gone and made him *mad!*"

Sordaak ignored him. "Buff up, people! This ends here." He watched the dragon carefully as the ranger and paladin did what they could to comply, augmented by the special skills of the cleric. Satisfied, the mage took a determined step toward the dais. "Let's do this!" He waved his arms. "Spread out as before, but stay within reach of the healer. Thrinndor, find that sword."

The paladin nodded as he resumed his trek toward the throne. This time, however, he had *Flinthgoor* at the ready.

The Platinum Dragon was fully in dragon form by the time the companions approached the dais. Thrinndor stopped less than ten feet from the dragon. "Move," he grated.

"Make me," the dragon replied.

He's actually enjoying this, Sordaak marveled. Suddenly his senses went on high alert; something was not right.

"Ward yourselves." Cyrillis whispered from her place a few feet back. Clearly, she felt it also.

It was then that Sordaak noticed a crown upon the head of the dragon and a scepter clutched in one of his claws. *Shit! He's got enhancement artifacts!*

Thrinndor started to go around, but the dragon moved to block him. "You shall not pass!" he shouted as he pointed the scepter at the floor in front of the paladin. A wall of fire erupted, and the big fighter was forced to take a step back.

Attack him from above and behind, the sorcerer relayed to his dragon.

On it, came the instant reply.

Sordaak waited until he saw Pentaath flashing into his field of vision, then he raised his staff and began to chant. Abruptly he slammed the shod heel of *Pendromar* to the ground just as Pentaath crashed into Bahamut from behind.

The ground began to shake beneath the raised part of the floor, causing the Lord of Dragons to stumble. Thrinndor dove through the wall of flames during the distraction and tumbled his way to the feet of the giant creature. Timing his tumble perfectly, he jumped back to his feet and swung Vorgath's axe with everything he had. The enchanted blade hummed in his hands as it passed cleanly through several scales and buried itself deep in the dragon's upper thigh.

Bahamut roared in pain, but he was too busy with another dragon to do anything about the pest around his ankles. Pentaath had succeeded in getting the bigger dragon's attention. Sordaak's pet sank claws and teeth into the back of the Lord of Dragons, dragging him backward off of the platform. But he'd underestimated the older, more battle-tested dragon. Bahamut threw himself into the younger dragon and both lost their balance. The bigger dragon landed on top of Pentaath, driving the air from his lungs.

The Platinum Dragon rolled over and stood, clearly favoring the leg Thrinndor had recently had moderate success with. Bahamut swung his scepter club-like at the head of the younger dragon.

Pentaath never saw it coming. Flashing pain exploded in his head as the scepter cracked both scale and bone.

Sordaak, his staff raised to again strike stone, felt the same exploding pain in his skull. He screamed and dropped like a sack of potatoes.

Cyrillis rushed to the mage's side, not knowing what ailed him. She reached her healing powers into his mind, finding the pain but not the cause. It was when she removed his skull cap that she saw the mashed spot on the back of his head. Blood, bone and gray matter comingled into a morass that matted his long hair. "No," she moaned.

Surprised by the mage going down, Bahamut smiled in satisfaction. "Ah, a two-for-one deal. I always figured they were somehow connected, and now I know." The dragon turned his attention to the paladin. "Three down and," he glanced around quickly, not seeing the rogue, "four to go. Without your caster, I will be able to deal with the rest of you in short order."

"Not so fast, blubber butt!" Savinhand shouted as he jumped from a column he had scaled down onto the dragon's back. As usual he held his vorpal sword and kukri before him, each sinking to the hilt under the rogue's weight.

Cyrillis remained oblivious to the others in the chamber, focusing her attention on the sorcerer. But as he was not harmed by direct contact, she decided he could not be healed by the same. Her one foray into direct healing got no results. A good sign was that he continued to breathe. However, it was the labored breathing of one seriously injured.

The three remaining men were in direct conflict with the Lord of Dragons now. The cleric reminded herself that she must keep tabs on their health while she continued her work here. She climbed back to her feet, brushed a wayward lock of hair out of her eyes and made her way quickly around the dais. As she walked, she touched up the health on the companions with varying degrees of heal spells.

When she approached Pentaath, doubt again seized her heart. She had no knowledge of dragon physiology—and that was required for her to be able to work her healing magic. On humans—and humanoids—the heart was always in the same place, as was the brain and many of the vital organs. On a dragon? She shook her head as she knelt beside the massive head of the creature that had become so vital to their mission. As on Sordaak, the dragon's chest continued to rise and fall with regularity.

A yelp of pain through clenched teeth from behind her caused the cleric to raise her hand, point in that direction and mutter a prayer of Healing at the paladin. Once again she automatically checked the other two, all the while never losing focus on the patient lying on the marble floor in front of her.

She could see the skull was severely damaged along the back of the crown. Shards of bone mingled with shredded skin, and there was the brain. She could see where it had taken a direct hit and had been damaged. There was also blood everywhere. Cyrillis took great care to ensure she did not come into contact with that blood—she'd heard too many stories as to what happened when one did.

Well, the brains are in the same place, and the damage done to both Pentaath and Sordaak seem to be related. The healer once again quickly checked the status of the others before diving in, knowing this might take her a while. She flipped the paladin another minor spell to stop some bleeding, but he would live she surmised.

Cyrillis took a deep breath, closed her eyes and began to chant. Feeling with her mind, she reached out her percipience and first removed the bone shards. The brain was bruised at the point of impact, but did not appear to be crushed or broken. She applied healing to the bruise and was gratified when the dull gray color returned, replacing the bluish-purple that had dominated the area. A deep calm settled over her as she worked; this is what she was born to do. Anyone watching would only have seen a blur of movement as her hands put the dragon's head back together. In the calm that was her workplace she could seemingly take hours to do what was necessary. Yet in real time only seconds would elapse.

Next she carefully moved the bone shards and placed them into the jigsaw puzzle that was the dragon's skull. Once all pieces were properly set, she melded the bone together with yet another healing spell. The cleric could see that her patient's breathing was less labored, and a quick stretch of her power showed the same was true for Sordaak. Good.

Lastly, she smoothed the shredded skin back into place and said yet one more prayer as the metallic white covering knitted together and became whole. She was about to revive him with a prayer of restoration when some instinct caused her to duck. Too late. A blinding white-hot pain flashed through her head and she pitched forward across her patient and lay still.

"You have undone enough of my handiwork," the Platinum Dragon said, a smug grin on his face.

The rogue lay unconscious in a heap over next to a column where he had been thrown, and the ranger, while conscious, was of no use with two broken legs and several broken ribs. Bahamut had masked these injuries from her—something the cleric had not even known was possible.

Slowly, deliberately, the Lord of all Dragons turned to face his one remaining adversary. "So now it is just you and I, O descendant of Valdaar. That is as it should be. And when I end your miserable life, so too will end this most recent threat to the peace that has encompassed the land for nigh two millennia." The dragon lowered his head so the two were eye to eye, keeping just out of range of that hated greataxe, *Flinthgoor, Foe Cleaver and Death Dealer*. Yes, that weapon would look good on his wall, the dragon decided.

"Say a final—short—prayer to a god that cannot hear you. I will allow you that bit of peace before I send you to be with him in the afterlife."

Thrinndor, bloodied and scarred, his left ankle mangled horribly, obediently fell to his knees. It was not, however, to pray to his god. He had one remaining paladin heal remaining, and he meant to cast that on himself as he sprinted to the only remaining weapon in the land that could slay his opponent.

During this the final battle he had kept one eye on the swords, crossing off in his mind those blades he knew could not be the one he sought off of the list. Now only two remained. Both were of the proper size and had the required skull affixed to the pommel. Both were wrapped in a sheath of purest Mithryl, and both had an enormous ruby as part of that sheath. There the resemblance ended. One was dull and lifeless, covered in the dust of disuse while the other glittered beautifully in the flickering light from nearby sconces. That blade glowed with life and vitality. The two were side by side, and clearly one was meant to mask the other

Thrinndor had made his choice and knew that he and his companions were going to either live or die by that choice. He had tried several delaying tactics, hoping the mage would awaken and again take up the battle, but he did not. The paladin no longer had any faith in that. *I am all that remains, and I place the outcome on our quest on my shoulders and my shoulders alone. As it should be.*

In one heartbeat the paladin poured the healing power into his own body and thrust himself to his feet, lunging toward the swords. He cast aside the greataxe of his friend knowing that its use was at an end. In the space of two steps he was sprinting at full speed, and the knowledge that the end was near— one way or the other—buoying him as he ran past the surprised dragon.

But only the paladin's sudden movement had caused that surprise. In fact, Bahamut had sensed the duplicity in the paladin's motions and knew something was amiss. "Choose well, O Paladin of the Paladinhood of Valdaar," the dragon shouted. "For if you choose poorly, I will dine on your flesh ere this day is done!"

The Platinum Dragon surged into motion, following the human at his best speed, which was limited by his recent encounters with said human. Still, he was only a few feet behind Thrinndor as the fighter neared the wall. In truth, he planned on ending this fight his way, regardless of which sword the paladin chose.

Instead of running to one sword or the other, the big fighter held out his hand as he approached and shouted, "*Valdaar's Fist*, come to me!"

Instantly, the unsheathed sword was in his hand and he spun to face his adversary, the sword of his god held before him in triumph. Grasping the pommel with both hands he whipped it around in an arc that severed the head of the dragon even as the jaws opened to end his life.

The body and neck minus the head stumbled back a few steps, the stump of the neck weaving around in chaos. There it collapsed and moved no more.

Thrinndor stared down into the eyes of the Lord of Dragons. "You have chosen well," Bahamut said as the life force ebbed from his eyes. Then his eyelids closed for the last time and his breath came no more.

Chapter Thirty-One

A New King

Breathing hard from both the exertion of battle and the thrill of at last holding the sword of his god, Thrinndor slowly raised the hissing, black flamed blade over his head with his right hand. The paladin glanced around and felt a momentary pang of regret as there was none with whom to share this moment of victory.

And then he heard two hands clapping together slowly. Breunne had been dragging his useless legs over to see if he could revive the cleric when the commotion behind the dais had caused him to turn and witness the death of the dragon. The ranger had twisted so that he could sit and was only then able to show his appreciation. His pain etched plain on his face.

Seeing the ranger's plight, Thrinndor looked around for the sheath for his new weapon and was surprised to find it tied at his side. There were no longer any other weapons in his inventory—only *Valdaar's Fist*. Quickly he sheathed the sword and rushed to give the ranger a hand. Seeing that his legs were clearly broken, Thrinndor tried to lower Breunne back where he was lying down.

"No," the ranger hissed through clenched teeth. "Help me get to the cleric. If she yet lives we must revive her. I have kept back a spell of healing for that purpose."

"Ease your own pain," the paladin admonished, chagrined that he had nothing left with which to aid his friend. "I will check on the cleric."

Breunne looked down at his broken legs and said, "One minor spell of healing won't help me much. For these, I'll need the aid of our cleric."

"Right," agreed the paladin. "Either way, remain here. I will check on Cyrillis."

"I don't think I'm going anywhere," the ranger said, wincing as he lay back.

The thinly veiled humor was wasted on the paladin, however. His attention was already on the cleric. He found her lying where she had fallen, her body draped across Pentaath's neck.

He knelt to inspect her bloody scalp, noting that she must have been warned in some way, because the enormous scepter the dragon had wielded should have crushed her skull, but it had not. There was a large knot on the back of her head and her honey-wheat hair was streaked with lost blood, but unless she was harmed far worse than he could see, she would live.

Thrinndor said a short prayer of thanks to Valdaar and gently lifted her slight frame and moved her to the dais. There he placed her on her back and waited as she began to stir. When her eyes fluttered open, he met her questioning gaze with a smile.

"What happened?" she asked, licking her dry lips.

Thrinndor smiled and pointed over at the mage, who had yet to move. "It seems the Lord of Dragons took exception to you undoing his hard work."

"Sordaak!" the cleric said and tried to sit up. But the room began to spin and she was forced to lie back down.

"Easy!" the paladin admonished. "That is a nasty bump you have there on your head. You are lucky to be alive."

"Lucky?" The healer's eyes narrowed slightly. "No, not lucky—I was warned." Her hand went to the sore spot on her head. "But it appears that warning came a bit too late." She winced as her fingers gently probed the knot.

"Late? I think not."

That caused the cleric to give the paladin a questioning look. But, she didn't have time to banter words with the big fighter, as he seemed want to do. She whispered a prayer and rubbed the knot until it was gone. Then, ignoring the continued protest of the paladin, she pushed herself to a sitting position and then to her feet where she stood shakily for a moment.

Cyrillis reached out with her percipience and noted the sorcerer was resting semi-comfortably and would soon awaken on his own. Savinhand was less comfortable with a couple of broken ribs and a nasty knot on his head. But he, too, would have to wait. And then there was the ranger.

The healer stumbled her way over to Breunne's side as quickly as she could. Her special sight told her that both legs were broken, that he had at least two cracked ribs, and his shoulder was out of joint. How he remained conscious she could only guess. But the pain—oh the pain! That pain had only recently been dulled somewhat by an empty wineskin that lay at his side.

First the healer eased his pain with a spell designed to do so. She chewed on her lip, knowing she had to set the broken bones before she could heal them—that and put his shoulder back in its socket. Suddenly she wished her patient was unconscious; this was going to *hurt*.

Breunne could see the conflict in her eyes. He reached out, grasped her arm and made her look into his soft brown eyes. "It's all right." His smile was so charming, so disarming. "Do what you must. I know it's going to hurt, but I want to dance again!"

Cyrillis returned the smile. "Very well." She looked around and, found a broken arrow and handed it to him. "Bite on this, then. I do not want your screaming to wake that dead dragon over there!" Her warm smile belied her words. "Thrinndor, come help me." When the paladin complied, she looked into his big blue eyes. Her voice stern and her face again worried, she said, "Hold him so that he does not move."

Thrinndor nodded grimly as the ranger put the shaft of the arrow between his teeth and closed his eyes. Neither bravery nor chivalry required him to watch.

Cyrillis set both legs, mended the bones, popped his shoulder back into place and tightened the ligaments there. She also healed the bones in his chest and soon had her patient on his feet.

Thrinndor went to check on the revived thief while she finished her work on the ranger. Savin patiently waited his turn. When the healer walked over, she reduced the knot on his head with her gentle touch and an empathetic smile. Next she mended his ribs.

She was reluctant to do what she knew must come next, and that was to check on her final two patients, neither of which had stirred. *They should have awakened on their own by now.*

Cyrillis knelt by the sorcerer's side and reached with her percipience into his prone form. She could see no further damage, and he seemed to be resting comfortably. However, she sensed that *something* was different. Part of him seemed to be *elsewhere*. It was nothing like she had ever encountered before. Yet his eyes remained closed. But when she looked hard at them, they fluttered like he was in the throes of a dream—not necessarily a bad dream, but surely something that held him elsewhere.

The cleric shrugged, stood and went to check on Pentaath. In him, she was even less certain. He also rested comfortably, and she could discern no pain in him. She finally surmised that he must remain unconscious because his master was unconscious.

When she brushed a wayward lock of hair from her face and turned to walk away, the dragon's eyes fluttered open. *Such huge eyes. When had Pentaath gotten so big?*

"Sordaak?" the voice of the dragon seemed to come from deep inside a cave. *When had his voice gotten so deep?* The single word was clearly a question about the sorcerer's health.

Cyrillis hesitated. "He will live."

"Where?" the dragon asked, raising his head to look around. "Aagh," he said as he closed his eyes.

"Go slowly," chastised the cleric. "You were hit on the head pretty hard. It may take a few minutes for you to get your legs back under you."

But Pentaath was not to be denied. He pushed to his feet, where he towered over everyone in the chamber.

When he spotted the sorcerer lying on the other side of the dais, the dragon quickly reverted to human form and hurried around the raised platform.

Thrinndor noticed the boy/dragon was wearing a tunic he had not seen before. It was brilliant white with a metallic sheen that glittered in the torchlight and was embossed at the collar, hem and sleeves with gold braid. It was simple but majestic.

When Pentaath got to his master, Sordaak's eyes flickered open. The mage licked his dry, cracked lips, smiled and said, "You're not who I was hoping to see."

Pentaath returned the smile. "It is good to see you alive as well, father!"

Cyrillis pushed the man/boy aside. Pentaath easily stood a head taller than even the paladin. When had he gotten *so damn big?*

"Ah," the magicuser said with a grin, "that's better."

The cleric threw her arms around his neck. When she pushed back, she demanded, "Where were you?"

The others in the chamber had no idea what she was talking about; the mage had never left their sight.

Sordaak knew. "That is for another story," he said with a wink. "One I will gladly relay one day, but that day is not now." He looked into her eyes. "Be content with this: I was in a far different land, and someday I will take you there. I promise."

He pushed away from the cleric, precluding further discussion, and looked around. "I take it we were victorious?" He turned to look at the paladin. "What about Vorgath?"

"Vorgath?" Cyrillis' eyes went wide and her hand went to her mouth as she looked over at where the dead Platinum Dragon lay. "Oh, no—" She rushed over to the decapitated monster as her hand dove to the rope tied around her waist. She pulled her ultra-sharp knife from its sheath and began carving around the scales at the dragon's underbelly.

It quickly became clear the task of baring Bahamut's skin was beyond what she could do with the knife in hand. Thrinndor took the two steps to be at her side, pushed her gently aside and began carving with *Valdaar's Fist*. The work went much quicker, then.

"Be careful that you do not hit Vorgath," the cleric said. Unconsciously she was biting her lip as she looked on apprehensively.

Sordaak thought to remind her that the barbarian was already dead, but he pushed that errant thought from his mind.

Breunne and Savinhand stepped in to help, and soon they had the dragon's belly open and spread on the floor. Thrinndor looked over at the rogue. "We are good here. Go get his legs."

Savinhand got a confused look on his face, but then he remembered that only half of the dwarf had been eaten by the dragon. "Right," he said as he stumbled away from the growing mess near the raised dais, going back toward where that part of the battle took place.

Sordaak gagged a few times and covered his nose and mouth to filter out some of the stench. His weak stomach overrode his desire to see the barbarian found and ultimately he had to turn away.

Savinhand returned to the group dragging the lower half of the dwarf just as Thrinndor announced success. Sort of. The upper torso of the barbarian was in a bad state. The dragon's stomach acid had dealt serious damage to the body, and much of the skin had been eaten away.

"Bring him over here," Cyrillis directed. She pointed to a clear space on the dais. Thrinndor and Savin hauled their carcass halves over and deposited them where told and stepped back to give the cleric room.

Cyrillis took in a deep breath and then moved to the barbarian's side. He was much further gone than she'd hoped. Too far gone, perhaps.

First she slid the two halves together, bowed her head and began to chant. Once again the companions felt the power in the room build around the cleric. Thrinndor also lowered his eyes and began to pray.

The healer applied her magic first to rejoin the two halves. The men were astonished to see the dwarf become whole before their eyes and the skin form again on his hands and face. That complete, Cyrillis reached inside her patient with her mind to begin repairing his internal organs. She was woefully short on spell energy and could soon tell she would not have nearly enough.

When the cleric staggered back a step, the ranger caught her by the elbow and steadied her. "Is he...?" He couldn't finish the question.

Cyrillis shook her head. "No. I am almost out of healing energy, and he needs far more than I have remaining." Her lower lip trembled. Thrinndor couldn't tell whether that was because she was exhausted or about to cry. "Even were I able to return life to his body, the damage I have not yet repaired would surely kill him again."

The chamber was silent for a few heartbeats before Thrinndor spoke. "Perhaps if you rested?"

Cyrillis turned to focus her eyes the paladin. "*It does not work that way!*" Her tone was scathing. "*And you know it!*" Her chest was heaving. Suddenly, she took in a deep breath and forced down her ire. When the healer spoke again, her voice was barely audible. "The longer his heart is not beating, the further into death he travels." Slowly she turned to look at the barbarian. "Even if I had the energy to raise him, I doubt that he would return to us even now."

"But you must *try!*" Thrinndor's eyes pleaded with her.

The cleric closed her eyes and bowed her head. A single tear escaped her right eye as she nodded slowly. She had held back just enough energy for a single raise dead attempt. *But would it work?* Cyrillis took in a ragged breath, leaned forward and placed her hands on Vorgath's chest. Quietly, she began to recite the words to her spell.

Again the men felt the energy in the room build as the healer called forth her power. "Here me o Valdaar. This man's time among us is not done. He has been instrumental to your cause thus far, and there is much yet to do that we need him for. Please return him to us so that together we may further your cause." Without opening her eyes she released every last remaining ounce of spell energy into her patient.

Vorgath's eyes sprang open, and his back arched at the influx of that energy. When the spell subsided, Cyrillis collapsed to the floor and the barbarian's body relaxed against the cold stone on which he lay, his eyes once again closed.

A deep silence followed that was finally broken when Breunne stepped forward to help the cleric back to her feet. She stood unsteadily, her eyes apprehensive as they drifted slowly over to the dwarf.

"Is he—?" Thrinndor began, hope edging into his voice.

Cyrillis reached out with her percipience as she, too, hoped against hope that she had been successful, all the while dreading finding out that she had not. The healer's shoulders drooped, and her hands fell to her side when she shook her head minutely. "No," she whispered. "There is no life in him." Her red-rimmed eyes turned to the paladin, pleading for him not to judge. "The damage done by the dragon's stomach acid was too much. His internal organs were almost nonexistent." Her eyes floated slowly back to the barbarian's body. "I tried everything I could!"

Abruptly, the healer pitched forward onto the still form of the dwarf and her knees sagged again to the floor. Sobs wracked her body as tears flowed from the emotional well of her soul.

Breunne took a step forward to give what aid he could, but Sordaak stopped him with a wave of his hand, a stern glance and a shake of his head.

An uncomfortable silence settled on the companions as the cleric's sobs subsided. Each dealt with the loss in his own way.

When he deemed it appropriate, Sordaak quietly stepped forward , leaned over and put an arm around the cleric's shoulders. He then gently raised her upright and helped her to stand. She buried her face in his shoulder, and the sorcerer thought she was going to break down again, but she didn't. Instead, she raised her head, pushed her hair back from her face and scrubbed the tears from her eyes.

"I am sorry," she said, straightening her shoulders as she pushed away from the magicuser. "I do not know what—"

"Shhh," Sordaak said, his right hand going to hers. "It's all right. We all felt the loss." He looked around at the others in the chamber to verify he was correct. There wasn't a dry eye in the place. He walked her slowly away from the dais.

Knowing he needed to change the subject, the sorcerer's gaze settled on the paladin, and he tried to smile. "You have the sword."

Thrinndor nodded and pulled his cloak aside, revealing the pommel of *Valdaar's Fist* high up under his arm. The paladin brushed away a tear, grasped the handle of the sword and slowly withdrew it from the sheath. As the blade was exposed, black flames engulfed the metal. When fully drawn, it hissed and popped slightly. Faint runes were etched into the blade, but the writhing of the flames prohibited them from being seen clearly. The metal was dark but not black; it was more of a tainted silver. Curiously, several veins of deep red coursed down its length, weaving no particular pattern that one could discern.

"It is beautiful," Cyrillis breathed softly, a catch in her voice. She was clearly grateful for the distraction. "But why are the flames black?"

When no one immediately answered, Sordaak shrugged and said, "It's said that the sword is so evil it taints even the flames." His tone was somber.

Thrinndor blew a disbelieving hiss though his lips. "I do not believe that to be true."

Sordaak smiled, breaking the tension. "Nah, me either. Although I didn't make that up—it's written in some of the old texts and stories I found back in the Library. The only thing I found that makes any sense is that the blade was enchanted by the ancient drow—purveyors of the dark arts. They must have found a way to darken the flames, probably for effect."

"Looks cool, though, does it not?" the paladin said, waving the sword back and forth a couple of times, causing the flames to splutter somewhat.

"That it does," agreed the ranger. His eyes had not left the blade since it had been drawn, and those eyes were thoughtful.

Thrinndor noticed the look. "Something bothering you?"

"Who, me? No." Breunne shook his head. He hesitated. "Well, what's with the second sword?" His eyes went to the wall of swords behind the dais.

"That is a fair question," the paladin said. He turned and walked over to the other sword—the shiny, alive-looking one that remained on the wall. "There have always been two—although seldom have they been found together." He sheathed *Valdaar's Fist* and removed the other blade from the hooks that held it to the wall. "This blade was forged at the same time and enchanted such that it resembles the original in every way." He pulled the blade, and it did appear the same, except the flames were the standard red of a flaming sword.

"That is how you tell them apart," continued the paladin, "red flames. That and this blade is essentially powerless. No enchantment other than the flames." He shrugged. "It has misled many a usurper of the power of our god—those wishing only to advance their own name or reputation. A true paladin of Valdaar—one with his blood in their veins—would know better."

"That explains why over the centuries the blade was reported found many times," Breunne mused. "But most recorded instances say the blade had red flames."

"Precisely," said the paladin. "The true sword of my god—*Valdaar's Fist*—is known to be able to disguise itself. Sometimes as a rusted piece of worthless iron, others it will act to resemble its twin—this blade."

"But, why?" Savinhand asked.

"Another good question. The blade of Valdaar is a very powerful artifact. In the wrong hands, much damage can be wrought in the name of another."

"But I thought the blade could only be wielded by one with the blood of Valdaar running in his veins?" Cyrillis said. She looked from the fake sword to the real one in its sheath at the paladin's side.

"Ah, I see where my explanation has gone astray." Thrinndor rubbed his chin and looked thoughtfully at the fake blade in his hands. "There are several who have the blood of Valdaar coursing through their veins, but not all of those seek to return him to the land."

"What?" The cleric was clearly more confused than before.

"Allow me to explain," admonished the paladin. "Our god spread his seed throughout the land—as did his brother Praxaar—in an effort to ensure his line never waned. But over the years more than one of those lines came to a halt, while others forgot the tales and only wished their heritage would be forgotten. Eventually it was. And in the intervening two millennia there were two or three who sought to use the blood in their veins and the sword of our god to unite the followers of Valdaar to try to take the land back by force. Those had to be prevented from gaining access to the real sword of our god."

Thrinndor sheathed the fake sword and cast it into a nearby pile of coins. He then unsheathed *Valdaar's Fist*, openly admiring the blade as he did. "Today there are only two—possibly three—of his line remaining that seek to return him to the land. Once we have succeeded in raising our lord, I intend to attempt to unite those of us that remain so that we can together serve our god."

"Well said," Sordaak interrupted. "But if we don't get on with raising this god of yours—ours—then they are merely words."

Thrinndor bristled at the rejoinder. "What are you trying to say?"

The mage held up both hands. "I'm not *trying* to say anything. We have been gone too long from the keep. I fear that they've been attacked in our absence, and our plans may now even lie in ruins." When no one spoke, he continued. "Look, I don't mean to throw a wet blanket over your little coming-out party, but we're only half done. We need to get back to Valdaar's Rest so that we can finish this. We can't do it here."

The sword surprised everyone by speaking. "Welcome to my personal Hell."

Sordaak was the first to recover. "What?"

"You think you are the first to make the attempt to rid me of this essence of a god that is contained within?" When no one answered, the sword continued. "Well, you are not. No less than five attempts have been made over the last two thousand years. All have failed. Do not expect me to get excited that you will succeed where so many others have not."

"Five attempts?" Sordaak was dubious. "I found no such records."

The mage was pretty sure the sword rolled its tiny eyes. "Morons! Who would have recorded such attempts?" Again no one replied. "Exactly. Would you record such an occurrence were you to fail? I think not."

"What is it you would have us do then?" Thrinndor asked.

"Do not get me wrong," the sword answered, "I sincerely hope you are successful. For, if you are not, I fear I will have to serve out my days with the essence of a god who is no more."

"Explain."

Sordaak was certain he heard the sword sigh in frustration. "Valdaar's life force was never meant to spend more than a century or two—three at most—trapped inside the gem affixed to my handle. Too many centuries his seen essence diminished. Now, two thousand years later, he is weakened to the point that he will not last until another attempt can be made. If you are not successful, Valdaar will be lost forever."

"We will succeed."

"Even if you do, you may be too late. It is uncertain whether Valdaar's spirit will be strong enough to survive once released."

Thrinndor puffed out his chest. "He will be strong enough. Valdaar will once again walk the land, and we will make it happen."

"See that you do." Then the sword went silent, and suddenly it was back in its sheath at the paladin's side.

Sordaak's eyes never left the sword. "As I said, we must return to the island to make the attempt. I require the power source hidden there to bolster our chances."

"But it will take you at least two weeks—probably longer if winter settles in—to get back to the island," Savinhand said.

Cyrillis turned to stare at the thief. "What?" he asked defensively.

"You said 'it will take you at least two weeks.' Are you not coming with us?"

"No," Savin said with a shake of his head. He went on quickly before he could be interrupted. "I signed on to this quest to help you find your sword. I've done so—and more. I have no part in the raising of a god, and I must to get back to running my guild before Bealtrive takes it from me. If she hasn't already."

"Would that be such a bad thing?" the cleric said.

"It would to me! Look, I ascended to the Guildmaster position the fair and proper way. Like it or not, that bunch of thieves, assassins and never-do-wells belongs to me. As does the Library of Antiquity." He looked around the chamber. "Some of this stuff probably belongs in there." He shrugged. "Either way, I have a job to do. And I need to get back to doing it before someone else does!"

Breunne could see the cleric wasn't buying it, so he decided to rescue the rogue. "This will be the end of the line for me, as well." All eyes turned to him as he turned to face Thrinndor. "I swore fealty to you and this quest of yours to regain the lost sword of your god. That we have done. I have never made a secret of the fact that I prefer to work on my own." The chamber got very quiet, and the ranger noticed the cleric's eyes seemingly getting darker and bigger. He was now regretting his move to save the thief. "Look, I too have obligations. I owe some people a bit of coin, and there's this girl back home that you remind me of that I've been pining for." He swallowed a couple of times before he could continue. "It's time I paid her a visit."

"Where is home?" Cyrillis asked quietly.

"Actually, it's not far from here. No more than two or three days' hard travel—once clear of this valley anyway."

"Wait! There is one more thing that I would like cleared up." Everyone turned to look at Pentaath, who turned to look at Sordaak, who shifted nervously under his gaze. "During the battle you said something about an 'Adamantine Dragon' and 'New Lord of the Dragons.'" He crossed his arms on his chest. "Please explain."

"Oh, that," Sordaak waved an arm dismissively and turned away. "I just said that to piss off Bahamut." He smiled. "It worked, didn't it?"

Pentaath didn't waver. Neither did his gaze.

"What is he talking about?" Cyrillis asked Thrinndor.

"I have no idea! I vaguely remember the discussion in question, but I thought nothing of it at the time." He turned and inspected Pentaath's raiment again. "Now I am not so sure." He joined the others and stared at the magicuser.

"OK, look," said an exasperated Sordaak, "I *may* have read somewhere that if The Lord of Dragons is slain, another dragon must step in to fill the void. And I *might have* stretched the imagination a bit in assuming that Pentaath was born for the position." He jabbed his finger at his protégé.

"And this robe?"

Sordaak cleared his throat. He was squirming now. "That was an embellishment on my part. I found that in the pile of stuff over there and it seemed the thing to do at the time. I switched it for your old garb."

"Adamantine?"

"That's what I believe that shirt is made of. It was the first thing that came to mind when I was searching for a name." Now it was Sordaak's turn to ask a question. "What about your scales?"

Pentaath blinked twice. "What about them?"

"Have you *looked* at them?"

"Ummm…no, not really." The dragon-boy shrugged. "They are white."

"They *were* white." Sordaak pointed a finger at his son. "Recently they've taken on a metallic sheen." He waited for that to sink in for a moment. "Kinda like that shirt you're wearing. The *Adamantine* shirt."

"That is *sooth*," Thrinndor said. "I noticed that before the battle."

Pentaath uncrossed his arms and rapidly began changing to dragon form.

"You don't trust me?" Sordaak asked. It was his turn to fold his arms on his chest.

"No."

"Ouch. That hurts! We share a mind, yet you don't trust me." When Pentaath didn't immediately reply, he added. "That's OK, I wouldn't trust me, either." His smile went from ear to ear as the boy became a dragon.

"Can someone *please* tell me what in the hell is going on?" Cyrillis asked, her eyes going from one man in the group to the other.

Thrinndor scratched his head. "I will try. It seems our magicuser friend here believes that Pentaath will replace Bahamut as the King of all Dragons."

"The King of all *remaining* Dragons," Sordaak corrected.

"That's true," Breunne chimed in. "There suddenly seems to be a shortage of those in these parts!"

"Well, there are plenty remaining in other parts of the land!" the mage said. "And that reminds me of the three we hold captive." He looked around the chamber and then said, "Wait here. I'll be right back." He waved toward the mounds of treasure in the room. "Count some coins or something."

The sorcerer sprinted from the room, limping only slightly because of a foot he was not yet accustomed to having. When he returned, he had the covered cage in his hand.

Slightly winded, he removed the cover. "Prepare yourselves," he said between breaths, "I'm going to release them."

"You're *what?*" Savinhand said.

"Relax," Sordaak answered. "Rest assured I'll have some answers first. And if this doesn't go well, we'll have to kill them." The mage looked over at the paladin. "Understood?"

The big fighter nodded and again drew *Valdaar's Fist* from the sheath. Others did likewise, preparing for battle.

Satisfied, Sordaak turned his attention to the cage. Inside the three canaries stood in a line facing the sorcerer. "Can you hear and understand me?"

The three birds nodded as one. They no longer looked beat-up or injured. They had found a way to heal themselves. "Good. Listen carefully, because your fate will hinge on your answers."

Sordaak drew himself up to his full height and motioned Pentaath closer. The boy in dragon form did so. "Bahamut is dead." He pointed to the carcass not far away. "Pentaath is your new King. Understood?"

"No," the boy dragon answered for them.

Sordaak rolled his eyes. "Look, you were born—hatched—less than six months ago, correct?" The dragon nodded. "Yet, here you stand, full grown in both dragon and human form, right?" Pentaath nodded again. "You were *born* to this role—it's the only thing that makes sense! You grew this fast *because you had to!* Bahamut had to die for us to gain the sword. But the dragons of the Land must have a leader. *You* are that leader."

"But—"

"No. No *buts*. You're here for that purpose, *period.* Is that understood?"

Pentaath wasn't ready to concede, but he had no arguments, either. He said nothing.

Sordaak hid his relief well. He turned back to the cage. "You three get all of that?" The canaries nodded again. "Good. I am going to release you. In so doing, I will be giving you a choice. Either you swear fealty to Pentaath as your new King, or you will die. Do you understand?" More nods.

Sordaak set the cage down and motioned for everyone to stand back. Once a space had been cleared, the mage began to chant. At first nothing happened, but then the cage began to slowly expand. After a few moments the bars were far enough apart that the birds inside could leave when ready.

Sordaak stopped chanting and waited. One at a time the birds hopped over and through an opening. Once clear, all three took flight and soon were high overhead. The companions could tell they were changing to dragon form.

That complete, the three ancient gold dragons, formerly of Bahamut's court, swooped in and each landed on a pile of coins amid a flurry of dust. It was not lost on the sorcerer that the three had Pentaath surrounded. But he was not worried. He had seen these gold dragons in battle, and knew that if it came to it, they would again be victorious. There was also no doubt his familiar had the size advantage were it to get ugly. *I'd like it better if I had more spell energy, though.*

Several tense moments passed before one after another each of the gold dragons dipped his head deferentially. That done, they raised up their heads and bellowed as one: "All hail Pentaath, Adamantine Dragon and Lord of All!"

Swords rattled against shields and staffs pounded the marble of the floor under foot in approval. Pentaath let out a huff and rapidly changed to human form, followed immediately by the dragons of his court.

"Why is it I do not feel like a king, father?" The young man glared at the sorcerer, clearly not ready to submit.

"See that you never do," replied the mage.

"Huh?"

"If you feel that you must work to earn your title every hour of every day, you will be the better for it. And so will those who serve you."

Pentaath turned to look at the paladin. "You have any idea what he is talking about?"

Thrinndor nodded slowly. "More so now than at any time in the past. Heed his words, young dragon, and your kind will again flourish in the land."

Chapter Thirty-Two

Hero of the Land

"We done with all this ceremonial shit?" Savinhand asked. "I must be on my way. But first we need to decide how to split the bounty." He waved an arm that encompassed the piles of gold and other loot in the treasure chamber."

"Hold on there," Sordaak said, a hand raised. "As heir to the throne, Pentaath has a claim to—and will need as the King of Dragons—this bounty. Or most of it."

Savinhand raised an eyebrow. "And by extension, *you* will have claim to it."

Sordaak puffed up his chest to explode, but Cyrillis beat him to it. "Gentlemen!" she said sternly. "Have we come to squabbling over some coin after all we have been through together?"

Both men glared at the cleric. "Have we?" she repeated.

"No."

"No," agreed the rogue. He pointed over his shoulder. "But you have to admit that is a bit more than some coin."

Cyrillis smiled. "Yes, I would."

"There is precedent for situations such as this," one of the council dragons said. He had stepped forward, and Cyrillis could see that he was not completely healed from his injuries.

"Go on," Sordaak said guardedly.

"You men talk, while I make the rounds and provide Pentaath's court as much healing assistance as I can do without spell energy," the healer said resolutely.

"That is not necessary, I assure you," said the councilman who had stepped forward.

Cyrillis puffed up to speak sharply, but Sordaak interceded. "Don't go there, old one. Let her do her work so that we all don't have to hear the tongue lashing that would otherwise follow." The mage smiled at the cleric, who released the pent-up breath with a soft laugh.

"Thank you," she said.

"Very well," said he who was apparently the lead councilman. "It appears there is something going on here to which we are not privy. We will suffer these ministrations."

"Thank you," Cyrillis repeated formally. "I promise that suffering is not part of my ministrations, and that this will not hurt."

The three dragons eyed her suspiciously while Sordaak breathed a sigh of relief. He had indeed not looked forward to an altercation between the dragons and the healer. "You were saying?" he spoke pointedly at the lead councilman.

"Yes." The dragon in human form returned his attention to the sorcerer. "While you have indeed slain Bahamut, and therefore have some claim to the bounty, as you call it," the old man wrinkled his face distastefully, "three of us remain of those who once held claim over that same treasure."

"Yet you abdicated your claim to that when you swore fealty to your new king," Sordaak said icily.

"Did we?" The councilman flexed his freshly wrapped arm and nodded his thanks to the cleric. He returned his attention to the mage. "You are correct in your assessment that the new King will need most of what is here—he has an appearance to maintain and other dragons to control." Savinhand made to speak, but the councilman raised a hand. "Patience, young man, I assure you the explanation you require is nigh."

The rogue released his breath noisily, crossed his arms on his chest and nodded.

The councilman returned the nod. "Again, there is precedent for an occurrence such as this. The new king as victor in battle has full claim over all that he has conquered." He held up both hands to forestall Savin, whose eyes were about to pop out of his head. "Yet if the new king permits, associates of this new king may take one item of their choice from the horde of specialty items—which I will point out to you in a moment—"

"ONE?" Savinhand bellowed.

"—and as much gems, coin and other non-enchanted items as they may carry with them when they depart."

That shut the thief up. His eyebrow lifted, and he smiled. "Now you're beginning to make some sense, ancient one. I will of course want to carry only platinum and gems."

"Of course."

"*Big* gems."

"Of course."

Cyrillis clucked her tongue, clearly disapproving of the direction the conversation had taken. "I would have thought that you would have access to whatever bounty you might want as leader of Guild Shardmoor."

"I do," Savin said, grinning at the cleric. "But I must show that this mission I have been on was worth my time as said leader of Guild Shardmoor, must I not?"

"Well said," Sordaak grinned.

"Men!" Cyrillis huffed with a shake of her head and went back to tending to any injuries she could find.

"Leader of Guild Shardmoor?" the councilman asked. The other dragons also took note of the comment and turned to stare at the rogue. "You?"

Savinhand had wandered off to take a look at a particularly big ruby that had caught his eye. It was about the size of his fist and his eyes glittered as he picked it up. He began flipping it nonchalantly into the air, his eyes never leaving the stone. "Yes," he answered with a sly smile.

"You do not appear to have adequate experience."

"Phinskyr—or Ytharra as you may have known him? No, he went missing years ago and is presumed dead. I won the Rite of Ascension tournament and am now the leader." He smiled big for the councilman.

"And the Library?"

"Safely hidden where only I may access it, I assure you."

The older man nodded. "And your name, young man, so that it may be recorded in our annals?"

"Savinhand: Rogue, Locksmith, Trap-Finder/Disabler and all-around—"

"Scoundrel," Sordaak interrupted with a grin.

"Scoundrel," Savinhand replied with a like grin. "And now Leader of Guild Shardmoor, at your service." He bowed.

"Well met, I am sure," replied the councilman, his tone aloof. However, he returned the bow. "The change in leadership is so noted."

"Now as to that treasure—"

"Wait." All eyes turned to Thrinndor. He cleared his throat and walked over to stand beside Vorgath's body on the dais. "There is one thing we must attend to first."

"What is that?" the councilman asked.

"Attend to a proper funeral for a Hero of the Land."

"Hero of the Land? I know of none that hold that title."

Thrinndor turned and faced the councilman. "You do now," the paladin's voice grated across his lips and his right hand suddenly rested on the pommel of *Valdaar's Fist*. "Vorgath Shieldsunder, son of Morroth of the Dragaar Clan, Hailing from the Silver Hills and Hero of the Land."

"Add Dragonslayer to that," Sordaak added.

"Note *that* in your records," Savinhand added, his arms folded on his chest.

Clearly flustered, the councilman looked from one to the other. He folded his arms on his chest and puffed up. "His blow was not the one that settled this battle," he said.

Thrinndor began to pull his sword from its sheath. "Do not!" commanded the mage. "I'll handle this." He walked past his friend to confront the lead councilman. The paladin reluctantly allowed *Valdaar's Fist* to slide home.

"Listen, you pompous windbag!' Sordaak began. "Vorgath has in his study the heads of not one, but two dragons!" He decided that stretching the truth a bit seemed in order. After all, the barbarian had *planned* to put the dragon heads in his study when he got a study. "Both Melundiir and Theremault fell to him and his greataxe in glorious battles! And were it not for his prowess in this fight, we never would have gotten to the point to where the only weapon in the Land that could finish Bahamut, *previous* Lord of the Dragons, did so!" He found he was breathing hard.

"So when Thrinndor, a paladin of the Paladinhood of Valdaar, hailing of Khavhall and a direct descendent of Valdaar, says he wants a funeral befitting a Hero of the damn Land, your only question shall be 'when can we make that happen for you, sir?'." Now he was definitely breathing harder. "Do I make myself understood?" Sparks flew as he tamped *Pendromar* on the stone floor to emphasize his point. Abruptly, he spun and strode back to stand next to Thrinndor.

The paladin leaned over and whispered, "Well said."

Sordaak nodded slightly. "So, what's it going to be?" he said, his emotions only barely under control as he, too, crossed his arms on his chest.

The councilman's mouth opened and closed a couple of times, but no sound came forth. Finally he was able to say, "Allow me to confer with the other members of the council."

"Be my guest," grated the mage as he made a sweeping gesture with his right hand.

The councilman's eyebrow twitched a couple of times and then he turned and walked over to the other two councilmembers. They spoke in subdued voices for a few moments, during which Pentaath fought an inner battle to join them—after all, he was leader of this council, right? But he did not.

The senior member returned to face the magicuser and paladin, still standing beside one another. "It shall be as you wish." He hesitated for a moment and then added, "When can we make that happen for you, sir?"

Sordaak fought the urge to smile. He hadn't wanted to push another fight, but it had been clear to him that he needed to make sure the dragons of the council understood their place in the new order. *Now I just need to figure out what this new order is.*

The paladin answered for him. "We require a day to rest and make preparations. Would tomorrow be too soon?"

"It shall be as you wish," the councilmember repeated stiffly. "Ponterruth will show you to a place where you may freshen up and rest. I will be by later to discuss the arrangements with you, if that would meet your pleasure?"

"It would," Thrinndor said.

Another of the councilmembers, presumably Ponterruth, said, "If you would follow me, please." He turned and walked back the way they had come.

298   V ANCE P UMPHREY

Sordaak looked up at the paladin, shrugged and said, "After you."

Together the companions followed, but they were stopped by the lead councilman after only a few feet. "Not you, my liege. We have much to discuss." He had stepped so that he blocked Pentaath's following of his master.

Sordaak made eye contact with his familiar and nodded slightly. *We will remain in communication this way. Don't allow them to take you far without letting me know, please.*

Yes, father. I sense no duplicity in them, so...

Agreed. But, only moments ago they would have slain us were they able to do so. Ward yourself and stay in communication.

"As you wish," Pentaath told the councilman. "Lead the way."

The two walked around behind the pedestal and through a door the mage hadn't noticed before.

"Are you sure you want to allow that?" Thrinndor whispered.

The sorcerer nodded, his eyes following the pair. "He'll be fine. They can't harm him without my knowing about it." He turned and looked into the deep blue eyes of the paladin. "He and I have agreed to stay in touch."

"I believe that to be wise." Thrinndor continued after the others.

Sordaak hesitated slightly. *I sure as hell hope so.*

*

Morning dawned without incident and with the companions refreshed. They had been provided fresh fruits from a hidden store that baffled the mage, but he chose to let that pass.

He and Pentaath had communicated several times through the night, but some of the information provided to the new Lord of all Dragons was going to have to come later, Pentaath warned. If at all. Some things were apparently not for the eyes of humans. Sordaak stated he understood. He didn't, but he decided to let that pass for now, as well.

The companions and the remaining dragons in human form gathered out in front of the entrance to the home of the dragons. There a large pool fed by some underground source lay still in the high mountain air. Snowflakes fell softly to melt on the clothing and armor of those who gathered there. On the lake was a small skiff in which lay the body of the dwarf.

The tone was somber, dampened further by the chill in the air and the snow that dulled the spirit. Each of the companions said the words that tumbled awkwardly from frozen lips and heavy hearts.

Thrinndor was last to speak. "Fare thee well, old friend, as you press on to the one great test you always feared, yet stood ready for: the afterlife. You were a good friend, a stalwart companion and the fiercest warrior I have ever known. Your courage kept body and soul together on too many quests to mention, and your exuberance for life will make mine the better for having known you." He paused as his control threatened to break. "Keep the path always before you until the day when we will once again chase our dreams together." He fought the lump in his throat. "Fare thee well, old friend."

The paladin dipped his head and threw the lit torch that he held into the vessel. The brand caught the tinder placed there as planned, and soon the flames crept up the small platform upon which rested the barbarian, swathed in clean linens and his armor, which had been retrieved from the Platinum Dragon's body. Several of his prized weapons adorned his form, but noticeably absent was his most prized possession of all: *Flinthgoor.* Sordaak had deemed that the greataxe's usefulness might not be at an end.

The paladin untied the single rope that kept the boat from floating away, tossed it aboard the craft and pushed it from shore with the toe of his boot.

Soon the entire boat was engulfed in flames as it approached the waterfall on the other side of the pool, beginning the stream that led from the Valley of the Damned. When at the last the funeral dirge disappeared over the brink, Thrinndor said one more time, "Fare the well, old friend." He then turned and strode quickly back down the valley with the others hustling behind him to keep pace.

Once inside the warmer confines of the dragon's home, he turned and waited for the others to join him. "What now?" he demanded gruffly.

"Now we go home," Sordaak replied. He turned to face the dragon council leader, whom he had learned was named Kreymeere. "I have one more request of you, if I may."

This time the councilman did not hesitate. "You have but to ask."

"Thank you," replied the mage, mildly curious as to the attitude shift. "As you may have overheard, we are to go our separate ways." Kreymeere nodded. "The two who are leaving us to return to their previous lives are on their own." He smiled at both Breunne and Savinhand, who shrugged. "But the rest of us—Thrinndor, Cyrillis and myself—must return to The Isle of Grief at utmost haste." He swallowed hard. "Would you be so kind as to provide transport for both of them? I will ride Pentaath."

Kreymeere nodded slowly. "It shall be as you wish. That is indeed a long journey, more than a thousand miles. Ponterruth and Leorandle will follow you and our king. I will take these two." He hesitated, and then a smile split his lips. "I will take these two scoundrels as far as they dare let a dragon do so. After all, surely the Leader of Guild Shardmoor and the great bounty hunter Breunne cannot be seen consorting with dragons now, can they?"

"You've got that right!" Savinhand said.

Breunne was less enthused. The memories of the last time he had ridden a dragon came flooding back, and that one didn't go so well. However, trying to scale these mountains as winter set in or going the long way through the caverns was not his idea of fun, either. He swallowed hard and nodded.

Sordaak fought back a smile. "Careful there, old one, you're close to busting out with a sense of humor!"

"Sonny, I had a sense of humor long before your kind ever set foot in this land." His smile vanished. "It was your kind that drove that humor from my soul."

The mage stepped up and offered his right arm for the traditional greeting. After a brief hesitation the older male took it, grasping arms in the old way. Sordaak's smile disappeared and he said solemnly, "I promise to do what I can to return that humor to you."

Kreymeere nodded as he released his grip. "We will see." He turned and faced the rest of the companions. "We have one task remaining before you depart."

Sordaak scratched his head. He was anxious to get back to the island. *His* island. He looked over at Cyrillis. *Well, I'm going to have to share it now, it seems.* He smiled and turned back to the dragon.

Kreymeere was still speaking. "Pentaath, Ponterruth and Leorandle and I searched through the artifacts at our disposal and came up with an item—or two, in some cases—that we believe will aid each of you the most.

"First for your healer, Cyrillis." He turned and accepted a large gilded bag from Ponterruth. This he presented to the cleric when she stepped forward somewhat shyly. "You already have the most powerful talisman a cleric can wield: *Kurril.* As you unlock its powers, it will make you even more adept at your craft." He pulled open the top of the bag and reached inside. When he withdrew his arm he held a breastplate—clearly made for a woman—made of a milky white metal that glistened brightly in the torchlight of the chamber. "This armor will better protect you when you stray too close to battle, while also allowing you to perform your healing duties without hindrance." He handed the armor to the cleric, who accepted it with widened eyes. He then reached back into the bag. "There are other pieces to that armor in here that you may or may not desire to use. It was a suit presented to one of Valdaar's mistresses—one that just happened to be a cleric." However, when the old man's hand re-emerged, it held a circlet. This he placed on the befuddled Cyrillis' head. "This circlet will certainly be a boon to your skills. It is enchanted such that it will enhance your already considerable wisdom and," he said with a wry smile, "it has a ward built into it that will keep you from being hit in the head."

Cyrillis turned beet red as she accepted the bag and the remainder of its contents from the council lead. "Thank you," she stammered. "If you ever have need of a healer, you have but to send for me."

"Thank you," Kreymeere replied. "Let us both pray for that to never happen."

As the cleric backed away slowly, the councilman accepted a similar bag from Leorandle. "Savinhand." The rogue stepped forward eagerly. "As Leader of Guild Shardmoor and curator of the Library of Antiquity, you should be wont for not much the rest of your life—short that it may be if your colleagues have anything to say about it." Kreymeere winked at the rogue, who grinned in reply. The old man reached into the sack and came out with an ornate crown. "This crown, while it is befitting of a king of any stature, has special powers that I believe you may find to be especially useful." He reached out and, grasping the crown with both hands, placed it on the rogue's head. "Indeed, this particular crown should probably be in the Library, but I think you may find some use of it before you intern it there. With it on your head, you will be able to see the true nature of any that you encounter, see invisible objects as if they were visible to all, and it will also increase your rogue-related skill abilities by several factors." The old man grinned at the thief. "However, it might seem a bit garish to wear out in public—especially when public is a thieves' den. So that crown also has the ability to disguise itself as a regular leather cap, similar to the one you were wearing earlier, simply by pressing the emerald on the front like so." The old man reached out and pushed the indicated gem and a faint click was heard. Suddenly the leather cap sat on Savin's head.

Again Kreymeere reached into the bag. This time he pulled out a long, flat, wooden box that was ornately carved and beautifully finished. He released the catch on the front and opened the box to reveal a pair of exquisitely adorned daggers. "These daggers are clearly special." He pointed to one of them. "This one is enchanted such that it will always return to you after you throw it—even after slaying whatever it was you were throwing it at. This other one becomes a brace of four daggers when thrown, and each will strike the target you threw it at. You will always be able to find them, but they do not return to you like this other." He looked up into the rogue's eyes. "These are sharp, *very* sharp. Take care where you keep them."

Savinhand accepted the daggers with a bow. "Thank you, Kreymeere." The council leader bowed in return.

"For you Breunne, Master Ranger." Kreymeere turned and accepted another sack from Ponterruth. "We had to search high and low because you already have the finest bow in the Land—*Xenotath*—to find something that would benefit your special skill set." His hand dove into the bag and retrieved a quiver full of arrows. "However, this is the quiver that once went with that bow." Breunne's eyes widened in wonder. "I see you recognize *Quill*, the quiver that is never empty?" The ranger nodded. "Yes then, I am sure then that you also know that these arrows are special—magically enchanted for sharpness and to be a bane to giants, minotaurs and most other larger-than-man-sized creatures." The ranger again nodded meekly as he accepted the quiver. The hand dipped back into the bag and when it emerged the councilman was holding some hardened leather pieces. "This armor was made for Markwonne, and it may have saved his life had he worn it that fateful day many centuries ago. But, alas, he did not know of its existence—it was to be a gift to him from his love. But I digress. This armor is enchanted such that it provides the protection of full plate mail, yet retains the suppleness of well-worn leather. It will also allow the wearer to breathe underwater and swim like a fish." He handed it to the ranger. "Use it well, First Mark."

Breunne nodded. "Thank you, Kreymeere. You are most generous." He took the items, including the bag, and stepped back.

"Sordaak—what can I give the most powerful sorcerer in the land who already wields *Pendromar, Dragon's Breath* and who learns from the spell book of Dragma?"

The mage stepped forward, and as he passed the ranger he whispered to Breunne, "You're going to have to someday explain that 'First Mark' title."

"Maybe someday," the fighter said, returning to his place with a grin.

"What can possibly aid the sorcerer who has it all? Why the intelligence to use his powers better and the wisdom to know *when* to use them." Kreymeere reached into the bag handed to him by Leorandle. When his hand emerged it held a ring and an amulet. "Both of these pieces were once part of Praxaar's personal collection. The ring is said to raise the intelligence of even a god." Sordaak raised an eyebrow. "And this amulet is paired with the ring to give the god the wisdom necessary to wield that power with impunity." Kreymeere handed both to the mage. "That is it. I have nothing more that could possibly aid you, young man."

"Thank you," the sorcerer breathed. "These will suffice."

The mage started to turn, but the council leader stopped him. "See that they do."

Sordaak nodded absently as he studied the two pieces on his way back to where he'd been standing.

"Thrinndor," the old man said as he accepted the final sack from Ponterruth. "Finding something that would aid you on your quest to raise your god was far easier than the others." When he reached into the bag, instead of pulling his hand free, he allowed the bag to drop to the floor. His hand was supporting a suit of black armor. "I see in your eyes that you recognize the armor of your god?" The paladin nodded. "Good. Then you probably know that its making took no less time than that sword you so proudly bear. The special alloy of adamantine and Mithryl makes the wearer impervious to any missile attack, grants additional resistance to all magical attacks and slowly heals any wounds and or injuries received during battle. It is also lighter by far than any alloy previously known, allowing the wearer to even swim without encumbrance. Finally," he picked the sack back up and pulled a helm from it, "this helm, which is also part of the suit, boosts your charisma—something I am sure you would agree is essential for a paladin, or a god."

Thrinndor didn't know what else to do but nod. "Thank you," he whispered.

"You are welcome. I truly hope that you gain what it is that you seek."

The paladin, who had turned to walk away stopped, turned and said, "What?"

Kreymeere waved his hand as if brushing aside the question. "Never mind, young man. Please ignore the ramblings of an old dragon."

The councilman's half-smile was not one the paladin would soon forget, however. Something in the way he spoke...

"You will each also note that the bag given to you is special in and of itself. It is what is called a Bag of Holding, size large. Inside you will find the items you were given, 10,000 in platinum pieces and an assortment of gems and other mundane jewelry. Enough to buy a king's ransom, should the need arise." Now his smile was positively jovial.

Kreymeere turned to face Savinhand. "I assume this loot will satisfy your requirements and ensure your guild-mates believe your endeavors were profitable?"

"Absolutely," the rogue responded with a huge smile.

"Good," Kreymeere said. "Are we ready to fly?"

"Yes," Sordaak answered. He had put on his items and couldn't tell whether he was smarter or not. He shrugged.

"That is well," the dragon council leader said somberly, "because The Isle of Grief has been under siege for these past two weeks."

Chapter Thirty-Three

Valdaar's Rest

With this new bit of knowledge, Breunne decided he needed to see the quest through until the end. If his girl still waited, a few more weeks wouldn't matter. Savinhand, however, remained adamant that he was needed back at Shardmoor. He also reiterated his point that he was of little or no use in a direct frontal attack. So a dragon switch had to be made. None of the older dragons could carry double—not with all their gear, anyway. Pentaath agreed to take Breunne and Savinhand, dropping off the latter at night not far from his guild headquarters. He would then use his superior speed to catch up with the others.

Every night at about midnight they stopped to allow the dragons to rest and get something to eat. The humans set up a dry camp and fell fast asleep. They were once again on the dragons' backs well before dawn. In this way they were able to circle the island from high above as evening approached on the third day, assessing the situation from that vantage point.

The companions minus the dwarf and rogue landed not far from the entrance to the keep after the light had passed from the sky to the west.

They were immediately accosted by guards, but not over aggressively. It seemed not many of them had ever seen a dragon, and certainly they weren't going to go in swinging with their swords. Not right away, anyway.

Sordaak quickly convinced his people that they were friendlies and was soon ensconced in his tower with his leaders for a briefing. That complete, he sketched out his plan and sent everyone to bed for the night.

Dawn broke with him again astride Pentaath and with the other three dragons in tight formation behind him. The others were left behind in the event his plan didn't work.

Sordaak sought out the largest vessels in the blockade, noting that one or two of them looked familiar. He vaguely wondered on which his sister waited. *It doesn't matter. She should've known better than to try again to stop me.*

The sorcerer sent the dragons diving on the ships he had selected, and before the sun was fully above the horizon eleven of the almost one hundred ships and boats of the blockade were aflame, with two of them already sinking.

Sordaak saw his sister—her long, raven black hair unmistakable even from high above—escape one of the sinking ships in a smaller boat. She shook her fist at him, and he shrugged. *What was she thinking? A siege? I suppose she thought the men wouldn't have time to work if they were worried about being attacked all the time. And maybe she thought she could starve us out. But the important work on the temple had been finished almost two weeks ago, and while the men were indeed getting grouchy about having to eat the same stuff day in and day out, they were far from starving to death. Surely she must know that...*

He watched her crawl into an adjoining boat and was satisfied to see the remaining fleet pull back. Soon it was clear the blockade had been broken, and their ships turned to sail away.

As he directed his dragon air force back to the island, an uneasy feeling settled over him. Something wasn't right, but he couldn't put his finger on it. Nevertheless, he was going to prepare the temple today. *I'll ask Pentaath to have the dragons search the surrounding areas in the event there was to be frontal assault.* That made him feel somewhat better. But the feeling that he was missing something wouldn't go away.

After the resounding defeat they had suffered only six weeks ago, he doubted an all-out attack was looming, but it was certainly possible. Regardless, the dragons would root out any possibilities along those lines. He'd ask Breunne to see if he could detect any unauthorized movements, as well. *He'll find them if they're there.*

Sordaak began to feel better. Nothing could stop them now, he thought

Later that day the mage was busy double checking all the dimensions and setting up the temple when he was summoned to the tower.

He wanted to rail at the messenger for the interruption, but he managed to keep from doing so. Barely. *While killing the messenger might make one feel better temporarily—at least until Cyrillis finds out about it—it seldom solves the problem.*

The sorcerer was again regretting not having finished that personnel elevator as he puffed his way up the last of the 124 steps it took to get to the top of his tower. *Damn, that's way too much like work.* He was waved over to the window opening to the west as soon as his head popped above floor level.

"What?" he wheezed, his hands on his knees as he tried to see what was amiss.

"Do you see that smoke?" Thrinndor pointed to the west.

"No," he complained as he squinted in the direction indicated. "Yes," he corrected, seeing a smudge on the horizon. "So?"

"So? That is Ardaagh."

"Ardaagh? Why would there be—shit!" *Pentaath!*

Yes, father?

I need you. Quick!

I am on the north side of the island. I am on my way and will be there in a few minutes.

All right, hurry!

Sordaak paced incessantly while he waited. Then, to save time he took the stairs back to the ground level two at a time. Pentaath arrived shortly after he got down and soon the two were again airborne. The mage directed the dragon west, and it was not long before they could see the source of the smoke: entire sections of Ardaagh were ablaze.

Why? The mage thought to himself. *Where are the Drow? There are supposed to be several thousand of the dark elves in the city rebuilding it as a support town. Yet I see no one! Where are they?*

Summon the other dragons, Sordaak told Pentaath. *Have them bring Breunne and Thrinndor. We've got to find out what happened to the Drow.*

Yes father.

Where is Rheagamon? Sordaak asked himself. He squinted to see the villa on the outskirts of town where the old man had set up shop, but he couldn't through the smoke. He directed his mount that direction. Pentaath obediently banked and soared lower for a better look.

As they approached the villa, both Sordaak's confusion and frustration grew. There was no movement anywhere in the vicinity. He signaled for the dragon to put down in the street, and Pentaath was quick to comply. The mage jumped down as soon as he could without injury and sprinted for the gate.

The gate from the street had been repaired recently, but it now hung from only one hinge. Sordaak ran through the gate, through the open doors and up the stairs to where he knew his master spent the bulk of his days: his library. No one was there. "RHEAGAMON!" the mage shouted. When he got no reply, he bounded back down the stairs and out into the street. Everywhere he looked there were signs of a hasty retreat.

But *why?*

He leapt onto his dragon's back and commanded him to go high—as high as he could. Something was obviously not right, and racking his brain had yet to reveal just what that something was.

As Pentaath used his mighty wings to work his way ever higher, Sordaak cleared his mind. He then closed his eyes and took in several deep breaths. He'd been told long ago they were called cleansing breaths. Whatever, they seemed to work.

What are the facts? No speculation, just the facts. One: They had broken the siege earlier that same day. Two: The Drow were missing. Three: Ardaagh—new home of the Drow—was ablaze. Four: I HAVE no four! What am I missing?

The sorcerer smacked his forehead with an open hand, knowing there was something just out of reach of his mind's eye. Suddenly he had it! *Diversionary tactics!*

He looked around, but they had yet to attain the altitude he needed. *As you continue to climb, head back toward the island.*

Pentaath didn't reply, but he changed course as directed. Sordaak could feel his dragon laboring as he clawed for additional height. The mage looked to the south and could see the blockade ships had stopped just out of sight of the keep. *What is that beyond them? Work your way south some.*

His dragon banked slightly right as he continued to work ever higher.

Damn! More ships! Minions of Set? Possibly. Dammit! What was she doing?

Now he and Pentaath were getting into thinner air, making it hard to breath. *That's high enough. Now get us over the island and to the west side. Recall the gold dragons and have them follow us. There's something wrong here, and I've yet to figure it out.*

You are giving up on Ardaagh and the Drow?

No, not giving up. I think their disappearance and the fires are part of a diversionary tactic to separate us now that we're back in the area. If I'm correct, we'll see another fleet of ships approaching from Pothgaard.

But why wait for us to get back? If they could have attacked while we were gone they would have stood a better chance of being victorious.

I know. It doesn't make sense. The only thing I can think of is that she is trying to separate us. Maybe capture or kill one of us.

She?

My sister. Shaarna. I'm certain she is behind this.

Why would she want to capture or kill one of you?

All three of us—Thrinndor, Cyrillis and myself—must be present to raise Valdaar. I'm starting to think she has figured that out.

Oh.

Is there any way for you to reach your mother or any of the other dragons?

No. The distance is too great. It is my understanding that we have to be back at Khandihaar to make the summoning. Why?

No matter. I am formulating a plan that might allow us to avert all-out war. The more dragons, the better.

I can try, but I do not think I can be heard at such great distances.

Yes, please make the try. However, even if heard, I doubt any of them can get here in time for what I have in mind.

Before he and Pentaath even got to the Isle of Grief Sordaak could see the masts of many ships advancing slowly from the direction of Pothgaard. *Dammit! That settles it! Shaarna is making an all-out effort to stop us from raising Valdaar. It's the only explanation that fits.*

Sordaak sat astride his dragon—now the Lord of Dragons. He hadn't gotten used to that yet—his mind whirring. What to do?

Take me down to the tower. Summon the other dragons and have them bring my friends. All of them. Now.

It shall be as you wish.

A disturbing silence whistled through the sorcerer's hair as Pentaath circled ever closer to the ground. *What to do? The options are too many!* As they approached the tower, the mage formulated possible plans and discarded the obvious failures.

Sordaak bounded up the stairs two and three at a time as Pentaath reverted to human form. In his chambers at the top, the mage rushed over to the table and swept everything from it to the floor with a single wave of his arm. He frowned at the stained wood that stared back at him and briefly searched the room until he found what he sought: a linen sheet from the bed to serve as a covering.

Quickly the sorcerer flipped it into place and smoothed out the wrinkles. The others began to arrive, and he waved them to silence as he began to assemble various fruits, carved figures and a large bowl on the table.

"Breakfast?" Breunne asked as he watched the frantic sorcerer place implements onto the table. He was the last to arrive.

Sordaak ignored him as he continued to work. Apparently satisfied, he stood back with his hands on his hips and studied his handiwork.

Thrinndor cleared his throat as the mage made a minor adjustment. "You have a purpose for all of this, I assume?"

Sordaak looked at the paladin as if seeing him for the first time, scratched his head and said, "Yes." He then returned his attention to the table and made a few adjustments, muttering all the while.

When the sorcerer finally turned back around, his troubled eyes sought those of the paladin. "We're in trouble."

Silence followed that statement for a few moments as the companions waited for the mage to continue. When that didn't immediately happen, they all began talking at once.

Thrinndor, however, recognized the look in the sorcerer's eyes, and that look concerned him. He'd seen it before. Sordaak was flirting with the edge. Again. The paladin held up his right hand, asking for silence. He got it.

"Calm yourself and explain."

"Calm? *Calm?*" Sordaak visibly tensed up. But then he closed his eyes and raised his face to the ceiling. He breathed deeply a couple of times, and when he opened his eyes, the walls no longer seemed to be closing in on him. When he brought his gaze back down to face the companions, Thrinndor could see the crisis had passed.

Sordaak waved them over to the table and pointed at the bowl in the center. "That is this island." Next he pointed over to a dozen or so fruit to one side. "That is my sister's fleet, waiting just over the horizon to the south." Then he pointed at a collection of wooden figurines on another side of the bowl. "That is a fleet of ships approaching from the direction of Pothgaard." Finally he pointed to a smaller bowl opposite the Pothgaard fleet. "That is Ardaagh. Empty." The troubled look returned to his eyes when he raised them to look at the paladin. "I don't know where the Drow have gone. It makes no sense."

"Does any of this make sense?" Breunne asked.

Sordaak looked at the ranger, but Breunne was not sure he was seen. "Are the dwarves here? What about the troglodytes?"

"The dwarves are present. However, there are rumblings among the rank and file that they didn't come here to fight a war." Breunne hesitated. "The troglodytes are also present, but they've retreated deep into their catacombs."

The mage looked down at his feet; indecision ate at his soul. When he looked up he sought out the lone messenger in the room. "Find Morroth and Gri'Puth. Have them report to me immediately." The dwarf nodded and then disappeared down the stairs.

"What are you thinking?" Thrinndor asked, again concerned for the sanity of the sorcerer.

Sordaak glared at the paladin. Abruptly his shoulders drooped. "I've narrowed down the possibilities to two. And with either of them, we're in trouble."

No one dared break the silence that followed. They all waited for the mage to continue. Sordaak complied by looking over at the table and pointing.

"Either these fleets intend to take the island by force—and I believe they have sufficient force to do so—or they are merely trying to divide our forces." Sordaak's eyes again sought those of the paladin. "Either way, they mean to prevent us from raising your god."

"Our god," the paladin replied evenly.

"Our god." The mage's eyes never wavered.

Thrinndor's lips were a thin line when he continued. "How is it you plan on thwarting their effort to prevent our raising Valdaar?"

"Ah, the question I've been waiting for," Sordaak said as he again looked over at the table. He took in a deep breath. "The chamber—temple—I had constructed to facilitate this raising has special properties that I believe will increase our chances of success." He looked back at the paladin. "We *could* leave under the cover of night and make the attempt at some other location."

"If the odds of success are reduced, then that is not an option."

The mage exhaled, and his shoulders slumped. "I thought you'd say that." He stroked the hairs on his chin. "That leaves us but two options as I see it. We get our shit together and fight the coming horde." He narrowed his eyes. "Or we make the attempt to raise Valdaar tonight before they have a chance to stop us. After that, regardless of the outcome of the attempt, I say we abandon the island—at least for the near future."

"Why?" Breunne asked.

Sordaak didn't immediately answer. Instead of looking at the ranger, he looked back at his makeshift war table. "Because if my estimates as to their numbers are correct, tomorrow they will come ashore with a force of around 10,000 warriors, all looking for a fight."

A fly was heard buzzing around the table in the silence that followed that announcement.

"How many men can we muster?" Thrinndor asked.

"By morning?" Sordaak shook his head. "Two thousand—and that's only if we can get the dwarves to come out and play. The troglodytes are too far away to get here unless we are able to prolong the fight. The Drow? I have no idea where they disappeared to. But *even if* we were able get every available body here in time for the defense, Shaarna's forces will outnumber us two to one."

The paladin's right hand shot out, and the buzzing stopped. He flipped his hand toward the open window.

"How long will it take for you to make the attempt?"

Again the sorcerer took in a deep breath. "I have no idea." He raised both hands to ward off the coming protests. "However, the spell itself is really nothing more than releasing the energy stored in your sword—and that shouldn't take very long at all." He tugged at the hairs on his chin. "The preparation? That's the hard part. I will need a few hours—minimum—to get ready."

"Do you have everything you need?"

Sordaak's answer to that was a simple nod.

"Very well." The paladin looked out the window to gauge how much daylight was left. "Gather what you require. We make the attempt to raise our god at nightfall."

Chapter Thirty-Four

To Raise a God

Sordaak stood alone in the chamber, verifying against a written list in his hands that he had everything he would need. Once begun, there would be no opportunity to get additional components.

What was soon to be designated as the temple had no furnishings as of yet. In fact, the only item on the polished black marble surface of the floor was a single raised altar on the far end of the chamber, which sat opposite the only set of doors in the room. The altar was unusual in shape and placement. It was hewn from a single piece of the same material as the walls and floors—black marble. Its surface was about two feet above the floor and it was roughly rectangular, with an elongated angle that formed the bottom toward the door. From that point to the top, it was just over six feet long. The two sides were roughly three feet apart, with the farthest points apart being away from the door.

The only other things in the chamber besides the magicuser and the altar were three curious black iron contraptions, one at each of the three corners opposite the door. They appeared to be supports—just what they were meant to support was not clear.

The six sconces—one on each wall without doors and one on either side of the doors—struggled mightily against the black walls, floors and ceiling to provide enough light to see by. It was as the mage wanted it.

One at a time the others trickled in. First was Thrinndor—Sordaak verified he carried both his sword and *Flinthgoor*. What the greataxe's part in this was to be, the sorcerer did not know. But he was fairly certain that it did have a part. Cyrillis came in next with her staff, followed immediately by Breunne. It was clear they had arrived together.

The mage pulled Breunne aside. "As you are aware, you have no part in the ceremony. I ask only that you remain completely silent and do not disturb us in any way." The ranger nodded. "I will seal the doors before we begin, and your sole task will be to stop anything or anyone that tries to enter—or exit—this chamber. Understand?"

Breunne raised an eyebrow. "Exit?"

Sordaak hesitated. "I don't know exactly what is going to happen here—no one does. *Nothing* must be allowed to enter or leave."

The ranger nodded and walked with the sorcerer to the doors. Once there, Sordaak turned to look at the others who were watching him. "Last chance. I don't know how long this will take, and once I seal the doors, no one is going anywhere until we are through. Understood?"

Cyrillis and Thrinndor nodded.

"Where's Pentaath?" the cleric asked.

"He is keeping an eye on the fleets with instructions to warn me if anything changes, like their coming ashore."

"You remain convinced they are going to try to take the island by force?" the paladin asked.

Sordaak nodded. "Yes. And I don't think they will wait for morning. Pentaath informs me that all ships seem to have on maximum sail and are only an hour away, at most."

Thrinndor nodded grimly. "Very well. It seems you have been correct in your assessment as to their intentions thus far. We will have to waste no time in evacuating once we are through here. What of the dwarves?"

"You may have seen some of them on your way here." The paladin and cleric both nodded. "I told them to go north under the cover of night and seek refuge with the troglodytes. Gri'Puth has agreed to provide shelter deep in their labyrinth until such a time as we are able to begin construction anew."

Cyrillis was chewing her lower lip. "This is hard for you, is it not?"

The mage took in a deep breath and allowed his shoulders to slump slightly. He nodded. "Yes. Surrendering the culmination of my life's dream does not come without regret." He lifted his chin and looked around at the walls. "Yet, these are only walls. Until they are complete and I reside within their fortifications, they can be rebuilt or repaired." He let a breath out noisily. "Surviving the day is by far the more important thing at this point."

The cleric nodded, partially mollified. "We *will* reside here one day." She tapped the heel of *Kurri* lightly on the stone to emphasize her point.

Sordaak nodded. "Yes, we will." Again he looked around the chamber. "Are we ready?" Getting the nods he expected in return, he continued. "Very well. Please move away from the walls and doors and refrain from approaching them until I give the all clear. Understand?" More nods. "Once I begin, there will be no questions, nor will there be further explanations. My concentration must not be broken for any reason. Speak not, not even among yourselves. Am I clear?" Again came more nods.

Satisfied, the sorcerer turned to face the doors. First he verified they were locked and then closed his eyes and bowed his head. If the paladin hadn't known better, he would have thought the mage was *praying!*

When Sordaak raised his head, he raised *Pendromar* as well. Slowly he began to chant. As he chanted, he sidestepped along the wall. When he reached a corner, he turned to follow it without looking, his chant remaining even through the turn. He continued this until he had made a complete circuit around the room. Once he was back at his starting point, he stopped.

The mage tapped the heel of his staff twice on the marble floor and raised it again in front of him. When he spoke, the language was unintelligible, but to the paladin the words resembled an old elven dialect. Blue light shot from the staff, and slowly Sordaak traced the edges of the doors with that light, including the small gap between the two metal-shod doors.

Satisfied, Sordaak then pulled his cowl over his head, covering his eyes, and then he again bowed his head. He remained like this for a time.

When he raised his head, Cyrillis almost betrayed her vow with a sharp intake of breath—the predecessor to a scream. However, she bit her lip and was able to force back the outcry. Sordaak's eyes could now be seen from under the covering of the cowl because they glowed a deep, dark red—the same color as the eyes on the pommel of *Valdaar's Fist.* The rest of his face remained hidden.

Sordaak raised both hands and began to chant. This chanting was different, however—darker and lower. The paladin thought he detected hints of the language known only to the gods.

This continued for several minutes, building in intensity until the mage abruptly dropped his hands. "It's not working!" he said loudly.

Startled, Cyrillis replied, "What is not working?"

Sordaak glared at her, his eyes back to normal.

"Sorry," she said demurely. As quickly as she said it, she realized the magicuser was not looking *at* her, he was looking *through* her.

"Something is missing!" the sorcerer shouted. His glare shifted until he had looked all around the room. *"DAMMIT!"* He snatched his staff from its holder and began to circle the altar. The others remained standing where they'd been told.

"What am I *missing!*" he hissed, not breaking stride. "We have representatives from the lineages of Dragma, Angra-Khan and Valdaar. The correct artifacts are also present!" He shook his head as he continued to circle.

Suddenly his eyes fell on *Flinthgoor*, and he stopped so quickly he almost tripped. "What? *What?*" He slammed the heel of his staff to the ground, drawing sparks. *"WHAT AM I MISSING?"*

Suddenly he stood up to his full height, spun on his heel and marched over to the doors. He waved his hand and the blue light tracings at the seams vanished.

"Wait here," he said as he opened the door on the right and stepped through without looking back. *Meet me at the tower,* he commanded his dragon.

On my way.

The magicuser noted that it was dusk when he passed through the outer chamber and into the courtyard of the keep. *Damn, this is taking too long! We're running out of time!*

When Pentaath landed amid a flurry of wind and dust, the mage wasted no time and jumped onto the dragon's back. *Take me to my sister's ship. If you don't remember which one, I'll guide you when we get close.*

The one with the command flag, right?

Yes.

Wings flapped and powerful legs launched the pair skyward. Pentaath banked to the north and soon they were over the water. *Go invisible. I don't want them to know we're there until I land on the ship.*

You land on the ship? Will I not be with you?

No. You're too damn big to land on such a vessel now. When we get close enough I'll use my fly spell to go the last distance.

Sordaak sensed the unease that request brought, but he knew of no other way. *I'll be fine. I'm pissed off enough that if I'm crossed, I'm liable to blow something up!*

The dragon chuckled as he began his descent. *Damn, the ships are getting too close!* He found himself hoping they had enough time remaining to accomplish their task. They must, for there would be no second chance.

Prepare yourself, Pentaath warned him, *the ship directly beneath us is the ship she crawled aboard when we sank hers.*

Stay close. Sordaak then cast his Fly spell and jumped off of the dragon, trusting his familiar not to steer him wrong. He hadn't. However, the mage narrowly missed getting tangled in the rigging as he slowly descended to the deck. His eyes had adjusted to the dark, and he spotted the form of his sister standing next to a male figure at the ship's wheel on the stern.

Deciding he didn't have time for diplomacy, Sordaak landed with a thud behind the pair. When they turned to see who was behind them, the mage hit his sister hard enough on the head with his staff to knock her unconscious, but not hard enough to scramble her brains. He hoped. *I'm still trying to get accustomed to this Giant Strength!* The man next to her opened his mouth to shout, but as the sorcerer caught the slight frame of his sister, he raised a booted foot and shoved the robed figure hard enough that he tumbled overboard.

The man's cry of surprise turned to one of fear as he hit the water. As an added measure, Sordaak spun the wheel as hard as he could to starboard. He felt the ship heel over as the rudder bit water. Just before he jumped back into the air, he cast a Wall of Fire spell near the mast, knowing the dry ropes and sails would quickly catch and soon the ship would be ablaze. *A nice distraction.* He hoped.

I hope you're still here, he told Pentaath as he jumped back into the air, *because it's going to get a bit hectic down there.*

Right above you—swerve a bit to your left.

Sordaak stifled a curse as he slammed into the body of the dragon, which caused him to nearly drop his sister. *It might help if you were to become visible!*

Right. And suddenly there was the dragon, easily illuminated by the light of the fire not far below. There were shouts from the deck as the crew gathered the bucket brigade in an attempt to save their ship. A quick glance told Sordaak that that wasn't likely. The mast was ablaze, as was most of the rigging. He noted with satisfaction that the fire-ship was heading straight for another vessel that was frantically trying to turn and stay clear. *That should keep them busy for a time.* He looked over at his sister in his arms. *Losing their commander might put a damper on their plans, too.* But he doubted it would delay them long.

The sorcerer dropped his sister onto the dragon's back when he got close and then settled next to her, wrapping an arm around her waist so that she didn't inadvertently tumble overboard. *Take us back to the Keep.*

Pentaath said nothing as he beat his wings to regain the lost altitude. While flying with two relatively light humans on his back was little or no trouble for a dragon of his size, gaining altitude with those same two without dumping them into the sea was much harder. But he managed.

The dragon settled back to the ground where he had picked up his human cargo, at the base of the tower. Without a word, Sordaak flipped his sister over his shoulder and jumped from the back of his mount. He heard a groan escape his captive's lips and she twisted slightly when they hit the ground. She was coming to.

The mage considered clobbering her again, but he decided against it since the distance to the temple was so short. *I might need her conscious for this.*

By the time he stepped through the doors that led back into the temple, Shaarna was fully awake and struggling mightily. *Damn, she is not as slight of frame as I remember!* "Be still!" Sordaak commanded as he dumped her unceremoniously onto the floor at the base of the altar.

"I will not!" his sister answered as she jumped back to her feet. "Oh, it's *you!*"

"You were expecting to be abducted by someone else?"

"No!" Shaarna spat. Suddenly, her eyes widened and she licked her lips as she looked around the room. "Where am I?"

"In my Keep," replied the sorcerer.

"For what purpose?"

"Good question," Sordaak said with a shrug. "I'll give you an answer when I figure out just what that answer is."

"You're mad."

"No. My mother had me tested." Sordaak smiled at his sister. He then turned to Thrinndor. "Make sure she doesn't try anything while I re-seal the chamber."

The paladin nodded as he moved to stand next to the sorceress. He smiled as he looked down at her. *Damn, she is beautiful!*

Damn, he's handsome! Briefly Shaarna considered trying to blast her way out, but she knew that would be a lost cause.

"I would not try," the deep voice of the paladin reverberated through the room. "Surely you know by now that your brother's power far exceeds your own."

"And I have *Pendromar*," Sordaak said from over by the doors.

"You are outmanned and outclassed, young woman. Resistance is futile."

"You really expect me to acquiesce?" Shaarna asked.

The paladin's mouth worked a couple of times without saying anything, and his eyes locked with hers. *Damn, she has beautiful eyes!* He shook his head. "No, I suppose that would not suit your style." He beamed his best smile at her.

Damn, he's got a killer smile! "Right," she agreed as she reluctantly turned her attention to her brother, who was again chanting as he slowly circled the room in the same manner as he had before. "Isn't that spell used to keep demons and/or devils from passing?" When she got no reply, she stamped her boot in frustration on the marble. "Just what is going on here?"

"*Silence!*" whispered the paladin, elbowing the young woman beside him for good measure.

When Sordaak finished his circuit and began resealing the doors she whispered, "That spell is designed to keep spirits—ghosts, wraiths and such—either in or out of someplace! *What* are you *doing?*"

Sordaak finished sealing the doors before walking slowly to confront his sister. "It is my belief that your presence—as a descendent of either Valdaar or Dragma, it matters not which—is required for us to raise our god." She tried to speak, but Sordaak silenced her with a raised hand. "You have a choice, of sorts." Shaarna raised an eyebrow—they were certainly related. "You can sit by quietly and allow me to perform my duties, or I can have pretty boy there knock your ass out. While I believe your presence is required, but I don't think you actually have to witness or do anything—a warm, breathing body should suffice." It was his turn to raise an eyebrow. "What's it going to be?"

Shaarna narrowed her eyes and crossed her arms on her chest. "You wouldn't dare."

"You're not as smart as I gave you credit for," Sordaak said with a shake of his head. He looked over at the paladin. "Thrinndor, if you would please."

The paladin licked his lips and hesitated. This had not been discussed. He hoped the sorcerer was bluffing. Striking a female in a non-combat situation was a distinct violation of his code. Yet the successful raising of Valdaar surpassed all code at this point. He uncrossed his arms and balled his right hand up into a fist.

"Wait." It was Shaarna's turn to lick her lips nervously. "Maybe you would. What is it you would have me do?"

"Stand at the end of this altar and hold onto this," Sordaak walked over and picked up *Flinthgoor*.

"Damn, that's a big axe."

Sordaak looked at the greataxe, admiring the craftsmanship of its makers for the first time. "Yes, it is." He held it out to his sister. "This is *Flinthgoor*, and it is one of the artifacts of great power from the Council of Valdaar. It belonged to his General of Armies, Kreithgaar, but was more recently wielded by Vorgath, Dragonslayer and hero of the land." His chin lifted as he spoke this.

"Who?"

An irritated look crossed the mage's face. *She could not know him*, he realized. "Never mind. Take this and stand over there." He stopped short of giving her the axe, however. "Know this: If you so much as open your mouth or make any move of aggression, I will not hesitate to put another knot on your head."

"That was you?" Shaarna asked, rubbing the knot she already had. "You should be more careful!"

"Your brains—what little there are—remain unscrambled, do they not?"

Shaarna's eyes flashed as her hand shot forward and grasped the haft of *Flinthgoor*. When Sordaak let it go, the weight of it caused her to bounce the end of the massive weapon on the floor. "Damn! That's *heavy*!"

Sordaak rolled his eyes as he returned to his place beside the altar. "Quit whining and get to your place, please."

As the sorceress drug the greataxe to her designated place in the chamber, the paladin leaned over and whispered, "Are you sure we can trust her? There is much at stake here."

"Of course I don't think we can trust her!" Sordaak snapped. He made sure his voice was loud enough for his sister to hear.

"Then why do you not ensure her silence?"

Sordaak turned his eyes to his sister. "Two reasons: One, if we are successful in raising Valdaar, I want her to report this to her people when we release her. Maybe she can then convince them that trying to overrun the island would not be in their best interest."

"Fat chance," Shaarna said wryly. "And the second?"

"Two, if we are unsuccessful in raising Valdaar, she would then of course report to her people as such, and they would have no further reason to try to take the island."

Shaarna shrugged. "Now *that* at least makes some sort of sense."

Sordaak walked over to stand in front of his sister. His eyes searched hers. There was intelligence there, possibly more than he had anticipated. "You will vow to not raise your hand in any way nor open your mouth. If you do this, I will allow you to act as witness to these proceedings for the purpose spoken. If you are unwilling to vow as such," he raised his staff. "I will take no chances." He set his jaw. "What's it to be?

Shaarna set her jaw in the same manner as before and her eyes searched her brother's for any sign of weakness. As expected, she found none. "Very well, I give you my word as a servant of that which is good and just in the land that I will not disturb you or your attempt to raise your god in any way." She smiled sweetly. "Will that suffice?"

Sordaak started to turn away, but then shook his head. "No. That was given too easily." His eyes again locked with hers. "This will ensure your silence." He spat an enchantment and pointed his finger as Shaarna's eyes flared wide. She tried to flinch, but a ray of blue energy shot from the mage's finger and engulfed the young woman. Instantly she froze, unable to move. Only her eyes moved, and that movement showed her to yet be conscious.

"I have extended that spell, and it should hold you for an hour or so if need be." The sorcerer looked over at Breunne, who remained by the door. "If she moves, shoot her." The ranger nodded. "Try something non-lethal at first. If she continues to move, kill her." Breunne nodded again.

Sordaak quickly stepped back to his place at the altar. His eyes swept the room. "Let there be no further interruptions." Without waiting for a reply, he placed *Pendromar* in the holder provided, reached back and pulled the hood over his eyes as before and bowed his head.

Sordaak raised his hands and began to chant. Dark and insidious, the words reverberated off the walls of the temple. As before Sordaak's eyes glowed red, their intensity startling those around him. This time, however, the eyes in the skull on the pommel of *Valdaar's Fist* matched that intensity.

As Sordaak continued to chant, the companions could feel the power in the room build. The mage's voice grew louder, and still the power built until the air in the room seemed fraught with electricity. Then the runes on *Pendromar* and *Kurril* began to glow up and down their length. Still the power continued to build.

Everyone in the room felt the energy as it crawled over their skin like a thousand insects. Finally, when Cyrillis was sure she could bear it no longer, Sordaak ceased chanting. The intensity of his eyes frightened her, and the cleric was certain she would never forget that look. Never.

Slowly the sorcerer lowered his arms. When he raised his right hand, he pointed at the skull affixed to *Valdaar's Fist* with his index finger and spoke several words in what Thrinndor was now certain was the language of the gods. As he spoke each word, his voice rose until he was shouting as the last one blasted from his lips.

A thick, searing ray of red energy leapt from his fingertip to strike the pommel of the sword full in the skull's face. Then the skull's mouth opened in a silent scream that produced flames instead of sound.

The flames launched into motion and bounced off of the first wall they encountered. From there they streaked to the opposite wall and again they bounced toward still yet another wall. This continued as the flames bounced from ceiling to floor and from wall to wall, leaving streaks of light burned into everyone's eyes until there were too many to count.

The mouth on the skull opened again, this time wailing with an intensity that built until it hurt the ears of all present.

And then, as abruptly as it began, the flames bounced one last time and went out. The skull went silent. Simultaneously the fires in all the sconces were blown out, pitching the chamber into utter darkness.

Cyrillis screamed and then a silence as complete as the darkness engulfed the chamber.

Sordaak's hands fumbled for *Pendromar*, finding it at last on the third wild swing of his arms in front of him. "Shield your eyes," he warned, his voice husky from the abuse of shouting. He then called forth light from his staff.

Quickly the sorcerer looked right and left. Thrinndor was to his right, Shaarna was where he had left her, and Breunne remained at the door, his bow in his hand with an arrow nocked. Cyrillis was the only one missing.

Sordaak jumped over the altar, narrowly missing the cleric where she had fallen when he landed next to her. Together he and Thrinndor knelt at her side. The paladin put his hand on her shoulder, but could not find anything wrong. *Perhaps she fainted.*

The sorcerer slid his arms beneath her slight form, easily lifted the healer and placed her gently on the raised platform. By the time her head rested on the marble of the altar, her eyelids fluttered open. "What—what happened?" she stammered, her hand grasping the arm of the mage.

"I don't know," Sordaak answered.

Thrinndor took the time to look around the chamber. "We have failed," he said, his voice strained. The paladin had been certain that his god would have chosen him as his vassal. It was obvious to him that that had not happened. They had failed.

"We have?" Cyrillis pushed herself up to a sitting position and swung her legs over the marble edge.

"I no longer feel his presence within me," it was the sword that spoke. "Valdaar has been released."

Thrinndor turned to the sorcerer. "Then your spells performed as expected." Sordaak nodded. "His essence must have been too weak from two millennia in captivity to finish the task." That proclamation returned silence to the chamber. A single tear wound its way down the cheek of the big fighter. "We have failed."

"His essence remains within this chamber," the sword spoke again.

"How can you be sure?" Thrinndor challenged. The paladin was bitterly disappointed that his years of service would come to this. Failure.

"He is here," the sword said stubbornly.

"Where?" demanded the paladin.

"I know not," admitted the sword.

"We have failed." Cyrillis repeated. Her heart sank until she was not certain she could call it back, nor was she certain she wanted to.

Abruptly the paladin spun and jabbed a finger at the sorcerer. "Your spells *must* have failed us, *magicuser*!" He spat the title as if it were distasteful in his mouth.

"They have not!" shouted Sordaak in return. "*I* have not! My spells functioned as required. Your god's essence was released from his prison. Two thousand years must have been too much for him."

"Bah!" shouted the paladin. He reached out his right hand and instantly *Valdaar's Fist* was in his massive hand. He strode to the doors and was about to kick them open when he remembered the sorcerer's warning. "Release them," he grated.

Sordaak waved his hand, releasing the binding spells he had placed on the doors and walls of the chamber.

Without waiting for an acknowledgement, the paladin grasped the mechanism on the doors, pulled them open and stepped through.

"Where are you going?" Cyrillis called after him. But she got no answer. She turned her tear streaked face to the sorcerer. "We have failed?" Her voice broke on the last word.

Sordaak didn't know how to answer that. Their god was certainly not present, but somehow this didn't *feel* like a failure. Confusion reigned supreme in his head. In answer he reached out and wrapped his arms around the cleric. Her shoulders shook as she sobbed silently within the folds of his robe.

Seeing that his sister remained trapped within the throes of his spell, he waved a hand and released her as well. She stumbled to her right, allowing *Flinthgoor* to clatter to the floor as she reached out to stabilize herself with the edge of the altar.

"Go. Call off your armies." Sordaak stroked Cyrillis' head as he spoke. "We will oppose you no more."

Shaarna's eyes searched those of her brother. She opened her mouth to speak but could not find the words. Finally she nodded and followed the paladin into the night.

Cyrillis continued to cry softly with her face pressed against the sorcerer's robes.

Breunne put *Xenotath* away, shuffled his feet nervously and cleared his throat. "Is there anything I can do?"

Sordaak shook his head and with a solemn nod the ranger followed the others.

Cyrillis pushed back and scrubbed at her tear stained eyes with the palm of her hand. "We failed?" she asked again.

Sordaak still didn't have an answer.

"Wait!" The cleric put both feet onto the floor and pushed herself up. She waved a hand and suddenly the mage felt better—and he hadn't even noticed *not* feeling this good. "If we failed, they why can I still cast spells?"

"What?"

Cyrillis rolled her eyes. "Silly, I just cast a restorative spell on you. I *know* that it worked. That means Valdaar remains with us!" Noting the sorcerer's confusion she added, "My healing power comes from my god." Sordaak's face brightened. "If he were no longer with us, I could not have cast that spell!"

"Right!" the mage agreed. He looked around. "But, where *is* he?"

"I know not," she replied with a shrug. "But that no longer matters." She looked up and into the magicuser's eyes. "He lives and he is free!"

Damn, that woman's smile could stop a war. Sordaak looked around quickly. *Or start one...*

A thought occurred to him. "What about Thrinndor?"

"What about him?"

"If you can cast spells and know that Valdaar yet lives, why doesn't Thrinndor?"

Cyrillis craned her neck so she could look through the doors exiting the chamber. "It is possible our paladin is not thinking clearly, right now."

"What?"

"Thrinndor had convinced himself that once his spirit was released, Valdaar was going to need a host body until such a time as he could regain his former strength." The healer turned her head slowly so that she could look into Sordaak's eyes. "And he assumed that host body would be his. His disappointment in that not happening possibly has blinded him to the possibility that he was not needed."

"So we didn't fail?"

Cyrillis shook her head. "No, we did not fail. Valdaar lives and he is *free*." Her eyes turned again to the exit. "Perhaps Thrinndor will see that when his anger wanes."

Sordaak helped the cleric to the floor and took her hand. "Let's go get something to eat. I'm famished! And, if we're going to have to leave the island quickly, I want to do so on a full stomach."

*

Breunne returned to his people, and he and his new mate visited his old friends on the island occasionally to say hello, sometimes staying for months at a time. The ranger had settled down in the shadows of Khandihaar and started a school for rangers—the first in the recorded history of the land.

Savinhand was doing well; he had even succeeded in expanding Guild Shardmoor until it was once again the premier information gathering—and trading, of course—source in all the land. He, too, stopped by for a visit when his duties allowed, which was not as often as any of them would have liked.

Thrinndor had disappeared. Rumors found their way back to the island that he had renounced his Paladinhood and lent his battle acumen—and sword— to the highest bidder in any dispute or war that offered. He was a mercenary. Sordaak had asked both Breunne and Savinhand to use their considerable skills to monitor the paladin and keep him informed as to his whereabouts and doings. Thrinndor worried the mage.

Cyrillis and Sordaak had weathered the winter in the tower as the dwarves returned to work building the keep. The Drow returned to Ardaagh with the explanation that an army of over five thousand had come upon them from the east. This army had marched through their town, setting fire to various buildings and ransacking the place in the name of Praxaar. Rheagamon had ordered the evacuation, and the drow had hid in caverns that honeycombed the mountains to the east until it was deemed safe to return. It had been from Ardaagh that the massive army had set sail on ships brought in from all over the land for that purpose.

Many a time Sordaak had thanked the gods—one in particular at Cyrillis' request—that his sister had found a way to turn the armies around. He hadn't wanted to find a place to hide until the armies dispersed. Of course, Pentaath had offered them refuge should the need arise, and as attractive as that offer had been just to drop off of the end of the world for the time being, the cleric and the magicuser had much to do, promises to keep.

Whatever it was that had required the cleric to remain reserved had been released that fateful night when he had performed the summoning. The two had exchanged vows to one another, and she had borne him a fine son. And now her slightly rounded belly indicated yet another child was soon to grace the halls of this, their home.

As the keep neared completion, the pair had kept their promise to the barbarians of Pothgaard and set up two schools. His taught the ways of the magic arts to those who showed sufficient aptitude. Hers taught the ways of healing, still in the name of Valdaar. Cyrillis' powers improved and grew as she taught. She knew that her god was back in the land and that his power continued to grow. She could *feel* his presence now, and her own skills improved dramatically with his presence among the living.

Sordaak shrugged. He no longer concerned himself with the goings on of the gods—Cyrillis did enough of that for the both of them. Fortunately she was not oppressive in her devotion to Valdaar, because the mage doubted he could stand any such behavior.

He paid homage to the friend he lost in battle by building the study that the barbarian had always wanted. Cyrillis protested only lightly when he included the mounted heads of Melundiir, Theremault, the gold dragon the barbarian had slain single-handedly and, over the massive stone hearth, the head of Bahamut, *former* King of all Dragons.

Pentaath returned to Khandihaar and called his first gathering. His power was unmistakable and went unchallenged. He formed a council of the highest-ranking dragons of each of the orders and vowed to his new followers that he would return the dragons to their rightful place of power in the land. Sordaak and his familiar honed their relationship so that even at great distances they could check in on the other and even see what the other saw if both were focused enough.

In the realm of man, the title of Dragon Master had been given to the mage. He fought it and refused to allow that title to gain hold on the island. He knew that no man could lay claim to being the master of those great beasts. He knew also that the fierce pride of those same beasts would not allow it, either. Yet, away from his island, the title not only stuck—it grew.

Shaarna had indeed succeeded in calling off the attack, and thus the land had narrowly avoided all-out war. Although that may have been only for the time being. Rumblings of late indicated the uneasy peace that had settled on the land might not last. Armies had been gathered and then sent home without being allowed to do what they had been gathered for: fight. There were hundreds—in some cases thousands—that remained banded together, looking for a cause for which to lend their swords. And then there were the rumors that factions remained within Praxaar's most devoted followers that there were those who did not believe the threat of Valdaar or those who served him had been eradicated from the land.

Which was, of course, the case...

Valdaar's Fist

Epilogue

Sordaak watched as his two year-old son Vorgaath chased a ball down the hill. It was a beautiful spring morning on the island—*their* island. He smiled as he turned to see Cyrillis, his mate for nearly three years now, hovering nearby to ensure their son didn't trip over some unseen stone or stick. Or, if he did trip, to ensure he was not seriously harmed. It had seemed fitting that they named their firstborn after their former companion. The mage frowned slightly at the memory, but he pushed that aside as he walked slowly over to join them.

Cyrillis glanced sidelong at her mate and smiled. They chatted idly about what was to be for lunch while she kept a mother's eye on her son. Sordaak walked away, headed back toward the keep. Quickly he disappeared over the hill and she was surprised when she turned to see a large eagle alight on the ground next to her son.

She nearly screamed, both to recall Sordaak and to scare off the bird that stood several inches taller than Vorgaath. However, something in the manner of both caused her to bite off that scream. Her son was talking animatedly to the bird while the bird bobbed its head as it apparently listened.

Kurril appeared suddenly in her left hand and she ran the few steps necessary to take her to her son's side. She raised the staff in the event it was needed, but Vorgaath turned his vividly green eyes on her and said in the sing-song voice of a two year-old, "No mother. Triang does not want to hurt me. I called him."

Confused, the healer stopped only a step away and lowered her staff. "Triang? You *called* him?"

The boy bobbed his head excitedly. "I saw him over there," he said, pointing to the peak of the mountain that stood behind the keep—at least two miles away, "and asked him if he wanted to play." The boy's smile beamed from ear to ear. "He said yes!"

Cyrillis didn't know what to say. Briefly she considered calling Sordaak back over, but decided not to bother him. He was leaving in the morning to inspect the northern holdings and had much to do. This did not appear like something she could not handle.

"OK," she said guardedly, "but *please* be careful! I will be right over here if you need me." The healer glared at the eagle for a moment and then took a couple of steps back. She could sense no malicious intent in the bird, but she wasn't going to take any chances. *He can talk to eagles?*

"Yes, mother."

When did this happen? The cleric had noticed several things odd about her son—at least as he related to Sordaak. The boy's eyes were a brilliant green, while her own were a bright blue and his father's a dark brown—almost black. Their son's hair color was like hers—a honey wheat color and very soft. Sordaak's was jet black. And thick. When she cared to think about it—she generally pushed these thoughts from her mind whenever they crept in—she noted that the boy was not much like his father at all.

Abruptly, the eagle launched skyward, his powerful wings blasting the seedlings from several nearby dandelions, where they were carried away by the morning breeze. Slowly, her brow furrowed in deep thought, Cyrillis walked back over to stand beside her son as the bird flew back toward the mountain. She wanted to ask what that was all about, but the cleric was sure she would get few answers that made sense from a two-year-old.

Curiosity got the better of her, however, and she asked, "How long have you been talking to animals?" She kept her tone unconcerned and gentle.

Vorgaath turned his eyes on her and his smile vanished. "Since I can remember," he said with all the honesty of a child in his voice. "Animal's thoughts are much easier to understand than people's."

Thoughts? Understand? What in the name of the seven hells is going on?

"Mother," her son's voice turned as somber as a two year-old's could, "Triang said that bad people are coming to hurt us."

"What?" Cyrillis' attention abruptly snapped back to her son. She had many more questions, but the appearance of one of the house servants caused her to forgo them for now. The servant explained that lunch was served. She nodded absent-mindedly, took her son's hand and followed the man back toward the keep. She made a mental note to talk to Sordaak about this.

As she silently chewed her food, she pieced together several other irregularities she had noticed with her son. Once she had seen him fall, skinning his knee. Cyrillis immediately healed him and wiped away his tears. That was normal. However, every time she saw him trip or almost fall from that point forward, he never fell to the ground. Instead he would float slowly until he was prone, where he always bounced back up and continued playing as if nothing had occurred. Another time she had seen him mimicking his father by throwing rocks into a pool in the hills high above the keep. Then Sordaak threw one in a way that it skipped multiple times before sinking below the surface. Vorgaath had tried to do the same, but failed miserably. However, the second time his rock had skipped nearly all the way across the pool. His father had missed this second toss as he had lost interested in the exercise and turned away, but she had watched in wide-eyed wonder as their son proceeded to skip several more before getting bored and following his father. There were other such occurrences. Separately they had seemed nothing to be concerned about, but combining those with this discussion with an eagle gave rise to more questions than she had answers.

I will talk to Sordaak about it upon his return from the northern reaches. He will know what to do if anything needs to be done.

The next day, having forgotten about the encounter between her son and the eagle, she was in one of the many storage rooms sorting through the paintings, tapestries and other decorative items brought to the keep by the others of the faith when they answered the summons. It was her job—one she gladly dealt with—to oversee the furnishings and decorations for the keep. She flipped the cover off of a large portrait and felt her heart stop. She almost dropped the painting as she stumbled back a couple of steps, tripped over a rolled-up rug and landed hard on her backside.

Rising, she sat the edge of the painting down on the floor and carefully brushed at the light dust that covered the canvas. The painting was *old—very old*. Dozens of centuries, at least. That is not what grabbed her attention, however. The portrait was of a handsome young man with shoulder length blonde hair and piercing green eyes. He also wore the same black armor that Thrinndor was given by the dragons after the battle with the Platinum Dragon. Valdaar's armor. The armor was unmistakable.

The portrait was of her god Valdaar.

However, that is still not what caused her surprise. The young man in the portrait looked exactly like an older version of her son. Identical down to the piercing green eyes.

The End

This ends the first series of books in the Valdaar's Fist Saga.
I hope you enjoyed reading them as much as I enjoyed writing them
and will join me as the adventures in the Land continue
with Shaarna (Sordaak's sister) and her entourage as they attempt
to wreak their havoc on the followers of Valdaar.

Thanks for reading.

The Valdaar's Fist Saga

Acknowledgements

In this the final book in this series, I want to acknowledge the role play-ing game Dungeons & Dragons for helping me to form the world that is contained within these pages. It was not forgetting all that this "game" taught me that originally forced pen to paper and brought these characters into being. Thank you for the fantasy that continues to play itself out in my head.

About the Author

Vance Pumphrey traces the evolution of his high fantasy novels from his Nuclear Engineering career in the U.S. Navy—not an obvious leap. He started playing Dungeons and Dragons while in the Navy, though, and the inspiration for the Valdaar's Fist series was born.

The Platinum Dragon is the fourth book in the Valdaar's Fist quartet. Retired from the Navy, Vance lives in Seattle with his wife of thirty-plus years.

To find out when the next Valdaar's Fist book will be released, check out VancePumphrey.com.